S Unprotected
Sax

Tony McFadden

&

Charles McFadden

Beach Nut Press

DEDICATION

Yo, Charles. Thanks for the idea.

DISCLAIMER

This is a work of fiction. All characters and events are the
product of the author's imagination

ACKNOWLEDGMENTS

Thanks for the tunes, Sophie Milman and Zoe Keating. They kept me writing when my fingers wanted to quit.

Chapter One

Vladimir Petrovski rolled the ash from his Cuban cigar along the edge of a crystal ashtray. He looked at the phone in his hand, slowly placed it on his desk and pushed the remains of his lunch to one side. His right-hand man, Stanislav Gorski, sat across his desk from him, head bobbing slightly in time to the music filtering through the strip joint's thin walls.

Petrovski knocked on his desk to get Stan's attention. "Sergei is in the club, no?"

"I saw him a couple of minutes ago at the bar. Why?"

"Go get him."

Stan nodded and left.

Petrovski sighed. He used the remote on his desk and lowered the air-conditioning temperature by two degrees. He leaned back in his chair and picked at his goatee, deep in thought. Sergei had been in his employ since 2008, then a young thug with imaginative ways of making money. Petrovski brought him in and entrusted him with many tasks others would normally shy from. It wouldn't do for him to share some of that information with the police. He liked his house on the Inter-coastal, and didn't feel like trading it for a small, dank and oppressively humid cell. This would be dealt with today.

He stood as Stan entered with Sergei. They were a contrast in body types. Where Stan was like a bull - a smart bull - Sergei was like a whippet: thin, a bit beady-eyed and always looking like he was about to be kicked. "Please, Sergei, sit. Stan, you stay. By the door, please."

Sergei sat across from his boss, realization slowly dawning that this wasn't going to be a normal discussion. "What's up, boss?"

Vlad smashed the side of his fist down on his desk, rattling the plate and cutlery. "Why?"

Sergei swallowed. "Why, what?"

"You were fucking turned. I will forgive anything else. Talking to the cops is a death sentence."

The air conditioning provided Sergei with no relief. Sweat stained his armpits and the neck of his shirt. "Whoever told you that, he's got to be lying. No way I'd do that. I'm not that stupid."

"You are worse than stupid. You are extremely unlucky. The cop you talked to also talks to me. Of *all* of the cops in Miami, you pick that one. *He* told me."

Sergei closed his eyes. "Fuck." He looked more like a whippet now than ever. "They're cracking down everywhere, boss. The nut-job in Homestead, what's-his-face Montana, he's behind bars, and his organization is pretty much gone. Smimov's crew are getting picked up every day. I'm just trying to protect myself. It's going to come, and sooner than later."

Petrovski slapped his desk. "Montana and Smirnov? Morons. They and their crews. Weaklings within their organizations went to the police. If nobody talked to the cops, we would be fine. They need fucks like you to make their cases." He leaned back in his chair and looked at the ceiling. "You know what I have to do."

"No. Don't. I thought," Sergei hesitated, "I thought it was the right thing to do. Right for me, anyway."

"You should avoid thinking."

~~~

Paul Coates, drummer and founder of the Coates Jazz Quintet, sat at the head of the table. Izzy, the restaurant owner's daughter, had just picked up the empty plates, leaving the remnants of the garlic bread. John Delacourte, the sax player, and Ned Franks, their prematurely balding pianist remained, sipping their coffees. The rest of the band had already left, taking advantage of their free afternoon.

Paul nodded at John. "What are you smiling about, JD?"

"Six months ago I was in Afghanistan. People shooting at me every single day. And you know it can get as cold as fuck there, right? Now here I am, in Miami in the late August heat, playing sax in your band. Haven't been shot at in a dog's age."

"You never told me how you know this runt, Coates." Ned winked at John.

"He played sax in the high school band I tried to run. Most of them were reprobates and shitty musicians. He was just a reprobate."

Ned leaned on the table. "Were you ever any shorter than this? "Cause, man, you're short."

"Yeah, and he had the mentality of a shortie when he was a kid. Had to prove to everyone he was tough. The number of times he almost got the crap kicked out of him..." Coates sipped his sparkling water and lemon. "Tough little nut."

"*Almost*, as in, I never lost a fight."

Coates shrugged. "If you don't want to share the number of times I covered for you when the cops were looking for a certain short, ginger perp, that's fine."

"Sandy, not ginger."

"Call it what you want." Paul popped the last remaining piece of garlic bread in his mouth. "I'm going to make a quick trip south and supplement my income if you know what I mean. You guys want to come along?"

Ned wiped his mouth and dropped the napkin on the table. "When have I ever gone with you, Paul? Ever? You're going to get caught one of these days, and we're going to have to find another drummer. Poaching alligators is a third-degree felony. Punishable by up to five years in jail, if you get an asshole judge."

"Drummers are a dime a dozen, Neddie. You'd find another one." He smiled, and he clapped his hands together. "Okay. You know where we are tonight, right? Off Collins. Be there at 7:00. That small place upstairs from the restaurant. Enjoy your afternoon. I'll see you tonight."

~~~

6

Sergei closed his eyes and pressed his forehead against the barrel. His hands were taped behind him. They were deep in The Everglades. He adjusted his knees to keep his balance on the airboat. "Be quick about it, okay? I don't want to feel anything." He rocked slightly as the wake of a distant boat or large animal moved the airboat. "Shit." He clenched his stomach muscles and let fly with a stream of vomit. It slapped against Vlad's lower legs and shoes and pooled on the deck of the boat.

Petrovski pulled the .22 handgun back from the informant's head and looked down at his shoes. "Really?"

Sergei's shirt stuck to his back, soaked with sweat. Petrovski waved away some mosquitoes. "You talked to the cops. Normally I would have someone else do this. Like Stan. But -"

"I'd love to do it, boss."

"Shut up, Stan. I am talking. Where was I?" He wiped the sweat off his forehead and wrinkled his nose. He sighed and pressed the barrel against Sergei's forehead. "I should just shoot you in the legs and let the alligators finish you off. That would be more fitting, no?"

Stan looked on from the airboat's elevated seat. "This is something I should be doing, and if it were me doing it, I'd stab the turncoat half a dozen times and tip him in. The snakes will take care of him. Or the 'gators. But it wouldn't be fast."

"Point noted, Stan." Petrovski wiped the sweat off his neck and pulled the trigger. The sharp report launched a flock of white birds off a nearby mud island as Sergei's body slowly tipped backward off the airboat into the swampy water. "God knows he deserved worse." He looked up at Stan. "Get us the hell out of here. I'll leave this to you from now on." He looked beyond his right-hand man and squinted. "Fantastic." He closed his eyes and shook his head. "Just fantastic." He looked at Stan. "You didn't hear him behind you?" He pointed over Stan's shoulder with the .22.

Stan twisted in his seat and watched with his boss as an airboat similar to theirs accelerated away from them toward the distant dock.

Chapter Two

The closing number before their last break wound down as Stephanie's smoky voice faded to polite applause from the small crowd. John placed his sax on its stand and stood to head to the back and a much-needed bladder release when a muscle head with a snout full of booze approached Stephanie.

"Hey, gorjus," he slurred. "We should hook up." He leaned a bit to his left and squinted at the diminutive singer. "I could show youse a really good time."

John took a step forward but stopped when she put her hand out behind her, palm out, stopping him without looking back at him.

"I'm flattered, sir, but you've had way too much to drink. Head home and sleep it off, okay? You've been over-served."

The man took a half step back and cocked his head. "You turning me down?"

"Absolutely. You're too much of a man for me, clearly. And I've got a headache. As I said, I'm flattered, but not tonight, okay?"

John crossed his arms and leaned against the wall and watched the show.

"Hey, lady, I'm going to take you home with me and show you how much of a man I really am. And I'm not going to take no for an answer."

"You're going to have to take no for an answer because that's the answer I'm going to give you."

"No."

"Exactly. No."

"No, I mean, no, you're not going to say no."

"I just did say no."

"No."

Stephanie shook her head. "You're just confusing yourself." She flicked a quick glance to John and shook her head.

He cracked half a smile and watched the tiny woman face down the belligerent drunk. Like a Chihuahua facing down a slobbering Rottweiler.

He leaned on the wall and continued to watch the show. There were only a dozen or so in the club. It was a Monday night. Not the biggest night of the week for audiences. Most had filtered out to the bathroom or left for home.

"If you'll excuse me, sir, I want to go grab a breath of fresh air." Steph moved to push past the drunk.

"I'll go with you. We can have a good time." He put his right hand on her left shoulder to stop her.

Stephanie looked down at the hand on her shoulder. "Stop touching me."

"Or what?"

John pushed himself from the wall and stepped forward to assist when she grabbed the drunk's right hand with hers, her thumb on the middle of the back of his hand, her fingers gripping under the fleshy part by his pinky finger. She took a quick step back as she wrenched his hand at the wrist, adding her left hand for strength. She continued to step back as she twisted. The leverage she had on his arm and shoulder drove his face into the hardwood floor, and John heard a crunch as his nose broke his fall. "Or what? Or this. I told you to take your hand off me, and when I tell someone to stop touching me, I expect them to stop touching me *immediately*." She punctuated the sentence with one final twist of his arm, straining the tendons in his shoulder.

"You fucking bitch."

She kicked him in the cheek with the point of her shoe and twisted his arm a shade more. "Watch your language, sir. I'm going to let go of you now, and you're going to leave. And never come back, right?"

She took a couple of steps back to clear herself. The man slowly stood, cupping his nose with his left hand, his right arm dangling by his side. "Yof fumpigbatd."

"Whatever. Piss off." She turned her back on the drunk and strode past John. "Didn't need your help, thanks."

He watched her walk into the back rooms. "Obviously." He walked toward the drunk who swayed, his nose bleeding down the front of his shirt and over his beer gut. "Hey, pal. You might want to get out of here before she comes back. I don't think she's in a good mood."

"Asshole."

"You've got one too."

The drunk kicked a chair on the way out, yelling something unintelligible back at him.

"What the hell was that about?"

John turned to Coates. "Ah, the oaf was harassing Stephanie. She cleaned his clock." He chuckled. "Didn't think she had that in her."

"She's a Midwest girl like us. Brought up tough. So the dude wasn't looking for me?"

John chuckled and looked his mentor up and down. "No, Paulie, I don't think you're his type."

"Why didn't you help her?"

Stephanie came back into the room and interrupted. "Because I didn't need any help. You okay Paul? You rushed the beat a bit. Are you off your game today? Under the weather?"

"Absolutely not. You're imagining it."

"No, I'm not."

"Don't cross her Paulie, she'll rip your arm off."

"I'm fine, everyone. Leave it alone." Paul moved back behind the drum kit and pulled the sticks from the snare drum's frame. "We're back on in five. Do what you've got to do and be ready."

John nodded and followed Stephanie. "Paul tells me you're from the Midwest, too. Why haven't you told me before? Where? I'm from Lincoln."

Stephanie took a deep breath. "Look, John Delacourte, you remind me of an especially slow schoolchild. I don't know how many times I have to tell you. You're wasting your time. Think of us as

12

team members. Business partners, even. You don't need to know anything about my history. You just need to play your sax, as well as you can - and I pray to God you will improve - and let me sing those few songs that actually need a singer. It doesn't matter where I've come from, what my favorite color is or who's my singing inspiration. I've got better things to worry about than a bantam rooster, a thinks-he's-a-hotshot-sax-player guy hitting on me. Okay? Now we're up in a couple of minutes, and it's one of the few songs where I'm needed more than you, a favorite student of our fearless leader."

"Hey, uncalled for. Paul helped me out a couple of times when I was a kid. So I helped him out when his sax player moved to Branson. No special favors here."

"I could walk out the door and be back with five better sax players than you in ten minutes. Very special favors."

"Ten minutes? That long?" John shook his head and returned to his chair, sax in its stand.

Sinnerman launched the set, Ned nailing the piano, Paul on drums, Stephanie on voice, Henry plucking bass and John listening. At least for the first three and a half minutes. Then he riffed the guitar part, arranged for sax. Bouncing off Paul and Henry's beats, and Steph's syncopated claps. Paul still sounded off, the high-hat work rougher than his perfectionism had ever allowed. Not like anyone in the audience would notice. There were only about six people left, and they weren't connoisseurs of good jazz music. They were Monday night drunks. And they'd pay for it tomorrow.

The song wound up. Ned freaked out on the piano, Steph hit the high notes, and they moved into the final minute of the drum solo.

It ended with a smattering of polite applause, and Stephanie took a sip of coconut water, and the rat-a-tat-a-tat of drums started as Paul launched *My Heart Belongs to Daddy*, Sophie Milman style. Ned tinkled the ivory and John played the full big band part, taking place of the trumpets, trombone and sax. Paul had arranged it pretty well, but John was still a very busy sax player.

They played to the end of the song and seamlessly segued into *La Vie en Rose*. As convincing as she sounded, John knew for a fact that Stephanie didn't speak a word of French outside those lyrics.

Back in high school band some twenty years ago - John felt a momentary twinge of oldness - his music teacher tried to impress upon his students the importance of letting the music transcend the notes on the paper and to live it, feel it, become one with it. He would have bet money that the guy was stoned most of the time. He didn't get it then, but he did now. That teacher sat behind the drum kit, living, feeling and becoming one with the music they were playing. He had to admit the old guy had skills.

Six months ago, when he hooked up with this group on Paul's invite, his sax skills left a lot to be desired. But they stuck with him, welcoming him into the group. Partially, he knew, because their sax player had just left for greener pastures, but in large part, because Paul had vouched for him.

Again.

Well, *almost* all welcomed him with open arms.

Steph was a bit of a harder nut to crack.

14

His fingers played the notes with minimal brain involvement, on autopilot. He noted, without realizing the significance initially, a commotion at the door, then the pattern recognition part of his brain zeroed in on the source.

The big guy with the broken nose, with two equally large friends, had pushed the security at the door to one side and was making a beeline for the stage.

"Fuckin' frog music now. Bitch, you're going to pay."

Stephanie had her eyes closed and her head tipped slightly back, in full croon mode. His bellow stopped her singing, and she took a step back, sticking the microphone back in the stand.

John dropped his sax in its stand and got between her and the oncoming threat. "I've got this. You handled one of them, and I'm impressed, by the way, but three is a bit out of your league."

He put his hands up in the universal 'stop' sign. "Boys, you really should leave. We're about to close, and the kitchen isn't serving food anymore."

"Outta my way, Red." He sounded like he had a bad cold and smelled of stale sweat and cheap whisky.

John looked at Nose and his two friends. "You want to leave now. This is not the singer you're looking for," he intoned, hoping for a smile. They didn't appear to get the reference.

Nose screwed up his face. "Look, shorty, if I have to go through you first, I will. Looks like it'll take me about ten seconds. Her, though, we're going to take our time."

"Wrong answer. And your last chance. Take your girlfriends and go find someone else to hassle."

Nose swung a haymaker so wide and slow JD had time to sigh before he stepped inside the swing and brought his right elbow up sharply under the guy's chin, snapping his head back and dropping him, flat on his back, his right arm still extended.

John looked at the other two. "Okay? You satisfied? Take your friend to a hospital and get the hell out of here."

"Lucky shot," said the one on the right.

"You two driving your friend to the hospital will cost nothing. But if I flatten the three of you, there will be ambulance charges, not to mention the humiliation of being flattened by a little guy like me. Be smart. I don't like fighting. Take him home and get the hell out of here."

He thought he convinced them. They stood looking down at Nose, passed out on the floor, and then at each other. Then they both came at him at the same time.

"Fuck, boys. You're going to make me work." John reached back and grabbed the microphone stand and swung the heavy base, catching the man on his left under his hanging ribs. He thought he heard a crack, but it could have been his imagination. The guy would know he made contact, though.

That assailant doubled over holding his side, so he continued the swing, dropping the base a foot and catching the second guy on the side of his knee, just as he had planted his weight to swing a punch. He let out a scream as he collapsed on the floor. John dropped the base of the microphone stand on his head, cracking his jaw. The cracked rib guy stood straight, gritted his teeth and winced as he drew a deep breath.

John placed the mic stand back on the floor. "Tough guy, eh? I don't need this now. Be smart and piss off. Your friends will be in the hospital tomorrow. You can stop by and tell them how courageous you were, taking on a girl and a puny guy like me.

"Or stay here, and the three of you will be sharing a room in the hospital later. Your choice."

The last big guy poked Nose in the ribs with the toe of his boot.

John shook his head. "No, no. He's out. Go."

"Maybe I stay here and avenge their beatings."

"Look, I'm sure you're a nice guy, loyal and all that, but you're not too smart. I've already shown you that you can't beat me. Take the hint and get out of here."

"Fuck that." He ran at John like a nose guard going for the quarterback. And, thought John, his technique seemed to indicate that perhaps in high school that was a regular activity for him.

Unfortunately for him, John wasn't a quarterback. He waited until his attacker had almost reached him and stepped to one side, swinging his elbow at the back of his neck. The momentum kept the attacker moving forward until he was face down on the floor, as unconscious as his friends.

John stepped back and took a deep breath. "Can somebody clean this up?"

Sirens sounded in the distance. Someone in the club had called the police.

Three suit-and-ties at a table in the corner stood and applauded. The rest of the band was still in their positions, except for Stephanie, who had moved by the piano.

Ned leaned into his mic. "That, ladies and gentlemen, was an extended solo by the incomparable Johnny D, Sax Machine. Tip your waitress. We're here all night. Which just ended. I think our set is over."

Stephanie frowned and walked backstage. Paul slid his sticks into the snare drum frame, and Henry started packing up his bass. The house lights went up as two uniformed officers came in through the front door.

John groaned. "Shit. I don't want to talk to the cops."

One of the suits walked over. "I saw everything. I can vouch for you if you want." He handed John a card. "Give me a call if you need anything. That was incredible. Like watching a Steven Segal movie."

John hated Steven Segal movies. He smiled and took the card and walked over to the policemen, mentally preparing for a couple of hours of his life lost to their questions.

Chapter Three

It was rehearsal time. Paul looked around the room at the rest of his band. "Folks, nothing about last night, okay? We don't need the distraction."

John nodded. "Fine by me. What do you want to go over first?"

Coates handed sheet music to Ned, Stephanie and John. It looked like an original. They'd only played standards until now.

"You write this, Paulie?"

He smiled, but it was a sad smile. "Yeah, I've been writing it for years. I think we're finally ready."

"Lyrics too? They're pretty mushy."

"Leave it, Rusty, I like them." Stephanie hummed the melody and mouthed some of the words. "It's really nice."

"No 'Rusty', okay? John, Johnny, JD, anything along those lines, but not 'Rusty'."

Henry chuckled deep in his chest. "I hope you were going for reverse psychology, because that's all she's going to call you now."

"Fantastic." JD looked at his music, then over at Henry. "Wait, Paulie, you forget something?"

Paul tapped the bass drum pedal a couple of times. "Probably. I'm old as fuck. Why?" He dropped his drumsticks at a sharp bang on the door. "Shit. Can someone see who that is?"

"I ordered food, Paul. Relax, will you? I've got it this time. Pay me back later." Ned stood from the piano and went out to the foyer.

Paul waited until Ned returned with the bags of food and pointed to a corner. "Leave it there, Ned. Back to the piano. We can eat after we lock this down. It debuts this weekend."

~~~

Detective Mario Cruz enjoyed working solo. He welcomed the freedom. His former partner, Detective Dan MacCready, had been reassigned as Miami PD liaison to the local FBI Organized Crime office. He hadn't been given a new partner yet, removing the need to explain his actions to anyone. Like why he answered the phone when one of the major Russian mob figures in South Florida called.

"Hang on a sec." He walked out of the station and turned left up a low-traffic road. "I have to be quick. What can I do for you?"

"Keep your eyes and ears open and let me know if you hear anything about a body being discovered in the Everglades."

"Anybody I know?"

Silence crackled down the line.

"Ah, right. So I'll ask around."

"Be far more subtle than that. And don't disappoint me."

Cruz looked at the phone in his hand, shook his head and hung up. He slid the burner phone into his suit pocket and slowly walked back to the station. He had no qualms about what he did. Survival of the fittest took many forms. He needed the money. His wife's taste in clothing, furniture, neighborhoods and everything else consumed more money than his detective pay-check provided. And her rich parents didn't like to share.

~~~

Detective Dan MacCready and his FBI cohort, Special Agent Stephen James stood by an examination table at the Medical Examiner's office near the University of Miami campus. An unlikely and friendly alliance had formed between the two, almost a year since they solved the double murder of a Jersey mob enforcer as well as an escapee from the Witness Security program. MacCready and James had gotten along so well, in fact, that MacCready accepted the offer to be the special liaison between the agencies.

Dr. Samantha Reese held court. As Metro-Dade Chief Medical Examiner, her court happened to be the morgue, which suited her just fine.

"What we have here, gentlemen is a merciful killing."

MacCready leaned forward and took a closer look at the body on the stainless steel table. "Merciful, Sam? He's been half eaten." Flesh had been torn from the extremities, and the torso looked crushed. The most intact parts were from the knees down.

"More than half, by the looks of it." Agent James had actually taken a step back. He'd get enough information from the eventually forthcoming paperwork. He didn't need a closer look.

"James is correct. More than half. Fortunately for me, his skull is still intact, even though most of the flesh is missing. This," she pointed at the small hole between and slightly above the eye sockets, "is the evidence of mercy. Also evidence of a crime. This guy didn't fall off an airboat. He was shot and thrown in, the shot certainly fatal. I'm assuming the killer wanted to make sure we would have no evidence of his actions. I've recovered the .22 caliber bullet. The only thing we may have to identify him with is the tattoo on his left calf." She turned the leg slightly and showed them the parrot-smoking-a-joint tattoo on his leg. "You'll have to find out who inks that."

MacCready took out his phone. "Hold it there for a sec." He took a couple of shots and confirmed they were good enough quality. "Okay. That should be good enough. Nothing on the body to tie him to his killer, I take it."

"Nada. If a tourist's airboat hadn't bumped into the carcass this morning, the killer would have succeeded in completely eliminating any trace of the victim. I estimate he's only been dead about 24 hours, but in another six there wouldn't have been anything to find. Lucky for us."

"Not so lucky for him." James wiped the sweat off his forehead. "Nothing else we can get from you, right?"

Sam smiled. "I've done all I can. You can escape now and bug Miss Harris for any trace she might extract from this poor schmuck's clothes. I'll send a better-resolution picture of the tattoo to her, and she'll run the database search.

"Copy us too." Mac looked at his phone. "This will only take me so far." He paused and looked at the body on the table. "One of these days I'm going to see my brother here."

~~~

Stanislav insisted on being called Stan. He'd moved to Miami ten years ago, found a home with Petrovski's crew and worked his way up in the organization, hell-bent on living the American dream and working very hard to assimilate himself. He'd been an enthusiastic user and abuser of every muscle-enhancing drug on the market over the last few years, inspired by his previous partner, Carl, an enthusiastic doper in the gym. Stan spent every waking hour trying to achieve the true all-American look.

He sat back in his Camaro, heading south back to the shack they'd been in yesterday, getting the airboat. Whoever had seen them had to have been there also.

He patted the car's dashboard. Not that long ago it belonged to Carl. Carl's head disappeared about a year ago while he chauffeured one of Petrovski's hit men around. Word was this hit guy, a real mean piece of work called Turk, shot Carl just before he himself took one to the head, courtesy of the FBI. Stan shrugged. No difference to him. He ended up with a sweet American car. And it felt to him like he had now filled the role the Turk had.

Life looked pretty good from where he sat.

He pulled the yellow car into the gravel parking lot and hopped out into the steamy heat. "Ah, this is beautiful." He closed and locked the door and ran up the stairs into the small hut used as a rental office. He could see a dozen or so boats through a greasy window behind the counter, resting against a dilapidated wharf. Petrovski killed Sergei on one of them. Another one held the witness.

The owner looked up from his Hustler Magazine. "You again." He looked past him. "No company this time?"

"Just me, Hector. I don't need a boat. I need some answers."

Hector closed the Hustler, dropped it on the counter and crossed his arms. "I don't usually have many answers. And I don't usually ask many questions. You may be out of luck."

"Someone else rented one of your little boats yesterday, around the same time as my boss and our guest and me. I need to know who that was."

"You going to take him out on one of my boats and kill him too?"

Stan crossed his massive arms and growled.

"Fine, really. I don't care what you do with him. Unlike you, who I trust implicitly, I took a copy of the other guy's driver's license and kept it with a copy of his credit card and that would be in this file right here hang on a second." He scrabbled through his file cabinet in a panic and pulled out a couple of sheets of paper. "Here. This is the guy. Take them, okay? I don't want evidence of these around here when you finally off him."

Stan grunted and took the photocopy of the driver's license and the rental agreement. He didn't care about the credit card info and left it on the counter. The address pointed to an apartment in Hialeah, but the photo difficult to make out. "How tall was this guy?"

Hector closed his eyes for a second. "He wasn't in here long and I see tons of people every day."

Stan looked around the empty shop. "Right. Just bustling. How tall?"

"Okay, maybe a bit taller than you. Not as big, though."

"Few are. The license says he was born in 1956. How old does that make him?" Stan hated math.

"Like mid to late fifties."

"Is he fit? Fat? Limp? Any tattoos? Tell me about him."

"I can't really tell you more than that. He comes by here every once in a while, poachin' 'gators. He's a little taller than you, middle-aged, a bit of a pot, balding, brown hair with grey at the temples. Can't tell you anything more than that. He's not as fit as you are if that's what you're worried about."

Stan folded the copy of the license and the agreement and slid them into his back pocket. "I wasn't here, you've never heard of this guy, and I'll kill you if my name ever comes up."

~~~

Stan headed back north into the city and landed in front of the apartment building just after 5:00 pm. He sat outside for a few minutes, watching the occupants come and go.

He got out and checked the witness's driver's license. Apartment 32. He pushed all the buzzers at the entry door and yelled "Courier". The door buzzed and he made his way upstairs.

Security in small apartment buildings tended to be strongest at the main door, the assumption being you could trust your neighbors in such a small community.

Stan wasn't a neighbor. He leaned against the apartment door, his considerable mass causing it to buckle slightly inward. He looked up and down the hall - no one was watching. He slid the blade of his knife between the door and the door jamb and jimmied the lock. The door swung into the small, one-bedroom. Nobody home.

He wandered through the kitchen and living room, neat but clearly a male's apartment. The bathroom provided nothing of interest. He pushed open the bedroom door. Also neat. "The guy's a nut job." He looked through the closet and chest of drawers, careful not to disturb anything. There was nothing. He resigned himself to a night of surveillance when he saw the flyer on the bedside table.

"Well I'll be damned." The flyer was for a jazz band. "The Coates Jazz Quintet," he read. "Featuring Johnny D, the Sax Machine and the delightful Stephanie Peters." He smiled and slid open his phone.

"Petrovski."

"Boss, this is -"

"I know who it is. Any luck?"

"Oh, yeah."

"Is the problem solved?"

Stan looked at the flyer. "In twenty-four hours. I know where he'll be tomorrow night. I'll introduce myself then."

"How can you be certain he'll be where you think he'll be?"

"He's invited me to one of his gigs. The man is a drummer in a jazz quintet. There's him on drums, some huge black dude playing that big upright fiddle thing, a pencil neck on piano, a short-assed guy on saxophone and a cutie singer. She looks kinda familiar."

"Keep your thing tucked away. Just have a 'discussion' with the drummer without getting nabbed and do not push your luck. Let me know when you finish."

Stan grunted and hung up. He'd seen the cute singer somewhere before. It would come to him. He'd finish off Coates then he'd track her down and introduce himself.

He waited by the clunky elevator and studied the band's flyer. The drummer looked very much like the picture on the driver's license. No question about that. A bit older now, and balder, and, though hard to be certain from the flyer, a bit fatter. Shouldn't be much of a challenge at all.

The elevator chimed, and the door shook open. He stepped on, still looking at the flyer, pushing past someone getting off.

He knew where the witness would be tomorrow. He'd prepare for it and finish him. Then, the girl.

Chapter Four

Detective Mario Cruz had two masters. Three if you were to include the Miami Police Department. In addition to feeding Vladimir Petrovski useful information, for a coin or two, he fed much of the same information to Rico Trattori, a Tamiami-based mobster and a competitor to the more abrasive Petrovski. Both arrangements had developed over the last three years, Petrovski first and then Trattori. It crossed his mind, once in a rare while, that Petrovski wouldn't appreciate the double dipping, and if he ever found out, Cruz would find his life a lot more complicated than it already was.

Trattori knew of the arrangement; he paid more and received better service from the young detective. Cruz took care not to share with Petrovski anything that might impact Trattori's business interests.

Cruz stood out by the fleet parking lot, sucking on a cig and dialing Rico's number.

"What the fuck, man? It's early."

"I'm not going to get a chance later, and I need to pass on some info. And I'm not sure about pest control, okay?"

He heard Rico sigh on the other end of the line. "Yeah. Got it. Spill your guts in carefully coached language."

"Your Russian friend is going treasure hunting."

"My Russian friend?"

"Yeah. The only Russian friend you have." Three months ago there were two Russian "friends", but one of them, Ivan Smimov, sat in a maximum security facility for various violent crimes, a year into a fifteen-year sentence.

That left Petrovski.

"Yeah, go on. I know who you mean. What do you mean by treasure hunting?"

"Let's just say he threw out some trash and he's concerned it may show up at an inopportune place or time."

"Ah. You're getting much better at this. Would this trash be potentially toxic?"

"To our friend, yes."

"Then it would be beneficial for me to make sure this trash is *found*. Take your time, find out more information and let me know how I can help. But make sure there's no pest problem the next time you call because, frankly, this double-speak is tiring me. You're doing well, kid. Keep it up."

~~~

MacCready leaned his head into the temporary office reserved for Organized Crime activities. "James, we've been summoned."

"Captain Sloan?"

"He's still in DC, brown-nosing some Homeland dude, trying for that cushy job. Sam called, and she's got Gloria with her. A break on the body in the water."

James folded the file closed and stood, grabbing his jacket. "So it *is* mob related or she would have tossed it to someone else. Are we missing anyone?"

"Nobody of any significance from around here."

James cocked an eyebrow. "Are Sam and Gloria at Sam's place or Gloria's?"

"Downstairs."

"Gloria's house. Good. It's too hot to go outside."

"You can always move back to Jersey."

"Hell with that. Lead on."

Gloria Harris, almost six foot tall, gangly, and very British, held court as the Chief tech in the crime scene lab. It occupied almost the entire lower floor of the station.

She and Sam sat at the large evidence table as Mac and James entered. Mac smiled. They'd been pretty busy lately, and he and Sam hadn't had a chance to see each other as much as they wanted to.

"Ladies. Good to see you. Something on the gator bait?" James looked around. "Must be the mob, right?"

"That's why we called you guys. The tatt id'd him. A mid-level low-life from Petrovski's crew."

"Not Simon, thank God."

"Your brother? No, Mac. I'd never tell you like this if he ended up on my table. Oh, God no. This guy went by the name Sergei Romanov. It's an alias, most likely, but it's the only name we have.

Your old partner reported contact with him a few days ago. Apparently, he had plans to spill the beans on Petrovski, then he shows up as gator bait. Coincidence? I think not."

"Mario? Why would Cruz have contact with a mob informant? That would be our domain. And I've known about this guy, but he wasn't on our list."

Gloria shrugged. "You'll have to ask him."

"Anything to tie his death to Petrovski? Mac and I have been trying to put that asshole away for almost a year now. Since last November."

Sam shook her head. "Any evidence of that is in the Everglades or an alligator's gut. Or possibly a python's gut if the crushing is any indication. Nope. We're going to need a witness, and the odds of that are slim to none."

"But he was killed in the Everglades, right?" Mac made notes in his notepad.

"Yeah, we're positive about that. The headshot killed him just before he was dumped in the water. If there were witnesses, they'd be hard to find." Gloria closed the file. "There's not much more I can do. If you find anything you think might be connected to the case, let me know, and I'll rush the analysis."

"*Mucho gracias*, ladies."

"Oh, look at that. The Yankee is learning the local lingo. Sam, Gloria, we'll catch up later. We'll check around. I think we need to make a trip to the 'glades, partner. You'll love it. Part of our National Heritage. And mosquitoes."

32

~~~

John had known Paul Coates for over twenty years as his high school music teacher, but as much more than that, too. John had no present father, and Paul had stepped in to keep who he saw to be a kid with potential on the straight and narrow. John had to admit it would have been a challenge some days. The number of times Paul had vouched for him, giving him an alibi when he didn't have to. He would probably still be in jail if Paul hadn't sorted him out.

Then after high school, he strongly encouraged John to join the military.

And until six months ago, that was the last he'd seen or talked to Paul. But he still knew him well enough to know something was bugging the older man.

The band gathered in a small room upstairs from the main dining room, a closer and cozier room than the open dining area downstairs.

They went on in thirty minutes. "What's up, Paul? You look freaked out."

"It's nothing. Didn't sleep well last night, that's all."

"You're jumpy."

"I told you, I didn't sleep well."

John considered his mentor. "It's more than that, but I'm not going to push it." He slapped the table. "We ready for tonight?"

"Why wouldn't we be? Same set as Monday night."

"Your new song. Thought we could give it a run tonight. I like it. Steph has nailed it."

"And I said we'd debut it on the weekend. It's not ready. We need one more session tomorrow."

"No prob. I get it. We've got a good crowd tonight."

"How many are we talking about?" Paul cracked open the door at the side of the stage area and looked into the crowd. He smiled and nodded as he scanned the audience sitting at the small round tables, nursing drinks, some of them picking at finger food.

Paul's eyes scanned the faces, then stopped and he paled.

"What is it?" John looked out in the same direction Paul looked. A couple of heavies sat at a table at the front. One of them had grotesquely large muscles, a product of EPO, steroids, *something* to enhance growth. "You know those guys?"

Paul pulled his head back and closed the door. "What?"

"I'll go have a chat with them, tell 'em to piss off, okay?"

"Johnny, my boy, what the hell are you talking about? Are you actually telling me you want to pick a fight with our audience? That dust-up the other night scramble your brains? You told me you were tired of fighting. Reinvigorated, are you?" He dropped into an old, overstuffed chair and ran his fingers through his thinning hair. "Get your head in the right space, kiddo. We've got a gig."

John frowned and poured himself a glass of soda water, added some lemon slices and ice cubes. Something stunk. He'd keep an eye on those two.

Because of the late start, they played only a single set. Twelve songs and no encore.

A Coltrane opening kept John focused on the music and by the end of "Lazy Bird" he'd forgotten about the two muscle-heads in the front row. He enjoyed starting gigs with a heavy sax song; it framed the rest of the night for him.

Stephanie took center stage for the next song with her rendition of "Summertime", echoing one of Ella Fitzgerald's performances, slowing the night down. John marveled at her voice; the range and control she showed at such a young age promised a very long career.

He leaned back in his chair, wiping the sweat from the back of his neck, and noticed the two in the front row again. They didn't seem to appreciate the singing or the flawless transition from the languid Ella song to Etta James's angry "It's a Man's Man's World". He had to take the guitar part - not an easy thing on the tenor sax - and he slid back into the music until the end of the set. When he finally looked back to the front row, specifically for the muscle, they were gone. He wasn't sure what time they left, but Paul would be relieved, no doubt.

The audience, getting drunk, met the final chord of the final song with loud and raucous applause, a never-ending surprise for JD. His career up to this job shunned attention. Army Rangers didn't look for applause, typically.

Paul leaned into his microphone. "Ladies and germs, the voice of the incomparable Stephanie Peters. Remember that name. Unknown except in the Midwest three years ago and now I expect her, any day, to tell me she's got a huge recording contract and will leave me and the $50 a night she's making for a more lucrative career. On bass is the gentle giant, Henry Collins, from just up the road in Boca. Gotta support local talent, right? Ned Franks, an escapee from Canada, tickled the ivories. Don't tell the INS, but I think he's overstayed his visa. And an old friend, John Delacourte, or as we like to call him,

'Johnny D, the Sax Machine' on saxophone. I'm Paul Coates, and you've been listening to the Coates Jazz Quintet. Thanks for coming out."

Paul pushed the mic back and made a beeline for the backstage. Nothing had to be torn down; they had a gig here tomorrow, a full three sets, and the management would let them leave their equipment on stage for the duration.

John followed Paul off stage. "Jesus, man, you okay? You were a bit rough tonight."

Coates' baleful glare set him back a step. "Leave it alone, kid. I've got to run. Catch up with you later, okay?" He slipped out the back door before John had a chance to reply.

Ned and Henry came in, followed by Stephanie. "Where's Paul?"

"He just took off, Steph. Something's up with the guy. Does he gamble any that you know of?"

She shook her head. "Not a chance. He calls it a chump's game. The odds are never in your favor, and you know Paul, he'll only play a rigged game. If he plays a game at all. Stacks the odds in his favor. Why?"

John scratched his ear. "Dunno, but I think there were a couple of gorillas in the front row looking for him. He saw them before the show and looked pretty shaken. Then after the show, he bugged out like his house was on fire. And did anyone else notice how badly he played tonight? Offbeat a couple of times, and missed a riff in 'Summertime'." He shook his head. "Something's funky. I say we sit him down tomorrow at breakfast and find out what the fuck."

Henry yawned. "He's a big boy. If he needs help with anything, he'll ask. I've got to blow, guys. Dead tired." He slipped out the same back door.

Ned followed him out. Stephanie took a pull on a bottle of water and wiped her lips. "What did these two guys look like?"

"One guy had arms on him like a freaking gorilla. Shaved head. Zipper tattoo around his neck. A smaller guy, relatively speaking, greasy looking, hair in a ponytail and a wispy looking goatee sat with him. Neither of them looked like they appreciated the show. Paul saw them through the door and nearly pissed himself. And then the way he played. I've known him for a very long time, and he's never been anything but perfect. Annoyingly so. Tonight, not so much. Very out of character."

Stephanie screwed the top back on the bottle and put it in the fridge. "I'll talk with him, see what's going on."

"We'll chat with him at breakfast."

"You don't know him that well if you think that's going to work. He's a very private guy. Four of us confronting him isn't going to get anything but denials. It's got to be one-on-one."

John looked at her in a new light. "Oh. Really? You and him? There's got to be a good thirty years difference in your age."

"Almost exactly thirty years. He's 57 and I'm 27. And no, we're not a couple. I have a good relationship with him for - other reasons. And I'll talk to him. Don't push it in the morning, okay?"

John opened his mouth to answer when the door opened and the manager poked his head in. "Where's Coates?"

"Bobby, how you doin'? Paulie left right after the set. Why?"

"Wanted to bust his chops. He sucked tonight. Better be better tomorrow. Big crowd on Thursdays."

"He's off his game. He'll be better tomorrow," said John. "Hey, did you notice the apes at one of the front tables?"

Bob shook his head. "I was in my office counting my money. Why? They cause any trouble?"

"Nah. Just didn't look like a typical jazz enthusiast. Metal or classic rock, if I were to guess."

"We don't discriminate. If they want to broaden their horizons with my three drink minimum, that's fine with me." He winked and backed out of the room.

Stephanie picked up her jacket from the back of a chair. "Why are you asking about these two?"

He shrugged. "They spooked Paul. Hard. I've seen him go face-to-face with punk gang-bangers when I was a kid without batting an eyelid. Kept me out of trouble a couple of times by standing up to the local thugs. Nothing scares him."

"Maybe you misread him."

JD frowned and picked up his coat. "I doubt it. He crapped himself."

The door opened again.

"What now, Bobby?"

The two big guys from the front pushed Bob to one side and stepped in. The bigger one spoke, and the smaller one stood guarding the door. "The man on the drums. Coates. Where is he?" He looked around the small room, and at the door out the back.

"You're a big fan, are you?" Stephanie stood toe-to-toe with the muscle. "He's under the weather. Had to go get some fresh air. Do you want to leave your name and number? I'll get him to call you. Or were you looking for an autographed photo?"

He looked down at her and scowled. "You must be the delightful Stephanie Peters." He looked at John. "And Johnny D, the Sax Machine. Cute. Tell him we'll be back." He nodded at his sidekick and backed out of the room.

Stephanie closed the door behind him. "Sure thing." John had a half smile on his face. "What's so funny?"

"Just imagining you taking that guy down like you did to the guy the other night."

She shook her head. "How did he know our names?"

He pointed at the poster on the wall. "Big isn't always stupid. Wonder what the hell that was all about?"

Chapter Five

Vladimir Petrovski rarely saw 8:00 a.m. His string of businesses didn't open before noon and most closed down at three in the morning. Chumps were up at 8:00 a.m. Chumps and working stiffs. He was neither.

He poured a strong coffee and debated the next course of action. He turned to the other occupants in this office, both of them looking as tired as he felt.

"Stanislav and Grigory. How did he slip by you? He is twice your age or more, and between the two of you, there is more muscle on your bodies than one of those Clydesdale horses. You let him get past you?"

Grigory raised his hand.

"This is not a school room. What do you have to say?"

He slowly lowered his hand. "He played in the band last night, but right after that, he disappeared. We waited outside for him. He didn't show up. We then went into the band's changing room area, and he'd already left. I saw another door in there, so there was probably a back way."

"Obviously." He steepled his fingers, closed his eyes and rested his chin on his fingertips. "Stan, you have been with me a long time. You are aware of the dynamics in this particular market. There were four of us. Montana no longer controls Homestead - he is gone away for the attempted murder of two FBI agents and a Miami PD Detective. His organization has disintegrated, and Rico Trattori has assumed control.

"Ivan Smimov is behind bars, as are four of his lieutenants. I have taken control of his part of the South Florida business. We have it split 50/50, Rico and I. The slightest sign of weakness and he will be in here like a piranha on chum. Do you understand me?"

"We need to get this Coates guy, and good."

Petrovski nodded. "If Turk were still here I could be assured of a very messy display. There would be no doubt I ordered the kill, but at the same time, no evidence. I need you to aspire to those levels. Do you think you can do that?"

"I may not be the Turk, but I'm not known for my kindness." Stan subconsciously flexed his biceps, straining his polo shirt. "He will be in a great deal of pain before he dies."

"You need to find him first. What is your plan?"

"We've got his address, and the band is playing at the same place tonight. Grigory and I will stop him at his apartment this afternoon. If we miss him, we will watch both exits tonight. He won't get away this time."

Petrovski leaned forward on his elbows. "You are correct about that. He will not, or you will pay the consequences."

"Yeah, I said I understand."

"I don't think you do. This man saw me kill another man. If he goes to the police and testifies against me, I will go to jail. I do not want to go to jail. There are guys in prison who would love nothing more than to stick me with a sharpened toothbrush while I take advantage of the hour of sunshine I am allowed. No, jail is not an option. And it does not matter what the police know; if they do not have a witness, they do not have a case.

"Kill the witness. Make sure he cannot EVER talk to anybody. Find any family he has and kill them too. I do not want a single strand of his DNA to exist when you are finished."

"I get it."

"Do you? You need to be my Turk. Can you do that? Absolute cold-blooded killer? You need to be my absolute cold-blooded killer."

Stan looked at Grigory and back to Petrovski. "It will be my absolute pleasure. You can count on me."

"I am not going to tell you what will happen if you disappoint me. Now leave. Come back when your job is finished."

～～

The band traditionally met for breakfast at a Denny's in Coral Gables. John wasn't sure who started this tradition. Fierce resistance blocked any attempts he made to move it to IHOP, so Denny's it was.

John squinted in the harsh morning sun and pulled his aging Honda into the lot. He stepped out of the car into the early morning heat, sweat beading on his upper lip almost immediately. Ten steps across the parking lot to the front door filled his heat quota for the day. He walked into the air conditioning and through the morning crowd to the back table. Ned, Henry and Stephanie were already there, nursing coffees. "No Paul?"

"Running late, I guess." Ned sipped his coffee and licked his lips. "He's been late before."

"Anyone talk to him last night?"

Henry nodded. "Quick chat after he got home. He was tired. Said he'd see us tomorrow. Very quick call."

"He sounded okay, though, right?"

"What, like was he suicidal? He was his usual self. A bit subdued, maybe, but not freaking. I don't think."

"So where is he?"

"Sit and order some food. He'll get something when he gets here."

John slid into the booth beside Stephanie. "Wonder what those guys wanted last night?"

"What guys?" Henry placed his cup back on the table.

"JD and I were accosted by a gorilla and his chimp sidekick last night after you two left. They were seriously intent on talking to Paul."

John laughed. "For a second I thought she was going to do a number on the big guy. Toe-to-toe. I'd say face-to-face, but it was more like her face to his navel."

Stephanie rearranged her cutlery. "He wasn't that big."

"Like hell."

"Steph, honey, why didn't you tell us about this when you got here?"

44

"Jesus, Henry, you sound like my mother. It wasn't anything. A couple of apes. We see those kinds of guys every week."

The waitress arrived with their food and took John's order.

He looked at his watch. "He's never this late. Something's going on."

"Bender?"

"Doubt it. He's been on the wagon for a couple of years now."

"All the harder the fall."

Stephanie shook her head. "Bullshit. Something's wrong. He's gotten himself into trouble. Those guys weren't that bright, they're just muscle. Someone is after him for something. Or maybe somebody already got to him." She sat back in the booth. "Maybe they tracked him down at his place this morning."

John pulled out his phone and placed it on the table. He dialed Paul's number and put it on speaker. It rang out to voicemail. *"Coates here. Leave it after the tone."*

"Paulie, it's JD and the band. Call me when you sober up. We're getting concerned." He pushed the button and hung up. "He's a big boy. If he needs our help, he'll give us a call. Let's eat."

~~~

MacCready reached past James and closed the door to their temporary office. "Time to reach out and touch someone, partner."

"Little brother?"

MacCready sighed. "Yeah. It's been a few months. Hate doing this. Every time we do I'm afraid we're going to expose him."

45

"Plenty of safeguards in place."

Mac grunted and dialed a paging service, then entered his mobile phone number followed by 9-1-1.

And sat back to wait.

His brother, Simon, caught in a tangled web about a year ago, agreed to go undercover in Rico Trattori's organization rather than spend fifteen years in jail for an unfortunate mugging that resulted in a dead senior citizen. He traded ten to fifteen years for manslaughter, for working for the Feds.

He provided the odd piece of information for them over the last ten months, but they agreed to keep him deep until he reached a suitably high position of trust in Rico's organization. Every contact with him carried the risk of blowing his cover, and perhaps getting him killed, something MacCready agonized over every time.

James looked at his watch. "You got anything else planned for the day?"

"Touching base with Gloria in a couple of hours, then we head down to the 'glades and try and track down an airboat."

"Sweaty and mosquito-bit. Fantastic."

MacCready shrugged. "You asked for it. Quit the bitchin'."

His phone rang. He placed it on the desk between them and answered on speaker. "MacCready."

"Me too. How's it going big brother, and what do you want from me now?"

"You're good to talk?"

"Wouldn't call you if I wasn't. I'm not an idiot. My first priority is to stay alive. Is James with you?"

"I am. We need you to put out feelers."

"What about?"

"We think Petrovski dumped someone in the Everglades on Monday."

"Sergei," interrupted Simon.

"You know about it?"

"Yeah. For talking to the cops. Like you."

"Did you witness it?"

"Hell no. That's Petrovski's deal. He did the shooting himself."

"That's what we're looking for, but you don't have actual evidence, do you?"

"No. Why?"

"Rumor has it someone witnessed the shooting. You hear anything about that?"

"Same as you. Rumors. You want me to sniff around about that?"

"That's why we're talking, little brother."

"And this witness, if he or she exists, will put Petrovski away?"

"That's the plan. You'll help?"

"Hell ya. And I'll have Rico's support."

"Because?"

"Because Montana and Smimov are gone. With Petrovski gone, we've got the whole place to ourselves."

"We?"

"You know what I mean. I'll put the word out and let you know."

"Appreciate that. Take care of yourself."

"You too, bro." Simon dropped the call on the far end.

"Your brother seems a bit too deep in. A bit too enthusiastic. Maybe we should pull him out."

MacCready shook his head. "No. He can handle himself. It's too early to yank him out yet."

~~~

John parked his Honda at the curb in front of Paul's apartment building. "He's probably fallen off the wagon and sleeping it off."

Stephanie got out of the car and slammed the door shut.

"Hey, take it easy. This thing is held together with gum and duct tape as it is."

"I'm concerned about him not showing this morning. He could be hurt. Or sick."

"Or drunk."

Steph pushed all the buzzers and called "Pizza." She pushed the door open when it was unlatched. "Come on, Johnny." She led the walk up the two flights of stairs and knocked on Apartment 32's door. "Paulie. It's me. And JD. You in there?"

John leaned against the door jamb and knocked. "Come on, Paulie." He rattled the knob. "Open up."

The door across the hall opened and a young woman stepped out into the hall. "You looking for Paulie?"

"How'd you guess?" Stephanie crossed her arms and looked the bottled blonde up and down.

"You're, like, knocking on the door and stuff?"

"And stuff. You have a name?"

"Amber."

Stephanie nodded. "Of course it is. Would you know where he is?"

"Paulie?"

"No, Carmen San Diego."

John bit back a laugh at the confusion on Amber's face. He let Stephanie take this.

Amber cocked her head. "I don't know any Carmen person."

"Okay, what about Paulie? You know where he is?"

"Paulie is a friend. I don't know you. I don't know if I should tell you anything."

"We're his kids. He's supposed to take us to the circus."

Amber beamed. "Really? How great to meet you all and everything. You look just like him, now that you mention it." She flicked a finger at John. "He doesn't. Did Paulie adopt him?"

John smothered his smile. Stephanie blushed. "Shh. We haven't told him yet. Paulie?"

"Oh, he left early this morning. Said he had to see a man about a thing. People say that all the time. Do you know who the man is? Or the thing?"

"What time did he leave?"

"Oh, about 8:00."

John pushed himself off the door jamb. "Was he alone?"

"Yes. Why? Is something wrong?"

He looked at Stephanie and shook his head before turning back to Amber. "No. Nothing to worry about. He must have forgotten that we were stopping by. Nice to meet you, Amber. Come on, sis. We've got to get going."

He followed her downstairs. "His kids? Where'd that come from?"

"I - " She stopped walking. "Look at that. Look." She pointed out a window in the stairwell. "Aren't those the guys from last night?"

A bumblebee yellow Camaro sat in front of the apartment building, behind John's car. The big guy and his sidekick walked toward the apartment. "Shit. What are they doing here?" He looked down the stairs. He could see the lobby door and the entryway to the elevators. "If they start coming up the stairs we duck on to the second floor. If they get on the elevator, we get out of here."

The front door opened. Looking down through the stairwell John watched the big guy poke the elevator button a couple of times. He looked at his watch and spoke. "Come on, come on. I ain't got all day."

He moved away from the elevator and toward the stairwell. John started backing up the stairs when the elevator dinged, and the doors slid open. He and Stephanie waited until the doors closed behind the two visitors, then ran down the stairs and out the door.

"What the hell was that about?" Stephanie climbed in the passenger side of John's car.

"Paulie owes someone some money." He wrote the license plate number on the palm of his hand. "Those guys are obviously the collection mechanism."

"So where is he?"

"If I knew that, we wouldn't have to look for him, would we?"

"It was rhetorical, asshole. We've got rehearsal. You better get us back there."

John started his car and pulled away as the two large visitors came out of the building. "They were quick. They knew exactly where to look, so they know him. Even odds they show up again tonight."

Chapter Six

The band rehearsed in the closed club. Ned plinked away at the melody part of Paul's new song, a melancholy riff that sounded vaguely French with a hint of gypsy and Russian folk song. Henry's bass played in perfect counterpoint. John and Stephanie had just arrived.

"Sounds nice. I need to work on the lyrics. I take it we have no drummer."

Henry leaned his bass against its stand. "You guys checked his place?"

John nodded. "Nothing. No answer. Bimbette across the hall said he left in a hurry this morning around 8:00. Said he had to see a guy about a thing."

"Nice and vague."

"And then the apes from last night showed up looking for him."

"Apes?"

"Two 'roid-fueled morons looking for him at the club showed up at his apartment."

Ned struck clichéd "dum-dum-dum" chords on the piano. "Something is rotten in the state of Dade."

"Dade's a county, you moron. So what do we do?"

"You pick up your bass, I'll pick up my sax, Stephanie can pick herself up and Ned, you can leave the piano right where it is. We run through the set, work on the transitions and get ready for tonight."

"Without a drummer?"

"He'll get here when he gets here. Pick up your bass. Until I see evidence to the contrary, he's just out running errands."

"You don't believe that any more than I do."

"Look, Henry, we could spend the next two hours putting together scenarios to explain why the old guy isn't here, but it's not going to do any good. We can't report him missing until he's gone for two days. That's Saturday morning. He's got something to do and I say we respect his privacy."

"That something to do has something to do with the couple of enforcers we saw. I don't think his being missing is as innocent as you're trying to pretend it to be."

"We've got a gig tonight. If he doesn't show, then I'll be concerned." John picked up his sax. "Now we've got work to do. The transition into 'Man's Man's World' is rough."

Ned looked up from his piano. "Hang on a sec. You think he won't show tonight?"

"He's going to be here." John adjusted the reed on his saxophone.

"Yeah, yeah, but what if? We can't do the gig without a drummer."

"He'll be here. He's never missed a gig."

"You just said that you wouldn't be concerned unless he didn't show tonight which means you're open to the possibility, however remote, that he won't show tonight."

"Really slim, piano man. Really slim."

Ned flipped open his phone. "I'll get a backup. Just in case."

"Like that?"

"Drummers are a dime a dozen."

"Yeah, man. But good ones are rare." Henry rubbed his face. "Larry's available, I think. He's not too bad."

"Great minds, and all that. He's the guy for me, too. Failing Paul, of course." Ned poked the numbers into his phone.

"He going to be pissed if he shows and Paul is here?"

"I'll let him know there's an outside chance he won't actually have to play. I'd prefer it if Paul actually showed. Fingers crossed."

~~~

"Well, boys, 100% confirmed that this is one Sergei Romanov, born Sergei Lebedev. We didn't need the tattoo. We caught a break. He's got a brother at FCI Marianna doing ten for money laundering. DNA match confirmed the body we found was the brother of the guy in jail."

MacCready smiled. "I'd say lucky you, but I know you'd punch me if I did. Great work."

Gloria wrinkled her nose and scowled. "Still don't know who killed him. I've got the bullet. Most of it. If you find a weapon, I can match it. But honestly, nothing short of a witness will get a conviction. Or a confession. There's precious little to connect the remains of poor Sergei to anyone or anything. Even the lead in his head is going to be difficult to match."

"Damaged?"

"A bit, but that's not the point. Whoever shot him no doubt tossed the weapon in the Everglades after him. If we're lucky. And that's a huge place to drag. If it's in the water, you'll never find it." She clapped her hands. "So it's either a confession or a witness. Do you have either?"

"Witnesses are so unreliable, aren't they, partner?"

James nodded. "Five witnesses will give you eight different versions of a story. No trace evidence tying the hump to a place any narrower than The Everglades? That's a pretty big starting place."

"Ah, I can help you there." She poked a couple of keys on her iMac and put the display on a screen on the wall. "The Everglades cover an area of over 5,000 square miles. Huge, eh? The main body of it is a huge river, about 60 miles wide stretching from Okeechobee down to Florida Bay. If that's all you had to go with you'd be out of luck. But," she pointed to an airboat wharf southwest of Miami, "that's the only place they could have launched from for the body to have shown up where it did. So, if you have a witness - I notice you didn't answer that - or want to track down who did it, you're going to have to head out to the swampy marsh. You're still looking at something like thirty or forty square miles to search."

"Yeah." James sighed. "I hoped to avoid it, but we kinda figured out we'd need to head out there somewhere. Thanks for narrowing it down. Should save us some time."

"I'm driving."

James tossed the car keys to MacCready. "Sure thing, Mac. I wouldn't know how to get there, anyway."

MacCready cruised south on SW 187th Avenue. "You awake?"

"Wasn't sleeping. Thinking about Gloria."

"Everything okay?"

"Yeah. Just thinking about her. I like thinking about her. Are we almost there?"

Mac pointed at a service station ahead on the right. "That would be it." He pulled into the parking lot and stepped into the hot, humid air. A thick bank of clouds skirted the coast to the east. Heavy rain clouds. "We're going to get pelted before the day is out. A massive storm is coming."

James nodded. "It's the end of August. What do you expect?"

"And it's Florida. Any plans for the long weekend?"

"I think we've got enough on our plates that we won't be getting a long weekend. I moved down from Jersey to escape the cold and ended up in a sauna working seven days a week."

"Bitch, bitch, bitch. So, what do we want to take out of this visit?"

"The name and address and phone number of the guy who shot Sergei. Failing that, something that will help us tie it all together."

Mac cocked an eyebrow. "Ever the optimist." He pushed the door open.

A shabby-looking guy, with grease stains on his shirt, an unlit cigarette in his mouth and a gut hanging over his belt stood behind the counter. "You looking for an airboat? I can rent them to you for your own use or, for an extra fifty, I can take youse on a tour."

Mac held up his badge. "I'm Detective MacCready and this is FBI Special Agent James. Not looking to go for a ride, yet. Would like to ask you some questions, though."

"Do I need a lawyer?"

"I don't know. Do you? We're just trying to find out if you've got the records of the rentals on Monday morning. You do have those records, don't you?"

"Why? What's going on?"

"Just a routine inquiry. Can I see your records for Monday?"

"I don't think anyone went out on Monday. It was a pretty quiet day."

Mac shook his head and smiled. "Do we look that stupid? Maybe my partner does. He is kinda young, but really, do *I* look that stupid? We know you rented out at least one, maybe two boats. Once we see your records, we're going to go over those airboats with a fine-toothed comb. James, call Gloria's office and tell her to get a tech crew out here before it rains."

James stepped to one side and placed the call.

"What's your name?"

The guy pointed at name stitched on his shirt. "Hector. I swear, nobody took a boat out Monday."

Mac held out his hand. "Show me your records for the past two weeks."

"You have a warrant?"

"I can get a warrant."

"Get a warrant."

"If I get a warrant, Hector, you'll be shut down for at least a week, maybe two. You'll miss the Labor Day weekend rush and frankly, by the look of this place, you can't stand the loss of income. Hand them over."

Hector grunted and grabbed a fistful of papers, shoving them in MacCready's direction. "This is fucking extortion."

"Thanks. It's just common sense, Hector. Glad you see it my way." He spread the papers across the cashier's counter." Let's see, Tuesday, Sunday, Wednesday, One here with no date, let's call it Monday and this one here. Only two on Monday? Slow day."

James slid his phone in his suit pocket. "She'll be here with a crew in thirty."

"Excellent. We've got paper." He handed one to James. "See this? Photocopy of a credit card for a Mr. Paul Coates. There's no rental form in that name, so we can assume it's missing. I'm going to place that as a Monday rental. Too coincidental." He handed a second paper to James. "And one for a Mr. William Clinton. "Slick" Willy himself."

"He's in Arkansas getting ready for the long weekend."

"I know that. Obviously an alias." Mac looked at Hector. "But not for you. You know who it was because you clearly knew it wasn't Clinton. So he was hiding from other people. Makes you complicit. Did you get a copy of a driver's license or credit card for Bill?"

"He left a large cash deposit, so I didn't ask for one."

"So tell us about this Mr. Clinton. What did he look like?"

"Average height, weight. Brown hair. No tattoos. Very average."

James looked around the inside of the shop. "You got any surveillance cameras in here? Security cameras?"

Hector held up his hands and shrugged. "I can't afford them."

"What's that up in the corner?"

"Just for show. It's not connected to anything. Regrettably."

"You don't say. I'm going to have to get that warrant, aren't I?"

Hector crossed his arms. "If dat's what you gotta do, dat's what you gotta do. You'll be wasting your time though. There ain't no pictures."

MacCready made a note in his little pad. "We'll see."

James folded Bill Clinton's rental agreement and slid it in an evidence bag. "Hand me that other one, too."

Mac passed the credit card copy and slid his hands in his pockets. "I say we get a head start looking at those airboats before the rain hits. Any of them out right now?"

Hector shook his head.

Mac smiled and leaned in, whispering. "You fibbing?" He held out a hand. "Maintenance records please."

Hector pushed the book across the counter.

Mac flipped to the front of the book and counted inventory. "James, it says here he's got ten. How many are out there?"

Hector held his hands up. "Hey, I've only got nine running. Some fucking tourists from Ohio totaled one of them. Here, look at the maintenance reports for it. Three months ago." He flipped to the appropriate page and turned the book around. "See?"

"Okay, fine. Nine. James, do a count please. Won't even have to take off your shoes."

"Cute." James left and Mac turned back to Hector. "So where's the missing rental agreement?"

"What missing agreement?"

"The one I've got the credit card copy for. There's a missing agreement and a missing driver's license copy. You throw those out? That's a Sarbanes-Oxley violation, you know. The IRS will not look kindly on it."

"Oxley who?"

Mac shook his head. "Never mind."

James pushed back into the shop, bringing a wave of warm, humid air and a cloud of mosquitoes. "Nine. Surprised some of them ran. There's one, in particular, I'd like Gloria's team to look at."

"Well, we'll go stand by it, just in case something may try to happen to it. You stay in here, Hector, erasing your security hard drive."

Mac and James wandered outside. The air hung heavy, perfectly still, save the clouds of mosquitoes and gnats. "Lovely place down here, James. You should find a place to live around here. Beautiful neighborhood, great neighbors. Very serene."

James batted away the insects swarming his face. "One thing about winters up north, they kill all these critters."

An MPD van pulled into the parking lot, disgorging Gloria and three of her young techs. "What did I do to you guys to deserve this? It's over 90 degrees and the humidity is stifling." She waved her hand in front of her face. "And these mozzies are killing me. What am I looking for here?"

"I think you were dead on about this being the launching place, and there's a boat I want you to look at. Residual blood on it. Might be the victim's."

Chapter Seven

Rico stopped at the table. "Where you guys playing tonight? And where's Paulie?"

The band had just sat for an early pre-gig lunch. Four of the band did, anyway. John looked up at the diminutive owner of the restaurant. "Missing. When you see him last?"

"When you guys were in here scarfing down my lasagna. Like animals."

"It's really good. We didn't see you here."

"I was in the kitchen, minding my own business. What do you mean, missing? When'd you see him last?"

They looked at each other. "After last night's gig. He bolted," said Stephanie.

"I talked to him a little while after that, but nothing since." Henry scrubbed his fingertips through his hair. "Not like him."

"Not lately, no. But the Paul I knew years ago would lose days at a time. Big partier. Maybe the wagon's bucked him off."

"You've know him that long then you'd know he's been dry for years now." Stephanie ended the conversation. "Can we see menus, please? We need to hurry up and get some food in us."

John nudged up against Steph. "Shove over a bit. I think our stand-in is here." He nodded at the door where a reedy-looking man stood, looking around the small restaurant. He smiled as he walked toward them.

"Have you ordered yet? I'm famished. Thanks for calling, guys. It's been a bit dry lately. Paul on vacation? Do I know you? I haven't seen you before."

John stuck out his hand. "John Delacourte. Call me JD. I play the sax."

"Ah, the saxamaphone. A replacement for our dear departed Wilson."

"Wilson died? I thought Wilson hit the big times."

"The bastard's dead to me. He needed a drummer to go with him, and he bypassed me." Larry sat. "So. What's for dinner? Can I get a freakin' menu here?"

John turned to Ned. "This guy ever shut up?" He tossed him his menu. "Izzy'll be by in a minute. Pick something quick."

Larry looked across the table at Henry. "He talks to you like that?"

"I'd pop his head like a grape." He laughed. "JD is cool, man. Plays a mean sax. And JD, you'll get used to Larry. He's not too bad on the skins, and he keeps his mouth shut mostly when we're playing."

Izzy did arrive and took their orders, Larry protesting that he hadn't enough time. He ordered chicken Caesar salad and leaned back. "So, Paulie. Is he dead? What's going on there?"

"Missing in action." Ned drummed his fingers on the table. "Not dead, not on a freaking bender, just fucked off somewhere when we needed him the most. Huge show this weekend, and he pisses off somewhere."

"You're forgetting the gorillas JD and I saw. At the club and the next day at his apartment. He hasn't just 'pissed off'. And he might be dead. We can't find him."

"What do you mean gorillas? Not real gorillas, right? Just big guys? Bigger than Mandingo here?"

Henry reached across and stuck a steak knife in the table between Larry's hands. "Watch it. You flap your gums a bit too much."

"Okay, big guy. Take it easy."

"And one of them was almost as big as Henry. The second one is not much smaller."

"Hey, size isn't everything."

Henry chuckled. "I've never had to say that."

John gently shook his head at the rest of the table. "And here comes Izzy with the food. Perfect timing." He helped hand out the dishes and leaned down, looking into Stephanie's eyes. Tears were flowing down her cheeks. "Hey, Steph, it'll be okay. Trust me. We finish this thing tonight, and I'll go checking his haunts tomorrow."

She sniffed and wiped her eyes. "Tonight. After the gig. And I'm coming with you."

"What? No. Absolutely not."

"Then I'll go on my own. Chicken shit."

"No, that's not what I meant, and you know it."

"Shut up JD, and eat. We'll talk about it later."

He grunted and bit into his burger. He had a pretty good idea what he'd be doing after the show.

~~~

Stan and Grigory sat at the same table they had sat at the night before, looking for the same person. Stan looked around at the others in the club. "Bunch of putz in there, Greg. You should go by Greg. Drop the Russian name. Become American."

"I am Russian. Don't call me Greg. My name is Grigory. This guy gonna be here tonight?"

"The boss will be really pissed if we don't do this. So he better be." He looked around again. "What kind of people come to this shit? Look at these people. And this isn't even real music." He looked at his watch. "And it's like 9:00 already. How late do these guys start?"

As if on cue, Bobby stepped to the mic in front of the setup. "Folks, thanks for coming by today. The Coates Quintet will be out in a minute. Please make sure to tip your server."

"About fucking time." Stan leaned back in the chair, straining its joints, and crossed his arms.

"We going to take him when they come out? Or wait."

"Greg, Grigory, we're in a packed club. I may not be a genius, but I'm not stupid. This time we don't let him out of our sight."

"So we follow him right backstage and do it there."

"Something like that. But we don't let him out of our sight."

"We may have to do the big black guy too.

Stan shrugged. "We do what we have to do."

66

The door opened, and Stan sat up. The singer walked out first, then the little sax player, the piano player, the big black guy and a drummer he didn't recognize.

"What the fuck?"

"Where's the drummer?" Grigory looked down at the leaflet in his hand and back up at the band. "He's not there."

"Yeah, no shit. Some pencil-necked dick is sitting in for him. The asshole is hiding from us. What the fuck?"

The band started playing an upbeat song that Stan hated. "Bullshit."

A middle-aged guy with a goatee and short-cropped grey hair leaned over from his table. "Ah, keep it down, okay? These guys are good. I'd like to enjoy the music."

In a smooth motion, Stan picked the glass off his table and smashed it into his face, splitting his lip and cutting him under the cheekbone. "You shut your fucking mouth, you asshole." Stan shoved him the rest of the way out of the chair and kicked him in the ribs. The music stopped. The other patrons stared at him and backed away. "What? Piss off." He turned to the band. "You think you can hide the drummer? It's not going to work. And after I finish him, I'm coming back and finishing all of you."

~~~

John reacted first. He dropped his sax in its stand, leapt past the floor speakers and squatted by the injured man. "You okay? Hey, you're the dude who gave me your card the other night. Shitty luck." He grabbed a clean napkin off the table and held it to the side of his head. "Where does it hurt?"

Steph dropped in beside him. "Idiot. His face and the ribs he's holding, I bet." She looked at the spectators. "Has anyone called an ambulance? The police?"

The club owner appeared. "Ah, shit. Just what I need. What the hell is all this about?"

"You've got security video, right?" John pointed to a camera mounted in the corner of the room. "I'd copy the section showing what happened and have it ready for the police when they show up."

The owner nodded and jogged back to his office.

Ned, Henry and Larry started playing a low-key jazz riff, slow and easy. John nudged Stephanie. "They are pros. We're pros. We need to still put on a show tonight, so don't get too bent out of shape."

"You saw who those guys were, right?"

"I saw. Not a coincidence. This has me as confused as hell. Why are they so intent on finding him and where in the hell is he?"

"If those two were looking for me I'd be in a Tibetan monastery as fast as I could get there. The big guy is scary." She shuddered involuntarily.

John shrugged. "It's just muscle. He's got the same pain points as everyone else."

"So tell me why you just sat there watching, instead of doing something?"

"The big guy hit too fast for me to do anything about it, then left. Jumping in after the fact is just adding fuel to the fire. No benefit to anyone if I do that."

The man on the floor groaned. "Gee, thanks."

"What did you say to him?" John lifted the cloth and looked at the damage. The guy would need a dozen stitches, maybe some surgery. "This is pretty ugly. You won't be the belle of the ball anymore."

"I just asked him to keep it down. I like your music. He was being a lout."

"What was he talking about?"

"He was pissed Larry was sitting in for Paul. Really pissed." He pointed to his face. "He must really be a big Paul fan."

John shifted his weight and ended up sitting on the floor beside him. "So you know both Larry and Paul?"

He nodded. "What's Paul got himself into? I'm kind of surprised to see the founder of your little group missing. Is he sick?"

Stephanie returned with some ice. "Put this on your cheek. It's starting to swell. Paul is MIA. And these apes are making me think it's not for a good reason. JD and I are going to canvass the rounds tonight after the gig."

The guy looked up at John. "Are you fucking nuts? You run into those two and steroid boy is going to crush you." He held his face and groaned. "It hurts to talk."

"So don't talk. Steph will go on her own if I don't go with her, and short of tying her up in bed, which has its appeal, the best I can do is go with her."

Noise at the top of the stairs, followed by the scraping of chairs and tables as the diners created a path, signaled the arrival of the paramedics and police.

Stephanie shook her head. "Great. We're going to be held up for an hour, at least, talking to the cops. I want to do this show. It'll help me unwind."

"Hang on a sec." John pulled one of the policemen to one side. "The girl and I are in the group that's supposed to be playing tonight, so we'll be here for at least another three hours. The owner has a tape of what happened. We were still on that little stage when it all went down, so we couldn't really comment on what anyone said, just what we saw. And the video is better evidence than any eyewitness account. Okay with you if we continue the set? We're here if you need us, and the owner has our contact information. That cool?"

The constable looked at the stage and the distance from them to the victim. "Yeah, makes sense. Your name?"

"I'm John Delacourte, and she's Stephanie Peters. Thanks, man. Appreciate it."

He popped back to Steph. "On stage. We're good for now. If they need us, they'll let us know."

~~~

They closed the night off with Woody Herman's "Body and Soul". John did a poor replication of the clarinet part with his sax and thought to himself, for at least the hundredth time, that he had to get his hands on a clarinet and teach himself. It wasn't that different from a sax, and it would add a bit of variety to the gigs.

They wound up, Stephanie thanked everyone for their applause, and the house lights went up.

70

"We're here for the long weekend, through to Monday night. Tell your friends. Come on back. We can't promise that the spectacle put on tonight will be repeated, but the entertainment will still be very high quality." She flicked off the mic and turned to the rest of the band. "I'm drained."

"So we aren't heading out?"

"I didn't say that."

Henry placed his bass in its stand. "What are you guys talking about?"

"Don't worry about it, big guy. JD and I have it covered."

"Have what covered? You're going out looking for Paulie, aren't you? Don't be idiots."

"She's the idiot. I'm just her sidekick."

"Seriously, man. He's obviously lying low until this blows over. You're either going to get yourself killed, or you're going to lead whoever is looking for him right to him. Back it off." Henry scrubbed his scalp with his fingertips. "This isn't funny shit anymore. You saw what happened. It's getting real."

Stephanie narrowed her eyes and cocked her head. "You know something, don't you?"

"I know that if that monster attacks you they'll be looking for pieces for weeks."

She shook her head. "No. You know something. Where's Paul?"

"I have no idea where Paul is. Your guess is as good as mine. Just let him go, okay?"

"I'm going. You coming JD?"

"I'm not letting you go by yourself."

"Oh, fuck." Henry rubbed his face with his hands. "I'm going too. Y'all are going to get yourselves killed."

"I don't want you coming with us until you tell us what you know."

"Lady, I don't know anything. And to be frank, I don't want to go with you. I could use my sleep. I'm not getting any younger."

"Time is linear, Henry. None of us are getting younger. Tag along and keep Steph and me out of trouble if you wish, but you're going to have to tell us what you know sooner than later."

Bobby came by with an envelope of cash. "I normally deal with Paul on this. Who's the second in command here?" He handed it to Stephanie. "You, right?"

Stephanie took the envelope. "Cash?"

He grinned. "You betcha. I put more on the books than I actually pay you. Paul records less in income. The IRS never matches it up. Win-win."

She took the envelope and fanned the bills. "I can't take this with me tonight. Can you hold it until tomorrow?" She handed the envelope back. "And how often do you pay us?"

"Mondays and Thursdays for the long gigs like this. In arrears. You sure you want me to hold this?"

"Yes, I am. We'll see you tomorrow night, okay? We'll just leave the kit set up.

John grabbed the reed off his sax, slid it into a holder and dropped it in his sax case. "Okay. Let's go get killed."

Chapter Eight

John pulled into Denny's parking lot with bleary eyes and a pounding head. "I had more fun in Afghanistan." He looked through the window: Ned, Henry and Stephanie were at their usual table. No Paul. No Larry.

He locked the car and went in.

"Son, you look like shit." Ned chuckled and lifted his coffee to his lips.

"Great. I'd hate to feel like this and look good." He waved at a server and mimed pouring a cup of coffee, then sat beside Stephanie. "You, on the other hand, look great. What's the secret?"

"So does Henry, and you're not hitting on him. Where's Larry?"

"We seem to be having a drummer's drought." Ned sipped again. "Larry sent me a text message and said he'd be joining us later, so no mystery there. No word from Paul?"

Henry lifted his head from the table. "Last night we hit every place in the greater Miami area that he could possibly be. And he wasn't at any of them. We did, however, almost get killed. Three times. And we have at least one big ugly asshole still looking for us. I haven't had this much fun since - ever. This may be the last day of my marriage. You realize that, don't you? Wife is mighty pissed."

JD accepted the cup of coffee from the waitress and thanked her. "Thanks for coming with us, big guy. Your bulk came in handy."

Henry laughed. "I knew it. You love me for my body."

"Well, your personality sucks, buddy."

Ned sat back and looked at the trio. "So you guys went on an adventure. Tell me what you discovered. What have you found out about our friend and fearless leader?"

"These two daredevils think he's in some sort of danger. They claim that muscle-bound idiot at the club last night has been around a couple of times threatening his life, but based on the absolute lack of anything we ran across last night, save the near beatings and the thug on our tail, I'd say Paul is somewhere sleeping it off. He looked pretty hard at that bottle of wine the other day. I'm sure you all saw that. He's been dry for a few years, but, folks, it's a disease, right? He's probably in his apartment, passed out."

Stephanie shook her head and yawned. "Sorry. No, we were at the apartment. He wasn't there."

John shook his head. "No, we knocked on his door and he didn't answer."

She sat up straight. "Shit. Then those apes showed up."

John closed his eyes for a moment. "But they showed up again later that night still looking for him." He scrubbed his face. "I don't know what the hell is going on." He slapped the table. "I'm going back to his place. Break in. See if he's there, if he's okay, whatever. At least we'll know that. Right now we have no data." He looked at

Stephanie. "And I don't want you tagging along this time, okay? Rest, or your voice will be shit tonight."

"Oh, that's so sweet of you. Ass-hat. But you're right. I'm dead. Henry, can you go with him?"

"Nuh-uh. I owe wifey for last night. I'm going to pass, brother."

Ned stuck up his hand. "I've been kinda bored lately, and you all are having all the fun. I'll tag along. As long as it's not dangerous or anything."

"It's break and enter, Ned. I think that's a felony, too."

"It's Paulie. If he's home, he invited us in. If he isn't, well, who's going to tell?"

The waitress arrived with their breakfasts.

"I don't need company. You don't have to come along, man. I'm good."

"Safety in numbers. Wow. I don't believe I just said that." Ned adjusted his plate, rotating it so the bacon sat at the front. "I'm going to come along for no other reason than I'm feeling left out, all the adventure you guys are having. Think of it as a bonding exercise, okay?

John shrugged. "Whatever, man. Dig in. We'll head out this afternoon. Hopefully, he's just plastered."

~~~

James yawned. "Too early, Mac. I need my beauty rest."

"And I don't?"

"It'll do you no good now. Too far gone." James held the door and let his partner through to the Crime Technicians' office.

"Very long day ahead of us. Early bird and all that shit."

Gloria Harris looked up as they arrived. "Good morning boys."

"Gloria. You're looking especially fine today."

She arched an eyebrow. "What do you want, James?"

"Hey, just a compliment." He half sat on an empty evidence table. "The Everglades killing. Did you get anything at all that can tie it to Petrovski? The victim was a member of his organization. He was also being groomed as an informant. When he shows up with a bullet literally between his eyes, I start thinking."

"So, that's the only time you start thinking? That explains a lot."

"I'm serious here Glor. He's looking good for it. Have you been able to find anything at all that points in his general direction?"

"Not a thing. You're stumped on this one, are you?"

"You're not helping any. What did you find out about that small amount of blood on the airboat?" Mac sat on one of the stools and flipped open his notepad. "Any match between that blood and our victim?"

Gloria laughed. "Not even close."

"And that's funny how?"

"Not the same blood type. Not even the same type of blood. That remnant of blood you saw in the crack came from an alligator. Somebody used that airboat to poach alligators."

Mac looked up. "Really?"

"So you're fish and game wardens now? Yes. Really."

"Did you lift any prints off the boat?"

"Seventeen different thumb prints alone. All up, about sixty unique fingerprints. Why?"

"We're going to have a set of prints sent to you later today. Can you prioritize a cross-check between them and the ones you found on the boat?"

"Sure. Looking for an identification or verification?"

"We know who owns the prints. We just need to confirm a statement he or she made about their whereabouts."

"Yeah, I can do that. Give me an hour or so after I get them. Can I make another suggestion?"

Mac spread his hands. "Always open to new ideas."

"Run some TV spots looking for a witness. The victim was killed Monday afternoon. It's the end of summer. There had to be people out in that area who saw something."

"Yup. There has to be." James looked at Mac. "Maybe an ad will look desperate? Like we don't have any idea what's going on."

"And maybe that's not a bad idea, partner." He kissed Gloria on the cheek. "Great idea. Thanks. We'll send you the prints electronically later this morning. I'll give you a call when we send them. James, I think we need to have a chat with our young detective Cruz."

"Why?"

"He was this informant's contact within the department."

~~~

Ned belched and pushed his plate back.

"How in the hell do you stay so skinny, eating like that?" Henry tore off a piece of roll and spread jam from a small individual packet on it. "You should be bigger than me."

"Magic metabolism. I burn it up faster than I can eat it."

"You know that metabolism stops eventually. And suddenly. You're going to wake up one morning looking like Michael Moore."

Ned grinned. "Not yet. Thank God. And as long as I don't end up with his personality. JD, you ready to go?"

"Patience, ass." He forked the last piece of sausage into his mouth and talked around it. "I don't inhale my food. And what's the rush?"

"I'm getting off on the idea of some excitement. I've led a boring existence up to now. No fights, no lawsuits, no unexpected babies -"

"You're gay."

"Whatever." He rubbed his hands together. "What do you expect to find? I expect to find a drunk Coates."

John shook his head. "Maybe. If not, I'm hoping I come across something that explains his disappearance."

"For Christ's sake, call the cops."

"He's not officially missing for another day. And I really think looking for a known drunk, the middle-aged man slides pretty far down their list of priorities." Stephanie rubbed her eyes. "JD, call me if you find anything, okay? I've got to go." She dropped a twenty on the table. "I'm completely beat. I'll see you all at the club tonight. I need to catch up on my sleep."

The three of them watched her walk out, a slight weave to her step.

"She looks beat," said Ned.

"We were out very late. And she's really worried about him."

John leaned forward. "Listen, I know I'm kinda new to the group and all, but there are some things I don't get. Like her and Paulie. Was there something between them before?"

"Jesus, are you kidding? He's about thirty years older than she is." Henry's laugh resonated in his chest, deep and gravelly. "She doesn't go for the older guys."

"Yeah, I know. That's what she told me."

"So you tried, did you?"

"I'm always trying. I like her." He worried some gristle from his teeth. "So nothing between them?"

"It's more like a father, doting daughter relationship. He stopped drinking shortly after she showed up."

"When?"

Ned looked at Henry. "What was it, big guy, about three years ago?"

"Roughly. Later in the year, so almost three years ago. She escaped from the Midwest somewhere. Tired of the cold weather. He kinda took her under his wing. We didn't have a singer prior to that. But we did have a clarinet player."

"I'm getting a clarinet. Easy to learn. We can put some Woody Herman into our repertoire."

Henry nodded. "That would be good. Although he's more big band."

"Paul has this magic ability to arrange the music to work."

"If we find him."

Ned stood. "Which we'll never do if we sit here all day. We need to get a move on."

~~~

Detective Mario Cruz sat at his desk, flipping through paperwork. MacCready walked up behind him and slapped him on the back. "What's going on, old partner?"

"Mac? What brings you here?"

"Thought we'd have a chat about one of your informants."

"I don't have many. Building up a base. Hey, I don't want you exposing any of them, okay? It takes a long time to get these guys to turn."

"Oh, this guy has already turned. Turned up dead, that is."

"Sergei. Damn shame, him. I planned on taking down Petrovski with him."

"He wasn't that high up in the organization though, was he? At least not in our files." James tapped the paper on Cruz's desk. "Did you know something we didn't?"

"I doubt it. And yeah, about half way up the totem-pole, but moving up fast. A very eager beaver. More than happy to spill the beans."

"Ambitious? What else can you tell us about him?"

Cruz shrugged and leaned back in his chair. "I don't know, Mac. Did a lot of odd jobs for one of Petrovski's henchmen, this gorilla named Stanislav."

"Ah, Stan. I know him well. He's a big fan of 'roids. I'd hate to meet him in a dark alley." MacCready looked at his watch. "Anything else?"

"Not really. Small-time player I groomed on his way up. He didn't really have much I could use now, but he was a willing talker and he was getting more visibility within Petrovski's organization. A perfect pigeon."

"Seems like Petrovski found out. Cancelled his contract." James snugged his jacket. "We need to hit the media folks before the next news cycle partner."

Cruz looked up at James, then MacCready. "Wait. What makes you think Petrovski found out. And why the media?"

"You said it yourself. He was still small potatoes. No reason for someone to take him out to the Everglades and put a bullet between his eyes. Not unless it was in retribution for something."

Mac nodded. "And the media is to get the word out that we're looking for witnesses. If we can link Petrovski to this killing, it will be enough to finally put that slick asshole behind bars."

"Really?"

"Yup. And then you can use whatever informants you have to work on his second in command." He turned to leave, then stopped. "Cruz, by the way, if your criminal informants have any relationship to any mob organization, you need to inform me and keep me completely in the loop. *Capice?*"

~~~

Petrovski flicked open the Miami Herald just as his phone rang. He looked at the incoming number, folded the paper shut and answered the call. "You can talk?"

"I can. I stepped out of the station. This is urgent."

"It must be. My phone is clean, I believe. Speak freely."

"The FBI is going to be running a TV ad looking for witnesses to Sergei's killing. They are trying to link his death to you, and if they do, they believe they will have enough to take you down."

"Really? How new is this information?"

"I just found out. They're heading to media relations as we speak."

"Very good. Thanks for giving me the heads-up. Forewarned is forearmed, they say. You are becoming very useful." He hung up and leaned back in his chair, thinking. This wasn't unexpected. He employed Sergei, and anyone who followed his line of business would be able to deduce that.

But he knew who the witness was. That gave him an advantage over the FBI and their police friends. He just had to find the guy.

Chapter Nine

Stan belched and wiped his mouth. "The strippers suck. Man, they're really dredging the bottom of the barrel."

"Stanislav," barked a voice behind him.

"It's Stan. Please call me Stan." He looked back over his shoulder. "Oh, excuse me, boss. Was just kidding about the girls. Join me for lunch?"

"No time for that, Stanislav." Petrovski pulled out a chair and sat across from him. "You're sitting there, gawking at the bottom-of-the-barrel girls and our witness is still, I believe, alive. Or have you killed him yet? Which is it? Alive or dead?"

"I've been by his place a couple of times, and by the club his band is playing at. He's nowhere to be found. Maybe he left town."

Petrovski shook his head before Stan finished talking. "No, no, no. That level of uncertainty is not acceptable. You and Grigory need to go now and not come back until HE IS DEAD. Am I clear on this? Perfectly clear?"

Stan balled up the napkin and stood. "Relax, boss. We'll find him and plant him. You want to do it again?"

"That's what got us in this mess the first time, so no. But I expect you to be as professional as if I was there. Understood? Now go find the guy and make sure nothing is left of him to testify."

Stan looked uncharacteristically nervous. "Um, boss, what do you suggest?"

"About what?"

"Finding this guy."

"You checked his apartment?"

"He wasn't there. I checked twice."

"He wasn't there, no. But did you look through his apartment for some clues as to his whereabouts? He didn't just vanish off the face of the earth."

"Would be good if he did, right?"

"He didn't. Check his apartment again and I'll do some calling around to my contacts. If he's holed up in a Miami hotel I'll find out about it."

Stan nodded. "I'll head over there now. I don't know what I'm looking for, but I'm sure I'll know it when I see it."

Petrovski drew a deep breath, shook his head and walked back to his office in the back of the club.

～～～

"We got two hours, max, man." John pulled up to the curb in front of the apartment. "We dicked around too much and we're running late. If we don't find him, we won't have time to go looking for him until late tonight, okay? No time to mess around."

Ned stretched his long frame out of the small car. "I feel like a sardine. When are you going to get a new car? This one smells funny."

"You heard what I said? In and out. And even then we don't have much time for lunch. I'm starving. In and out."

"That's what he said."

"She said."

"I'm gay, remember?"

John cocked an eyebrow. "And you've never hit on me. Should I be offended?"

"You're straight. Very. And even if you weren't, you're not my type. Too short, too butch. I'm more of a bear guy."

John put his hands up in surrender. "Fine, you've made your point." He shook his head and pressed all the buzzers. "You'd think they'd have figured this out by now." The door buzzed open.

"Too many trusting people in this world, Johnny. Warms the heart, doesn't it?"

"How are we going to get into his apartment?"

Ned winked. "My fingers are for more than the piano."

"That's what he said."

Ned laughed and trotted up the stairs, two at a time. "Two flights, right?"

"Right-o." John followed one step at a time. "Turn right when you come out of the stairwell. Why didn't you take the elevator?"

"Not keen on getting trapped in a small metal box. Odds are huge that its maintenance schedule hasn't been met for years, if not decades." He turned up the second flight. "Really hard to get trapped in a flight of stairs."

"You've got a point there." They popped into the hallway on the second floor, Apartment 32 on their right. "So show me your magic."

Ned slid a credit card out of his wallet, leaned against the door and popped the lock. "Easy."

"What if he had the deadbolt locked?"

"I've been here before. He has a chain. No deadbolt."

"And if the chain was in place?"

"That means he's in there. But it's not." He swung the door open.

"You know, man, I've been here dozens of times and I never noticed the deadbolt thing."

Ned shrugged. "I'm observant. So what are we supposed to be looking for?"

John walked into the apartment beyond the small kitchen on the right and into the small, spotless living room in front of him. To the left a small hall led to the bathroom and bedroom. "Cozy. Start looking around."

Ned plopped on the sofa and put his legs up on the coffee table. "That's your job. I'm just company. Man, this is a nice television." He looked around and spotted the remote on the lamp table beside the sofa. "What is this, 56-inch? Must be new. Football games must be great on this." He turned it on and flicked through the channels. "Wonder if Ellen is on."

John shook his head and wandered back to the bedroom. "This place is immaculate."

"What?"

"Never mind." He stood in the center of the room and slowly turned. "You'd never guess that an overweight, frequently whiskery middle-aged man lived here."

"What? Can't hear you."

"Talking to myself." A stack of flyers for the band sat on the bedside table beside the well-made bed. "Hospital corners. Huh". He opened the bedside table top drawer. Paul's wallet sat in the bottom beside a pack of condoms and his mobile phone. He opened the wallet and rifled through it. No cash, but credit cards and driver's license. He slid it into his back pocket and the phone into his front.

The closet held a couple of suits and dress shirts. Three really ugly ties adorned a tie rack. Two pairs of cheap dress shoes were on the floor of the closet. A small safe sat in the corner, the door open, empty.

"Double-huh."

Paul wasn't here, and by the looks of the light layer of dust, it had been a couple of days. "Hey, Ned, we should be able to report him missing now. It's been more than 48 hours."

"Not until tomorrow morning. And fat chance of them doing anything. If he was an eight-year-old blonde, blue-eyed girl, there'd be a task force. A middle-aged man with a history of drinking problems? It'll go to the bottom of the pile if they even take it."

"Bit of a cynic, aren't you?"

"Realist." He flicked the channels until he hit ESPN. "Hey, Braves - Jays game. I didn't know they were playing a day game today." He settled back on the sofa. "Keep looking for clues, detective. There are two innings left, and it's tied."

John wandered into the small kitchen. The counter opened to the living room. A refrigerator, dishwasher and oven were crammed into a space three people couldn't comfortably stand. He wrinkled his nose and looked in the sink. "Dishes."

"Huh?" Ned kept his eyes on the screen. Bases were loaded and a Brave's batter sat on 1 strike and 3 balls. "What about the dishes?"

"There's dirty dishes in the sink."

"So?"

"So look at this place. Does it look like he leaves a dirty anything, anywhere? He probably puts his clothes in the washing machine when he takes them off for the night. Speaking of which, where's the washing machine?"

Ned pointed over his shoulder. "Stackable units in one of the closets in the hall. Fuck. Braves hit a bases-loaded homer."

John opened the closet and looked at the very small washer/dryer set. "Cute. Wait, what's this?" He reached in and pulled out a rifle. "Ned, what the fuck's this?"

He twisted on the sofa. "What do you think it is, a tennis racquet? It's a rifle. A .22, if I remember correctly."

"Personal protection with a rifle? First, I wouldn't have expected him to have a gun, and if he did, it should be a handgun, shouldn't it?"

"You can't shoot alligators with a handgun. You'll get your hand bit off, like Cap'n Hook. They use a .22 to minimize the damage to the skin. But because it's a small caliber they have to get close. So it's got to be a rifle."

John hefted the .22. "So he's killed alligators with this thing?"

Ned nodded. "A few. This game is shit. Braves are up by 5 and the Jays have fallen apart. Screw this. I hate day games." He scrolled through the channels until he got to a local news station. "Hey, JD. Check this out."

"Miami Police are requesting the witnesses to the shooting of a Sergei Lebedev, also known as Sergei Romanov, in the Everglades this past Monday afternoon to come forward."

John sat on the sofa beside Ned. "When was he -"

"Yeah. Monday afternoon."

"Mr. Romanov is an associate of Vladimir Petrovski, a member of an organized crime family known to the FBI and the local police. Romanov was shot between the eyes and deposited in the Everglades. Fortunately for the police, the body was found relatively intact and the .22 bullet retrieved from his skull."

John looked at the rifle in his hand. "Shit."

"Police believe a witness or witnesses to the shooting are in the community. They are strongly encouraged to go to the nearest police station immediately, for their own protection. It's highly likely that whoever shot Sergei Romanov will not hesitate in killing the witness or witnesses. Again, if you are watching this and witnessed the killing, or you know who witnessed the killing, you are urged to contact Detective Dan MacCready at Miami PD, or Special Agent Stephen James at the local FBI offices. Phone numbers are displayed at the bottom of the screen."

"Son of a bitch. You think he shot this Russian dude? By mistake maybe?" John put the rifle down and backed away from it. "Shit."

Ned stood. "I think the shit just got real, as the kids say."

"The kids haven't said that for years. But you're right. Paulie's in some serious shit." John stepped over to the window. "And it looks like some friends of Sergei want to avenge his death. Shit."

"Yeah, shit."

"No, new shit." John looked at the bumblebee color scheme on the Camaro. Neither the muscle-head nor his colleague were anywhere to be seen. "Double-shit, we need to get out of here, now. The gorillas are in our midst."

"Funny."

"No so funny. Their car is here, and I can't see them. It won't take them long to get up the stairs. There has to be another way out of here."

"Other than what?"

"The door, Ned. The door which is going to be filled with -"

Heavy steps stopped outside the door. John put his finger to his lips and picked up the rifle. He pointed to the kitchen and motioned for Ned to go in there and get down below the sight line. He quietly slid a shell into the breech and held the rifle to his shoulder.

They heard a grunt, and the door popped open. The muscle head filled the frame.

"Stop right there, big guy. What's your name?"

"Stan. You're JD, right?" He looked around the apartment. "I thought this was where Coates lived. You his boyfriend?"

Ned stood. "You homophobic?"

John shook his head. "Man, you didn't have to pop up like that. Complicates things. Hop over the counter and get behind me."

Stan took a step forward.

"Hang on there, big guy. You're not coming in."

"You going to stop me with that pea-shooter?"

"Probably."

"I've been shot before, and by guns a lot bigger than that. And I'm still here."

"I might not kill you, but you'll hurt, and I'm confident you'll be spending some time in the hospital after I drop six in your gut. So save yourself the pain and back the fuck out of here."

Stan stuck his hands up. "I'm not looking for you, JD. Or you, piano player. I'm looking for Paul Coates. This is his address. Where is he?"

John shrugged. "Who knows? Could be anywhere. But he's not here so you can leave."

"He's your friend, is he? Well, I've got to kill him. And I'll go through you two to get to him if I have to."

Chapter Ten

"Do you know where you're going?" James looked from the map on his phone to the GPS in Mac's car. "We've got to be there in five and it's like we aren't even close yet."

MacCready chuckled. "You really don't know your way around here yet, do you? And it's been almost a year. We're here." He rounded a corner and stopped in front of the Miami Federal Courthouse. "We've been here half a dozen times and you still can't find the place? Good thing I'm the Detective." He parked and stuck his card on the dashboard.

"It's a nice day today, Mac."

He looked out over the coast. "That weather is going to break soon. We're due for a storm. Thunderheads pounding Bimini. They'll be heading our way."

"You think?" James slung his jacket over his shoulder. "This is beautiful."

A block from the Federal Courthouse was the local office for the Federal government. Mac oriented himself with the buildings and pointed east. "That-a-way."

"So why'd we park in front of the Federal Courthouse if we're going to walk two blocks to the Federal Building?"

"We're going to end up at the courthouse, and there are even odds it'll be raining before we're finished. Planning, James. That's the key to a happy life."

James slipped his jacket on as they walked into the air-conditioned lobby of the Federal Building, sitting at a federally mandated 72 degrees. He waved at the security guard at the desk. "Department of Justice still on 6?"

The ready-for-retirement guard nodded. "Hasn't moved yet. Long time no see, James. What you up to these days?"

"I'd tell you, Wally, but then my partner would have to kill you. Catch you later."

The guard's gravel laugh echoed off the marble as they stepped into the elevator. James pushed '6'.

"You come here often?"

James cracked a smile. "You trying to pick me up?"

The elevator 'dinged' and the doors slid open to the South Florida offices of the Department of Justice. James looked at his watch. "Cutting it close."

"It's the Federal Government, partner. When have the Feds ever been on time for anything?"

The receptionist looked up from her computer and smiled. "Be nice, or I'll make you wait." She checked her schedule. "You must be MacCready and James, here to see Agent Furness about a WitSec application. Have a seat and he'll be here -"

"I'm already here, Karen. Thanks." A gray-haired portly man held out his hand. "I'm Agent Dave Furness."

James shook his hand. "Special Agent Stephen James and this is my partner in crime, Detective Dan MacCready."

Furness led them to a small meeting room and had coffee brought for them. He opened a buff file folder and slid out a piece of paper. "I've gone over the application form. You've actually got a witness for this shooting? We saw the plug on TV less than an hour ago. This came across the fax machine half an hour ago. No way you got someone that fast."

Mac smiled. "A bit of misdirection. We've had this guy since yesterday morning. He's obviously under intense pressure, and we're pretty sure the Russian is after him. He's more than willing to testify, but he needs protection. The plug, hopefully, will keep the black hats guessing."

"Reliable?"

James shrugged. "He came to us. He was poaching alligators when he saw the event. We've confirmed that part of his story. Alligator blood and his fingerprints on an airboat put him there, and fingerprints on a second airboat put Petrovski, the victim and a third party there. We have nothing to confirm they were at the same place at the same time, except for the witness's testimony. But that testimony should be enough to put Petrovski away for a very long time."

Furness nodded. "Sounds like a good case. The Marshall's office needs to buy in and we need to interview the guy before we make a recommendation to the Attorney General's office, but it's looking solid."

"We've got a meeting with the US Marshall's office straight after this. You both need to be part of the interview, right?"

"Works better that way."

"We want this to move fast. What kind of schedule are you looking at?"

Furness looked at the clock on the wall. "It won't be today. And we've got a long weekend coming up, but I can move things around and get out there Tuesday morning."

"You federal types don't work weekends?"

"You're a federal type too, James, and you know how it works. Overtime is only approved if it's an active case. This isn't active, for us, until we get AG approval. Then we'll be all over it." He handed them both cards. "After you've worked out a time with the Marshall's office, give me a call, any time, and I'll make sure I'm available. Best I can do."

Mac flicked the card and slid it into his shirt pocket, stood and held out his hand. "Thanks. We'll be in touch. Let's go, James. We've got a Marshall to see."

~~

John backed the two thugs up a step at a time. "Keep it moving, Stan. And if either of you move your hands out of my sight, I'm shooting."

"I could rush you. You might get one shot off before I got to you."

John shot a hole in the floor just in front of Stan's left foot, and recycled the bolt, pushing another shell into the chamber in a fraction of a second. "I doubt it. I've actually been trained in the use of firearms. And I'm pretty good at it."

The door behind Stan and his friend opened and Amber stuck her head out. "What was that? Did you guys hear a shot? I'm going to call the police."

"Amber, get your ass back in your apartment and lock the door."

"Is that you? Did you find your father? What's going on here?"

"Closed the fucking door, you stupid bitch. You're going to get yourself killed."

Stan moved to grab her and John shot him in the elbow, cycling the bolt and holding the rifle steady on his head. "I warned you, Stan. Amber, close your door, now, and stay in there until long after you hear any noises, okay? Now. I apologize for calling you a bitch."

She squawked something, backed up hurriedly and slammed the door shut.

"Fuck you. You shot me."

"You'll live."

"You won't." Stan held his arm. "Flesh wound." He nodded at Grigory to leave. "We'll be talking to you again. Greg, move it before the cops show up."

John held the rifle on them and followed them out. "Ned, watch the window. Make sure they drive away. Yellow Camaro."

Ned scurried to the window. "Still there."

"Yeah, they're still in the building, Ned." He followed them down a flight. "Keep moving, boys. And don't bother coming back here." He watched them out the front door. A minute later he heard Ned call out that the car had pulled away.

He flipped the rifle over his shoulder and walked back upstairs. "What a fuck of a day." He knocked on Amber's door. "It's all clear, Amber. Have you called the cops?"

"I just did."

"You know my name, right?"

"No. What does JD stand for," she asked through the door.

He ignored her and went back into Paul's apartment. He grabbed a tea towel off the counter and wiped the rifle from one end to the other. "Ned, we've got to fuck off out of here. We don't want to be talking to the cops right now."

"Why not?"

"I shot a guy. I don't need the hassle. We've got a couple of minutes. Don't worry about your prints being in here, we're Paul's friends." He slid the rifle back into the laundry room. "Don't want them on this, though. Let's go."

~~~

James followed MacCready into the Federal Courthouse. "So, you planning anything this weekend?"

"We're going to be busy."

"Come on, Mac. All work and no play and all that."

"Lot of work to do."

"You're kidding, right? Labor day weekend. Celebrating the working man. An extended period of rest and you're going to make me work? Dictator."

"That's not nice."

"Hey, I added the '-tator'."

Mac laughed. "Okay, you make a good point. Let's do a barbecue on Sunday. Get Sam and Gloria over, maybe some other friends."

"That's more like it."

Mac pushed the elevator button. "Went well with the DoJ. Hopefully we get the same kind of response here."

The receptionist escorted them to a meeting room where they waited for a few minutes before a shiny young agent in an ill-fitting suit barged into the room. "Ah, here you are. I went the wrong way. New around here. Sorry for the delay. I'm Agent Spooner. I was just on the phone with Furness, and he's brought me up to speed. Sounds like a good case. I'm available Tuesday morning if you are. Where've you got the guy holed up, a hotel somewhere?"

"Slow down Sparky. I'm Detective MacCready."

"Gladtameetcha. And you must be James. How far do we have to travel Tuesday? Gotta make plans."

James looked at Mac and shook his head. "Yeah, let's talk some details first. Mac and I want some assurances that there will be protection for our witness while all the paperwork goes through. I understand it might take a couple of days to get everything lined up, and I don't want him disappearing before we get him in front of the grand jury."

"Absolutely. In fact, I can have a couple of guys on him now, before we close this thing."

"That's not standard procedure."

Spooner shrugged. "We've been hearing about Petrovski a long time now. Just as anxious as you are to shut him down. I can have at least one agent with him at all times, maybe two during the day."

Mac nodded. "Sounds good. A friend of mine owns a trailer park, one of those retirement places, west of Davie. He's letting us use a property there. Hotels are too dangerous. The mob has its fingers in all of them at one level or another. And it gets him out of Dade, also."

"Brilliant. Excellent idea. Get me the details, and I'll have a couple of guys head over there now."

MacCready wrote out the address and the name of the manager. "She's cooperating with us because the owner told her that she had to. I don't know her and can't trust her. Tell her your men are friends or relatives. I'll contact our witness and tell him that your guys are on the way and to let the manager know they are cousins or something coming for a visit. No overt display of badges or guns. Use unmarked cars, keep it really low-key."

"Yeah, definitely. Hang on while I make a couple of calls."

Spooner left them in the meeting room.

"Well, James, that's a level of cooperation from our Federal Government I wasn't expecting."

"He's young. Still a newbie. Wait until he's been in the job a few years and grows a thick shell of cynicism."

"Ha. How's your shell doing?"

James smiled. "Just a thin crust, yet. Your idealism seems to repel the growth process."

"*My* idealism? You're like a fucking Howdy-Doody doll."

Spooner came back in before James had a chance to reply. "They're on their way. Should be there in about thirty minutes. You call your guy?"

Mac placed his phone on the table and pressed the buttons. The phone rang on the other end twice, and then a voice answered. "Who is this?"

"Detective MacCready, with Special Agent James."

"You told me this phone didn't work."

"Incoming calls only."

"Of course. What the fuck do you want now? And how long do I have to stay in this shit-bucket?"

"Hey, good to hear your voice, too. A couple of US Marshall's agents are going to stop by and provide close protection. At least one will be with you at all times. Tell Linda, the manager, that you have a couple of cousins coming by to stay with you. She has no idea what's going on, but she'll cooperate. We just want to avoid questions, okay? They should be there in half an hour."

"Tell them to bring some pizza. I'm starving and the cupboards are bare. Listen, Mac, how long is this going to take?"

"How long is what going to take?"

"The whole thing. I want to get relocated with a new identity before those assholes find me."

"Early stages yet. We need the Attorney General's approval on this first. Then you need to testify in front of the Grand Jury, and possibly in court. It could be a couple of months before you are free and clear of this. A lot of Federal government bureaucracy. And you know how that goes. Slow wheels grinding things out."

Mac listened to silence long enough to think the call had dropped. "You still there?"

"Yeah."

"You okay?"

"I may have jumped into this a little too fast. But I was scared shitless. I'm really going to be given a new identity? And I won't be able to contact anyone from my old life?"

"The new identity is your choice, and that's why we need the AG's approval. This doesn't come cheap. And we strongly recommend avoiding contact with your old life once that happens. There will be bad people looking for you."

"And they'll be looking for me through my friends and family."

"You didn't mention family when we first talked."

"There's family." He paused. "How long before backing out is not an option?"

James looked at Mac and leaned into the phone. "Look, we really need you to testify. This guy is scum and we need to get him off the street. His alleged sex-trade alone should be reason."

"No, no, don't worry. I'll testify. I'm just not sure I want this whole new identity thing. It seems to be a really big disruption."

Spooner's leaned into the speakerphone. "Ultimately it's your choice, but I know these guys you're testifying against, and they won't hesitate to cut you up in little pieces and throw you in the Everglades. You and everyone you care about. The option is there.

But we need to talk about the family angle. They'll obviously be included also. Right now my concern is that your family members are in more danger than you are. Tell me who they are."

Chapter Eleven

"What took you guys so long? We're on in less than half an hour." Stephanie had her hands on her hips in full mom mode. "And did you find anything out about Paul?"

Ned shook his head. "Last time I volunteer to go with this guy. Let me know if any cops show up. I need a bit of a head start making a run for it." He swept by her and into the back room.

She placed a hand on John's chest. "Hold on. What's he talking about?"

"Paul's in a spot of trouble. We're not sure what he did, but it's related to some mobsters who are trying to track him down and shut him up. It wouldn't surprise me if he's taken off to that Tibetan monastery you talked about earlier."

"How do you know?

"One of the mobsters told me. Showed up at Paul's apartment when Ned and I were there. We had a bit of a stand-off. Those two guys who were here last night and at the apartment yesterday."

She shook her head. "So how did you manage to get away from them unscathed?"

Ned came back through the door with a glass of scotch. "JD shot the biggest one. Didn't shoot him hard enough, though. The guy's still standing. He'll probably show up here tonight and kill all of us." He looked at the drink in his hand. "This isn't going to be enough." He walked back into the back room, the door swinging shut behind him.

John looked at the look on her face and shrugged. "What he said."

"Shot him like with a gun?"

"Is there any other way?"

"Did you hurt him bad?"

"No. Like Ned said. Not hard enough, I'm afraid. Flesh wound on his upper arm near his elbow. Hurt him a bit, and he'll lose some blood before they patch him up, but I think I may have just angered him. Maybe we call off the gig tonight."

Stephanie shook her head. "I talked to Bobby earlier. He's got extra security on. He did even before I asked him to, because of the glassing last night. He doesn't want to lose business over the bad publicity, so he's advertising the extra security to offset the bad news."

"Good. Stan, that's the big guy's name, was some pissed off at me. Hope security is big."

"A couple of Samoan guys who looked enormous to me, but it's all relative. Who's Stan?"

"The muscle-bound gorilla. Don't know the other guy's name."

"What did you shoot him with? I didn't think you owned a gun."

"I don't. Paulie has a rifle for killing alligators. He had it stashed beside his washing machine, next to the broom and what looked like an old metal detector. Fortunately he kept it loaded, or I'd be playing sax with my jaw wired shut. Unfortunately, I think I've just delayed the inevitable. He's going to come looking for me."

"And no idea where Paul is?"

John shook his head. "Nobody seems to know. I should probably go to the police tomorrow and report him missing and tell them what I know. Well, part of what I know." He grinned and shook his head. "Won't mention shooting the big guy."

"He might."

"Doubt it. It wasn't much of a wound. He'll come across like a pussy, and besides, these guys aren't known for liking the authorities. He'll just try and take it out on me later." He clapped his hands. "We need to do something this weekend." He smiled at the look on her face. "No, not 'we' like you and me, 'we' like the band. It's a holiday weekend and the end of summer. Need to head out to the beach or something."

"How long have you been here? Six months? Summer doesn't end. This isn't Nebraska where everything is under snow by October. Besides, it wouldn't feel right without Paul. Get your sax ready. We're on shortly."

~~~

Rico led Simon up the stairs from the restaurant below the small jazz club. It had been a while since he'd seen and heard Paul's group. He wasn't a huge fan of jazz, but they did a pretty good job, and

Stephanie's voice, a throaty, smoky purr, turned him on just listening to it. "You'll like these guys, Simon. Pretty crisp."

"More of a classic rock guy, myself, but the food downstairs is good, so it's not a total waste."

Rico grunted and sat. "The food wasn't as good as mine."

"You're right. It wasn't. Why did you ask me to come along?"

"Thought you might like these guys." He looked at Simon. "Open mind, okay? It's not classic rock, but it's good music. Soak it in." He waved at a server. "Honey, open a tab and bring me a Jameson, neat, would you?" He handed her a credit card. "What do you want, Simon?"

"Bailey's and ice, if you're buying. Double."

"Make it so." He winked at the server. "Come by often. I've got a big appetite."

Simon watched her walk away, her hips swaying. "So, how do you know these guys? They affiliated with the mob?"

Rico shook his head. "All above board. A friend hooked me up with them. I love good live jazz, and these guys are good. There's quite a lot of good jazz in Miami, but these guys are unique. Plus that Stephanie - she could give a dead man an erection."

Simon watched her organize the rest of the band as they set up. "Yeah, she's pretty good-looking. You may have overstated the case a bit, though."

"No, my boy, it's not just the look. Wait until she starts singing. What a thick, lusty, sexy and beautiful voice. Man, this is like aural sex, except the aural that means hearing and not with the mouth."

Simon laughed. "Rico's got a crush."

"From afar, boy-o. From afar."

"So that's why we're here tonight. You've got a woody for the little lady."

Rico sat back in his seat and accepted his drink from the server. "While that in and of itself is a good enough reason, no. That's not why we're here tonight. The drummer has gone AWOL, and the owner has told me about a couple of guys causing disturbances here, looking for that same drummer. I thought I'd stop by and see what I could see." Rico pointed to the man coming out of the kitchen, heading toward the mic. "That's Bobby. It's his joint." He gave him a little wave and got a nod in return. "Good guy, overall. Clean as a whistle, though."

Bobby tapped the mic lightly. "Good evening people, we've got a really nice crowd tonight. The Coates Quintet will be out shortly, but without, again, Paul Coates. My informants tell me that he's come down with a nasty flu and he doesn't want to share with anyone. Larry is sitting for him and promises an exciting evening."

The band came out, and Simon nodded. "Very nice looking girl."

"Wait until she starts."

The set went fast, and the band didn't seem to have the relaxed fluidity Rico had heard in the past. At the break he approached the pianist. "Ned, old boy, you guys sound strained. Everything okay?"

"Missing Paul, is all. What brings you out of your man cave? Hardly ever see you this far into town."

"Wanted to hear some quality jazz, is all. Still waiting, truth be told."

"Ouch. That hurts, Rico."

"Just saying." He waved Simon over. "This is a good friend and colleague. He's a classic rock fan, himself, but he said you guys sounded good. Gives you an indication of his tin ear."

Simon stuck out his hand and shook Ned's. "Don't listen to him. You guys sounded good." He nodded toward Stephanie. "Her voice is like pouring Bailey's on velvet and wrapping it up in moss."

Stephanie smiled and walked over. "I heard that. Nice meeting you, Simon. Good to see you too, Rico. What brings you out?"

Ned shook his head. "Don't ask him that. He'll just insult us."

"Actually, to be honest, I heard about the dust-up last night and thought I'd come by. I think I know who the big guy was. Wanted to confirm it."

"Who was he?" Stephanie leaned against the piano and crossed her arms.

He shrugged. "I haven't seen him yet, so I'd be guessing. I take it the Samoans downstairs have his picture and won't be admitting him."

"I guess. If it's who you think it is, why would they be looking for Paul?"

"Hard to say. Has Paul pissed off anyone lately?"

Ned jumped in. "Just some alligators. But we don't talk about that much since it's technically a felony and we don't want to get him busted." He cocked his head. "You've got me intrigued now. This guy who you think you know, why would he care about Paulie? You seem to know both sides of the equation. What's the connection?"

"Damned if I know."

Simon held up a finger. "Hang on. Paul poaches 'gators?"

"Keep your voice down, man. What of it?"

"In the Everglades?"

"No, in the meat department at Publix. Of course in the Everglades."

"When did he last go out?"

"Monday afternoon."

Simon nodded. "I wonder."

"What?" Stephanie crossed her arms. "What are you thinking?"

Ned interrupted. "The guys at the house said Paulie saw something he shouldn't have. Are you saying that he may have witnessed the killing of that guy in the 'glades? The one on TV? JD and I thought maybe he actually shot the guy by mistake."

Rico shook his head. "No, I've got it on petty good authority that he was killed by the head of that crime family personally, for talking to the police. Paul must have seen that and now he's on the lam."

"People still say on the lam?"

"I do."

"How bad are we talking?" asked Stephanie.

"Petrovski? Very bad."

"Petrovski?" She took a slight step back

"Yeah, Vladimir Petrovski. Very bad. Ruthless. My guess is the big guy who busted the poor schmuck up last night was his number one muscle head, Stanislav Gorski."

"JD did tell me the guy's name was Stan," said Stephanie.

"How did he find that out?"

Ned interrupted. "He asked him just before he shot him."

Rico stared at Ned for a second before answering. "Dead?"

"No, I would have said he killed him. He shot him in the arm. Flesh wound designed to make him back off."

"Oh, that's not going to go over well. Stan's a bit of a 'roid junky. He's not entirely stable."

Stephanie shook her head and left to the back room.

~~~

MacCready stretched out on his sofa, cold beer in one hand and a roast beef sandwich in the other, the television playing an old Wesley Snipes movie about parachutists, only paying half attention when his phone rang. He looked at the display and swung his feet to the floor, put down his beer and answered. "What's up, Simon?"

"Something interesting. Not sure if it means anything to you."

"Everything cool?"

"Yeah. I'm out the back of a jazz club in town. Rico's upstairs drooling over the singer, so I've got a few clear minutes."

Mac sat forward. "What band?"

"Coates Quintet, I think. Not bad. And the singer is hot."

Mac wiped his face. "So why are you checking out that particular band, so far out of your normal stomping grounds?"

"Well, that's why I'm calling you. You know that Sergei guy who got himself shot in the Everglades?"

"I do." Mac leaned back and closed his eyes. "What about him?"

"Turns out that this Coates guy who plays drums for the band may have seen it. He's been the target of a couple of big guys from

Petrovski's stable. Looks like he may have poked his nose where he shouldn't have."

"Really? Is this theory carrying any weight?"

"Seems to fit. He was in the right place at the wrong time. And Petrovski's boys are trying to track him down."

"They getting close?"

"Doesn't sound like it. They're still flailing around like a couple of ADHD chimps."

"Thanks for the info, bro. Having a barbecue on Sunday afternoon. Stop by if you want. It'll be good to see you legitimately."

"Sounds like a plan. I should get back before I'm missed."

Mac hung up and took a long pull on his beer. "Shit. I've got a smart brother."

~~~

Rico looked up as Simon slipped back into the club. "Got you another drink. Thought you left."

"Had to take a call."

"From who?"

"My brother. He's invited me over to a barbecue at his place on Sunday. I think I'll go."

Rico cocked an eyebrow. "Do some digging for me, okay? See what he knows about the Sergei killing. Might be good to see what his slant on this is, being a cop and all."

"Yeah. What do you think about this Petrovski thing?"

Rico smiled. "Would be a blessing. Could help me sew up the whole of South Florida. If your brother can help us get to that point, by all means, help him."

Simon took a sip of his Bailey's. "I'll see what I can do. Would be good to get the Russian out of the way."

"It would. Now shut up and let me listen to the girl sing."

Chapter Twelve

Paul Coates opened his eyes, at first unsure of his surroundings. Then a palmetto bug crawled across the ceiling into his eye-line and it came back to him. The trailer park. Surrounded by about fifty retired snowbirds, most from Canada. Quebec, specifically. A bunch of old, cranky French-Canadians.

When he approached the FBI on Thursday morning, they'd hooked him up with Agent James and MacCready. They listened to him and, apparently, believed him. He expected to be stowed in a nice hotel suite for the duration.

He'd watched too many movies. The Feds categorically ruled out a suite. Something about them not being that secure.

So they stuck him in this horrible trailer park in Broward. "If I wanted to live in Broward I would have moved to Broward."

Then yesterday they sent a couple of minders. He had to pretend they were friends.

One sat in a chair outside the door. Paul squinted through the screen. "You want a coffee or something? What's your name again?"

"Darrel. I'm your cousin, remember?"

"You're black as the ace of spades."

"By marriage, pal. A coffee would be good. Double-double."

Paul grunted and made his way to the bathroom for his morning piss. He turned on the coffee machine as he walked by, pre-loaded the night before. "I don't know if I've got any sugar," he called. "I haven't checked."

"I'll survive. What is it you're supposed to have seen or done to warrant this kind of protection?"

Paul stopped half-zipped and laughed. "*This* kind of protection? I hoped for a nice suite." He pulled the zipper the rest of the way up. "Instead, I get this. A bug-infested death trap, surrounded by angry Canadians." He pointed across the narrow street. "Jean-Claude there thinks I'm a Russian spy. I'm the youngest guy here by twenty years, excluding the manager and I think Linda's an illegal Canadian immigrant getting paid under the table."

"You done?"

"Not even started." He rinsed his hands in the sink and finger combed his thinning hair. "I'm starting to question this whole thing, anyway."

"How's that?"

"What do I care if some asshole shot another asshole? No skin off my nose."

"They care. And they won't stop until you're dead. Real dead. So my friends and I will keep an eye on you until you testify in front of the Grand Jury and these guys are behind bars."

"But they'll have friends."

"And you'll have a different name, living in a different city, living a different life."

"Without any of *my* friends."

The guy in the chair shrugged. "The price you pay."

"I'm not sure it's a price I want to pay anymore." He shook his head. "What's your name again?"

"Darrel."

"Right. Darrel, so who do I talk to, to back out of this?"

"MacCready. James. But you won't get them until Monday. No, Tuesday, being as it's a long weekend."

"Great. What say we head to Denny's and get some breakfast?"

Darrel stood and stretched. "My shift change should be showing up in a few minutes." He looked at his watch "Coming up on 9:00." He smiled at Paul. "Thanks for the offer, though. Very nice of you. Reconsider reconsidering, okay? This Petrovski asshole is a very bad guy. We really need to put him away."

~~~

Petrovski slammed the handset back in its cradle. "Dammit." He slammed it down again for good measure.

Stan rushed in. "What's going on?"

"I have literally had every hotel and motel in the greater Miami checked over the last twelve hours and there is not a single person checked in over the last couple of days matching the description of the witness. We need to spread the net wider."

"You think he's still in Florida?"

"I don't know where the hell he is. But for our sake, I have to assume he hasn't gone far. If he's left the state it could take forever."

"Yeah, but if he's left the state he's less of a threat to us."

"Explain."

"The biggest threat is him being a key witness in our prosecution, right?"

Petrovski nodded.

"It's really hard to be a witness for the prosecution of someone in Miami if you're in New Hampshire."

"True. So, erring on the side of caution, I assume he is still in Dade, Broward or Monroe counties."

"I'd include Palm Beach, too, boss."

Petrovski nodded. "Okay. Get the word out."

"Okay, so this is awkward, but there are guys out there who can help, but don't like you very much. You want I should approach them, too? They may think this is a weakness they can exploit."

"Impress upon them the urgency of this. If I get taken in, the Feds will have access to all my guys, some of whom may have information about rival organizations. It's in everybody's benefit to get the Coates guy off the streets, preferably in a body bag."

"Got it. I'll get right on it."

Petrovski waited until he left, then picked up the phone and dialed.

"Rico speaking. Is this you, Vladimir?"

"We have a problem."

"We do?"

"There is a man on the streets who has witnessed a crime that could prove to be inconvenient for me."

"That's terrible. I should find him and buy him a drink."

"It's worse than you think, Trattori. If I go down, some of my men will go with me, and it's very possible that some of them will have enough information to bring *you* down."

"Is that a threat? You woke me up on a lazy Saturday morning to threaten me?" Rico started laughing. "You're starting to sound desperate, my friend. If you're looking for my help, save your breath. You're not going to get it."

The call terminated, and Petrovski sat at his desk for a minute looking at the phone. "I need sleep."

~~~

Paul sat in a cheap lawn chair in front of the old single-wide trailer. The previous tenant built a low brick wall around the hitch area and painted it Art Deco pink and green and filled it with potted plants of some sort. Paul hated it. He hated the perfectly trimmed lawns, some no larger than a Buick, and he hated the perfect little gardens tended by the blue-haired women from Canada. He hated everything about the trailer park.

Darrel had left, replaced by Stella, a middle-aged, hard-as-nails-looking agent with, as far as Paul could discern, absolutely no sense of humor.

"You're gay, right?"

Stella looked up from her paper. "What?"

"I mean I've got no problem with that. My piano player is gay. It's just that I'd feel real sorry for you if you were straight, looking like you do. Be really hard to get a man."

"You know I've got a gun, right?"

"Hey, just saying. I'm cool with it."

"I'm not gay, and I've been married for twenty-five years. Are you always this obnoxious?"

"Really? Shit. Never would have guessed." He lifted his cup. "Empty. Can I get you a coffee?"

"I don't think so."

"Yeah, I probably shouldn't have another, either. I'm really thinking about backing out of this."

"Why?"

"I've got a great jazz band. We should be playing this weekend. Huge jazz festival in Miami. This will be a very good payday for us. And I miss the band. They're my friends. Family. Like a very close family. They're worried about where I am, I'm sure, and I can't let them know I'm okay."

"Petrovski's boys find you, and you won't be okay."

"I'm willing to take that chance."

"If you saw some of the things he's done, you wouldn't."

"He shot a guy."

"He was being very merciful. Must have liked the kid."

"Liked him so much he shot him between the eyes? I saw it. The Petrovski guy pressed the handgun against the kid's forehead and pulled the trigger. Bam."

"If he hadn't liked him he would have cut him enough to injure him and thrown him in the Everglades for the alligators. Or lit him on fire while he was still alive, then hung the charred remains from a light post. The bullet was a mercy killing. The FBI has been trying to drop this guy for years. You represent the best hope to do that."

Paul slumped in his chair. "You're not making it any easier."

A golf cart rolled up in front of the trailer and turned into the short drive.

"Ah, crap."

Stella subconsciously checked her shoulder-holster. "Who's that?"

"Linda. Manager. Pain in the ass."

Linda hopped out of the golf-cart and grabbed a clipboard from the other seat. "Good morning Mr.," she checked the clipboard, "Calvin. Paul Calvin, right?"

"Um, yeah. If that's what it says."

She looked at the clipboard again. "It says here you have a guest, a cousin named Darrel." She looked up from the board at Stella. "This doesn't look like a Darrel."

"This is a Stella. She's another one of my cousins. She gets her looks from the other side of the family. What difference does it make?"

"The rules for this community are very clear. We can't have just anyone staying here."

"Didn't the owner tell you to give me a bit of lee-way?"

"He told me nothing of the sort."

Paul looked at Stella. "You going to help me out here, cuz?"

Before she had a chance to respond a man across the street let out a bellow.

"Linda, you need to come over here, eh?"

Paul smiled as Linda closed her eyes and mouthed an expletive.

"Jean-Claude. What is it now?" She looked at Paul. "I'll be back."

She backed the golf-cart out and drove the six meters to Jean-Claude's trailer.

"I can't stand much more of this."

"You've been here two days."

"Not even, and I'm ready to do the rounds and mercy kill every single one of these fucking retirees. Half of them would drop stone-cold dead if the battery in their pacemaker died."

"You don't like old people."

"Damn, you're observant."

"You're going to be one, eventually. Unless you back out of this WitSec thing. You do that and you'll be lucky to make it to Thursday."

~~~

John walked into Denny's, gave the waitress his order and grabbed a cup of coffee. "You guys look like shit."

Henry frowned. "Come on. It's getting a bit weird, don't you think? Nothing at all from Paul? I called the cops this morning and officially reported him missing."

"So that's good, right?"

Henry shook his head. "The lady taking my call told me that since he is a healthy, adult male the effort would be minimal. I emailed her a picture and she said they would put out a bulletin, but the realistic view was that there wouldn't be many resources put on it."

"Great."

"You said yourself that would happen."

"Yeah." John stirred his coffee. "Damn, I almost forgot." He dug Paul's mobile phone and wallet out of his pocket. "Slipped my mind after the altercation yesterday."

"Paul's?"

John nodded. "In his apartment. I doubt he go anywhere voluntarily without these." He tried to turn on the phone. "Dead."

Henry tapped on the table. "What's in the wallet?"

John pulled the cards out of the pockets and spread them on the table. "A couple of credit cards, driver's license, all his ID is here. Weird. Business card for the clubs we play and one for an airboat rental place down south of the city."

"Amber said he left in a hurry Thursday morning," Stephanie pointed at the phone, "but if he left without that, he must have been planning on coming back." She rubbed her forehead. "I'm not feeling good about this."

"I'm heading down to the Everglades today."

"Why?"

"That's the last place he went before he disappeared."

"So you're a cop now?"

"The cops aren't going to do anything. I'm not going to sit around. And I'm going by myself. I don't to put anyone else in danger."

Ned laughed. "Nice of you to think about that now, after I've had a run-in with the apes."

"You got out of it unscathed."

"Barely."

"Man up, Ned." John sat back as the server brought him his pancakes. "It was just a bit of noise. Nobody got hurt."

"You fucking shot the guy. I bet he wouldn't agree with your assessment."

John waved him off. "I don't care what he thinks. I meant nobody in our tight-knit little team got hurt."

Stephanie sliced off a piece of her pigs in a blanket and appeared to be ignoring everybody.

"You okay, Steph? Awfully quiet."

"Fine."

Ned and Larry and Henry all laughed. "Careful JD."

"Not in the mood, guys." Stephanie pushed her plate back and left without another word.

"She's taking this pretty hard." John watched her walk out and get in her car. "What's going on?"

"Women stuff, maybe. Who knows? Paul's disappearance has really hit her. You sure you don't want someone to go with you?" Henry cracked his knuckles. "I'd be better use to you than Ned."

"You can have it, man. You should have seen me climbing over the kitchen counter. Looked like a complete ass."

John looked at his friends. "I appreciate the offer Henry. Just popping down for a look."

~~~

Paul prepared himself for another onslaught from Linda. She had her fists on her hips, getting into it with Jean-Claude, president of the resident's association. He stood on his front step in a too-small pair of swimming trunks, white socks and sandals, yelling loud enough Paul should have been able to understand everything he said, and would have if he understood French. Linda was going to be in a bad mood.

He adjusted himself in his chair and turned to his minder. "How long do you stay here? Want to go get some lunch? There's an Arby's around here somewhere. I can smell it."

She chuckled. "Appealing as that may be, my replacement is going to be back here shortly. Darrel says he's looking forward to it. Most boring assignment he's had - we've had - in years."

"Darrel fits in here like Chihuahua crap in a swimming pool. I don't think the old folks here like him very much. He's a little too, shall we say, dark for them."

"You think all these old happy grandparents are racist?"

"It's kind of obvious. You should hang around for a bit and watch."

"You'll be here for, at the most, another week. I wouldn't stress about it."

"Oh, I'm not stressing. This is funny, actually. If it wasn't for the fact that some fucking Russian mobster seems to want to kill me and that I'm missing one of the biggest gigs of my career tonight I'd be having a fucking ball."

"Sarcasm doesn't wear well on you."

Chapter Thirteen

Stephanie pushed into the club in Miami, near the airport, coming in from the hot, bright sun to the dank, cool bar. Strippers gyrated on a harshly lit stage to an audience of not more than a dozen.

She leaned on the bar. "I need to talk to Vladimir."

The bartender took one look at her and turned his back, focusing his attention on the already clean glasses. "No-one here by that name."

"I didn't ask you. I told you. His car is outside. He's here. Tell him Stephanie needs to see him." She looked around the place. It had been over two years since she'd been here last, but it hadn't changed much. The girls were younger and the bartender uglier, but it otherwise was the same shit hole she walked out of, she thought for good.

The bartender tapped on the counter. "Back here."

She followed him back into the office.

Petrovski met her at the door, thanking the bartender and closing the door after she came in. "Stephanie Peters. To what do I owe this distinct pleasure?"

Steph had been rehearsing all the way from the restaurant. "I understand that you may have a grievance against Paul Coates. I'm asking you, as a favor to me, to let it go and to back off of him." She took a deep breath. "This is very important to me."

Petrovski smiled. "What on earth would you know about what I do these days? And why should I care what you think?" He took a sip from the drink on his desk. "Can I get you anything?"

"You can stop hunting Paul."

"So you know where he is?"

She shook her head. "And if I did, you know I wouldn't - couldn't - tell you. I'll find him and talk to him. I'll tell him to leave you alone. I understand he witnessed something you did. I'll make sure he never talks about it."

"So will I, young Stephanie. So will I."

"What do I have to do to get you to back off? I'll do anything."

Petrovski's smile broadened. "You should never promise what you can't deliver. What's the Coates chump to you anyway?"

Stephanie pulled at her earlobe. "He's the drummer in the jazz band I sing with. He's the leader. And he's like a father figure to the group. He's old, he's harmless, and you don't need to chase him down. Let him be, and he'll eventually surface, and I'll talk to him, okay?"

"He'll eventually surface all right. And when he does, I'll make sure he doesn't testify. Are you sure I can't get you lunch? You're tiny. Need to put a bit of meat on your bones." He leaned forward and steepled his fingers. "You know where he is, don't you? Tell me. Don't make a stupid mistake that could cost you your life."

128

~~~

John's Honda rattled too much. He slammed his hand on the dash, trying to make it stop. It didn't help that he was traveling on a road wash boarded from years of heavy rain. He punched the dash once more.

His phone rang and it took him three tries to touch the right place on the screen to answer it. "What is it, Henry? I'm driving."

"You actually went down there?"

"On my way now."

"You do know we start at five today, right? Planning on opening strong again and can't do that without you."

"This'll only take a couple of minutes. Just want to talk to the guy."

"It's the 21st century, Johnny. I'm pretty sure even he has a phone. I don't care how isolated he is."

"Have to do it face-to-face. I can't read people on the phone. Like I can't tell right now if you're pissed, concerned or just going through the motions. And since I can't tell, it doesn't matter so I'm going to hang up now. I'm almost there, and I'll be back on time. Trust me."

He jabbed at the screen and hung up the call. He felt the feeling in his gut again. The feeling he had going into combat, hyper-aware and trusting only his troops. And even then, with the spate of green on blue attacks before he left, his trust was mostly in himself.

Paul's mobile phone sat on the seat beside him, charging, getting ready for the next time he examined it for useful and helpful information.

He pulled into the parking lot, and the Honda almost seemed to sigh in relief when he turned off the engine. He'd thought the air conditioning in the car had failed, but when he stepped out into the unbearable heat, he recalibrated his expectations. The heat amplified the smell off the Everglades, rotting vegetation in a boggy soup. He noted the lack of cars in the parking lot. This should be fast.

~~~

Stan kept the Honda well in front of him. By the time the beat-up car had turned south on 187, Stan knew the destination. The air-boat launch. He'd meet him there. And he'd end him there.

"You've been quiet, Stanislav. What are you thinking about?" Grigory rolled down the passenger window and lit a cigarette.

"The amount of pain this little runt is going to be in." He leaned his arm out the window and winced when he touched the wound on his left arm. "Shit. I owe him. That stings."

"Bad?"

"I've been hurt worse before. The bitch slap to my pride hurts more."

"I don't get what you mean."

"That little prick had a gun on me. Could have killed me easily."

"But I thought you said you could rush him and not get hurt."

"All bluff. And he knew it. And when he had the chance to take me out, he shoots me in the arm with that fuckin' pea-shooter. If he had shown me even the slightest respect, he would have done more damage than this."

"So you're pissed at him because he didn't shoot you worse? You're nuts."

"You wouldn't understand. It's a respect thing." He smiled. "And when I catch up to him, I'm going to show him a lot of respect."

~~~

John pointed at the man behind the counter. "Hector, right? I'm looking for a guy."

"You need to go to South Beach for stuff like that." Hector picked a tooth with a toothpick. "Don't have none of that around here. Sorry."

John slid Paul's driver's license from his shirt pocket. "No, I'm looking for this guy." He dropped it on the counter. "Seen him around lately?"

"Never laid eyes on the guy before."

"You didn't even look at it Hector. Look at it, Hector." He pressed his index finger on the license. "It's important that you look at it and tell me when you saw him last. I know he's a regular, coming down here and popping alligators for their hide. Did you help him find buyers? Accessory to a felony would shut you down, wouldn't it?"

"Look, little guy, I just mind my own business, take the money and provide a service. I don't keep track of who comes in here."

John dropped the business card on the counter. "I found this in his wallet. Your name and number are on the back. You're not doing a very good job of convincing me."

"Fine. It's Paul. I don't know where he is, honestly. The last time he rented a boat was Monday. He came back off the water early and bugged out of here like he had an ex-wife on his tail. And since then some real heavyweights have been hound-dogging him. Like the FBI or something."

"How well do you know him?"

"Why the hell should I tell you?"

"Don't be a dick. I'm concerned about the welfare of a friend. I don't want to make a big deal out of this. Tell me what you know."

"Get out of my shop. I see you around here again I'm going to mess you up."

John laughed. "Right. Relax, man. Just tell me what you know about Paul. Where would he hang out? Where do 'gator poachers hang out? I haven't seen him in a couple of days, and I'm getting concerned."

Hector stepped out from behind the counter with a baseball bat in his hand. "Out."

"Are you serious? You're a walking, talking cliché. I don't want to do this, Hector. I don't want to put you in the hospital. You've got a nice business here. If you're laid up for any length of time, your customers will go to the next guy down the line."

"Heh. You're shitting me, right? Little guy like you? Lots of bluff, I'll give you that." He started twirling the bat in one hand. "Gonna crush your head like a melon." He advanced a few steps. "Take a fucking hike."

"Now, now. Language. You kiss your mother with that mouth?" John took a step backward toward the door. "It's not bluff, buddy. How about you put that bat down, and we talk like reasonable men."

"Get out." He swung the bat in front of John's face, just missing his nose. "Next one connects."

John shook his head. "It won't.

Hector adjusted his grip and stepped in, swinging wide.

John simultaneously stepped forward and blocked Hector's swing with his left arm. He grabbed Hector by the throat and placed his right leg behind Hector's and kept pushing forward. The bat flew past John's head and bounced off some shelves. "Whoops. I think you broke something." He squeezed harder on Hector's larynx and followed through, pushing him onto his back. "Don't fuck with me." He squeezed. "Tell me what you know about Paul and what he saw on Monday. And quickly. I've got a gig to get to."

Hector gargled something and grasped at John's hand on his throat.

"Oh, sorry about that." John eased off. "Were you trying to say something?"

"Jesus." He coughed. "I can't tell you anything. They'll burn my place down with my body in it. If I'm lucky they'll kill me first."

John let go of his throat and put out a hand to help him up. "That bad? Is one of the guys a big oaf who goes by the name of Stan? Serious steroid user. Thick as a brick."

"You've met him? He's not that stupid actually. Him and his boss. You let this go. Maybe you can handle me, and I gotta admit, that was slick. And quick." He coughed and rubbed his throat. "But these guys are at another level. Vicious."

"So where can I find the boss man?"

"Petrovski?" He shook his head and backed away. "No way. I'm not telling you anything else. Nothing you can do to me can compare to what they will do to me if I tell you anything else. Give me a break and get out of here, okay?"

~~~

Stephanie watched Petrovski eat his lunch. "I want to leave now."

Petrovski looked at his guy standing at the door, blocking her exit. He smiled around the mouthful of steak. "We're not finished talking." He dipped another piece of steak in the mushroom gravy. "You could leave in a second. Just tell me where he is."

She sat back in the chair and looked to her left at the man in front of the door. "I don't have a clue where he is. I'm looking for him too. I just want you to back off." She looked at the door again. "You really need that brute at the door to stop me from leaving? That's a nice compliment. And a waste of a man." She looked at her watch. "I've got to get back to a gig soon, so I hope this doesn't take too long."

"Sure you don't want some food?" He pointed at his plate with his fork. "This is good. The cook outdid himself. Again." He smiled. "I've got all day. I don't have a gig to get to. But I'm sure they can manage without you. They found another drummer. They can find another singer." He placed his cutlery on his plate and snapped his fingers. The guard at the door left his post and collected the dishes and placed them on a table near the door and resumed his post.

"If I can't interest you in food, perhaps you'd like a drink. Ice-cold *Stolichnaya*. Only the best." He opened a small refrigerator near his desk, took a half-full bottle out and poured himself a drink. "No? You sure?"

She opened her phone and smiled. "I've still got three levels of Angry Birds: Space to get through. That'll take me a little while." She looked up at him. "I'm not going to interrupt any of your business, am I?"

"Listen, my little *plemyannitsa*, you're as stubborn as your mother. I don't know whether to believe you or not, but it's clear that I won't get any information from you without physical threats and, frankly, I'm not in the mood to damage your precious little frame. Not today anyway." He nodded at the guard. "You may leave. We'll talk again."

Steph closed her phone and slid it in her pocket as she stood. "I hope not. You're going to continue looking for someone who means you no harm. I know about your reputation. You don't want to do this. It's wrong. He's harmless."

Petrovski leaned forward, his weight on his fists. "Make peace with the fact that you will never see your drummer alive again. When I find him, and I will, he will cease to exist."

Chapter Fourteen

John helped pick up the merchandise the bat had knocked down. "You seem like a pretty decent guy, Hector. How'd you get messed up with these guys?"

"Right place, right time. I guess I'm just lucky that way. And the shut up money is good."

John grunted. "Luck like that..."

"I'm really sorry, but I can't tell you anything else. It's not going to help you anyway. I'll tell you where Petrovski is and you'll just go there and end up dead. You should be thankful I don't tell you."

"You forget what I just did to you?"

Hector actually laughed. "Look at me, man. I'm overweight. The most exercise I get is lugging a dozen beers from my car to the kitchen. Taking me out was pretty easy. My only advantage is that I'm kinda big. Big plus a swinging bat tends to make people back off. It's mostly all a bluff."

"At least you're honest." He placed the last box of tackle on the shelf. "Give me a hint. Don't actually tell me where he is, just give me a hint. Be a man."

Hector closed his eyes and shook his head. "I'm an idiot for telling you this. Look for high-end strip clubs near the airport. He tends to hang there. You didn't hear it from me, okay? He'll kneecap me if he finds out."

~~~

Stan stopped his car short of the airboat launch.

Grigory opened his eyes. "We here yet?"

Stan scowled. "Hand me my phone." He held out his hand. "Got to call the boss."

"Sure thing." Grigory passed the phone over and rolled down his window. "Hot as shit out here."

Stan flexed his left elbow as he dialed with his right hand. "Getting stiff. Asshole's going to get some payback."

"What's the call for?"

"Want to know how hard I should go." The phone rang on the far end. Twice before Petrovski picked up.

"What is it, Stan?"

~~~

Stephanie stopped her exit when she heard the name 'Stan'. Petrovski had his back to her.

He nodded. "Yes, go very hard. But don't kill him. Make sure he survives. At least long enough to pass the message on to this Coates guy before he dies."

She watched him as his shoulders slumped a fraction, like he was tired of having to explain himself every time.

"What message? What do you mean, what message? After you've thrashed that midget to within an inch of his life, make sure he knows to tell Coates that he's next. That the only thing preventing us from killing him would be him pulling a Tony Scott." He shook his head. "Tony Scott. Movie director. Jumped off a bridge. Fuck it. Tell him his only option is to kill himself. Clear enough for you?"

He dropped his phone on the desk and swore in Russian.

"Everything okay?"

Petrovski spun around. "You're still here? I thought you had left. You seemed very intent on leaving."

"I'm nosy. Your conversation caught my interest. Who would Stan be planning on beating up? Anyone I know?"

"Maybe he's found your drummer."

She shook her head. "No. And you know I'm not that stupid." She pushed open the door. "If it's who I think it is, you might want to send Stan some reinforcements."

"He has Grigory with him, and he's a big boy. He doesn't need any more reinforcements."

Stephanie smiled. "Okay, if you say so." The door latched behind her and she made a beeline for the exit before he changed his mind about letting her go.

~~~

The door crashed open and Stan and Grigory strode in.

Hector started to come around to the front of the counter, then stopped when he saw who it was. "Stan. What's up? You gonna pay for the door?"

John leaned back against the counter and held his hands loosely in front of him. "Fancy meeting you here, big fella. You come here to talk to Hector or were you following me?"

"Cheap shot with the pea-shooter yesterday. I owe you."

John looked around. Cramped space and a lot of potential weapons for both him and Stan and his friend. "Let's say we take this outside. Hector has enough grief in his life." He backed into the counter. In front of him were a few racks of supplies one might use while air boating - sunscreen, hats, snacks - and to the left a bank of coolers held beer and soft drinks. To the right a wall of snacks - potato chips, chocolate bars, beef jerky - crowded most of the floor space. There wasn't much maneuvering room. "You got a back door outta here, Hector," he asked, speaking over his shoulder. "Might get messy in here."

"Straight through and turn left."

John nodded and spun around and ran for the back. Stan let out a bellow behind him. He heard crashing as he launched over some boxes and through the door to the back. He ducked left and saw the exit. He hit the door without slowing and crashed out into the parking lot, Stan hot on his heels.

"Chicken shit. You've got nowhere to run." Stan barreled out through the door behind John, his friend right behind him.

John slowed and turned, his hands spread. "I like a bit of space around me. And really, Hector didn't need you smashing the place up. He seems like a good enough guy."

"Did he tell you anything?"

"Nothing useful. You can tell your boss that he kept his mouth shut even while I beat on him."

Stan barked out a laugh. "You were beating on him? He's twice your size."

"Lucky for you and your 'roid shriveled nuts, size isn't everything. What's your friend's name? I like to know who I'm fighting."

Stan flicked a glance to his left. "Grigory. Maybe I'll hold you for a while so he can punch on you."

John shrugged. "Whatever it is you think you're going to do to me, you're wrong. Either do something or piss off. I've got a show to do in a couple of hours, and I'm running out of time."

Grigory let out a yell and charged. Stan dwarfed him, but he still had about fifty pounds and six inches on John.

As he got closer, John adjusted his stance a little wider and at the last moment squatted, ducking his head forward and under Grigory's center of gravity. As they connected, he used Grigory's momentum and stood, flipping him onto the ground behind him, landing him on his back, knocking the wind out of him.

As John stood upright, he noticed Stan coming at him. He ducked the first swing and came around behind him, driving a fist into his kidneys, like punching a wall.

Stan rotated off balance and came at him again. The strength in his arms and legs would be what killed him, and there was no doubt in his mind that was what Stan wanted to do. A kick or a punch would end it.

But that much muscle is heavy. If he could keep him moving, Stan would tire out. But there would be no dope on a rope. A couple of direct hits from Stan would be all it took.

John stayed moving, just outside of Stan's reach. The mountain in front of him was still just a person. He had weaknesses. John wasn't stupid enough to try and hit him in the nuts; getting a foot or fist that close to Stan's center of mass just asked for trouble. No, the weakness he would target would be the joints.

Steroids help build muscle mass, but they do little for the tendons holding the joints together, and the knees were the most susceptible to injury. Ask any NFL player.

Two objectives: tire him out and do his knees.

And not get tagged in the process.

"Grigory, get off the fucking ground and help me stop this asshole." Stan shuffled in a circle. When he came close to his friend, he kicked him in the ribs. "Come on."

Grigory groaned and rolled over to his stomach and slowly pushed himself up. John had a third objective now, one that went to the top of the list: take the friend out for good.

He stood with his back to the store, about ten yards behind him. Stan stood to his left, between him and his car, Grigory to his right, a bit wobbly and not appearing to like this game much anymore. "What's wrong Greg? That's your name, right? Not up to it? Come on. Show me what you've got."

The smaller assailant approached with more caution, and as he came within reach, Stan came in also.

John jabbed the stiffened fingers of his left hand into the space between Grigory's jaw and neck and turned, lashing a kick backward into Stan's kneecap, connecting with his heel. He heard the patella crack as Grigory's right elbow swung back and caught him on the side of the face.

He saw stars and hit the deck in a controlled tuck and rolled to his feet. He touched his lip with his tongue and tasted blood. He wiped at his chin and looked at his palm filled with blood. "Lucky shot, comrade."

Stan flexed and roared. The cracked patella probably hurt but, reasoned John, it didn't stop him from putting all his weight on that leg. Grigory was not as well off. The punch to the carotid artery had slowed him, the impact causing more distress than pain. Grigory stumbled to his feet, disoriented. John drove the side of his foot into the back of the smaller assailant's knee, collapsing one leg, and then drove his fist into the right side of Grigory's neck. Out of the corner of his eye he saw Stan's approach, fast and hard. He slipped to the far side of Grigory, now completely stunned and on his knees, and brought his knee up under his chin. As he fell, Stan ran into him, finishing John's job.

One down.

One much bigger one to go.

He stepped to one side and drove the side of his foot into Stan's left knee. He mistimed the kick, though, and Stan got a hand on his foot and lifted, knocking John on his back. He had to roll away fast to avoid the boot coming down on his head. He continued the roll, up and onto his feet. "You're fast for a big guy. But you'll tire out."

"You're the one bleeding, not me."

"Lucky shot from your bitch friend." John circled with Stan, both looking for an opening. "And it looks like you're on your own now, big guy."

Stan drew deep breaths. John smiled and winced and continued moving, not giving his large assailant an opportunity to rest. "You thought I'd be done by now, didn't you? Well, didn't you?"

Stan roared and lunged, his fist scything through the air like a wrecking ball. Getting inside the punch would be suicide. Stan would crush him.

So he ducked under the punch, driving his right fist up into his armpit, an area filled with many nerves and few layers of protective muscle. Then he smashed the side of Stan's knee, the one with the cracked patella, with the side of his foot and all of his weight. The leg buckled and John slipped out of reach.

Stan tried to stand, but his knee wouldn't hold his weight. He balanced, weight supported on his right leg, left just for balance and held his hand under his right armpit. "Come on. Let's do this."

"I'm doing it, big guy. Haven't you noticed? I'll keep doing it until you see the foolishness of your ways and leave me alone."

An injured animal is dangerous, especially so when they have the capacity of thought. "You'll die."

"We all die. You going to back off now?"

"I'm going to fucking kill you." He lunged again at John, who was now much quicker than his attacker. He grabbed Stan's outstretched hand and echoed the move Stephanie had used on her attacker, giving Stan's hand a sharp pull and twist. He heard the wrist break as he followed through. Stan fell to the ground, face first, arm twisted behind him. JD gave the arm an extra twist and felt something give. He gingerly licked the corner of his mouth, tasting blood. "Stay down Stanley, or I'll have to hurt you more." He dropped Stan's arm.

Stanislav let out a moan. "Asshole. I'm going to kill you."

"You've got a trashed knee, and that shoulder is going to need surgery. How are you going to -"

Stan rolled to his side and slid a knife from his boot and jabbed it at John, slicing his calf.

"Son of a bitch." John grabbed his leg and fell on his back. "That's going to leave a mark." He ripped his pants up the seam and looked at the wound on his right calf. Stan had cut deep, but he missed major arteries and tendons. Stan made to move again. John lashed out with his left foot and drove his heel into the side of his head. "I said stay down." He pulled off his t-shirt and tore it into strips. He used the bulk of the shirt as a bandage and tied it tight around his leg. The pressure would have to hold until he got back.

He stood and tested its strength. He placed his weight on his leg and bounced. "Shit. I won't be running any races today." He hobbled back to his car. Grigory and Stan were still unconscious, and he had no desire to be around when they came to.

He awkwardly got in his Honda, it for once in better shape than him, and backed it out of the parking lot. He looked up at the shop as he left. Hector stared at him, then turned his back the window, talking on the phone.

Chapter Fifteen

John pulled into the restaurant's parking lot. He grabbed a jacket from the back seat and ventured in, limping. Rico, sitting at his usual table, looked up from his paper and nodded, then looked down again. He limped to the counter. "Hey, Izz. Seen the band anywhere?"

She closed the till and smiled. "They left about fifteen minutes ago." She stepped from behind the counter and looked at him closer. "You okay? You look like hell."

John grinned and winced as his lip split again. "I look a lot better than I feel."

"What happened? Should I call an ambulance?"

"Jeez, do I look that bad? No, I'll be okay. I think. Leg's kinda sore."

"Were you in a car accident?"

"Nothing like that. Ran into a guy who disagreed with me living."

Rico pushed himself up from his table and ambled over. "Yet you still are." He clapped him on the shoulder and looked him up and down. "Boy, you look a treat."

"You should see the other guy."

"I shudder to think. What happened to your leg?"

"Got sliced. Nothing important got cut, but it's going to be a while before I run anywhere."

"Deep?"

"I think, yeah. I'd head off to the hospital, but we've got a show tonight. I'll go after."

"How you going to explain that?"

"What do you mean?" John looked down at his calf, blood seeping through his torn t-shirt.

"The emergency room doctors will have to call the police if they believe the injury is related to a crime. Hard to explain a cut on the back of your leg like that. Not like you cut yourself shaving or anything."

"It's deep enough I have to do *something* with it. I've got a few hours. I'll think of a story."

Rico shrugged. "I may have an alternate suggestion for you."

"You going to staple it shut for me?"

"I could, of course, but I have a doctor on retainer. He'll be able to sort you out, no lines, no waiting, no questions."

"Really?" He chuckled. "Lawyers on retainer I can understand, but a doctor? In case the cook cuts something he shouldn't?"

"Sure. Something like that. Interested? In and out in thirty minutes."

"They take my insurance?"

Rico waved him away. "My treat. You guys bring a lot of business my way. Least I could do."

"I don't know."

148

Rico took him lightly by the arm and guided him through the back of the restaurant kitchen. "Look at it this way: You'll save hours in the ER, and a bucket of money. This isn't negotiable. I know what I'm doing."

"I'm glad one of us does."

Rico grunted. "Now tell me about the guy who did this to you."

~~~

Petrovski sat in the back of his C300 with a battered Stan. Grigory rested in the front passenger seat, eyes closed.

"Who did this to you?"

Stan lifted the bag of ice from the side of his face. "I don't think he knows where the drummer is."

"Who?"

"That little shit, the sax player. The guy who shot me."

Petrovski rubbed his temples with his thumb and forefinger. "How bad?"

"Bumps and bruises. I might have a torn ACL."

"No, him. How bad is *he* damaged?"

"I cut him."

"And he's still alive?"

"Sorry, boss. The guy is fast."

"Super-fast," said Grigory from the front seat.

"When I want your side of the fucking story, I'll ask it. Shut up." Petrovski turned back to Stan. "Let me understand this. You, Grigory and our friend Hector could not manage to damage that runt more than a cut? What did you cut, his hair?"

"I got him in the leg. And Greg is right. That guy is fast. He's got some specialized fight training or something." He tried straightening his leg and winced. "He really may have done my ACL."

Petrovski looked at the hulk of a man beside him. "This is disgraceful. This saxophone player is half your size. Less than half your size, and he took all three of you out."

"Oh, he knows he was in a fight."

"He should be dead. And you tell me he just drove away."

"You're missing the important thing here, boss."

"I am? What is this important thing I'm missing?"

"He really doesn't seem to know where this Coates schmuck is. Maybe the guy is dead."

Petrovski shook his head. "I have not seen a body. You have not seen a body. Nobody has seen a body, so the guy is not dead. Find me his body and I will believe he is dead."

"Well then, he's an awfully good hider."

Petrovski leaned back in his seat and closed his eyes. A good hider. An exceptionally good hider. None of his contacts in the greater South Florida area had even a sniff of the witness's whereabouts, and he had guys everywhere. No hotels, hospitals, or even youth hostels had anyone by his description check-in since Thursday. He'd gone to ground like a professional.

Or like a professional helped him.

"Oh, shit." He shook his head. "Stan, I am thinking you were a bit too slow off the mark."

"I don't know what that means."

"You were late. You took too long to do your job. You fucked up."

"I don't understand."

"Of course you don't. We can't find the drummer because someone is helping him hide."

"So we find the someone and beat the shit out of them."

"I'm afraid, Stanislav, it might not be that easy. I'm afraid our friend is being hidden by the police. And if that's the case, then we are all well and truly fucked."

~~~

John winced as the doctor applied a dressing. "You are lucky, Mr. Saxophone Player. Whoever did this kept their knife very sharp. No tearing. Clean cut. Don't let me see you again." He picked a pill bottle off the table and tossed it to him. "The white ones in here are an antibiotic. Take one twice a day with food or your tummy might get upset. The light green ones are a strong painkiller. They should only be dispensed by a script, so don't get caught in a compromising position with them, okay? And don't take any more than you really need to. They could prove to be addictive and we wouldn't want a nice boy like you becoming an addict."

John looked at the bottle and slid it into his pocket. "Thanks Doctor…" He let the title drag out.

"Call me Marcus Welby if you want. Doesn't matter. It's not my real name, and I'm not going to tell you my real name."

Rico stepped in. "Okay, that's enough. Let's get you back to my place so you can get your car, chief." He winked at the doctor. "Maybe you can pay this guy back by getting him into one of your shows for free."

"The quality of work that I did on your leg, I should get into a dozen of your shows for free."

"Hey, doc, any time we're playing just stop by. Any time. Thanks again."

John limped out, led by Rico. He slid into the passenger seat of Rico's car and leaned back with his eyes closed. "So that was interesting."

"Yeah, kiddo, there are certain regulations concerning the practice of medicine and dispensing of medications that the doc may have breached back there. Just keep it to yourself, okay?"

"I'm starting to think that maybe running a restaurant isn't your only source of income."

"Would that be a problem?"

John thought about it. "The place we eat at, is that a front for something else?"

"No. I wouldn't put my daughter in a position like that. It's completely above board. Pay my taxes, file everything with the government, all clean and legal."

John grunted. "Yeah, well as long as I don't know what's going on, I'm good. Don't tell me about any of the other places you've got."

"Six other joints around town, actually, with a couple more on the drawing board. You'll have to tell me how you got out of that scrape alive. He's a big motherfucker."

John gingerly touched his lip. "Playing sax is going to be fun tonight."

"Take a green pill. They're good, trust me."

"Nah, a couple of Tylenol will do. Don't want to get into the heavy stuff. I've got an addictive personality. It won't end up good."

"Well, if you're looking for a couple extra bucks, you can get about $10 a pop for them on the street." He looked at John's face and laughed. "No, you're not that kind of guy, are you." He turned off the car and turned in his seat. "Petrovski and I have competing interests. I really don't like the guy and would go well out of my way to torpedo the commie bastard, so if there's anything I can do to help, you let me know, okay?"

"Okay. Right. I've got to get going. Music beckons." He got out of the car and limped to his Honda, still a beat-up piece of shit. "What a wonderful pile of crap I've gotten myself into today. Shit."

~~~

Petrovski dialed the number, let it ring once and hung up. He repeated the action two more times, then sat back and waited.

Fifteen minutes later his phone rang. "Hello. Clean?"

"Yes. You?"

"Of course I'm clean. I check every day."

"Well, look, it's 6:00 on a Saturday evening. What do you want from me?"

"I think the drummer I'm looking for is under police protection somewhere. I need you to go in right now and see if there is anyone in any holding cell who really shouldn't be there. The name may be different, the appearance may have been altered, but I want a list of all males in custody with little or no reason to be there and I want that list tonight."

"I've got a date with my wife, man. I was just getting ready to go."

"Cancel it. Tell her something of critical importance has come up at the station and you need to go in there now."

"This can't wait until morning?"

"If it could, I would have called you in the morning. But I called you now because I want you to take your overfed ass into the station now and do as you're told. Call me back at this number in two hours or I'll come looking for you."

~~~

John arrived at the club just before they were meant to go on. He grabbed some ice from a bucket and wrapped a linen napkin around it and held it to the corner of his mouth.

Henry looked up and did a double take. "Shit, what happened? Can you play?"

"Probably."

"You got beat on?"

"It's been a wonderful day, so far. Pounded on by the gorilla of all gorillas, had my injuries tended to by a doctor I'm almost positive is on the mob's payroll, and still no closer to finding Coates. He's buried deep."

154

Ned sauntered in. "Whoa, wait. Mob doctor? This sounds good. What did I miss?"

"Ran into Stan and his sidekick, emphasis on kick, at the airboat place. They tried to do a number on me."

"If that's tried, man, what's succeeded?"

"I'd be dead, I think. Anyway, we got everyone here?"

"Yes. Don't change the subject. The mob doctor. Spill."

John squinted and carefully touched the corner of his mouth. And winced. "My embouchure is going to be messed up tonight. Gonna have to play out of the corner of my mouth, like a hillbilly." He pressed the ice to the lip. "You guys ever wonder about Rico?"

"Wonder what?"

"He always seems connected. Hangs around with some big guys. The revenue from that restaurant wouldn't be enough to support his lifestyle. It's rarely more than half full."

"I've heard he's got six others."

"Yeah, he told me the same thing, and a few more on the way." He nodded. "That was about the time he introduced me to the doctor he has on retainer. The one who stitched up my leg and gave me prescription pain meds without a prescription. I think Rico runs a bit deeper than we think he does."

"Pain meds? What kind of pain meds?"

"Green ones. Where's Steph?"

"She said she had to run an errand, but that she'd be back in time for the show." Henry looked at his watch. "So, like in the next fifteen minutes."

At that moment she pushed through the door. "My ears are burning. Everyone set?" She saw John's face. "Oh my God, are you okay?"

"Couldn't be better. You have any luck on your errand?"

"Luck?"

"You were looking for Coates, right? He's gone well and truly to ground. I haven't had a sniff of him. And the gorillas aren't having any luck either." He pointed to the bruises on his head. "They seemed to think they could beat his location out of me."

Henry sat in a chair and crossed his arms. "You've got to tell us what happened. I'm actually not going on until you *do* tell us what happened."

"I was in a scrap. Nothing else."

Ned shook his head and chuckled. "With the big guy? The one you shot? He must have been in a good mood."

"Okay, fine. The big guy, his sidekick, and Hector, the out of shape schlep at the boat launch. But the big guy, Stan, was the only real fight. Kinda feel sorry for Hector. He's got himself in way over his head. Can't be comfortable for him."

"Screw him. How did you manage to beat the big guy?"

John looked at the rapt faces. "You guys are sick. I just fought a guy like a caveman. Evolution took a big step backward today."

"Fine, fine. How do you go nose to nose with someone that much larger than you, and come out on top?"

"He's not a machine. Steroids do wonders for bulk, but all that extra weight tires most people out. And his joints are still susceptible to attack. Steroids don't help them any. Look, enough. He lost. This time. I expect he'll try again so travel in groups and pretend you don't like me, okay? He's really going to be pissed off now."

Chapter Sixteen

Stan looked like the walking wounded. He *felt* like the walking wounded. The cast on his right wrist and the brace on his right knee were constant reminders of being bested by a man half his size. He shuffled into his boss's office in the back of *The Natalia*, his club by the airport. "Doc says that the knee is just a strain, not an actual tear. It should be good in three or four weeks. The wrist, though, could be at least eight weeks. Longer if I'm not careful." He raised his arm above his shoulder. "Rotator cuff is strained, but nothing is torn. Hurts like hell."

Petrovski stared at him for a few seconds before talking. "Have you heard anything about the location of our witness?"

"What? No. I've been at the hospital for the past five hours."

"You have a phone?"

"You can't use a phone in the hospital. You know that."

"So you have been a complete waste for me today. What did you tell them caused your injuries?"

"A motorcycle accident."

"Did they seem convinced?"

"I guess. They treated me. Didn't call the cops." He slowly lowered himself into a chair. "I have contacts in Florida also. Here, south, Broward, Palm Beach, there are friends, and friends of friends I can draw on." He dug into his pocket and pulled out the band's flyer. "I've sent the picture of the drummer from this to a lot of people and told them to pass it on. The word is out, and it's spreading. It doesn't matter where he's holed up, I'll find him." He cleared his throat. "I may have intimated that there would be a favorable response from you, monetarily, to the person who locates him. Hope that's okay."

Petrovski studied the flyer. "Yeah, that's fine. Forward to me the picture you took. Where's Grigory?"

"He's pretty seriously concussed. He's still at the hospital under observation." He held up his hands. "I told them he was on the back of the bike. We're okay."

Petrovski nodded. "I need you to leave."

"Understood." Stan levered himself from the chair. "I'll be outside if you need anything."

Petrovski waited until the door closed behind his temporarily useless muscle then extracted a burner phone from his desk drawer.

It rang four times. Petrovski pulled it away from his head to hang up when he heard Cruz answer. "What is it? I'm at dinner at my in-laws."

"You didn't go to the station as I asked?"

"I did. Nobody fitting your description there. I sent you a text message. I really had to go to this dinner. You know what it's like."

"No, fortunately, I don't. Can you talk freely?"

"Yeah, what is it?"

160

"Shortly I will be sending you a picture of a man I am looking for. His name is Paul Coates. It is extremely important that I find him, and soon."

"I already checked the station. What is this going to accomplish?"

"He's hiding too well. I expect he's been getting some help from your organization, or, heaven forbid, someone a bit more federal. Sniff around. See what you can learn and tell me."

"Tonight, right?"

"You learn fast, Cruz. Tonight. Tell your moneybag in-laws that there's an urgent crime thing you need to attend to. I'm sure they will understand. It's Miami. And be fast. My patience is wearing thin."

~~~

John remained seated throughput the gig. He had the mouthpiece hard to the left to avoid the split lip, a technique Coates had lectured him against repeatedly in his high school years. A brief disturbance at the back of the club caught the band's attention, collectively, but it was a mousey little guy with too much gin in his system being rebuffed by a girl, and not taking it too kindly. When the disturbance started, John noticed Rico and a colleague at a table near the front stand and look toward the noise. He smiled to himself. In addition to the large men at the front door it appeared that they had a couple of security in the joint too. Other than that, the first set was uneventful.

When they closed off the last song of the first set, John stowed his sax and joined them at their table.

Rico stood and extended his hand. "You still look like shit. You've met Simon, right? I'm looking at investing in this place. We're calling this due diligence. That way I can expense my meals. Love the tax code. If you know how to use it."

John shook Simon's hand and sat across from Rico. "The conversation we had, about you offering to help. Is that for real?"

"Absolutely. Why?"

"That's what I want to know. Why? Why help take down Petrovski?"

Simon smiled, sat back and crossed his arms. "This I gotta hear."

"Yeah, well, Vlad and I have been butting heads for a coupla years now. There were four of us in South Florida, me, him, a wing-nut named Tony Montana running Homestead and south - yeah, Tony Montana. I said he was a wing-nut, right? - and a hard-assed psychopathic Russian called Ivan Smimov. I got them all together for a very nice dinner and proposed an alliance; we work together and gain economies of scale. Went over like an ex-girlfriend at a wedding.

"When Montana was arrested for attempting to kill a coupla FBI agents and this guy's brother," he hiked a thumb in Simon's direction, "I kinda, sorta consolidated his organization into ours. Petrovski naturally picked up Smimov's business when he was picked up."

"So now it's just you and Petrovski in Miami?"

He shrugged and waggled his hands. "We've got the bulk of everything south of Okeechobee, fairly evenly divided. Six months now. Both of us consolidating our power and watching and waiting for an opportunity to torpedo the other. This sounds like a great opportunity for me. And you. Win-win."

John's head swam. He'd got himself in the middle of a mob war. "Hang on a second." He looked over at Simon. "Your brother is a cop?"

"Long story. He thinks I'm business development manager for Rico. Or something equally prosaic."

"And funnily enough, he does do a lot of that. So you see where I'm coming from. If your buddy is a threat to Petrovski, then your buddy is my best friend. I'll help you find him and then exploit whatever threat he has against Vlad."

"Like what, a traffic cop?"

"Huh?" Rico looked puzzled.

"This guy's brother, what kind of cop is he?"

"Homicide detective, currently assigned as liaison to the FBI's OC division. Organized Crime." Simon smiled. "Makes life kinda interesting."

Henry walked over and rested his hand on John's shoulder. "Everything okay here?"

"Yeah, thanks Henry. Catching up with these guys. I think they're going to help us find Paul, right guys?"

"Whatever we can do to assist."

"That's great, guys, but I've got to steal JD. We're on in a minute for the second set. Remember to tip your server."

~~~

Rico sipped his drink. "This could be it, Simon. Taking advantage of these opportunities when they arise is what has got us to where we are."

Simon nodded. "I want to find him just to find out why the Russian has such a hard-on for him."

"I want you to reach out to our friends around Miami. Make it all of South Florida." He handed Simon a flyer. "Take Paul's picture off this and send it to them. We need to know where he is. Need to find him before Petrovski or one of his mutts do. Make it a priority."

Simon folded the flyer and slid it in his back pocket as he stood. "I'll get on it now."

"Don't want to stay for the show?"

"No. I'll stick to Zeppelin and The Doobie Brothers." He tossed back his drink. "I'll call you later and let you know how it's going."

Rico nodded and turned his attention to the band. The replacement drummer, if he worked hard, barely came close to Coates on a bad day. And John labored with his injuries. He had the sax in the corner of his mouth and definitely wasn't his best. He shook his head and marveled at the toughness of the little guy. To go up against big Stan and not come out of it a greasy spot on the road was a true accomplishment.

The band wound up with a big number Rico didn't recognize - the only song he recognized all night was "Sinnerman" - and the house lights came up to a room full of applause. He stood and waved John over. Henry joined him.

"Gentlemen, have a seat." He flagged down a server. "Bring me a bottle of 18-year-old whisky and glasses for these two." He looked to John. "You taking those pain meds?"

"No. Tylenol only."

"Good. This Irish pain killer works better anyway."

"I can't stay long, Rico, but I appreciate the drink."

"What, you got another gig tonight somewhere?"

"No, but it's been a helluva day."

"Exactly. You've got to regale us with the battle. I've heard through the grapevine that Stan is worse for wear. Much." He poured generous drinks for Henry and John. "You fucking near ripped his arm off." He pointed at the glass. "Drink."

John took a mouthful and winced, placing the glass gently on the table. "I'm a lucky guy."

"Oh, bullshit. I know Stanislav pretty well. He's no slouch. You took him apart. And he wasn't alone. Grigory is almost as big as Henry here and if the stories are true he barely slowed you down."

"No." He took another drink and topped up the glass. "Never an afterthought. And it's not something I enjoy doing. I spent too much time fighting for a living to ever enjoy it, if that's what you think. And even now it's a last option. I really don't like doing it."

"You may not like it, son, but you sure are good at it."

John pointed to the bruises on his head and his split lip. "Not that good." He swallowed another mouthful of the Irish Whisky.

Rico grinned and topped up his glass. "This elixir costs almost a hundred a bottle. Slow down and appreciate it." He topped up Henry's also.

"Works better than Tylenol."

"Yeah, but not as good as the Percocet I gave you."

"That's what they were? Wouldn't know. Haven't touched them."

"Don't let them go to waste, Johnny. But not tonight. I think those little green pills won't go well with the booze in this big green bottle."

John inspected the contents of his glass. "A hundred a bottle? Very smooth. Packs a punch, too."

"You're tiny," Henry slurred. "Be a cheap drunk, I think."

"Not cheap if we keep drinking this." John took a more restrained sip. "Very smooth." He closed one eye and squinted at Rico. "Don't drink much, but when I do I think I'll be sliding this my way. Thanks for drinks." He stopped suddenly and sat straight up. "Hang on. Is this one of those 'I may call you some day for a favor' things? I'm not comfortable with that."

Rico laughed. "I'm as much of a fan of "The Godfather" as anyone, but that was decades ago. And not entirely accurate." He leaned forward as if confiding in him. "This is hugely to my benefit already. Now come on, how'd you take out Stan?"

He watched John struggle with the idea of bragging about a feat certainly worth bragging about, but one he was no longer comfortable taking part in.

"I don't enjoy fighting."

"I know. Rare thing to see in a man these days. Stan, I happen to know, does enjoy it."

"I noticed." He gently touched his lip. "Too much. That was his downfall."

"He's literally a foot taller than you and at least a hundred pounds heavier." It wasn't a question. Just a statement of incontrovertible fact. John had bested a giant.

He took another drink and looked at Rico. "It's just physics. Momentum, leverage, knowing the weak spots on any human body."

Henry barked out a laugh. "So you nailed him in the nuts, did you?"

"Dumbest thing you can do. Especially against someone that big. It's too small of a target," Henry and Rico started laughing. "No. Seriously. His thighs, his quads, are massive. It's nearly impossible to get a direct shot. Not worth the risk."

"The guy is slab after slab of muscle." Rico shook his head. "There is no weakness."

John took another mouthful and re-filled his glass. "Always a weakness. Everybody." He put down his glass and started counting off his fingers. "One, he's really heavy. It may be muscle, but it's heavy. Keep him moving, and he tires. Steroids don't do a thing for your cardiovashl - cardiovlasc - heart and lungs. And they don't do anything for your tendons." He took another mouthful. "I know what they mean now by 'feeling no pain'. Much better than Tylenol."

Rico smiled. Tylenol wouldn't be mean to him tomorrow like the whisky would. "So what about the tendons?"

"Relatively speaking, they are weakened by the steroids. The bulk of the huge muscles strains against the tendons and makes it easier to hurt them. So I did. Plus a few well targeted attacks to places muscles don't tend to accumulate."

Henry shook his head. "Few people surprise me these days. But you, you really surprise me. Like a rat terrier going after a Doberman."

Rico leaned forward and rested on his elbows. "Unfortunately the Doberman is still alive. He's not going to make the same mistakes twice."

Chapter Seventeen

John cracked open his eyes. The sun shone into his bedroom, reflecting off a glassed picture on his wall and onto his face. He'd forgotten to close the curtains before he went to bed. Not surprising, since he didn't actually remember the events leading up to getting into bed. He went to sit up and groaned, holding his head. It started to come back to him.

The gig went okay. There were no more disturbances, at least not from any gorillas. He played with a sore mouth, but he'd had to perform in his past life with more painful injuries than that, so it wasn't that big of a deal.

After the show he made the decision to forego the painkillers the doctor had provided and go for the ones Jameson provided. Henry matched him drink for drink until he got to the point he couldn't remember feeling any pain.

He had no idea how he got home.

He squinted against the glare and stepped out on his balcony. From there he could see his assigned parking spot. No car. "Shit." He took a deep breath, wincing against the pain in his ribs, and tried to settle his thoughts.

"Maybe a hot shower."

He stripped off in the bathroom and surveyed the damage. In addition to the sliced calf - under a waterproof bandage - and the split lip, his head, neck and upper torso were painted purple with bruises. He took another slow breath against the pain, pushing through it. "No cracked ribs, anyway. Jeez, why does it always hurt more the next day?"

The hot shower beat on his neck and back, pounding away the pain. He continued the deep breaths. The fact that he got out of the fight with no broken bones was nothing short of a miracle. He'd cracked ribs in the most innocuous ways in the past. Not having a cracked rib was a rarity for a good three years of his Ranger life.

He showered and shampooed and decided to leave the shaving for a couple of days until the swelling on his lip went down and the bruises cooled off.

He dressed, then looked at the bottle of pills. They tempted him. He hurt everywhere.

He slipped them into his back pocket and took two Tylenol. If they didn't work, he had the little green pills as back up.

He sat on his balcony and tried to remember where he left his car, sweat beading on his neck.

"At least I didn't drive it," he muttered.

He half closed his eyes to relax when his phone rang. "JD."

"Henry here. You okay?"

"I'll live. Where's my car?"

"At the club. I'll swing by your place in a couple of hours and pick you up. You were hammered last night, man. Never knew someone your size to put that much away."

"Huh. My head hurts when you talk. And when I talk. I'll see you in a couple. Thanks."

He hung up and thought about what had happened at the boat launch. He wasn't an idiot. And certainly Stan and company had a lot of resources to draw on. And if nobody could find Paul, maybe Paul really was getting help.

Rico mentioned that he and Petrovski had competing interests in a similar business. He thought hard and tried to push the haze away. He'd mentioned something last night about helping find Paul and using him to take down Petrovski.

He limped into the kitchen and rummaged through one of his kitchen drawers until he found the take-away menu for Rico's restaurant.

"Italiano Kitchen, how can I help you?"

"That Izzy?"

"Who's this?"

"JD. Is your dad around?"

He waited for a minute until Rico picked it up. "How's the leg, champ?"

"Stiff and sore, but your doctor knows his stuff."

"I only retain the best."

"Rico, I'm not going to beat around the bush. You and Petrovski are competitors in an Organized Crime family way, aren't you?"

"Son, I'm a respectable businessman, running a successful string of restaurants in South Florida. I don't know what you're talking about, should anybody be listening in on this call."

"Ah. Right. So, would it be accurate to say that your business interests may overlap those of a certain Russian we were discussing the other day?"

"You don't remember any of our conversation last night, do you?"

"I remember very little of anything yesterday, except the smack down Stan gave me."

"I've been doing some calling around. Stan is in a very bad way. Sprained rotator cuff, broken wrist and a torn ACL. He's useless as a weapon for now. The conversation will come back to you later as the booze filters out of your system. When you remember what we talked about, give me a call. And if there's anything I can do for you, let me know. Anything."

John rubbed his face, winced and contemplated the alliance he now apparently had with Rico. He'd gotten into bad ones before, but they always seemed a good idea at the outset. It wasn't like he had much of a choice, though. "Anything?"

"Really. Any way I can help you, just ask."

~~~

Paul Coates paced in the screened-in porch. Four steps, turn, four steps, turn, repeat as necessary. "Three days I've been here and I haven't heard a thing from you guys yet." He stopped and looked at the US Marshall sitting in the cheap patio chair. "I thought you guys wanted Petrovski gone. He's probably got his army out looking for me. I'll be shot in my bed."

Darrel Lund put his finger to his lips. "Keep it down. The old folks living around here are the worst gossips you've ever seen. And relax. Nobody knows you're here. I want to keep it that way. Can I get you a beer?"

"No. I don't drink. Told you that yesterday, and the day before." To the east, somewhere over the Atlantic, a rumble of thunder promised a much needed cooling rain. Paul took a deep breath. "It's the heat. And my stupid luck to come to you guys on a long weekend."

A screen door slammed behind him, startling him. Jean-Claude stepped out on his porch across the street and waved. "Some hot, eh? *Tabernac.* I come down too early this year. But it was some friggin'' cold in Montreal, I tell you."

Paul gave him a half-hearted wave. "Yeah. Guess so." He turned his back, not wanting to make conversation.

"But this rain, she'll be good. We need it." Jean-Claude opened the screen door, letting himself in. "So, where'd you say you came from?"

"Nebraska, okay?"

Darrel stood and got between Paul and the septuagenarian. "We're just leaving, sir. Perhaps you could go outside."

Jean-Claude squinted past Darrel at Paul. "Okay, sure." He nodded. "Dat's fine." He pushed out the screen door and walked back to his trailer, his flip-flops slapping against his feet as he looked at the screen on his phone, then put it to his head and started talking.

~~~

John waited in the entryway of his apartment building. He had two Tylenol extra-strength in him and the pain in his head had reduced to a dull throb. "How can something that tastes so good cause so much damage?"

Henry pulled up in front of the apartment in John's Honda and blew the horn. He hopped out and jumped in the passenger's seat as John walked out.

"You didn't have to hit the horn, pal. Mother of God my head hurts."

"You drank over half the bottle. I'm truly impressed. Thought that would have killed you."

"I feel dead." John licked his lips and put the car into gear. "Who drove me home last night?"

"Rico had one of his guys take us both home. You got a very important friend there."

"Not the kind of friend I'm looking for. Denny's?"

"Not IHOP."

"Yeah, I've always wondered about that. Why not IHOP?"

"Blueberry syrup is an abomination. We all voted about a year and a half ago. No more IHOP."

"It can't be that bad."

"Early in the morning, it looks exactly like maple syrup. Ever bite into a pancake expecting maple and getting blueberry? One time too many and we've never been back."

John pulled into Denny's parking lot. "Harsh. Everyone here?"

"Looks like it, man." They sat at the table with the rest of the band. "So how were your evenings last night?"

"Well if it isn't 'piss-holes-for-eyes' Delacourte. Hanging out with mobsters now, are you?" Larry drummed a beat on his legs. "You be careful. He only seems nice. He can be a real nasty prick."

"He said he'd help us find Paul. I'll take that. If he turns out to be a prick later, I'll deal with that then." John waved for some coffee. "Biggest concern now is finding Paul. The band, the gigs, everything else is secondary." He pointed at his bruised face. "If they did that to me, imagine what they'd do to him. I've run out of ideas. I've looked everywhere I know he'd be. I don't know what else to do." He stopped and sat back. "Hang on a second. I forgot about something."

He limped out to his car and checked the glove box and under the seats. "Shit. It's in here somewhere." He stuck his fingers down between the passenger's seat and the center console and felt it. "Yes." He carefully extricated Paul's mobile phone from the gap and ran back inside with it.

He sat and stretched his leg in an attempt to relieve the pain in his calf. He dropped the phone on the table. "Paul's mobile. Anyone know the code to unlock it?"

Stephanie took it, swept the screen to bring up the security prompt and entered a four-digit code.

"What was it?"

She handed the phone back to him. "If he wants you to know, he'll tell you. What do you expect to get from this?"

He scrolled through the recently called numbers. "Here's two I don't know." He dialed one and placed the phone on speaker.

"Miami Police Department. How may I direct your call?"

They looked at each other, then John leaned in close to the phone. "Sorry, wrong number." He hung up the call.

"When was that call?"

John looked at the call records. "Wednesday night. Late. After the gig." He flicked to the next one. "Here's the other. Thursday morning at 7:45."

Again he dialed and placed it on speaker. "MacCready."

"Simon?" John looked at Henry and shrugged.

"No, Dan. Detective Dan MacCready. Who's this?"

"My name is John Delacourte. We're looking for a friend. He dialed this number just before disappearing. Do you know a Paul Coates?"

There was a pause on the line. John could hear chatter in the background. "I have no idea who you're talking about, sorry. He must have called a wrong number and I've forgotten about it."

"You're with the Miami PD, right? Homicide?" John strained to remember what Rico had told him about Simon's brother last night.

"Liaison with Organized Crime. Do we know each other?"

"No, I don't think so. Saw something in the news about you a year or so ago. Somebody tried to kill you, and he ended up in jail."

"Right. Great memory you have. I'm afraid I've got guests and need to go. If you have any police-related questions, please call the station and go through the appropriate channels."

John hung up and looked at the band. "He knows something. I'm sure of it."

~~~

"Who was that, bro'? You looked a little rattled." Simon leaned against the counter and watched his brother prepare steaks for that afternoon's barbecue.

"Strange. Someone called looking for -" he stopped. "For someone who shouldn't be connected to me. At least nobody outside a very small circle should know he's connected to me." He added some beer to the marinade and dropped the steaks in. "Said he knew my name from an old newspaper article from when we picked up Tony Montana."

"You get the guy's name?"

"John Delacourte." He shrugged. "Never heard of the guy."

"And he thought you knew where this mystery person would be?"

"Wrong number."

"I don't think so. He's looking for someone who, according to you, is connected to you, but very few people know he's connected to you. Sounds like a fishing trip. This guy have enemies?"

Mac nodded and placed the steaks in the fridge. "Some big ones. Enough about this. How's it going with you and Rico?"

"You make it sound like we're dating."

"You know what I mean. Does he have any clue that I'm your handler?"

"Nope. Other way around. Keeps asking me to sniff around for info for him."

"What's he looking for now?"

"Some guy named Paul Coates. A drummer in a jazz band." He pulled the flyer out of his back pocket. "This guy here." He pointed at the drummer."

Mac's head spun. "Who? Why? Why is he looking for him? Let me see that." He grabbed the flyer. "What's his interest?"

"Whoa, back it up a bit, bro'. You're coming across really intense, like."

Mac took a deep breath and a closer look at the flyer. "Have you looked at this closely?"

"No, why?"

"That guy who just called is in this band." He jabbed a finger at the sheet. "John Delacourte. The sax player."

"So he's looking for Coates, too? Seems natural enough."

Mac slowly folded the paper and handed it back. He'd just revealed information that he shouldn't have, albeit unintentionally. That actually made it worse. He should know better than that. "Simon, you can't talk to anyone about this. Tell Rico you haven't found out anything from me."

"That serious?"

"Very. He's stashed for now, and I need to keep him stashed for the rest of the weekend."

"Around here?"

"Drop it, little brother. And tell your boss to drop it." He thought for a second. "Actually, tell him that I told you I had him arrested for fraud in Ohio and extradited him back to Cleveland."

"But he's around here somewhere."

Mac leaned in and placed his index finger on his brother's chest. "You need to drop this now."

"Drop what?"

Mac and Simon turned together. Detective Cruz leaned on the door jamb, hands in his pockets. His wife stood behind him, over made-up and looking bored.

"Hey, Cruz. You been here long?"

"A coupla minutes. James let us in. We got here at about the same time. Great idea this barbecue. Hot as hell weather. Due to break soon. You got any beer?"

Mac nodded at the fridge. "Help yourself." He looked at Simon. "Don't forget what I said."

"We'll talk later."

"There's nothing to talk about. It's over. You'll keep your mouth shut about it."

"Boys, calm down. It's supposed to be a party. Brothers fighting is so cliché." Cruz fished a beer out of the fridge for himself and handed one to his wife. "Can't we all just get along?"

Chapter Eighteen

Detective Mario Cruz left Mac's kitchen and wandered outside to the backyard. He drifted over by some trees in the corner of the yard and took out his burn phone. He called Petrovski first.

"On a Sunday. It must be important. What do you have for me, Cruz?"

"That Coates guy."

"What about him?"

"I overheard a conversation between Detective MacCready and his brother. Apparently, a lot of people are looking for him. Some guy named Delacourte has called around, and Rico's looking too."

"Delacourte? He's the sax player in that band. How'd he know to call MacCready?"

"Got me. I'm just passing on the info."

"Try and find out why. And Rico? You sure?"

"The cop's brother works for Rico, right? Which way do you think that's going?"

"What do you mean?"

Cruz sipped his beer. "Is the Simon guy spying for Rico or are the cops working him against Rico?"

"I really don't give a fuck. Are you sure Rico's looking?"

"Yeah, yeah. The cop's brother quizzed him hard. Full on, like. And MacCready told him to drop it. To back off."

"Anything else?"

"Nah, they saw me then."

"Where are you, at the station?"

"No, Mac's place. He's having a barbecue. Invited us all over."

"If you're going to be there for the afternoon, keep feeding him beer and see what else you can get from him."

"Taking all the fun out of this. It's supposed to be a relaxing day."

"Just do it." Petrovski hung up.

Cruz looked at his phone and dialed Rico's number.

"Detective. What can I do for you this hot and sweaty afternoon?"

"Might have something on Coates."

"Really? How's that?"

"I'm over at MacCready's for a barbecue. His brother, Simon, is here. He works for you, right?"

"Yeah, he does. Why?"

"I sometimes wonder whether he's actually working for you or if he's just pretending to work for you while all along he works for the cops."

"I believe it's the other way around. He pretends to work for the cops while all along he works for me. Continue about Coates."

"Right. The cop and his brother were having a heated discussion about Coates. Mac the cop told your boy to back off and leave it alone. A dude named Delacourte was looking for him also."

"Ah, Johnny D the Sax Machine. Interesting he should get to MacCready so fast. Clever and tough. Good info, Cruz. Now go enjoy yourself. If anything else comes up, give me a call."

"Will do." Cruz slipped the phone in his pocket and walked off to rejoin the rest of the party, Rico's orders to enjoy himself in stark contrast to Petrovski's "just do it". He knew which one he'd push under a bus first if he had to choose.

~~~

Rico sent a text message and sat back, waiting for the call. Izzy stopped by with a fresh cup of coffee. "You going anywhere today?"

"Don't think so, why?"

"Barry and I are hitting a movie this afternoon. Need someone to cover for me for about thirty minutes while my backup isn't here."

"Well, that's shitty planning."

"Can't be helped." She kissed him on the top of his head. "Thanks for the help." She walked back toward the kitchen.

"Hey, I didn't say anything about helping." She either couldn't hear him or ignored him. "Kids."

His phone rang. "Rico speaking. This Simon?"

"One and only. What's up?"

"You at your brother's barbecue?"

"What, are you spying on me?"

Rico laughed. "No, Cruz just called me. And since he does feed shit to Petrovski, make sure you send some absolute horse-shit his way once in a while."

"Absolutely. Is that why you wanted me to call?"

"No. Cruz told me that you and your brother had a discussion about Coates."

"Yeah, very freaky. Like everything is connected to everything else in a weird sort of way."

"That'll be all, Dirk Gently."

"Who?"

"Not important. What did you learn of the conversation? You can talk freely, right?"

"Should be good for a few minutes. Mac got a call from JD looking for Paul. I have absolutely no idea how JD connected this to my brother, but he's involved somehow, based on the conversation he had with him on the phone and the subsequent conversation with me."

"Your brother's in that new place, right? Out of the apartment?"

"Yeah, why?"

"Don't worry, Simon. Your brother's interests align with mine. I'm not going to do anything to mess that up." He hung up and stretched out his legs. This was getting better.

~~~

John took a deep breath and sighed as the pain in his ribs cut in near the full lung mark. He looked at Stephanie, sitting on his sofa in deep thought. "You okay?"

"Yeah, thanks. How are the injuries?"

"I've had worse."

"I'm sure you're used to all this fighting."

"When people over the age of sixteen fight, unless it's a sanctioned fight in a ring, the primary intent is to kill or maim seriously enough to make the other guy wish he *was* dead. Not my bag. I had more than my fill of that with the Rangers. If I never lift a hand in anger again I'll be happy. But sometimes you don't have a choice."

"You always have a choice. You could have walked away from Stan."

"I would have had to run away, and that would have led him right back to the rest of you. No, I'm not going to do that."

Stephanie didn't answer, just sat on the sofa and looked at the ground.

"What's wrong? It's like your cat is dead."

"I'm allergic to cats."

"You know what I mean. You're usually Stephanie the feisty, or Stephanie the bubbly, or Stephanie the "get-the-fuck-outta-my-face-or-I'll-break-your-nose". I don't think I've ever seen a Stephanie the morose."

She cracked a half smile. "I've got some things I've got to sort out, but mainly, I'm extremely worried about Paul."

"Me too. I think I'm going to call in a favor. Rico said he'd help in any way he can."

"You're playing with fire, JD. He's going to want a lot in return."

"I can worry about that when the time comes." He slid his phone out of his back pocket just as it rang. "Hello?"

"JD? Rico here. Can you stop by the restaurant? There's something I need to talk to you about."

"Speak of the devil. I had my hand on the phone, just about to call you. I need your help finding -"

"Stop. Talk face to face. Here. Only way to do it. See you shortly."

John looked at his phone, locked it and slid it in his back pocket. "That solves that. I've been summoned. Rico's looking for me and wants to tell me something face to face."

"I'll go with you."

"Why not? You look like you could use some fresh air. Or something."

She stood and stretched. "Some sleep, some easing up on the stress. Some relaxation. Lots of things I could use."

"I'm more than willing to help you achieve a Zen-like state of relaxation."

"I'm sure you are. So where are we meeting Rico?"

"The restaurant. Our home away from home."

"Do we need the rest of the band?"

"He only mentioned me. You can tag along, but I'm not getting the others involved."

"Oh, I can 'tag along', can I? How generous of you. I've known Paul for a very long time. Probably longer than you."

"I've known him since high school."

186

"I know. So my interest in finding him is as least as strong as yours, and probably stronger."

"This isn't a contest, Steph." He grabbed his keys off the counter and held the door for her. "There's no meter to determine who's more concerned. I'll defer to your level of concernedness, if that makes you happy." He locked the door behind them. "Just don't be silly about it."

She punched him in the shoulder. "I'm never silly."

"Hey, ouch. I've got a bruise there."

"You've got bruises everywhere." She followed him out of the apartment. "You know I went to visit Vladimir yesterday."

"Who?"

"Vladimir Petrovski. The guy Stan works for."

He stopped by his car. "What? What the… How in the hell do you know him? What were you doing there?"

"How I know him is irrelevant. It's from a long time ago. We don't keep company any more. I thought I'd pay him a visit and tell him to stop looking for Paul. That I could guarantee he wouldn't do anything against him, whatever Petrovski was concerned about."

"Are you crazy?"

"Apparently so. He wasn't very amenable to my suggestions and I'm lucky to have gotten out of there unscathed. I think I heard him talking to Stan just before you and he got into it." She smiled a wan smile. "Glad you got out of it relatively unscathed."

"Yeah, me too." He got in and started the car. They drove in silence to Rico's restaurant, ten minutes away.

"You won't tell me how you know him?"

She shook her head as he parked. "Maybe someday. It's not important. No big conspiracy or anything."

"That's comforting." He eased out of the car. "Damn, it always hurts more the next day."

"You're a yellow-ish purple all over. Kind of a nauseating color."

John grunted and walked into the cool air of the restaurant. Rico sat at a corner table reviewing something that looked official. He looked up and waved them over.

"You brought Steph with you."

"She has an interest in all of this that's a bit deeper than I understand. And she looked bored. What did you want to talk about?"

"You look like death warmed over. Sore head?"

"You're evil."

"Want a shot? Hair of the dog and all that?"

"That dog had rabies. What's this about?"

"You called a detective today, Simon's brother, right? Looking for Paul? What made you call him? How'd you know about his involvement?"

John dropped a phone on the table. "This is Paul's phone. That number was the last number he called. Nothing magic. What do you want to share that needs to be shared face to face?"

Rico looked at Steph. "So you called that detective, twigging something. His brother, my loyal right-hand man, was there also. He had a chat with his brother and it would appear that Paul is under the protection of the police."

"Got that from one call?"

"I got that from a couple of calls."

"Why?"

"Why what?"

"Why is he under the protection of the police? Or is he arrested?"

"No, he's not arrested. That seems to be pretty clear. He's in protective custody. I suspect he witnessed Petrovski killing Sergei, but I haven't had that confirmed yet."

Stephanie leaned forward in her chair. "So he's not hurt in any way?"

"Don't know that, but he's not in any hospital in South Florida. I've had them checked."

"But he's alive."

"Yes, Stephanie, he's alive. Guaranteed." Now Rico leaned forward. "But Petrovski is going to move heaven and earth to find him, and kill him, so it's imperative we find him first."

"How? I've looked everywhere. Steph visited Petrovski yesterday trying to get him to back off."

Rico let out a low whistle. "Into the lion's den. And you returned without a single bruise. You could teach this young man a thing or two." His phoned buzzed. He looked down and held up his hand. "Excuse me for a sec. I've got to call a guy back."

He levered his large frame out of the chair and walked to the back of the restaurant.

"I still can't believe that. Into Petrovski's lair and not a scratch to show for it."

"I can't believe you're comfortable using the resources of a mobster."

"Whatever works. You want to find Paul as much as I do."

"The ends justify the means? Really? I never took you for one of them."

"One of what?"

Rico re-entered before John could find out.

"Kids, I have some news. But first we need food." He waved Izzy over. "Chicken parm all around and some soft drinks." He turned back to John and Steph. John thought he saw some kind of triumph in his eyes. "I have some news. Not bad news."

"So, good news then."

"Not bad news. Whether it's good or not remains to be determined."

"Spill it." John balled his fists. "Where is he?"

"Relax, kiddo."

"I'm thirty-seven. You're what, forty at most? Stop calling me kiddo. Where is he?"

"I need you to promise you won't go to where he is."

"Why?"

"Petrovski and his minions are looking for him, too. And his net spreads pretty wide. There's no guarantee he hasn't also found him."

"Where in the fuck is he?"

Stephanie put her hand on John's arm. "JD, take it easy."

"Yeah, JD, take it easy." He held up his phone. "Is this him? It looks like him to me."

A picture of a middle-aged man in shorts and a t-shirt sitting in front of a single-wide trailer took up half of the screen. A large black man sat beside him in what looked like uncomfortably warm clothes.

"Looks like him. In a trailer park? That's not something I'd expect him to do." Stephanie leaned closer to the phone and took it from his hands. "Who's with him? I don't recognize him. Why would he take off and hide with someone we don't even know?"

"That's what I'm trying to tell you two. Paul never knew that guy before Thursday. I can guarantee it."

"How?"

Rico took his phone back and poked on the screen. "I know this guy. He's a US Marshall. If he's with Paul, Paul's in the witness protection program. WitSec." He grinned. "And that means he's got something that'll put Petrovski away for a very long time."

Chapter Nineteen

John pointed at Rico's phone. "Send me that picture."

"Say please."

"Seriously, I need a copy of that picture."

"You think you'll figure out where he is by comparing that trailer to every other trailer in South Florida? These places all look the same. Depressingly boring and cookie cutter identical."

"Don't make me beg, man. I just want to be able to prove to the rest of the band we weren't bullshitting when we tell them he's okay.

"You have a habit of bullshitting?"

"It'll take you two seconds. Just forward the picture to my phone. I'll even enter my phone number for you."

Rico sighed and handed him the phone. "So what are you going to do with this information?"

John pressed the buttons and sent the picture to his and Stephanie's phones. "I don't know what I can do. I'm glad he's alive, but to be honest I'm kind of afraid that he's too easy to find. If you found him that quickly, anybody can."

"Nah, I doubt it. I don't think Petrovski has the blue-haired set looking at things for him."

"The what?"

"Biggest gamblers as a percentage of disposable income in the state. Oldies. Bingo, Keno, betting on horses and jai alai. It's good to know your customers. I'm tapped into every retirement park south of Orlando. I host big Christmas and 4th of July parties. It's a small investment to have one of the largest, and nosiest, segments of the population on my side."

John slid Rico's phone back across the table. "Very clever. So some old biddy took this for you."

"I've been told the president of the resident's association took it. Some French-Canadian named Jean-Claude something or other. Thinks he's James Bond. Works for me. He passed it through a couple of hands before it got back to me."

Stephanie held her hand over her mouth. "Shit."

"What?"

"So at least three other people besides us know where he is. And you're right, they are nosy. Gossips. Everybody is going to know where he is. We have to warn him." She made to stand.

Rico reached across the table and took her hand. "Hang on. He's got US Marshalls on him. I'd bet that there's more than we can see here, also. Probably some guys in cars around the corner or something. I wouldn't stick your nose in there. Stay well clear. If you draw too much attention to him, Petrovski *will* find out where he is. And then there'll be nothing you can do."

~~~

"Cruz, what in the hell have you done for me lately?" Petrovski sprayed spittle, leaving flecks on the mobile phone he held to his head.

"Excuse me?"

"You have the resources of the Miami PD at your disposal and you can't find one single middle-aged man. Are you any good at your job?"

"I need a reason to be looking for him. I'm in Homicide. He needs to be dead,"

"I only wish it to be true."

"...or a suspect in a killing," continued Cruz.

"Is that all? Hang on a second." He held his mobile phone by his desk phone and dialed a number from memory.

"Missing persons."

"I'd like to report a Paul Coates, C-o-a-t-e-s, missing, and presumed dead."

"Who's speaking, please?"

"Oh, my name is of no concern. I'm a close friend who is worried about Paul. It's very uncharacteristic of him to be missing like this."

"And why do you think he's dead, sir?"

"It's a gut feeling I have, based on the type of company he keeps. He's been known to frequent a restaurant owned by known organized crime figure Rico Trattori. And we haven't seen him since Thursday. Isn't that reason enough?"

Petrovski listened as the clerk on the other end of the line typed something on her computer.

"Mr. Coates has already been reported missing by a John Delacourte. I'll be sure to add your information to the file. It would be very helpful if we could have your name and contact number in case we have follow-up questions."

Petrovski hung up and returned to his mobile phone and Detective Cruz. "There's already a missing persons file open for him? And you couldn't find a reason? You suck at your job. Get out and find him." He hung up the mobile phone and poured himself another glass of Stoli.

~~~

John called everyone together at the club. "We have news about Paul."

"He's eloped with a waitress and is living the debauched life of an expat in Cozumel."

"Not even close, Ned. It looks like he's going to be a witness in a mob case. He's hiding in a trailer park somewhere in the state with a US Marshall guarding him. So basically he's in Witness Protection." JD opened the picture on his phone and passed it around. "The big dude with him has been identified as a guy by the name of Darrel, a US Marshall."

"You guys see *Eraser*? The Schwarzenegger movie? Bad shit can happen to people in WitSec." Ned looked excited that something new was happening in their lives.

"Thanks," said Stephanie. "Just what we needed to hear. It's not a movie, asshole. For now, it's enough that he's safe. We can get on with what we're doing and put on a show tonight."

Henry held up the phone with the picture. "So who took this? And can we trust them?"

"A resident at the trailer park, and yeah, I think so. I hope so." John took the phone back. "So we do the show tonight and let well enough alone, okay? He's got something to do. It must be important or he wouldn't have left us like this."

Steph stood. "You know how I feel about it, JD. We do the show tonight, but I may be out after that. We don't have a show tomorrow. See if you can dig up another singer. I need a break."

~~~

Cruz opened another bottle of beer and handed it to MacCready the elder. "So, former partner, how's life in the OC department?"

Mac accepted the bottle and placed it on the counter beside him. "Okay. Not boring. Never boring. You're on the phone a lot tonight, neglecting your beautiful wife and missing out on James's bad jokes. Everything okay at the station?"

"Yeah, yeah. This and that. You know how it goes."

"Long weekend. Must be important to be paying you overtime. Open case? Anything I can help with?"

"Don't want to burden you with it. You've got your job and I've got mine." He wandered away with a nod and a salute with his bottle of Bud.

"What's he on about?"

Mac turned and nodded to his younger brother. "He's young. Got as much common sense as a - no, nothing. I can't think of anything with as little common sense as he has."

Simon laughed and pointed out the back door to the patio. "You should be out there with your guests. And your lady. Too nice a day to be in here."

"Getting the steaks, numb-nuts." He pointed at the beer. "Want this? I think Cruz is trying to get me drunk."

Simon took the bottle and dropped half of it down his throat. "Do you trust him?"

"Who, Cruz? Why shouldn't I?"

"Well, I didn't say anything, but I think an internal investigation might turn something up."

"Says who?"

Simon held his hands up in surrender. "Hey, not me, that's for sure." He walked to the back door. "Hurry up with the steaks. I'm starving."

Mac watched him leave and shook his head. Some of the shit his brother tossed him from out of left field surprised him. Stuff he couldn't really ignore. He sighed and opened his phone and scrolled through his contacts. He paused before pressing "send", then thought to hell with it, better safe than sorry.

"Sloan speaking. What are you doing bothering me on a Sunday? You don't even report to me anymore, technically."

"Great to hear your voice too, Sloan. How's the weather in DC?"

"I think I'm going to get malaria. As hot and as muggy as 'Nam. You call me for a weather report?"

"No. Need to know the protocol for something, but I don't want to ask around the office. Thought you'd be the best guy to trust."

"Well, the policy on dating co-workers is pretty clear, but with you transferred, on loan to the FBI, I guess you can keep seeing Sam. You're still seeing her, aren't you?"

Mac scratched his head. "Yeah. Didn't know it was that obvious. And that's not it. I got a tip that one of the detectives may not be entirely trustworthy. I want IA to investigate, but I want it kept quiet. There's suspicions he's leaking information and if he is, I want to use him to leak disinformation."

"Without him knowing?"

"That's the plan."

"That's tricky. A subject can usually tell when they're being investigated by Internal Affairs."

"That's because they're a bunch of ham-fisted amateurs when it comes to surveillance. They couldn't spy on Helen Keller."

"You're not wrong."

Mac listened to Sloan breathe down the line.

"Okay, I think I know the guy to talk to. Talk to him directly and tell him what you want to do. I'll send you the contact information. So do I want to know who the potentially dirty cop is?"

"My old partner."

"Shit. Really? I didn't think he was smart enough to pull something like that off. Talk to my guy and tell him to put everything on this. And tell him if his boss gives him a problem to call me. Take it easy, Mac. And thanks for calling. Hate dirty cops. Now I have to go and get ready for an ass-kissing ball. My wife is loving the shit out of this."

"You're not?"

"I didn't say that, did I?" He chuckled a thousand miles away. "I could get used to this schmoozing." He hung up.

Mac walked into the backyard. James and Gloria were over in a corner talking about something. That relationship seemed to be going well. He and Sam were still well below the radar, or so he thought. Sloan surprised him with that crack. Times like this he wondered what a normal life would be like. Cruz and his wife were like the odd men out at a fancy dress party, except in reverse. He told them to dress casually for the barbeque. She probably overruled her husband. Mac had shorts and a T-shirt on, and he was overheating. Mario and his wife had to be melting.

Mac looked down and his skinny legs and smiled. Too much desk work, not enough work in the field. Simon was in shorts and a t-shirt, as was Sam. She actually looked good in shorts, in comparison to everyone else.

Cruz and his wife, though, they looked very uncomfortable in their formal clothes, Mario in a suit and tie and his wife in a gown.

Very out of place.

His phone vibrated an incoming message. The name of the IA agent to contact. Doug Horn. "Well, Dougie. Let's see if you can pull this off."

"Wazzat?" Cruz had a glass of something cold and icy in his hand. "You talking to me?"

"No, De Niro, I wasn't. Be back in a minute. I need to make a call." Cruz watched him as he went back into the house.

He called the number supplied by Sloan and let it ring out to voicemail. "Horn, It's Detective Dan MacCready. I need to talk to you urgently. Please call me back at this number ASAP. Thanks."

He slid the phone into his back pocket and rejoined his party. IA didn't work weekends, apparently.

~~~

The gig ended, everyone played satisfactorily, or in Stephanie's case, sang satisfactorily, and nobody beat anybody up. Not a disappointing night, all in all.

John stowed his sax and stretched his sore muscles.

"You still feeling it?" Stephanie sat in his chair.

"Not as bad as yesterday. You've got to reconsider."

She shook her head. "I need a break. This Paul thing has really hit me. More than you could realize. You guys can find another singer. I'll send you some names. This is a good band. I know a lot of singers who would love to be part of this. Some of them are better than me."

"Nobody sings better than you."

She smiled and kissed him on the cheek. "That's sweet of you, and you know it's not true. I may head back to Lincoln. It's been too long. I'll send you some names tomorrow, okay?"

He watched her walk away. "Lincoln? Really? Small world. Is that how you know Paul?"

She walked away without responding. He shook his head, finished stowing the sax and walked to the back room. "Guys, take it easy tomorrow. And Steph says she's going to head back to Nebraska. Needs a break. Says she'll send us some names for singers. You guys might want to do some calling around tomorrow too, just in case she forgets."

Ned sucked back on a water bottle. He squinted in thought and screwed the cap back on. "She's serious, isn't she? Damn shame. Her voice brought the boys to the yard. It'll be hard to find a good replacement."

Henry grunted. "I'll do some checking around. Maybe get a sister up in there."

"Don't care if she's white, yellow, black or plaid, as long as she can sing." John left his sax in the back room. They were playing there all next week also. No point in lugging it around.

Henry called out. "John, you up for a drink?"

"Not like the other night."

"Hell no. A beer at the counter. Just want to have a quick chat."

John nodded. "I'll buy."

"Great. Becks."

John sat at a table and waved over a server. "Becks and a Corona." Henry sat across from him. "What's up, big guy."

"This whole idea about Paul going into WitSec sounds hinky."

"Hinky?"

"How'd you find out he was in WitSec?"

"I know a guy who knows."

"And you trust him?"

"Come on, it was Rico."

"And he cares, why?"

"He just does. This is solid information, Henry. You can trust him on this."

"I don't trust him as far as I can throw him. Nice enough guy, but ulterior motives out the ass. You're nuts."

John shrugged. "Maybe. But it's my call. The Feds are looking after him now."

"You believe that? Some guy shows you a photo and tells you that the other guy is a US Marshall? It could be anybody."

"You've got a point there. But Rico has nothing to gain by lying about it. He's a good friend of the band, has known Paul for years, right? So why would he lie about it?"

"The guy's a certifiable sociopath. He'd tell you anything if it furthered his cause."

John took a drink of beer and pushed the bottle back. "Maybe. I'll have to ask him about it the next time I see him. Enjoy your day off, Henry. I know I will."

Chapter Twenty

Paul stretched spread-eagle on the mattress in the trailer, the window-mounted air-conditioning unit rattling its last breaths before its imminent death. Sweat pooled in his navel and in the hollow where his collarbones met his neck. The place stunk of bug spray, but it kept the mosquitoes at bay, at least for a few hours.

Crickets loud enough to drown out the air conditioner added to the noise. "Fuck this. It has to be ninety degrees in here. Darrel, you out there?"

"Keep it down, chum."

"I'm not your chum. We're heading to a sports bar and watching some sports."

"What sports are on at 11:30 at night?"

"I don't give a shit. It'll be cool in there and, dammit, I may fall off the wagon for a cold beer."

Darrel cracked the screen door into the trailer. "You ain't goin' nowhere, chum. One more day here then the DoJ will fast-track your application. Can't have you compromised before that."

"You're a dick."

Darrel smiled, white teeth gleaming in the dark. "That's the nicest thing you've said to me all day. Stay strong."

"Get fucked."

Darrel laughed and moved back to the porch and his permanent position in front of the door.

"Go ahead and laugh. I'm going to reach out and touch someone."

~~~

John sat on his sofa and looked at the picture on his phone. Rico had a point. It looked like every other trailer park he'd ever seen. Not that he'd seen many. He smiled as he examined the picture. Paul looked to be in full throat, yelling about something. As usual.

Henry's comments worried him. Rico could have been bullshitting. Nothing on Paul's companion identified him as a US Marshall, or anyone else. He could just as easily be throwing out disinformation. He did have a way of finding out, though. He could ask Rico.

He opened his laptop and plugged in his phone. After a few seconds of synching the photo app opened. He imported the latest pictures, including the one Rico had sent to him. He took a deep breath. He was banking on the long shot; that the person who took the picture had used a smartphone that had location enabled, and that the camera had been set up to geotag all photos.

He clicked the small "i" at the side of the photo and waited for the window to open. Date, time and yes, co-ordinates. He clicked the button to "show on map" and presto-gizmo, a red pin dropped on a trailer in a park west of Davie, just outside of Fort Lauderdale.

He zoomed back on the map. It wasn't far from the junction of the I-595 and the Sawgrass Expressway. Maybe an hour to get there. He looked at the time. Almost midnight. Too late to go now, but it would be a very early start tomorrow.

~~~

MacCready sat back, relaxed, on his sofa, Sam Reese beside him. She tucked in under his arm. "That was fun. We should do this more often."

"No argument from me. Want to hit the beach tomorrow?"

"Almost today, actually. And yes. I'd love that. Just us, though."

"No James and Gloria?"

"Just us."

Mac opened his mouth to answer when his phone rang.

"Great." Sam pushed away. "Who's calling at midnight?"

Mac looked at the screen. "IA."

"What?"

"Don't worry. He's returning my call. Stay quiet, okay? Don't want him to know you're here." He held up a finger and answered. "Mr. Horn. You're calling back awfully late."

"I was sailing this afternoon. Phone went in the drink. Just checked my messages about ten minutes ago. If it's not urgent, my apologies. I'll call you back in the morning."

"No, I've got you, I may as well do this now. Sloan told me that I could count on you. There's a guy at the station who I strongly suspect is selling information."

"Tell me who. We'll crawl so far up his ass he'll think he's the mayor of colonoscopy central."

"No, I don't want you to do that. We believe he's feeding a mob guy info. This is a guy we've targeted for over a year now. I'm a liaison with the local FBI Organized Crime office. I want to use him to feed his guy bad information. Disinformation. It'll ultimately bring them both down, but if you just shut this guy down hard, Petrovski will find someone else and we'll be starting from square one."

"Petrovski? What's the detective's name?"

"We need to reach an agreement on the investigation. Low and below the radar, okay? Extremely soft touch. You'll get your guy. Don't worry about that. I just need to use him to get my guy too. You've heard of Petrovski, right?"

"Yeah, yeah. Bad-ass."

"Baddest. You up for it?"

"I'll have to explain it to the boss."

"Just tell him it's a request from Sloan. I talked to him earlier and he'll back this 100%."

John waited for an answer. He heard breathing and the soft pat of sippers on hardwood floor. Finally, "Okay. Deal. When it's all finished it'll make other criminal elements think twice about trying to turn cops. Who are we talking about here?"

"Okay, great. Glad you're seeing it my way. They guy's name is Detective Mario Cruz, my former partner. When we've finished all this, I want to find out what involvement he had in getting me shot last year. And when I'm finished with him you may have to run an investigation on me."

"Cruz? Not that surprised. Everyone assumes the car and watch are because the wife is rich, but half the time he opens his mouth he's complaining about what tightwads his in-laws are. I'll start something in the morning, and I'll keep you across things. A bit out of the ordinary, but since you'll be using him for disinformation you need to know where we are in our investigation."

"Thanks, Doug. I'll catch up with you tomorrow sometime." He hung up and turned to Sam. Her hands were over her mouth.

"Are you kidding?"

"About Cruz? No. And not kidding about using him to feed fake info to Petrovski. This may be the year we shut these guys down for good."

"But Cruz? I trusted that asshole."

"You trust everyone in the station. As you should, us being all good cops. But he managed to fool me, and I was his partner. If I find out he had anything to do with me getting shot last year I'll kill the guy."

"Right behind me."

"That's sweet of you. I got first dibs on him. There won't be anything left of him when I'm finished." He rubbed his face. "All this is good fun, but we really need to keep it straight around him. No idea that he's under investigation, no idea he's feeding info to the mob."

"No idea he's going to die a horrible death." Sam grinned. "I think I can do that."

"Seriously, hon. You might want to avoid him for the next week or so."

She nodded in agreement and took his hand. "It's late. Bed time."

"You're staying the night?"

"Well, I assumed. It's late. I'm here."

"I concur."

Mac pulled her close for a hug and his phone rang again. "Jesus, what now?" He looked at the display. He didn't recognize the number. He sighed. "I've got to take this."

She disengaged as he answered the phone.

"MacCready. Who is this?"

"Hey, Mac. Did I wake you?" The voice on the other end whispered.

"Worse."

"Oh. What's her name?"

"None of your business. This is Coates, right?"

"Yeah."

"What are you calling me from? I know you left your phone behind and I specifically instructed that the phone in the trailer be blocked for outgoing calls."

"Got Darrel's cell. The asshole is asleep. Some protection he is."

"Shit. Stay inside and I'll contact the Marshall's service and have him replaced."

"No, no. Don't do that. The guy's been here eighteen hours, sitting in the sun. He's blacker than when he got here, if that's possible. Take it easy on him. This is a big crock. Fucking waste of time. I'm changing my mind. I want out of this. I'm leaving too much behind for too little gain."

Mac sat back on the sofa. "You saw what Petrovski did to Sergei. How can you let him get away with that? And that pales in comparison to what he's done, or has had others do for him. I need your help putting him away."

"He shot the guy. Find the gun. Do that CSI shit I always see on TV."

"The gun's dumped in the Everglades. Or he's got it. We'll never find it. Barely circumstantial evidence places him there, and we need your testimony to put him away."

"Would you need me if you had the gun?"

"We don't have the gun."

"But if."

"If we had the gun we could probably put him away for Sergei's killing. But we don't. Have. The gun."

"Yeah, I get it. Look, I'm going to sleep on this and make up my mind tomorrow. Although I doubt I'm going to change my mind. You can't actually hold me pris -"

A deep voice interrupted Paul. "Sorry, Darrel Lund speaking. Who's this?"

"MacCready. Dozed off, did you?"

"Just laying a trap for the asshole."

"Well he sprung it. Put a pin code on your phone, for Christ's sake. And drink more coffee. Put Coates back on, would you?"

"Hang on." Mac heard some sharp words and Paul Coates was back on the phone. "Thought you were finished with me."

"Leave Darrel alone, get back to bed and call me tomorrow. Promise you don't bolt on him."

"Yeah, okay. I've got a bad feeling about the guy across the street from me. Can you run a background on him?"

"What's his name?"

"Jean-Claude something or other. That bitch manager would know."

"Whatever. Give the phone back to Darrel and I'll talk to you tomorrow."

Darrel came back on the line. "MacCready, my replacement just arrived. Sorry, but this won't happen again. I've got to go. If you need to report this I completely understand."

"Nobody's dead and you were there more than twice the length of time you should have been, so I don't know what you're talking about."

"Thanks. I'll talk to you tomorrow."

Mac hung up and turned to Sam. She was asleep on the sofa.

~~~

Darrel slid his phone back in his holster. "What the fuck kinda trick was that?"

The porch light came on across the street. Paul put his finger to his lips. "Shh. Don't attract Jean-Claude's attention. He's a nosy prick."

Stella pulled into the short drive and killed the headlights and ignition. "Sorry I'm late. Family issues. Let's move it inside." She ushered the other two into the trailer. "What the hell is going on? This place is lit up like a Coney Island fairground. I thought we were supposed to be low-key."

"Buddy McDrummer here wants to walk. Thinks the hardship of a new life isn't a fair trade for getting one of the worse scumbags in South Florida off the street. Poor guy."

"Keep it up Darrel, and I'll have to pound on you."

"You couldn't beat an egg."

"I'll riff off your head like it's a snare, high-hat combination and you'll never know what hit you."

"That'll be the day."

"Darrel, go home. I've got Coates covered."

"My lucky night. Sorry, Stella, you're not my type."

She made a puffing motion with her hand. "You hittin' the weed?"

"No, I'm just tired. I could use a couple of long hours of sleep. And I miss the band. And playing with the band. And sleeping in my bed. And eating good food and not being surrounded by crazy, nosy old people." Paul's voice rose at the end. "I'm fucking tired of this."

"Keep it down Paul. This is normal. Kind of a culture shock. It is difficult, but it's necessary. Get some sleep. Take a fresh look at it tomorrow."

They both jumped as someone hammered on the outside screen door.

Stella placed her hand behind her back and rested it on the butt of her gun. She cracked open the main door, looked, then opened it and walked out. "It's Linda, right? What can I do for you?"

Paul looked out the door, shook his head and closed his eyes. Crazy lady.

"Is Paul Craven here?"

Paul stepped out onto the porch. "We making too much noise?"

"I've had numerous complaints. Curfew is 10:00 pm. I'm sure you know that. You ticked that box when you signed the rental agreement."

"I certainly did. And I apologize for the noise my cousins made." He glared at Stella who tried to hide a smile. "I have great news for you, though."

"It's after midnight, and I've been woken to discuss breaches of the curfew with the newest tenant in this trailer park. I doubt you can have good news for me."

"Surprise. I'm not going to be here that long. I'm gone either tomorrow or the day after. Probably tomorrow."

"The deposit is non-refundable."

"Of course it is. I don't care. I just want to get out of here. How do you deal with all of these old farts, day in and day out?"

He pointed across the street at Jean-Claude's trailer, then dropped his hand. The old French-Canadian stood on the porch watching. And listening. Then he turned and headed back into his trailer, turning off the light as we went in.

Chapter Twenty-One

John looked at his watch. Almost midnight, but if he didn't call tonight he'd lose her to Nebraska tomorrow. And that wasn't an appealing thought. He closed his eyes, took a deep breath, and dialed.

She answered after four rings, just as he reached for the disconnect button.

"What are you doing calling me at midnight?"

"Sorry, but I had to."

"No you didn't."

"I couldn't let this go until tomorrow and risk you leaving before I had a chance to tell you."

"Oh, give me a break. You going to propose or something?"

"God no. No, I didn't mean it like that. I know where Coates is."

"You what?"

"Coates. He's in a trailer park in Davie. I'm going there first thing in the morning. You should come with me."

"No, no. Wait. How do you know this? How could you possibly know this? Rico said it - there are hundreds of trailers just like that in South Florida. No way to identify it from the picture."

"The picture itself didn't help, but the underlying data did. The phone used to take this picture geo-tagged it. I uploaded the shot from my phone to my laptop and looked at the geo data and extracted the coordinates. You going to come with me?"

"Is that smart?"

"Why not? We want to see where he is, make sure he's okay. We'll go incognito." He listened to silence. "Hello? You fall asleep?"

"I'm almost there. Call me in the morning. I want to see him, but I don't want to put him in danger."

"We're not going to put him in danger. I'll pick you up early, nobody will know it's us. You can put on a pair of Groucho Marx glasses and I'll put a skull cap on. Completely incognito."

"Johnny, call me tomorrow. I'm beat."

"Just don't get on a bus or a train or an airplane tomorrow and leave town without talking to me."

~~~

Petrovski jabbed the disconnect button with his finger. "Son of a bitch." He paced in his office, trying not to pace in time with the music pounding outside its walls. "Son. Of. A. Bitch."

Stan sat across from his desk, damaged leg extended by a brace and a cast on his wrist. His boss paced behind him. He continually shifted to the left and right trying to keep him in view. "What now?"

"He's disappeared. There are whispers that he's getting prepped for WitSec, but I can't find him. We're lucky it's a long weekend. He's not in the program yet so he doesn't have a full complement of

216

protective detail around him, wherever he is. Although a large security detail would make him stand out like a sore thumb." He shook his head. "No. We've got one more day to find him before he's wrapped up in a cloak of blue."

"Yeah, but we've checked everywhere."

Petrovski frowned. "Except where he is."

"Obviously. If we knew where he was, we wouldn't have to look."

Petrovski held the bridge of his nose and took slow, deep breaths. A headache formed, one that would put his worst hangover to shame. "But we don't, so we do."

"Huh?"

"I need some outside of the box thinking from you, Stan. You're one of the smartest guys on my team, believe it or not, and I need your help. And it's about time you showed me you can use your brain, what with your body being almost completely useless to me right now."

"So, okay. The problem is we can't seem to find someone you desperately need to find."

"Not just me. If he testifies you'll be caught in the crossfire also."

"Yeah." Stan nodded. "So it's in all of our interests to plant this guy."

"Exactly. Thoughts?"

"We've checked off hotels and motels, hospitals, campgrounds. Have you checked people's boats?"

"We've asked around at the marinas, yes. And you've told me where he isn't. That's not anywhere near good enough. I need to know where he is."

Stan nodded. "And we eliminate where we know he isn't to narrow down the search. The only place I can think of that we missed is a personal one. A friend's house, hiding under our noses."

Petrovski scratched the back of his neck in thought. "You suggesting we barge in on them in their homes and shake them down?"

"Much as I'd love to, even though physically I can't right now, no. The guy's got to get out for beer, food, entertainment. He's not going to stay holed up there 24/7." Stan warmed to the idea. "We stake out his friend's places. Not a bad idea, right? But we need to find out where the friends are, and we need to do that tonight."

"Then we better get to work. Any idea how we get their addresses?"

Stan slid the band's flyer across the desk. "You've got a guy inside the MPD. Give him these names and faces and get him to run their driver's licenses."

Petrovski took the flyer from him and smiled. "Very good. There's hope for you yet." He looked at his watch and his smile broadened. "Cruz will be upset. It'll be good to remind him who he really works for." He picked up his mobile phone. "You know I give him more money each month than his legitimate job does?"

He dialed and interrupted the garrulous answer. "Shut up. I know what time it is. I will be scanning and sending a flyer to your personal email address. On this flyer are five faces and five names. I need address for all of them. And I need them yesterday."

He half listened to Cruz's complaints and cut him of half way through. "Save it for your wife. I don't want to hear any more bitching. Do it. I expect an answer back within the hour, or our business relationship is terminated."

He hung up and looked at Stan. "So now we wait. I hate waiting."

"We use this time to get our resources ready. I'll check out that skinny little fucker's place, because any excuse to off that asshole is good enough for me."

"Fine. Call four others. They need to be here within half an hour for a briefing."

"Got it. Grigory is in the club, so that's one. And I can get three more, quickly."

"Then do it."

A couple of minutes later Grigory walked in, accompanied by a young black guy who Petrovski recognized, but whose name he didn't know. He pointed to the sofa and they both sat, silent. Stan made a couple of more calls then placed his phone on the desk. "So we got Grigory and Scott here. I just got off the phone with Al and his buddy JJ. They've all got cars and know what they have to do."

"Explain to me what you've told them they have to do."

"They meet here where we give them addresses. They will each be assigned one. This isn't going to last longer than twelve hours, because that fuck Coates will pop his head out in the morning for a bagel and a coffee, I'd bet money on it."

"And if it takes longer?"

"In the morning I'll chase up five more to relieve these guys." A knock on the door followed by two more men completed the team. "But I don't think we'll need that. When we see him, we kill him. No discussion, no warning, just three in the head." Stan looked at the other four. "You guys armed?"

They all nodded.

"Great. Wipe the gun and drop it where you shoot them. Walk away, don't run. Get in your car and drive away within the speed limit. Don't draw attention."

Grigory raised his hand.

Petrovski closed his eyes and shook his head. "It's not a classroom, Grigory. What's the question?"

"Where are we going?"

Petrovski circled his desk and sat. "I will have addresses for you within the half hour. Are you all clear about what you need to do? Crystal clear?"

Scott held out his hand. "You got a picture of the dude we're supposed to do?"

Petrovski handed him the flyer. "The older guy. Drummer. Memorize the photo and pass it on."

Scott looked at it and took out his phone and took a picture of it. "My memory is shit." He handed the paper to Grigory who passed it on.

"I know the guy."

"Give it back to Grigory. And Grigory, either take a picture or memorize the face." Petrovski leaned forward. "Fuck this up and we'll be handing around your picture next time."

Grigory took the flyer back and snapped a picture of his with his phone. "Got it. Don't worry, I won't mess this up. Just give us some addresses, or this is all a bunch of talk."

Petrovski's phone vibrated. "Just in time." He opened the message and scrolled through it. "He's come through. Hang on a sec." He read through the message carefully. "The big black guy lives in Boca. You, Scott, go there. You'll blend in."

Scott started to laugh, then stopped. "Right. Okay."

Petrovski wrote out an address. "Stan, the sax player lives here. You take him. Don't kill him until after you've killed Coates." He scribbled out another. "Grigory, you take the singer. She's a bit west of us."

He smiled. "The best looking, too."

"Get caught peeping and I'll shoot you myself. At least not until after."

He handed papers to Al and JJ. "The piano player and the back-up drummer." He looked at them. "What the are you waiting for? Get the fuck out of here."

Petrovski watched them leave. He scrubbed his face with his hands. He'd been in tight places before, and he made it through them, too. He had to shut down Coates before WitSec had him completely covered or they would have enough to put him away. Maybe enough to inject him.

Coates looked out of the window above the kitchen sink. It faced out over the street toward Jean-Claude's trailer. The old guy's lights were still on, and Coates could see him puttering around in his living room in a pair of boxer shorts and nothing else.

"Shoot me if I end up like him when I get old," he muttered. He checked his porch. Stella leaned to one side, trying to read a paper under dim light, just in front of the main door. He had to get out and talk to the Frenchie. He'd move immediately if the guy turned out to be a threat. Stella didn't believe him. Scoffed at him, even.

He turned out all the lights. "G'night, Stella."

All he received in response was the rattle of the paper and a "Shh".

He walked to the other end of the trailer. A back door near the end opened out to the side yard behind the porch off the front door, only twenty feet, at most, from the front door and Stella's back.

He stood in front of the back door and took a deep breath. Any squeak would give him away. He took another breath and grasped the handle, turning it slowly.

No squeak.

He closed his eyes and slowly pushed the door open, thanking the previous resident for keeping the trailer well-maintained. He stepped out onto the grass barefoot. He could see Stella to his left, through the screening, sitting with her back to him guarding the front door. He shook his head. This wasn't a very nice thing to do to her, but sometimes a guy's got to do what a guy's got to do.

He turned right and slipped around the back of the trailer. He walked across the open space between his trailer and the park entrance, acutely aware that Linda could see him from the office. Likely she wasn't there at this time of night, but his luck hadn't been holding up lately. He ran along the far side of the trailer under the streetlight. He stopped at the corner near the road. Frenchie's shadow passed in front of the light in his kitchen. He was still up.

Coates took a breath and ran across the road and up on the old guy's front step. He tapped on the door frame. "Hey, Frenchie."

The old guy slowly walked to the door, head cocked, looking into the dark. "The name's Jean-Claude. You're the new guy from across the road, no?"

"Yes."

"Why you whispering?"

"I don't want to wake up my cousin. Can I come in?"

Jean-Claude looked out the door and across to Paul's trailer. "You mean that cousin who never seems to sleep? The one reading a paper by your front door?"

"Shh, okay? I've got to ask you a question."

"So ask. I don't got to answer you."

"Why you so fucking nosy? You're peering over at my place all the time. Coming over uninvited, then calling people right after you leave. What the fuck does my business have to do with you?"

"Hey, chief, cool it down, eh? I'm old. I'm nosey. We're all nosy. It's as boring as the prairies in winter around here. You're the only new thing we've had around here in months. And you're young."

"Linda's young."

Jean-Claude waved him off. "Don't talk to me about her, with her rules and curfews and violations. She's supposed to run this place, but *you* try and get her to get the pH balance right in the pool. Impossible." He scratched his belly. "So, ya gotta tell me, what are you really doing here?"

"What do you mean?"

"What do I mean? What I said. What are you really doing here? Too young to be retired, you've got security around you all the time. Whispers on the street are someone is looking for you. You a mobster turning state's evidence?"

Paul blanched. "You're crazy, old man. Is that what everyone's saying?"

"There's speculation. Yours isn't a normal situation. The guy in that trailer up and disappears and the next day you show up. Not like I miss that other guy. Didn't like him much. Antisocial as hell. And you got these cousins showing up at all hours, including one so dark he'd be invisible at night if he didn't smile. You're not being that subtle."

"So everyone's talking like this, are they?"

"I told you, it's boring around here. Anything for a bit of excitement." He chuckled. "A couple of the more desperate have you as a trained assassin setting up for a hit on someone in the park. Except I know most everyone here, and there ain't any worth the price of a bullet. Most of us will die on our own in the next coupla years anyway. Sure you don't want to come in for a drink?"

Paul looked across the street at Stella, still engrossed in her paper. "What the hell. Soda water and lime is fine."

Jean-Claude gestured across the road. "Won't she miss you?"

"What she doesn't know, won't hurt her. I've been getting pretty bored, too."

Chapter Twenty-Two

John finished dressing and stood, flexing his calf. It felt much better. He'd have to thank Rico for his genius doctor.

Five hours sleep, yet he felt fresh because he was actually doing something instead of sitting around. He checked the time. 5:45. He had to get to the airport and rent a car, pick up Steph and get up to Davie this morning. Pretty straightforward day.

He ran down the stairs instead of waiting for the lift. Better to push the leg now when he didn't need to, than wait until he *had* to run to find out its limitations. It felt good.

He came out of the stairwell into the front lobby and had his hand on the front door when he stopped. He could see his car in its parking spot. And beyond it about 100 yards he could see the bumblebee Camaro. Stan sat in the driver's seat, watching his car.

He backed away from the door. The sun, low in the sky and directly in front of him would be reflected off the glass door and into Stan's eyes. He hoped.

He walked around to the other side of the alcove and ducked through a side door that took him to the loading bay. He'd been there once before when he moved in. The driveway out of it exited on the other side of the building. He jogged up the ramp, testing his calf a little bit more, and left Stan to watch his beat up Honda.

He grabbed a bus to the airport and picked up a cheap subcompact rental. A tiny white Toyota replaced his shit-bucket for the day, maybe two. He headed north to Stephanie's apartment, calling her on the way. "You ready?"

"I will be when you get here."

~~~

Stan tried to get comfortable in his car. He pushed his seat as far back as he could and stretched out his stiff and sore knee. He rolled down the window and leaned his head out into the fresher air. He could see the Honda across the parking lot.

He leaned back, tilted the seat back a bit and made do as best as he could. Sweat pooled under the constrictive cast. He thought maybe the doctor didn't know his job and put it on too tight. He scrambled around the center console and side pockets until he found a pen and used it to try and relieve the itching.

"Ah, shit." The digging seemed to only make the itching worse. "This thing has to come off. Fuck the pain."

Seven-thirty in the morning and sweat trickled down his back into his ass crack. He wiped the back of his neck with a cloth. The sun had moved across the sky until it spilled across the nose of his Camaro. He watched it creep slowly up the hood toward the windshield. "Shit." He looked around the apartment building's parking lot. Shade in the far corner, but he couldn't be sure if the Honda would be visible from there.

He got out and hobbled to the one empty spot where he could see the tail end of the sax player's car. It would do. The guy had to back out of his space. He'd be fine. He hobbled back to his car and drove to the far side of the lot. He reached the spot and turned to back in when a small sports car stole the space.

Stan stopped his car and got out, yelling. "Hey, jizz-tube. That's my spot."

A young guy, toned from regular gym use, popped out of the car. "Your name isn't on it, pal. Piss off."

Stan placed his good hand on the guy's chest. "Move the car."

The guy looked down at Stan's hand. "You sure you want to do this?"

"Positive. Move the car before I put your head through the windshield."

The guy looked, pointedly, at the cast on Stan's arm and his knee brace. "Seriously?" He went to push Stan's hand away and met with resistance.

Stan smiled. "I warned you." He grabbed the guy by the throat and shoved him hard onto the hood of his little sports car. Continuing to squeeze, he stepped to one side of the car. "I really warned you." He leaned into it and rammed the guy's head into his sloped windshield, cracking it with the back of his head. Blood streamed down the glass and hood of the car. Stan shoved him off the side of the car and looked down at the guy. He poked him with the toe of his boot. "Move the fucking car or I'll do that again."

The owner dragged himself to his feet. "I'm fucking calling the cops."

"Do it and I'll come back and break each bone in your body, one at a time." He stepped out of the way as the guy got in his car and moved it.

"Asshole!"

"You got one too, buddy. Thanks for understanding." Stan laughed and backed into the parking spot. It was in the shade, and he could see the rear quarter panel of the Honda.

And he put a beating on someone. It just might be a good day after all.

~~~

John stopped the Toyota in front of Stephanie's apartment and buzzed her. "Ready to go?"

"Two minutes. I'll be right down."

"Want me to come up?"

"No need. I'll be there shortly."

John sat on the front step. She lived in a nice neighborhood. Lots of trees, green grass, high-end cars in the driveways. He pulled his shirt away from his skin. At this time of day and already over eighty. In four hours, with the sun above their heads, it would be unbearable.

He stood as the door opened. Stephanie came out in Capri's, a no-sleeve shirt and Egyptian sandals. "So where are we going?"

"You look great."

"Where's your car?"

"Back at my place." He pointed at the little white car at the curb. "Hop in."

"At least we'll know it runs."

"What made you change your mind? You weren't sure last night."

"I need to see him. Make sure he's okay."

"We get there and say hi, make sure he's okay and then decide what to do from there."

"What do you mean, "what to do from there"? We get him to a better hiding place. Rico found him too easy. Petrovski can't be far behind."

John grunted and pulled away from the curb. "Petrovski's nowhere near this."

~~~

Grigory leaned forward, staring out his windshield. "Son of a bitches." He dialed Stan's number.

"What?"

"Stanislav, you have eyes on that sax player?"

"I can see his car right in front of me. He hasn't gone anywhere."

"Is that so? Then how it is that he just showed up and took off with the singer girl?"

"Fuck me. Really?"

"Yeah. They're going somewhere awfully early. He showed up in a little white rice burner. Must have rented it."

"Follow them."

"Petrovski made it pretty clear that we should keep an eye on where they live. This Coates guy could be inside."

"No, no, no. The sax player and the drummer are very close. He'd have gone inside if the drummer was in there. Maybe he's bringing her back here. You follow them, and I'm going to check inside his apartment before he gets back. Call me when you get close." He gave Grigory the address. "If you're within a block or so, give me a heads up.

Grigory started his car. "If Petrovski gets pissed, this was your idea."

"Yeah, whatever. I've got to go."

Stan half jogged, half limped to the apartment building. A smartly dressed couple left as he arrived and he slipped in behind them. He looked at the address written on his cast. Apartment 312. Up two floors in the elevator, turn left out of the doors and he stood in front of the apartment. He listened first for some activity. Dead silence.

He knocked lightly on the door. "Coates?"

Nothing.

He hit it a little harder. "Coates, you in there?"

A door opened across the hall and a frumpy head looked out. "Who is you looking for? That's where Johnny lives."

Stan crossed his arms and leaned his back against the door. The woman, who he estimated to be in her mid-forties, stood with her arms crossed, in a bathrobe and ugly slippers. "You know Johnny? Any idea if he's got a guest? I'm looking for his friend, Paul Coates. I heard he was here."

"Paulie? No, He's not here. I know Paulie, too, and he's not here."

"How do you know? How can you be sure? This is important. I've come to give him a large sum of money." Stan smiled. Manipulation was easy. And fun.

She licked her lips. "I can hold it for him if you want. He'll probably be by later. He visits here quite often."

"Oh, that's quite kind of you, but no." He reached behind him and hammered on the door again. "Absolutely positive he's not in there?"

She nodded. "Sorry."

"Okay. Best you go back in your apartment. Wouldn't want anything to happen to you."

"Why?" She looked down the hall. "What could happen to me? It's safe in here isn't it?"

"You just never know who could sneak in."

~~~

Grigory hung back a few car lengths. A couple of times he thought he lost them, the white Toyota being a very common car, but he inevitably caught up with them at the next set of traffic lights.

After about ten minutes it became apparent that they were not heading to the address Stan had given him.

He picked up his phone and pressed redial.

Stan answered after half a ring. "They getting close?"

"They're getting farther way from where you are."

"Where are you now? I'll try and catch up with you."

Grigory looked at the passing street signs. "Heading north on 441, just past Miami Gardens."

"Where the hell are you going?"

"I'll know when I get there, idiot."

"You're going to be out of Dade soon."

"No shit."

"Why is he staying on 441? Why didn't he get on 95?"

"What am I, a fucking mind reader? Shut the fuck up and let me follow these assholes. They are in one of the most common god damned cars in this state." He banged on his steering wheel. "*Sookin syn.* Where in the hell are they?" He yelled into the phone. "You know my car. I'll call you if I can figure out where we're going."

He hung up the phone and threw it on the passenger's seat. "Son. Of. A. BITCH."

He pulled to a stop at the intersection of 441 and W. Hallandale. On the other side of the road, the white car appeared as the bus behind it pulled to the side of the road at a stop.

"Assholes." He wrenched the wheel and pulled into the left turn lane and accelerated across traffic against the red light, swerving at the last minute to avoid a pickup truck heading west on Hallandale. The guy laid on the horn like it would actually change Grigory's course of action. "Shut up, you dick."

He flipped the bird at another car coming straight at him in the oncoming turn lane and swerved right into the correct lane. The sax player and the girl were half a block ahead. He accelerated to within two cars of the Toyota. He'd have to find another car after he finished all this. No way the red light camera missed him. "Fucking Stan will pay for this."

~~~

Stan started his Camaro and thought about the route ahead. He wasn't sure how far north they were going, but he knew they were on their way to see Coates. They'd be in Broward County somewhere. And west. If they were going to the east side of the county, they would have gone up 95. It would have been faster. So, to get in the general area of Grigory and his prey in the fastest time he'd go east a couple of blocks to 95 and pound it north. Stirling might be a bit too far north, but it beat getting off the interstate too early. The V-8 in his Camaro was wasted on the surface streets.

He tooled out of the parking lot, smiling as he passed the sports car with the bloody and cracked windshield. Even with one hand and one leg he still had it.

Traffic on a Monday morning, during a long weekend, was very light. He had an unobstructed run north, about fifteen miles to Stirling. Twelve minutes in his car.

He pulled off 95 onto Stirling and turned west. He called Grigory.

"Where are you?"

"Still going north on 441. Wait, turning west on Hollywood."

"Shit. I'm north of you. Heading west on Stirling."

"Keep going. Just as good a chance that we turn north again."

"Or they could be going to North Perry Airport. I'll head south next major cross street and catch up to you. Keep calling me every once in a while and let me know where you are. What's their tag?" Stan scribbled the license plate number on his cast. "Okay. I'll call you when I'm closer."

"I'm hanging up now before I lose these assholes again."

~~~

Grigory swore and tossed the phone on the passenger's seat again, keeping his eye on the Toyota.

Hollywood Boulevard changed names to Pines Boulevard just west of the Florida Turnpike. And they kept driving due west along the flat road.

They continued past the small airport without slowing, continuing further into the west of the county.

Grigory squinted at the sun reflecting off his rearview mirror and into his eyes. And off his wing mirror. "*This* is why I'm never up at this fucking time of day." He flicked the rearview mirror to one side and kept his hand up blocking the reflection from the wing mirror. "Annoying as hell."

He tried to fold in the side mirror, losing concentration with his driving. At the last second, he looked up and jammed on the brakes, just missing rear-ending the white Toyota.

The sax player looked in the rearview mirror and Grigory saw recognition in his eyes.

Chapter Twenty-Three

"You know where we're going?"

John checked the rearview mirror. "What's that?"

"I haven't been this far west in Florida since I got here. Beach girl myself. I'm expecting to see cows any minute."

"I know where I'm going. And we have company." He checked the rearview mirror again. "The smaller ape."

Stephanie twisted in her seat. "Who?"

"The guy who showed up with big Stan. Can't remember his name. Greg something or other. Positive that's him behind us."

She sat sideways in her seat, squinting into the glare of the sun, trying to make out the face of the driver. "You sure?"

"He almost crawled up my ass about a block back there. 99% sure."

"Damn."

"Yeah." John changed lanes and headed for the I-75 North on-ramp.

Stephanie sat forward again, adjusting her seat belt. "You know what that means?"

"We're in deep shit?"

"He either followed you to the airport to get the rental, then followed you to my place, or he was sitting outside my place waiting."

"I didn't see him before this. I'd be surprised that he followed me." He remembered. "Shit."

"What?"

"I saw the yellow Camaro outside my place this morning. They were staking us out. Expecting us to go to Coates."

Stephanie held her face in her hands. "Or find us and kill us while finding out where he is."

John shook his head. "He'd have done that by now. This thing can't outrun his car. He's following us. Doing a poor job of it." He pulled onto I-75 North and floored it. The little car got louder and imperceptibly approached 55 mph.

Stephanie rolled up her window. "Too fast for open windows. Ruining my hair."

John rolled his up too and Stephanie reached to the center console and turned on the air conditioning. The car slowed noticeably.

"Seriously?" He beat the steering wheel. "This is a piece of shit. I won't complain about my Honda anymore." He looked in the rearview mirror. "He's backed off a bit. Obviously following us."

"And we obviously can't lead him to Paul. What are you going to do?"

"What I should have done the first time he showed up."

~~~

Grigory picked up the phone and redialed again.

Stan answered. "Still going west?"

"North on 75. Heading toward Davie, I think."

"He hasn't made you?"

"I thought he did. Almost got in the back seat of that car I got that close. But he's not acting like he knows I'm back here."

"Okay. I'm going to Davie. Good place to head him off. Don't let him get too far ahead of you."

"I don't think that thing can go any faster than the 50 it's doing."

"So you're real obvious then. I-75, that's hitting 70 mph at points, isn't it?"

Grigory watched cars flash by. "Or faster, yeah."

"So you've been made."

"But he's not acting like it."

"Every other fucking car on that road is doing at least 70. You're doing 50 and the only other person on the road doing 50 is the car you're following. He made you, *durlak*. He's not going to lead you to anything or anyone. Where exactly are you?"

"Griffin Road. Hang on, he's getting off. Heading west on Griffin."

"Be careful. I'm about ten minutes behind you. Don't let him out of your sight."

~~~

Stephanie looked behind them. "He followed us."

"Good."

"What? We don't want him finding Paul. Turn around and head back."

"Paul is farther north. I'm taking him away from him. I'm getting tired of this shit. It's got to end."

Griffin rapidly petered-out from a multilane in each direction road to a narrow, two-lane, black top trail. "So what's out here?"

"Nothing. And then Everglades. More Everglades."

"What are you going to do?"

"Convince him to back off."

They crossed State Road 27. Theirs were the only two cars on the road now. "You're going to get us killed."

"I don't think so."

"Don't *think* so? That's heartening."

"You stay in the car and keep the engine running and the doors locked. If it looks like I've lost my touch, and little Russian appears to be gaining the upper hand, you get out of here. Call Detective MacCready at MPD. He seems to be involved with this."

John turned a hard left down a dirt road without slowing. The car behind them bounced over the ruts as it followed. "Remember, stay in the car. I know you can fight - I've seen it. But this isn't the time or place."

He slammed on the brakes and opened the door. "Lock it behind me." He turned and walked toward the car following him. "We got a problem asshole?"

~~~

Grigory had the phone up to his head. "He's led me down a dead-end dirt road. You're right. He knew." He heard Stan sigh.

"Any witnesses?"

"Other than him and the girl? No."

"Then kill them both. And burn the car when you're finished."

"Mine?"

"Theirs. Jesus. West on Griffin?"

"Yeah, then after a long right-hand turn, a dirt road off to the left." Grigory paused. "He's out of his car. How far away are you?"

"At least fifteen. He's good, but he's beatable. Go in fast and hard. Don't give him any time to think. I'll be right there."

Grigory dropped his phone on the seat and got out of his car. "I didn't hear what you said. My windows were up. Could you repeat?"

~~~

"I said, do we have a problem, asshole?"

"My asshole is fine. You have a problem with yours? Your name is Johnny Delacourte, right? JD?"

"Cut the crap. Why are you following us?"

"I hoped you'd lead me to the drummer. I need to talk with him."

"Get back in your car and get out of here. Leave all of us alone."

Grigory smiled. "Oh, I can't do that. I'm not going to stop until I'm absolutely positive that he can't testify against my boss."

"That would be Petrovski?"

"That would be no concern of yours. You should be more worried about what I'm going to do to you both right now. You're standing between me and what I need to get to." He reached behind his back and pulled out a handgun. "Tell her to get out of the car."

"You must think I'm a mouth-breathing troglodyte. Just like you."

"Tell her."

"Fuck you."

Grigory stepped forward and pressed the barrel hard between and slightly above the sax player's eyes. "I'll splatter your brain all over your rental. Tell her now."

JD pressed hard back, taking small steps to his right, making Grigory adjust his position with him. The instant Grigory countered by pushing back harder, John pulled his head back sharply, dropped below the barrel line and came up with a hard uppercut. Grigory's head snapped back and he fired the gun into the air, scattering a flock of pelicans. He staggered back and tried to get the gun down for a second shot.

John got under the gun arm, grabbed Grigory by the wrist and turned while extending it, elbow on his shoulder. He pushed up with his shoulder while simultaneously pulling down on Grigory's wrist. He heard a pop as the ligament tore and the elbow joint dislocated.

Griory's screamed in pain and lost all control of his hand. The revolver slipped from his grip and onto the dirt.

John let go of him, kicked the gun away and took a few steps back. "Just warming up."

Grigory let out a bellow and charged.

John was too close to evade and Grigory hit him with his full weight, the fifty extra pounds pinning him to the ground. John brought a knee up and caught Grigory in the ribs, twice, before Grigory shifted position and grabbed John by the throat with his left hand, his right arm hanging useless by his side.

"That's it, you asshole midget. I'm killing you. The bitch will tell me where the drummer is after I finish using her." He squeezed tighter as John scrabbled at his hand. "My grip is stronger than yours, little fella. You don't have a hope."

John smiled and grabbed him by the wrist, pulling the hand harder against his throat. He grabbed Grigory's pinky finger and in a smooth movement wrenched it up and out. He heard bones break. Grigory tried to squeeze tighter, but the combination of the pain and the fact that the pinky finger is far more important than many realize, prevented him from doing further damage. Then John grabbed the ring finger of the same hand and smoothly wrenched it up and out, breaking it also.

Grigory rolled to one side holding his partially broken left hand to his chest, his right arm hanging uselessly by his side. He looked at his gun in the dirt about fifteen feet away and got to his feet and staggered over to it. As he bent to pick it up, John plowed into him, broadside. Grigory instinctively put out his right hand to break his fall and yelled in pain as his arm bent the wrong way.

John lashed out with his foot, catching him in the side of the head. The Russian fell as he grabbed the gun and let a shot go, missing by a mile.

JD slipped in behind him and arm locked him across the throat, squeezing like his life depended on it.

Grigory scratched at the arms with his left hand, tried dislodging them, and tried to break the grip, but unsuccessfully.

Technically he died from a heart attack. John wasn't willing to risk a miraculous recovery though, so he wrenched the head hard to the right and up, fracturing his vertebrae and severing his spinal cord. He let the body slump to the ground and picked up the handgun. A little .22 pistol.

Good for close up work, but useless more than ten yards away from the target. He wiped his prints off it and slid it down the back of Grigory's pants. Let the cops try and figure out how the Russian managed to get killed while armed.

He wiped as much mud off himself as he could and knocked on the window. "Unlock."

The four lock buttons popped up, and JD eased himself into the car. "Tore the calf, I think." He slid his pant leg up and looked at the blood slowly seeping through the bandage.

"Is he - dead?"

"As a doornail."

"Did you have to kill him? Really?"

JD started the engine and backed the small car in a three-point turn and headed out of the scrub and back to Griffin Road, backtracking to I-75.

He weighed her question and his answer. "It's not a game they're playing, you know. They intend on killing us. And there are more out there. The big guy, Stan. Petrovski. And we'd be stupid to think that was all of them. If he had eyes on me and you, then it's sure he had eyes on the rest of the band."

He pulled on to I-75 heading north to Davie, the little car laboring in the heat.

Steph combed her hair back with her fingers and looked out the back of the car. "No way we can continue to wherever Paul is now. You've got to turn around, JD."

He responded by pressing harder on the accelerator. It acted more like a volume control, the car getting louder but not much faster. "No way. If I could find him this easily with Rico's help, Petrovski could find him. We've got to get to him and warn him, maybe get him out of there and to somewhere safer."

"Where? He knows where we all live, obviously. What do you suggest?"

"You want to leave him in the trailer park, surrounded by old farts, to fend for himself?" He shook his head. "I don't think so." He looked over at Stephanie and smiled. "It's an adventure, right?"

He navigated through the concrete spaghetti to 595 East and took the first exit, making his way to the trailer park. "Once we get out of here with him, we'll figure out what to do next. He can't handle himself like I can. And Petrovski's going to come at him with everything he's got."

Chapter Twenty-Four

Paul jolted awake, someone kicking at his feet. "What the hell?"

Darrel looked down at him with his arms across his chest. "Wake up gorgeous. Stella had a freaking heart attack when you weren't in the trailer. Called me, freaking her ass out." He laughed. "What in the hell are you doing over here? Getting drunk with Frenchie?"

Paul swung his feet of the small sofa and sat, running his hands through his hair and groaned. "I don't drink." He looked up at Darrel. "I told you that now, what, six times? Seven?" He puffed his cheeks. "Up until 5:00 listening to the old guy tell me stories of his rum-running days. St. Pierre to Newfoundland and back. Fuck, that old guy can talk the ears off of an elephant." He stood and stretched. "Apologize to Stella, will you?"

"Apologize yourself. She's back at your place and man, I'm glad I'm not married to her. She's going to rip you a new one."

~~~

JD handed his phone to Stephanie. "The blue dot on the map is where we want to be. The red dot is us." He drove past the sign instructing all visitors to register at the office and turned down one of the main roads.

Stephanie looked out the window, then back at the map on the phone. "Left at the next road. Then turn right at the t-intersection at the end. The dot is a few trailers down from there."

John followed her directions and pulled in front of a double-wide trailer surrounded by beds of flowers. "This place?"

"The dots line up."

He stopped the car and got out. He took the phone from Steph and loaded the picture of Paul and the agent. He held it up and slowly turned until the picture on the phone was similar to the view toward one of the trailers. "That one."

Across the road stood the singlewide, hideous pink and green bricks protecting half a dozen nearly dead flowers. "Yup. That's the one."

They walked over and rapped on the doorframe.

A pudgy but hard looking woman opened the door. "Who are you?"

John looked at the picture on the phone, then at the trailer. "This is the right place. Who are you?"

She slid her jacket opened and displayed the badge on her belt. "Agent Stella Harding, US Marshalls office. Who are you?"

"We're looking for Paul Coates. It's not safe here."

She drew her gun. "Get in here." She held the door and closed it behind them. "Sit down. Keep your hands on the table and start talking."

~~~

Darrel stepped out of the door with Paul in tow, then stopped abruptly and put his hand up. "Stop."

"What?"

"I just saw Stella escort two into your trailer. She had them at gunpoint. Stay here."

"What if it's a trick? You go over there and see what's up and two more come in here and kill me and Jean-Claude here?" He pointed to the French-Canadian, still sleeping off the rum.

"Fine. Come, and stay behind me. Son of a bitch, this was supposed to be an easy assignment." Darrel drew his sidearm and crab-walked across the street. "Tuck in close behind me. I don't like this."

Paul complied. "Maybe both of us should get the hell out of here."

Darrel shook his head and put his finger to his lips. "Not leaving Stella behind."

"Then call back-up?"

"Radio's in your place. We wouldn't have this problem if you didn't wander at night. She's going to be pissed you snuck past her."

He slid up to the kitchen window above the tiny flower garden, trampling the peonies in the process. The two inside had their backs to him, facing Stella.

Paul pushed past him and looked in. "Who is it?"

"Back up."

"Wait. No, hang on a second. I know them."

He hopped off the trampled flower garden and pushed through the door. "Put the gun away Stella. This is all good." He turned to John and Steph. "We got rehearsal or something? What are you two doing here?"

Stephanie pushed her way past Stella. "Dad. God, I'm glad you're okay."

John looked between the two. "Hang on. Dad? Like for real dad?"

Paul hugged Stephanie and smiled over her head at John. "It's a long story. Want some ice lemon tea?"

~~~

Stan slowly drove west on Griffin Road. Grigory wasn't answering his phone. He found the dirt road to the left as described, after a slow right-hand turn in the road. He turned in, no other traffic around, alone in the scrub. He carefully navigated his Camaro through the ruts until he saw the back of Grigory's car.

He hopped out. "Hey, Greg. What the fuck, over?" He knocked on the fender of Grigory's car. "Where are you? Where are the two schmucks?"

He stepped around in front of the car and almost tripped over Grigory. "Oh, shit." He dropped and checked the pulse on his neck. He touched him under the jaw, and the head rolled loosely to one side. "Shit, shit, shit."

He got on the phone to Petrovski.

"What is it, Stanislav?"

"Grigory is down. For good."

"Coates?"

"Still unknown. Greg followed the sax player and the singer down some dirt road to nowhere. We think they were on their way to see Coates. They must have gotten the drop on Greg. What do you want me to do with his body?"

"Remove anything that might connect him to me or help in identifying him, torch him and the car, then get well away."

"But -"

"No but. Do it."

Stan licked his lips and looked down at his dead friend. "Okay. Have you heard anything about where Coates is?"

"He's in a trailer park, but I don't know where."

"Davie."

"What? Davie who?"

"No, the place. There's a huge trailer park in Davie. A bit west of Davie. Greg thought they were heading that way. They were going north on I-75 before they pulled off on this side road. Toward Davie. Ten bucks says they're there."

"It's worth a lot more than ten to me. Find all three of them and kill them. But clean Grigory's body first."

Stan slid his phone in his back pocket and looked at down at his friend. "Hard luck, buddy." He leaned over, his knee screaming, and checked his friend's pockets. Took the wallet, the mobile phone and loose pieces of paper. He hobbled back to his car and popped the trunk. From the toolbox he took a pair of wire cutters and two plastic re-sealable bags. Petrovski said clean him, he'd clean him.

Back at Grigory's body he half squatted, injured leg extended in front of him, and methodically cut off the end of each finger at the first joint. Thumbs also. As he cut each one off, he held the plastic bag under them and caught them. Identification would be difficult, but not impossible. This would buy them some time.

When he finished, he sealed the bag, placed it in the second bag and sealed it also. He wiped the cutters off with Grigory's shirt and placed them, and the sealed bag, in the back of Grigory's car.

He looked at Grigory, lying dead on the muddy ground. He shook his head and lifted him by the armpits. The small handgun fell from the waist of the dead man's pants into the mud. "You were armed? Jesus, man, you're an embarrassment."

He muscled him into the car, into the driver's seat, leaving the door open. He took the reserve fuel can from the back of the car, splashed the contents over the seats, and Grigory, placed the can in the back of the car and closed the trunk. He tossed a lit book of matches in the window. It ignited with a "whoomp".

"Sorry, pal." Stan retrieved Grigory's gun and wiped the mud off of it. He got in his car, stashed the gun in the glovebox and left. It would be at least ten minutes before emergency services showed up -

he'd be well gone from there by then, on I-75 North heading toward the trailer park.

~~~

Darrel officially relieved Stella of her duties and parked himself outside the trailer. John kept his distance until she left. "I think she wanted to hurt me."

Darrel chuckled. "Oh, be certain of it. So, Paul, how come you didn't tell us you had family? Changes the whole dynamic."

"It happened too fast, man. MacCready had me moved in here so fast my head spun. No intention of leaving Stephanie behind. But I had no intention of involving her, either."

John shook his head and scrubbed his face. "You never told me you had a daughter. Shit, neither of you ever let on you were related. I actually thought you two were dating."

"Well, that would be kind of weird, dating a guy 30 years older than me."

JD counted off on his fingers. "So you would have been in primary school when I had this old guy as a music teacher. Paul, I'd been to your house dozens of times. No kids. What gives?"

"I told you, it's a long story." He looked out the window. "And it'll have to wait."

Linda pulled into the short drive on her golf-cart at full speed, about 6 mph. She got off almost before it stopped and hammered on the aluminum frame of the screen door. "Mr. Calvin, I need to speak to you immediately."

"Come on in," said Paul. "It's open."

She wrenched it open, glared at Darrel and stepped into the trailer proper. "I have had numerous reports of men running around with guns. That is absolutely not tolerated on these grounds. I will have to ask you to leave immediately."

Darrel stepped forward and displayed his identification. "Excuse me, but he won't be going anywhere. He is a designated secured witness. We'll be here for a week at most. I expect your full cooperation. If you have any concerns with that, please take it up with the local US Marshall's office tomorrow." He leaned forward and lowered his voice. "And I expect full confidentiality from you. Any breach of that confidentiality is a federal offense punishable by up to 10 years in prison."

"Well, I never," she sputtered.

"You better not. Now if you could leave, we have confidential matters to discuss."

She looked between them, opened her mouth as if to say something, closed it, turned and left.

Darrel watched her drive away, then turned to Paul. "I'll be back on the porch. I don't think she'll bother you again."

John chuckled. "Ten years?"

"I may have bullshit a bit." Darrel grinned. "Don't tell, okay?"

"Mum's the word." He turned to Paul. "So tell me again how you had a daughter?"

"When a man and a woman really love each other, he puts his thingy in her and -"

"Seriously."

"Seriously, I didn't know until three years ago. Actually, two and a half years ago. Her mother didn't tell me she was pregnant, and if I'm honest, at the time I don't think it would have made any difference. I wasn't big with responsibility." He shrugged. "She was a fun time for a few weeks, then I moved on. Many, *many* years later Steph came to Miami looking for me. We decided not to make a big deal about it, first, because I didn't want people thinking I gave her the singing job on anything other than merit and second, because we're both emotional retards."

"That's a little harsh."

Stephanie smiled. "But not inaccurate. And now that you know, please keep it to yourself."

"It won't really make that much difference. WitSec will have you relocated after the trial, and nobody will be the wiser. Or care, wherever you end up."

Stephanie looked up at Paul. "You're going through with it?"

"I'm of two minds. We've got a good thing here and I'll be damned if I'm going to let some psychopathic bastard dictate how I'm going to live my life."

"They mean business, Paul. They will try to kill you. They may succeed."

"I'm safe here until the Feds sort something out."

John looked at Stephanie, then back at Paul. "We would have been here half an hour earlier if it wasn't for the guy following us who tried to kill us."

"Who?"

"Some thug working for Petrovski. Remember those two guys you saw sitting up front the other night? The smaller of the two."

"At least it wasn't the bigger one."

"Oh, I've already tangled with him. Stan. Regretting not killing him now."

Paul sat back in his chair. "What about the guy today?"

John looked out the window at the US Marshall. "Well," he drew his thumb across his throat, "he won't be showing up anytime soon."

"Really? You have to?"

Stephanie nodded. "He had to. And we believe the big one is closing in on your location."

"Hey, I meant to ask that. How did you find me?"

JD showed him the picture on his phone. "Someone in this park took it. A guy named Jean-Claude, Rico said. It ultimately ended up in Rico's hands. He'd very much like for Petrovski to disappear."

"Jean-Claude lives across the street. The old folks here had me pegged pretty fast." He scratched his chin. "Why would Rico want this Petrovski guy to disappear?"

"He's Petrovski's direct competition."

"What, the friendly, short and fat Italian is mob? What a cliché." He laughed and looked at Stephanie, then back to JD. "No joke?"

"No joke. His feet on the ground got this picture. It could have just as easily been Petrovski's feet on the ground. You're not safe here."

Paul stood. "Darrell, get your ass in here."

"What?"

"You hear anything we said in here?"

"Not much. Should have I?"

"JD, show him the picture."

Darrel grabbed the phone. "Who took this?"

"The old dude across the street. That's not the question you should be asking."

"How did you get it?"

John snapped his fingers. "Exactly. And how many digital copies are making their way around the state, waiting to be picked up by the wrong person?"

"You can't tell this is here from this picture, though. It could be anywhere."

"The coordinates are embedded in the picture file. Jean-Claude's smartphone has GPS. Very easy to find if you're looking."

Darrel nodded. "Stay put. I've got to make some calls."

"Can you get any traction today? Long weekend."

"I can try." He stepped out to the porch.

John looked at Stephanie. "So we're like brother and sister?"

"How do you figure that?"

"Paul was like a father to me, since I didn't have one, and he's your actual father, so we're like brother and sister."

"Not even close, and if you mention it again I'm going to beat the crap out of you."

John shook his head in mock disappointment. "Paul, you didn't bring her up very well. But I can tell where she got her temper from."

Chapter Twenty-Five

"So what actually happened to get you stuck in a trailer park in Broward?"

"I saw Petrovski shoot a kid in the forehead and dump him in The Everglades. The big guy who showed up at the club, Stan you said his name was, handled the airboat controls. I saw Petrovski calmly press the gun between the kid's eyes and pull the trigger. I shit myself when I saw that. Came back, called the cops and ended up talking to -"

"A guy named MacCready."

"Yeah. How'd you know?"

John pulled Paul's phone from his pocket. "You left this behind in your apartment. You called him just before you took off."

"Jesus. They told me to leave it behind because its location could be tracked. And you brought it right to me."

"I shut off the GPS. Should be good." He tossed the phone to Paul. "Easier to reach you when you've got one of these."

Paul placed it on the table. "You know what you're doing, technical-wise?"

"I do. I think."

"Well we'll just leave this here for now."

"They didn't have enough other evidence to convict?"

"I don't know if they have anything more than my word. I'm the prime witness. I've been watching too many movies. I expected to be put up in a suite and fed steaks while being guarded by big men with huge guns. Instead, I've got Darrel or Stella. And Jean-Claude across the road bending my ear." He looked at the phone. "I don't know what I was thinking. This isn't working for me." He leaned out the door. "Hey, Darrel, we're outta here."

"What?"

"Can't do this. Make the case on your own."

"This Russian dude wants to kill you."

Coates shook his head. "Nah. I'll tell him I don't give a shit what he did and don't intend to testify."

Darrel crossed his arms. "You think that'll work? These guys aren't real understanding. Once they make up their mind to kill you, they don't often change it."

Coates scowled and shook his head. "Bullshit. He's human. He can be reasoned with."

John interrupted. "Maybe we should give that MacCready guy a call. He's the one who set this up, right? Should get his input on this, Paul. It's a big step you're making."

"What are you, a pussy? There have been asshole thugs in the world since the beginning of time. Hiding isn't going solve anything. And I don't feel like changing my life because of something they might do."

John clenched a fist. "Paul, I've run across these guys a couple of times already." He lifted his pant leg. "Stabbed by one of them. Ran into another one just before we got here and if I hadn't stopped him he would have found you and killed you."

"And where's he?"

"That doesn't matter. You need to resign yourself to the fact that these guys won't stop until you're dead."

"Or they're in jail."

Steph shook her head. "I don't think you're getting it. I've seen these guys."

Paul Coates looked at his daughter and the guy he thought of as a son, then asked Darrel, "You can't force me to stay here, can you?"

"You can leave, but until I'm told differently, I have to stay with you. And I'd be pretty damned upset if you try to shake me."

"Who has to tell you differently?"

"Special Agent James, Detective MacCready or my immediate supervisor, Spooner."

JD grabbed Paul's phone from him and dialed, putting it on speaker and placing it in the middle of the table.

"MacCready."

"Detective MacCready?"

"Yes. Who is this?"

"My name is John Delacourte. We've talked briefly before. I'm with Paul Coates in the trailer park in Davie. I'm a close friend. I'm with his daughter, Stephanie Peters, and the US Marshall here to protect him. Paul wishes to back out of the witness security program. I'd like you to convince him of the error of his ways."

"How'd you find him? And he never mentioned anything about a daughter."

Paul leaned into the phone. "Hey there Detective. JD is an enterprising young man. Ex-Army Ranger. Apparently tracking me down wasn't that difficult. I didn't mention my daughter because, well, long story. Anyway, what JD said. I'm out. This is stupid. You guys can't protect me. JD found me in a couple of days."

"Who the hell is this Delacourte guy. Can you trust him?"

Paul laughed. "My sax player. And I've known him since he was fifteen. Yeah, I can trust him."

John interrupted. "Tell Paul the danger of going out on his own."

"Sax player? Ex-Army Ranger? I can't protect you, sax. You're treading on dangerous ground, and I can't help you. Coates, I can help, but unless you were a witness to something also, or Coates's long lost son, I can't help. Shit. If you found him that easily, Petrovski and his boys are probably not far behind. Coates, I'll make a couple of calls and find a better place to put you. Maybe I bring you in and place you in protective custody."

"A jail cell? No fucking way. And there's my daughter to think of. If they find out I have a daughter she'll be a target, too."

"Yeah, I've got to amend the paperwork tomorrow to include the both of you."

"You're not listening. I'm out. I'm going to get into JD's car, with my daughter, and leave the godforsaken trailer park and its quasi-zombie population of degenerate French-Canadians. And if Darrel follows us I'm going to call the local cops and tell them I'm being followed by a large man of color and he's scaring the hell out of me."

They heard MacCready sigh on the other end of the line. "I can't put Petrovski away without you. We don't have enough physical evidence to make the case, but with your testimony, we should be okay."

"So what are you missing?"

"If we had the gun he used it would be a much better case."

"If you had the gun, would you need me?"

Silence.

"You there, Mac?"

"We don't have the gun. We believe he dumped it in the Everglades, and that's a big-assed place to look."

"I've watched movies. Why don't you bug his phones or put a tail on him and catch him in the act?"

"What the hell do you think we've been doing for the last year? He's not an idiot. He rarely gets his hands dirty and he's got someone doing regular electronic sweeps."

"You can tap the phones without a bug, with the phone company's cooperation. Go right in at the switch."

"Chicken and egg. That kind of warrant needs evidence of a prior crime, and he's kept himself clean enough, so far, that we haven't been able to get one."

Coates leaned back and crossed his arms. "Your problem, not mine. Johnny, take me home."

"Wait, Coates, reconsider this, okay? If you voluntarily walk away from this, I can't protect you, either."

Coates leaned forward, enunciating carefully. "I'm out. Find the fucking gun." He stabbed the end button and pocketed his phone. "Let's go, kids."

Darrel slid his hands in his pockets. "You're making a mistake, buddy. I'm not going to stop you, unless I get a call from someone soon. But watch your back, right?"

John got behind the wheel, Paul beside him and Steph in the back. "Where to, boss?"

"My place?"

"We could do that." John started the car. "How do you manage to live across the hall from Amber without cutting your own throat? She's not that bright."

"Eye-candy. Fastest way back, okay? I miss my place."

"There is no 'fastest' in this car, but okay." He moved the gear into reverse and jumped when Jean-Claude knocked on his window.

"Shit." He rolled down the window. "What? Who are you? We're leaving."

"So tell me the truth then, eh?" He pointed at Paul. "He's a mob informant," he pointed at Darrel, "big black guy is US Marshall and I'm not sure who you are, shorty." He leaned down and looked in the back of the car. "And a cutie in the back seat. I haven't had this much excitement in years." He leaned in the car window, preventing them from leaving. "So it's all over then, is it? The bad guy get offed? Why you breaking camp?"

Darrel walked over and pushed him away from the car. "Because nosy assholes like you have compromised the mission. Get back to your trailer."

Jean-Claude crossed his arms and moved to the back of the car, blocking it in. "I happen to know that you can't order me around."

John let off on the brake and slowly moved back. "I can't tell you what to do, and you can block me in, but let me out, okay? This is serious."

Steph leaned forward. "What's so serious?"

"I'm kind of worried that I found Paul so fast. Petrovski has more resources."

"I can call him and tell him to back off again."

Coates twisted in his seat. "Call him? And what do you mean, again?"

She sat back in her seat. "I should have told you a long time ago. He's my uncle. On my mother's side. My last name, "Peters", is "Petrovski", anglicized."

~~~

Stan pulled off I-75 east onto the Port Everglades freeway, then took the first exit onto SW 136th Avenue. He was near the trailer park. He pulled over and called Petrovski.

"Are you getting closer, Stan?"

"Can you call your friend in blue? Give him the license number of the guy I'm looking for and see if there's been any sign of him?"

"You lost?"

"I know exactly where I am, but I have no idea where I should be."

"He is in a rental, right?"

"I'm assuming he is. He's not in his car, or the girl's."

"Speaking of her, you get rid of everything?"

"Everything?"

"The guy who followed her. You get rid of everything?"

"Yeah, yeah. Fingertips, torched the car. Should be clean."

"Good. I will call my guy and see what we can do. The fact it is a rental might make it easier."

~~~

Mac paced in his kitchen. "Double shit." He called James.

"Working on a long weekend?"

"Surprised?" Mac took a deep breath. "I think we lost our witness."

"So, define lost. Is he dead? MIA? What?"

"I just got off the phone with Coates. He's got a daughter and a change of heart."

"Tell him how important this is."

"I have."

"And a daughter?"

"He says it's a long story. And Darrel called me just after he left. So he's left. I don't think he liked the trailer park that much anyway. But we're back at square one. Without Coates, we don't have anything." His phone beeped in his ear. "Hang on, I've got a call coming in."

He switched calls. "MacCready."

"Gloria here, Mac. Enjoying your weekend?"

"Up until about twenty minutes ago. And I assume you're not calling me to thank me for the fantastic barbecue yesterday."

"Something's come up in Broward that might be related to one of your cases."

"I've got James on the other line. Hang on while I bridge." He pushed the right buttons. "James? I've got Gloria here, too."

"What's going on," asked James.

"We got a body in Broward, far west. Partially burned in his car. Local fire service got to it before the fire completely consumed the body. The victim's fingers have been cut off and his neck broken and his pockets emptied. Sam believes the neck is the cause of death." She gave them the address.

"Obvious question is why you guys were involved?" Mac tugged on his earlobe. "Broward guys didn't want to pay their crime scene techs overtime on the long weekend?"

"The Broward guys were fast. The car had Dade plates, and is owned by a known associate of Vladimir Petrovski."

"Stan?"

"The big guy? No, this guy is smaller. Grigory something or other."

"He had a broken neck?" MacCready tapped the kitchen table. "With a struggle, or a clean break?"

"She called it a clean break. Very professionally executed in her opinion."

"And then they cut off the fingers and burned the car? Or were the fingers cut off peri-mortem?"

"No, he was dead when they were removed."

Mac shook his head. "That's more mobster crap. And those guys are more blunt force trauma or rapidly decelerating lead to the head."

James interjected. "Two people? One kills, the other cleans up?"

"Possibly. So who's Petrovski's natural enemy in the wild?"

"Rico."

"Exactly, James. Gloria, thanks for the call. We've got some stuff to do now. Appreciate the heads up."

"Okay, boys. Call me if you need me."

Mac waited until she dropped her leg of the call. "I've got to call Simon, and see if he's involved."

"You think he's killing to stay undercover?"

"I hope not. The one kill I know he did was an accident and it wrecked him for weeks. Maybe he did clean up."

James groaned. "Even that's pretty gross. Cutting off the fingers? Even when the guy is dead, that's gross."

"You're soft, James. Got to get you out to more smelly crime scenes."

"Some other day. What do you think is going on?"

"It's an uneasy balance right now. A hard enough shove in the right direction could spark an all-out war. The last thing we need. I'll find out where it is and let you know. Meet you at the station. I'll call Simon on the way, figure out what the hell his involvement is."

~~~

Petrovski drummed his fingers on his desk, waiting for Cruz to respond to his page.

Finally, his phone rang. "What took so long?"

"It's a long weekend. I had family stuff. Not that easy to just duck out of the in-laws."

"You're a cop. Make shit up. I need you to find a car. A rental." He reeled off the make, model and license plate number. "And I need it now."

"Why?"

"You don't ask why. I pay you money and you do. If you become more of a liability to me than an asset, I stop paying for you and your wife draws widow's pension. Call me in an hour with what you know."

Chapter Twenty-Six

Paul opened a beer and passed it to John who passed it to Stephanie. "None for me, Paul. I've got something to do. But you, Steph, you have one. Might loosen your tongue a bit. Why didn't you tell us your uncle is one of the most vicious mobsters in Miami? Especially since two of his goons were after Paul?"

"I don't think of him as an uncle. And I never made the connection. It wasn't until the other day when Rico mentioned they worked for Petrovski. I went and talked to him right after that, trying to convince him that Paul wouldn't testify, that it was all a mistake and that he should just back off."

"And how'd that go?"

"I'm lucky to have gotten out alive." She ran her fingers through her hair. "I heard him tell Stan to kill you. I wanted to warn you, but I couldn't make a call without him knowing." A small smile flitted across her face. "I'm glad he didn't kill you."

"He'll try again, don't worry."

Paul took a long pull on his soda "Your uncle is trying to kill your father. This is a full-on Maury episode."

"Think we can get all three of us on the same stage?" Steph took a more dainty sip of her beer. "Would make a few people's job easier, wouldn't it?"

"Yeah, maybe. Listen, Paul, can you remember where you were in the Everglades when you saw Petrovski shoot the kid?"

"Why?"

"Going to find the gun, if he did actually toss it."

Paul snorted. "Don't joke like that when I've got a mouthful."

"No joke. Can I use your metal detector?"

"It's in the laundry room behind the rifle."

"Might take the rifle with me, too." He opened the mapping software on his phone and placed it on the table in front of Paul. "Show me where the bad man shot the kid."

Paul pushed the phone away. "I've got charts. I mark them where I've tagged the 'gators, so I don't go back to the same place that often. Don't want to be too obvious." He pulled a cardboard tube out from behind his fridge and unrolled the charts on the kitchen table, holding diagonal corners down with condiment bottles. He jabbed the map near a red "x" and a recent date. "Right here. This is where I sat, looking for the ugly critters. I drifted a little, just south of this bit of land." He pointed at a slightly raised marshy island called 'Gator Hammock'. "As soon as I passed the southern tip of it I could see him. So that would have him about here." He marked the map just west of the southern tip of the hammock of land.

John took his phone and navigated the map until he located the same hammock. He zoomed in. "Right here?"

Paul looked at it and nodded.

"Okay. I'll mark it on mine. Makes it easier to navigate to." He looked back at the chart. "Does it say here how deep the water is?"

"Rarely more than two feet. Usually closer to one. That's why we use airboats. No draft."

John dug through the back of the small laundry room and pulled out the metal detector, a disc at the bottom of a six-foot-long shaft, with a battery pack and set of headphones. "Do you know if this is waterproof?"

"I've used it in the rain, and it's had surf wash over it. Not sure how much it will take, but give it your best. Don't care if I ever see it again. A toy from days gone by."

John grabbed it and the rifle. "I'll be back a bit later tonight. I shouldn't have to say it, but don't let anyone in."

~~~

Cruz looked around the station. None of his regular contacts worked this shift. No one paid much attention to him. He dug the scrap of paper out of his pocket with the car information and called the rental agency. "Good morning, my name is Detective Cruz of Miami PD. Could I talk to your manager please?" He drummed his fingers and looked at an old warrant sheet. He tucked the phone between his shoulder and ear and started typing on his laptop. The manager came on the line. "Good morning, you're the manager?"

"Yes, what can I help you with?"

"I'm detective Cruz, Miami PD. You've got lo-jack or other type of tracking on your cars, right?"

"They have GPS tracking, yes. Why?"

"There's a suspect in one of your cars, a known sex offender and he has a young boy with him. We need the location of that car immediately."

"We have a procedure that needs to be followed, Detective, as I'm sure you're aware. You need to fax us a copy of the signed warrant and the make, model and license plate of the car."

"Absolutely. I'm just calling to get your fax number. I'll include my number on the bottom. Call me back as soon as you get something." Cruz dropped the phone in the receiver and forwarded the desk phone to his mobile. He finished typing the phony warrant body and printed it out. Careful cutting and the judicious use of tape and a photocopier and it looked just like the real thing. He wrote the station number and his extension on the bottom and faxed it to the car rental agency.

He peeled the fake body off the real warrant and shredded it and the copy. He deleted the file on his laptop, closed it and left the station.

Halfway to his car, his mobile rang. "Cruz."

"Hi there, it's the rental agency. That car you're looking for? It's heading south on SW 187th. It's still moving. I can disable the car remotely if necessary."

"No, don't do that. I may call again later for an updated location. Keep this confidential, okay? We don't want the perp to be alerted. He may do something stupid."

"Of course. You can count on my discretion."

Cruz snapped his phone closed and got in the car. "I sure as hell hope so." He started the car and his phone's Bluetooth paired with the car's audio system. He called Vlad.

"You have something for me Cruz?"

"The car is heading south on SW 187th. I can get there in about thirty minutes."

"No. You're driving now?"

"Yes."

"Back to the station and wait for further instructions."

"But, I've -"

"No, no buts. I'll call you when I need something."

Cruz punched his steering wheel. The call had been terminated. He pulled a U-turn and re-entered the station parking lot. "What an asshole."

~~~

Petrovski hung up and looked at his phone for a second. He dialed a number from memory. "They're going back to the airboat launch."

"How do you know?"

"The rental is heading south on 187. You know any other reason to go down that godforsaken road?

"Good point. And you want me to do what?"

"Why do I pay you, Stan? Why are you on my payroll? What is your one, unique skill?"

"Yeah, okay. Got it. Except I'm kind of injured. I would have a hard time healthy."

"You've got an equalizer, right?"

"Always."

"So use it. Why you didn't use it before is beyond me. Use it today and make sure this is the last I ever hear about them."

~~~

John pulled into Hector's parking lot and hopped out of the car. A sheen of sweat coated his neck and his short hair matted against his scalp. The dark, overcast sky promised rain later in the day, and it looked like it was going to be a helluva a storm.

He ran up the steps to the store.

Hector met him at the door. "Not today. I've just finished cleaning up and fixing the mess you assholes made last time." He looked past John. "Where are your friends?"

"No friends of mine, Hector. I just want to rent one of your airboats. Legit."

Hector looked up at the sky. "Not a good idea. Big one coming. You get caught out in that and I'll lose a boat."

"You got insurance, right?"

"Yeah."

"And you're open for business?"

"Well, yeah."

John pushed past him into the shop. "Then rent me a goddamned boat. I don't have all day."

"You're going to have to sign a waiver."

He held out his hand. "Give it." He scrawled his signature across the bottom. "You can sleep easy now if I drown or get eaten." He dropped his driver's license and credit card on the counter. "Let's get the paperwork done."

"What are you going out for? You're not a tourist, and you're not going out for the same reason Petrovski did. You popping 'gators too?"

"You don't seem to be too worried about that."

Hector shrugged. "Can't stand the things. Living dinosaurs more than happy to eat you. Could kill them all and it wouldn't bother me." He ticked a couple of boxes and spun the papers around for John's signature.

"Can't argue with that." He scrawled his name a couple of more times. "Point me to the boat."

Hector led him to the one at the end of the wharf. "Look, buddy, you gotta get this thing back within the next couple of hours or they'll be dragging the 'glades for your remains and I'll be putting a claim in for another boat."

"You need to ease off on the coffee, Hector. Relax a bit."

"It's my business, buddy. I never relax."

"That's too bad. Relaxing is good."

Hector expelled a deep breath. "Fine. You ever drive one of these things?"

"No, but how hard can it be? You can do it." He smiled, waiting for a response to the jibe.

None was forthcoming. "I'll start it for you. It's a pushbutton on the back. The throttle's on the floor like your car. Hang on to this handle with your right hand. It'll keep you from separating from the boat if you do something stupid. And you will do something stupid."

"How does this thing steer?"

"This upright shaft on the left. Keep it straight up and you go straight. Push it forward to go right and pull it back to go left."

"Seriously?"

"Yeah. Don't get lost. I don't want to have to come looking for you."

John held up his phone and a plastic bag and pulled out a roll of duct tape. "GPS. I'll be fine." He taped the phone inside the plastic bag and attached it to the seat beside him. "Fire this puppy up."

~~~

Stan slid his seat back as he drove and tried to straighten his leg. The persistent dull ache of the strained ACL drove him to distraction. The itch under his wrist cast was nothing compared to the knee. He dry swallowed another Percocet and shifted into fifth and floored it. Thunder rumbled in the east. The storm built off the coast and the wind promised to blow it onshore.

He slid into the parking lot beside the rental. Petrovski's guy came through. An airboat bounced across the rough water, heading west.

"Shit."

He hobbled into the shop. "Hector, you fat fuck. Where are you?"

The owner stepped out of the back room. "Oh, fantastic. It's a party. What do you want?"

"I'm taking a boat. Who's on the one out there already?"

Hector shrugged. "Hey, I'm trying to run a business here, Stan. Take it easy, okay?"

Stan grabbed him by the throat with his good hand. "Fuck with me and your kids will go to bed tonight without a father. Who took out that boat?"

"The little one." He rubbed his throat and looked at the rental agreement. "Delacourte. John Delacourte. The guy you and Grigory fought, remember?" He couldn't help it. He glanced at Stan's cast.

"You laughing at me?"

"No. God, no, Stan. Take a boat. On the house. Find him and do whatever you want with him, okay? Just stop using me for a punching bag."

Stan grunted. "Just him, not the other two?"

"What other two?"

"A girl, smaller than him, and an older guy, a bit overweight and balding. The older guy was out here Monday afternoon, a week ago."

"You mean Paul Coates. No, he wasn't here today. Haven't seen him since Monday."

"Fuck. I'm taking the boat on the end."

"You sure you're okay to ride one of those things with the cast?"

"I'll manage." He leveled a finger at Hector. "Tell anyone I'm out there and I'll personally kill you myself."

Hector put up his hands in surrender.

Stan pushed out the door. A gust of wind caught it and slammed it against the outside wall. He took out his phone and called Petrovski. "Coates and the girl aren't with him. It's just the little guy."

"So kill him, like you want to do so badly, and I will see if I can find out where the witness is. I have suspicions, but I need them confirmed. Stay on your phone."

~~~

Cruz sat at his desk, clenching and re-clenching his jaw. Like a servant. At Petrovski's beck and call. He slammed his fist on his desk.

"Hey, pardner, what are you doing in here on a holiday? Looking for overtime?" MacCready slid into his old seat.

"Case I'm running. Things are popping up. I'll only be here for an hour or so. You?"

"Same-same. Gotta sit out here while they paint our new OC office. We seem to have lost a witness. One who cemented a case for us and now, without him, we need to find something as compelling or start from scratch."

"That sucks. What case?"

Mac smiled and waved a finger at him. "Can't tell you that, pup, or I'll have to kill you."

Chapter Twenty-Seven

Petrovski called his personal detective again. "I need to know where Coates is."

"I can't talk freely right now."

"Just listen and say what you can. Can you find Coates?

"How?"

"You're the detective. Do some detecting. Put some effort into this, Cruz. I'm going to need to know within a couple of hours."

"Are you kidding me?"

"I don't kid, Cruz. Have you not figured that out yet?"

"Yeah, yeah. I'll find him."

"Good." Petrovski hung up and sat back at his desk, smoking a Cuban. He needed to start cultivating some more cops. Cruz took too much effort for too little gain.

~~~

MacCready waved James over to a spare desk while he flipped through the directory on his phone. "Hey, you got Coates's home number?"

James pulled a scrap of paper from his jacket pocket. "Here." He handed it to his partner. "You going to try and sweet talk him?"

"Yeah, it's worth a try." He punched the number into his desk phone. "We've got nothing else right now."

"Why are we out here? Why not our new office?"

"Getting painted. They didn't expect anyone in over the long weekend. I stopped by earlier. The fumes will take you to a very happy, brain-dead place." He shook his head. "We'd be higher than a kite inside half an hour." The phone rang at the far end. "Help me out, okay?"

"Who's this?"

"Coates?"

"That's me. I asked who you were."

"You don't recognize my voice?"

"You're on speaker. Is that MacCready?"

"Bingo."

"And you think you can change my mind."

"Bingo again."

They heard him belch. "I ain't gonna. Not worth it. I'm home, with my girl, sitting back watching golf. So save your breath."

"Let's put that to one side for a moment. Someone killed a known Petrovski associate named Grigory something. Since Petrovski is the guy trying to kill you, I thought perhaps you might know something about it."

"Are you serious? Really? I don't know this Greg guy and I sure as hell didn't kill him." He hung up.

James picked his teeth with a corner of paper. "That went well. So we gotta find the gun."

"Good luck with that. We're back at square one, and I've got to make another call."

~~~

Cruz's desk was half way across the room. He sat with his back to MacCready and his FBI buddy. He didn't hear everything, but he'd heard enough. A quick text message to Petrovski and he'd be able to leave for the rest of the day.

~~~

Petrovski looked at the incoming text and smiled. Cruz actually came through. Wonders never cease. He replied: "Thanks. You should probably go home and not attract attention in the office on your day off."

~~~

The spray soaked John, and it stunk. Trial and error for the first five minutes steered him way off course. Adjusting the touchy throttle while steering took practice. Holding the steering stick straight up propelled him straight forward, but straight was relative. As he hit the swells the lever would move forward and backward, causing the boat to describe an "s"-track through the marsh grass until he caught on. He backed off the zoom on his phone and adjusted his course slightly south toward Gator Hammock. He swung around the southern tip and slowed, centering the dot on his phone screen. He reached back behind him and turned off the engine. He tied a length of rope to his wrist and the angle frame of the boat. The wind had picked up and the last thing he needed now was his boat drifting west. Forever.

He stepped into the water. It came to just below his knees, but he needed to tread carefully across the soft, sucking bottom. He taped his phone, map app open and in a plastic bag, on his right forearm. He slung the rifle off his shoulder, barrel down, easy to bring to bear quickly in the event an alligator decided he was afternoon snacks. He pulled the headphones on and turned on the metal detector, testing it against the barrel of the rifle. It seemed to register fine.

He looked at his surroundings. A bank of clouds swept in from the Atlantic, about ten miles to the east, darkening the sky. The wind whipped small whitecaps around his knees. He took a deep breath and looked around. He estimated about a half square mile of area to grid. "Just like minesweeping, without the risk. If you exclude the alligators and pythons." He dropped a pin on the map showing his current position and started sweeping. It was going to be a long, boring afternoon.

~~~

Stan instinctively knew the sax player's destination on the Everglades, but he didn't know why he would be heading to the scene of the crime. The scene of many crimes. It would take him ten minutes to get there from the wharf, maybe slightly faster with the stiff onshore wind.

The spray from the whitecaps soaked him, his cast getting wetter than it should.

His pants pocket started vibrating five minutes into the trip. He slowed the boat and pulled out his phone. Petrovski.

He reached back and shut off the engine and answered the phone. "What's up?"

"Where are you? Have you finished what you went to do?"

"On the way. Had to shut down the boat so I could hear you."

"The real target, the one you really need to visit, is in his apartment."

"Whose apartment? Non-specific pronouns piss me off."

"The real target is in the real target's apartment."

"Much clearer. Do you want me peel off and go for the primary?"

Stan sat on the silence coming down the line and let him think. The wind continued to blow him in the general direction anyway.

"No. Finish what you went to do. He is a thorn we could do well without anyway. Finish that task fast and then head back to the primary."

"Sure. Why in the hell would he go back there?"

"Who knows? Maybe the girl did not bullshit me, and he has decided against testifying. No matter. He knows, he needs to go. Do not make mistakes this time."

~~~

John wished he'd brought a net, or a long stick or something. The metal detector pinged every third or fourth sweep. Miller Lite cans, Bud cans, even a Pabst Blue Ribbon can; there had been a lot of beer consumed on The Everglades. The excitement at the first ping had rapidly disappeared to a desperate delve into the murky waters, rewarded with annoying consistency by the retrieval of another piece of trash. The floor of the airboat quickly started to look like a *garbarge*.

His clothes dripped water and the wind chilled him, even with the temperatures in the high eighties. He dropped a crushed and half-torn beer can on the boat when an earlier one disappeared. He looked to the left and watched it drop into the water, then felt the metal detector wrench from his hand. The metal pipe dropped into the water, pulling the connected headphones off his ears. He could now hear the airboat approaching from behind him.

And the ricochet as another shot whined just in front of him.

He dived to the far side of the airboat and brought the rifle to his shoulder in a smooth movement. Stan approached at a fast speed, his airboat less than twenty feet away. If the guy had been a little more patient and waited until he got closer it would have been a single-shot job.

John untied the rope that attached him to his airboat. He carefully sighted and shot the engine housing of Stan's airboat. Black smoke billowed and the boat lurched to a stop just as it collided with John's. The edge of the boat caught him on his knees. He staggered and dropped the .22 as Stan launched forward off his and landed among the beer cans.

Stan landed on his wrist, his cast now almost a paste from the incessant wetness. John saw him wince and smiled. The big guy still had a weakness.

He scrambled to get on the relatively stable footing of the airboat deck and came face to face with the muzzle of a 9mm Beretta. Stan didn't look comfortable holding it with his left hand, but he didn't have much of a choice.

"You're not getting the jump on me this time, Army boy."

John raised his hands. "Stan, fancy bumping into you out here. Paul is going to want you to replace his metal detector. It's going to set you back a couple of hundred."

"I'll pay him back personally. He's my next stop."

"If you can find him."

Stan laughed. "He's home. Safe and snug in his apartment." Stan looked smug. "We got you all this time."

"Maybe you got bad information."

"Maybe you'll never know because you're going to be dead in a second."

"Maybe."

John weighed his chances. Stan wasn't the greatest conversationalist he'd ever met and he bet he'd grow tired, both of talking and of getting wet in the marsh, sooner rather than later. The fact that he held the gun with his weaker hand was promising. His muscle memories and reactions were built into the right hand. The left hand was an untested infant as far as killing people with a gun was concerned.

But John had to be fast, and there wouldn't be a second chance.

Stan held the gun at full extension, the weight of the gun multiplied by the length of his arm, producing the strain, however slight, on his left shoulder.

John moved his hands slowly from the "I surrender" position to the supplicating "please sir can I have some more" position as he talked. "Stan, buddy, you're wasting time and ammo. Paul has told me to my face that he has no intention of testifying about something he may or may have not seen, and is in fact planning on heading to Europe for an extended engagement in the finer French jazz clubs. This is all just a big misunderstanding."

He waited until Stan opened his mouth to talk then hit the inside of Stan's left forearm hard with his left hand while his right hand simultaneously hit the back of Stan's left hand. The combined action forced a hard bend to Stan's wrist, opening his gun hand just as he pulled the trigger. The shot went over John's left shoulder, grazing his ear, then the handgun fell to the deck.

They scrambled for the weapon, Stan's injuries offset by his bulk. He wrapped his legs around John's waist and squeezed as he tried to extend his reach to the gun.

John grabbed the torn beer can and drove it with all of his strength into Stan's right knee, the one damaged behind Hector's shop.

Stan bellowed, forgetting about the handgun. He punched at John with his right hand, re-injuring his wrist, then switched to his weaker left hand, punching John around the head, trying to land something on target.

John grabbed at Stan's right hand and gave it a twist as another left landed on his cheek, splitting it.

The skies opened, rain pounding them. John's hands were slick with blood. He tried to grab at Stan's arm again, trying to deflect shots that were just too much for him. He tried to push himself to his feet and Stan kicked him in the ribs.

He heard a splash behind him. A large splash. He pushed himself onto his hands and knees and reached for Stan's gun. Stan placed the sole of his foot on his back and pushed him down again. John slipped and knocked Stan's large handgun into the water.

"Stay down, you fucking freak. Why aren't you dead yet?" John winced as Stan kicked at him again. He saw an alligator tail in the water about fifteen feet from the boat.

"You had your best shot already, music boy. Now you're dead. The alligators can finish you off. I've got another job to do now. Your buddy's next. That big fucking 'gator will eat well today." Stan caught him with another kick under the ribs and one more kick under the chin. He faded as he slipped off the boat.

Chapter Twenty-Eight

John heard the roar of the airboat fade as it drew Stan farther away. He coughed out a mouthful of water and winced as a sharp pain drove through his chest. "Ah, crap." Thrashing in the water behind him spurred him on. He pulled himself onto the small deck of the boat and laid on his back, face to the rain. The alligator bashed into the boat but then left him alone.

He took stock.

Cracked rib on his upper left chest. Maybe two. It hurt like a son of a bitch to breathe, but nothing felt broken. Stan hit him in the head pretty hard, but as far as he could tell, he'd avoided a concussion. The moderately blurred vision was probably from the rain beating on his face.

He reached for the phone strapped to his arm. Nothing. He lifted his arm and looked at the single remaining piece of duct tape. He grunted and dropped his arm across his chest and winced.

His left ear stung. Blood poured down his neck from that wound, but that was the least of his problems. He looked at the smoke still pouring out of the engine housing. "Well, shit. It just gets better."

He sighed and looked at the water surface around the boat. He had no desire to go toe-to-toe with an alligator, but he needed a way to propel the boat. He slid off the boat again, feeling the mud with his feet, hanging on to the airboat for balance and continually looking around him for signs of movement. He crab-walked looking for the metal detector, or the rifle; anything he could use to propel the dead boat back to shore. Lightning snapped followed by almost immediate thunder. He ducked instinctively and kept crab-walking until his foot hit a tube of some sort. He ducked down and grabbed it and pulled the metal detector to the surface. He took another step sideways and felt the rifle. Maybe his luck had turned.

He plunged into the water and retrieved the rifle and as he stood, the unmistakable smell of burning grass wafted past his nose. He looked west. Smoke rose from the grasses less than a mile away. Right now the easterly wind blew it away from him, but no telling when it would shift. He clambered onto the dead boat and started pushing it east, using the metal detector as a gondoliers pole.

He made slow progress against the headwind, but that same wind kept the fire from getting closer, so he couldn't complain about it too much.

Not that there was anyone to complain to.

He continued to push east, the wharf now in sight, seemingly an impossible distance away.

~~~

MacCready looked out the window at the storm. "Good thing I did the barbecue yesterday, James. Getting really shitty out."

"About time. Break this heat." James sucked on a fruit smoothie. "We any further ahead?"

"No. I can't get any kind of approval to drag the Everglades. The tech laughed at me. Gloria pulled him up, but still."

"I can talk to her, try and persuade her to approve it."

Mac shook his head. "She'd be going too far out on a limb for nothing. Tens of thousands of dollars to do that, with a probability of success in the single digits. If we could narrow the location down some, maybe."

"How's the Grigory murder related?"

"Let's see if we can find out." He called Simon and waited for his brother to answer. "Can you talk?"

"Yeah. Free and clean. What do the boys in blue want today?"

Mac looked down at his shirt. "Actually, I'm wearing a light yellow oxford shirt and a red tie. Fashion aside, what do you know about the death of a Russian guy who worked for Petrovski, hung around with that giant Stanislav, name of Grigory. He's dead. What do you or Rico know about that?"

"Whoa, bro. I haven't killed anybody."

"You know who I'm talking about?"

"Stan's faithful companion, yeah. I do."

"Companion like, you know?"

"Gay? No. Thug brothers." Simon laughed. "I'll let Stan know you think he's gay, though. That'll go over well. How'd he die?"

"Broken neck. Then his fingers were cut off and his car burned. With him in it."

"Where? I would have thought I'd have heard about that."

"West Broward. Nothing's coming up on it.

"The broken neck isn't something the local thugs would normally do. Too up close and personal. The fingers and car though, that's a pretty common tactic to delay the identification of a victim. It never stops it completely, but it delays things."

"So Rico didn't arrange this?"

"Hang on. I'll put him on."

Mac looked at James and shook his head. "What the fuck?"

"What the fuck indeed, Detective. I'm assuming you're calling Simon to see if he can weasel some information from me concerning Grigory's unfortunate death."

This slid just a little too close to the line for Mac's comfort. "I know some of your business activities, Rico, and I know that you and Petrovski have an uneasy split of South Florida. When one of his lieutenants ends up dead in Broward, I start looking at the obvious."

"And the obvious would be that I'm knocking off the competition."

"Well, now that you mention it."

"I'll save you some time, Detective. It wasn't me. And it wasn't someone acting on my behalf. I barely knew Grigory. If I were going to leave a message for Petrovski, I'd do Stan. Or burn down *The Natalia*. And last I checked, both Stan and the club were still standing. But maybe I can help. How did Grigory die?"

"I'm not sure that's pertinent."

"Of course it is. The style of killing could be unique to certain people and I might be familiar with those techniques."

"Is that so?"

"Come on, Detective, it can't be that confidential. You told your brother. Tell me now and I can share whatever information I have with you, and not whatever other cop I talk to."

James leaned close and whispered. "Where's the harm? Maybe he can help."

Rico's voice crackled from the phone. "Special Agent James, is that you? A very good point you made. Where's the harm?" Another crackle interrupted the phone line. "You guys getting this storm? Epic in its proportions."

"You're right, I've already told Simon. You'll know as soon as I hang up. He had his neck snapped. Our ME says it looked professional. Very well executed. And then his fingers were cut off."

"Post-mortem is confirmed?"

"About the fingers? Yeah. Why?"

"Well, he wasn't tortured, then. And that is a quick killing."

"There were fresh bruises indicating a bit of a fight first."

"And then someone broke his neck. Anybody in his sphere of influence who has specialist killing skills? Green Beret? Ninja?"

"Thanks for your time, Rico." Mac punched a button on the desk phone and hung up the call. "Hadn't thought of that."

"Of what?"

"Ex-Army Ranger sax player."

"That Delacourte kid?"

"Out of the Rangers only six months, so he'd still have the skills."

"And Petrovski is trying to kill his good buddy, the drummer."

Mac nodded, half a smile on his face. "We have a vigilante on our hands."

~~~

Stan crashed into the wharf at almost full speed and used the momentum to run up to the parking lot, his game knee making the whole exercise look ridiculous.

"You lash that thing down?"

"Fuck off, Hector. I'm in a bad mood. Do it yourself." He stopped by the rental the sax player had driven.

He slid his knife out and stabbed all four tires, then broke the driver's side window with a sharp strike of his elbow. He snarled, reached in and popped the trunk.

He grabbed the jack from the back and systematically destroyed every window in the car.

Hector ran back up the wharf, soaked. "What in the hell are you doing that for?"

"That asshole really pisses me off. It was supposed to be a clean kill and he fought me again. I'm already injured. Lucky shot, but it's going to mess me up for weeks. Maybe even months."

"Now it's going to be on my property and I've got to explain it."

"Call the cops after I leave. Tell them there's an abandoned car some vandals got to. Whatever. I don't care. Just wait until I leave." He shoved a finger under Hector's nose. "Until I leave, understand?"

~~~

The wind swirled and the smell of smoke abated. The fire didn't catch. The critical mass of heat necessary to maintain a grass fire in the rain hadn't been achieved. Rain poured from the sky, soaking him to the skin, but he didn't have a chance to cool off. He had to stop Stan. He had to get to Coates and Stephanie first or die trying.

He dug into the bottom of the marsh and pushed again and again.

He'd developed a rhythm. Drive the bottom of the broken metal detector hard into the bottom, push it to the back, pull it out of the sucking mud and continue. Sweat poured off his face and mixed with the rain, the salt burning his eyes. He could taste it on his lips.

His ribs screamed with every stroke. But he'd fought against worse pain before, and they felt like cracks, not breaks. They hurt, but he wouldn't puncture a lung. He grit his teeth and continued to push. Push against the headwind that had picked up speed.

Stan had almost an hour head start on him. He resigned himself to the fact that Coates and Stephanie were almost certainly dead.

He shook his head. No. "Almost certainly" still left a small sliver of hope, and that's what drove him.

His shoulder and his pecs started to cramp from the workout. He could see the wharf clearly, now almost spitting distance. The final push brought him alongside. He grabbed Paul's rifle and ran to the car.

The tires were slashed, and the windows broken.

Stan didn't take any chances.

Chapter Twenty-Nine

John leaned against the car and looked up at the sky, the deluge pouring over his face. "SHIT!"

Hector ducked out of the shop, hood pulled up tight, shielding his eyes from the driving rain. "What the hell is going on?"

He pointed to the wharf. "Brought your boat back. It's broke." He sighed and patted the rear quarter panel of his rental. "But this isn't going anywhere. Stan just tried to kill me and now he's going after two of my best friends and I've got to stop him. Again. Lend me your car."

Hector scratched his head. "You might want to call triple-A, buddy. That car is a mess. But you're not borrowing mine. I don't care what you say. Now about the boat."

"Forget about the fucking boat. You've got insurance."

"What happened to it? Run into a submerged log?"

"I shot it."

"What the hell are you doing shooting the boat you're in?"

"That's the one Stan took out, Hector. I'm running out of time, man. Stan came at me in that one, and I shot it to stop him from ramming me. He thought he killed me. Now he's going after Coates. Are you listening to me? He tried to kill me."

Hector backed up with his hands up in the "I surrender" position. "I don't want to get involved. I'll file an insurance claim for the boat and call you a taxi."

John grabbed Hector by the throat. "Give me your fucking keys before I rip your goddamned arms off and beat you to death with them."

Hector dug in his pocket and pulled the key to his car out and threw them on the ground. "Never come back here, okay?"

JD scooped the keys. "Around the back?"

Hector nodded and backed away.

"Thanks. I owe you one. Sorry about the boat."

~~~

A uniformed officer walked into the squad room, took a quick survey of the occupants and headed toward MacCready. "Hey, you were looking for this Delacourte guy, weren't you?"

Mac looked up from his computer at the constable. "Yeah, why?"

"Just got a report of vandalism, a shot boat, physical assault and car theft from the owner of an airboat tour company south of town. The guy says John Delacourte was responsible for all of these acts. He's in the owner's car heading north." The constable dropped a sheet of paper on MacCready's desk. "Here's the car details. There's an APB out on him."

"Thanks." Mac took the paper and looked at the details. "Any ideas where he may be headed, James?"

"I'm more curious about why he went back to the Everglades. Anyone else from Petrovski's 'family' missing?"

"Not that I know of." He rubbed his chin. "Coates didn't want to testify, right? And he asked if finding the gun would give us our case. You think this sax player went down there looking for the gun?"

James snorted. "If he's insane, maybe."

Mac stood and closed the file. "Saddle up. I think we need to check out some of Petrovski's haunts. See if we can head him off at the pass."

"Kinda want him to get rid of a few more of Petrovski's crowd before we find him though, ya know?" James took his gun and badge from the desk, holstered his handgun and stood. "Although I do realize that's unethical of me, I appreciate the help. We aren't having much luck shutting that asshole down."

"I'll forget you said that. I'm driving. Let's hit *The Natalia* first."

~~~

Stan's phone rang. "What's up, boss?"

"How you feeling?"

Stan turned the volume up on his phone to compensate for the rain hammering on the hood of his Camaro. "Sorry, what did you say? Too noisy with all this rain."

"How are you feeling? How are your injuries?"

"The sax player fucked my knee up even more, and my cast is a soggy mess, but I've got a couple of Percocet in me so I'm good. On my way to the drummer's place to kill him too."

"So the sax player is dead?"

"Left him bleeding out in the swamp with a dead airboat and an alligator sniffing at his ass. The 'gators will be burping up his aftertaste by now."

"So he's dead? You didn't actually answer me."

"Okay, fine. He's dead."

"Good. When you get to Coates" place, I don't want you to kill him. I want you to bring him to me. Beat him up a bit if it makes you feel better, but I need him alive. Understand? That guy has been on my nerves. He needs the personal touch."

"You sure about that?"

"What's that? Am I sure?"

"The last time you took matters into your own hands we ended up in this mess. That's why you pay me. I do the killing, and you keep your hands clean."

"Bring him to me."

Stan looked at his phone and tossed it on his seat. He reached across the car and took Grigory's small gun from the glove box.

~~~

John pushed north on SW 187th and then east and north and east again as he zig-zagged his way back to Paul's apartment, wipers flailing at the rain, trying to keep the windshield clear. Hector's car wasn't in much better shape than his Honda. He scrambled for his phone before remembering it rested among the sludge and discarded beer cans at the bottom of the "glades.

He pressed the pedal harder to the floor, hydroplaning as he passed the slower cars in his path. Learning to drive in the Nebraska snow turned out to be a good thing.

He ran an old yellow light and yanked the wheel to the left, turning north on S. Dixie highway. Ten minutes to Paul's apartment in good weather and easy traffic. The rain and influx of old northern retirees made it a slog. He'd be lucky to do it in twenty.

He veered left around a bus pulling from the curb and glanced off a light standard. Paint scraped off the driver's side of the car as he corrected and continued north. He snaked his way past traffic, horn in full throat, until he had the apartment building in sight.

~~~

Petrovski let the police wait for a few minutes. His place, his rules.

They stood by the bar, wet and bedraggled looking. He raised an eyebrow and smiled. "Ah, MacCready and his Yankee friend James. You look like shit. I expected beat cops. This must be very important for actual organized crime boys to show up."

"We're here to warn you." MacCready shook rain off his coat.

Petrovski laughed. "You threaten me?"

"Is that what I said, James?"

"No, I think you said you warned him. Hey, Russkie, your boy Grigory, he's dead, no?"

"So I have heard. It is unfortunate, but that is price that occasionally needs to be paid."

"Do you know what happened?"

Petrovski shrugged. "He met an untimely death. I will miss him. He was a good kid."

"That's not what we heard. He's a psychopathic asshole. Was."

Petrovski cocked his head. "How did you confirm his identity? I understood that you *suspected* him to be Grigory, but his fingers had been cut off. That would make identifying him difficult, wouldn't it?"

"You are well connected. Easy to identify him. We found him in his car, for one thing. And the fire didn't totally consume him. You know, if you didn't order the car to be torched his body wouldn't have been found for weeks. Good of you to light the pyre for us. And thanks for confirming his identity."

"Is that why you came here? A cheap trick like that?"

"No, actually. We think we know *who* killed him and believe he might be on his way here, right now, to kill you."

Petrovski smiled. "That would be something special. This person who killed Grigory, if it is who I think it is, experienced a terrible accident this afternoon in the Everglades. Or so I've been led to believe, so unless either of you believes in zombies, or the walking dead, I think I'm pretty safe."

James looked at MacCready. "That make any sense to you?"

Petrovski studied the Detective's face. The smugness in it unsettled him. "Why doesn't it make sense?"

"I don't know that I want to lay all our cards on the table yet. We came here to try and head the guy off at the pass, but if you're comfortable that he's no longer a threat, I guess we could leave. I'm sure you can handle anything that comes up. You've got that reputation."

"I want to make sure we're talking about same guy."

"I'm afraid we can't share any details of a currently active case. As I said, we're just here to head him off. Since he's dead, there's no need."

"Didn't we get a report that this person shot up an airboat, beat up poor Hector," he turned to Petrovski, "that's the dude who runs the airboat place," he turned back to MacCready, "and stole Hector's car? Does that sound like a dead man to you?"

"Maybe Hector got it wrong. It doesn't matter, really, since he's not here and by my calculations, he should have been by now." He nodded at Petrovski. "We'll be seeing you around. I'm sure of it. If the sax player does show up, tell him we said hi. And good luck."

Petrovski watched them walk out, a blast of weather getting in when they opened the door. "No. It cannot be."

He walked back to the privacy of his office and called Stan.

"Can I call you back boss? I'm in the parking lot and about to go in."

"The sax player is dead?"

"Didn't I tell you already? Gator food."

"Then how is it that he's in Hector's car heading this way, with me in his sights? Can you tell me that?"

"Says who?"

"Our friends MacCready and James. They just left the club."

"They're fucking with you. I wouldn't be surprised. If this guy does show up, let me know. But I've got to go now and fetch a drummer for you."

Petrovski hung up. It wouldn't be the first time the cops had lied to him, trying to provoke him into doing something stupid. He'd never bit before, though, and that's because he could read a face very well.

And the look on MacCready's face wasn't the look of someone trying to mess with his head. It had the look of someone who knew something that tipped the scales in their favor.

"Shit."

He dropped into his chair and checked his gun. He flicked the safety off. If the sax player showed up he'd shoot him on the spot.

~~~

John beat on the dashboard in frustration. He could see the apartment building, a block away, less than a two minute drive from his location. But a tow truck, sideways across the road removing a car wrapped around a light pole, had stopped everything. A cop directing traffic had just told everyone to wait. The temptation to leave the car and run was overwhelming, but he knew as soon as he got out of the car the traffic would start moving.

So he waited.

When the tow truck had finally removed the car, the cop let the cars proceed. He pulled into the parking lot and ran for the apartment.

Chapter Thirty

Paul looked at the bottle of scotch in the cupboard. "Awfully tempting, Steph."

"Leave it there. You're doing great."

"Yeah." He took the bottle of sparkling water instead and poured a glass with ice and dropped in a couple of slices of lemon. "This is boring as shit, though."

"But you're alive."

Paul nodded and sat at the table across from his daughter. "If I kept drinking like I was, I'd be pickled by now. So there's that." He gulped some of his drink. "I don't want you to leave the group. You're the draw. We're just a bunch of schmucks playing tunes. Your voice, your looks, your voice."

"You said "voice" twice."

"Should have said it three times. Your fantastic voice is what draws the crowd. The rest of us are just competent."

She shook her head before he finished. "No, I think I need a break. I'm burned out. It's not fun anymore."

"That's just all this bullshit going on around us. I'll renounce any statement I made, make peace with the Russian dude and life will be back to normal."

"It doesn't work that way. I know him." She reached across the table and took his hand. "I really know him. He's bent. My mother warned me that he was a psychopath. That's one of the reasons she changed her name."

"I only knew her as Peters." He cleared his throat. "So why didn't you tell me about your relationship to Petrovski right from the beginning?"

"Would you have hired a singer linked to the Russian Mob?"

Paul shrugged. "I wasn't lying when I said you have a hell of a voice. I could have overlooked it."

"No way."

"You'll never know, now. You're leaving. If you stayed, you'd still be in the band, and you are most emphatically linked to the -"

The door crashed open, splinters of wood flying into the living room. Stan stood in the entry and looked at the two sitting at the small dining table. "We meet again."

~~~

MacCready sat in his car, wipers trying to beat the rain away, the inside of the window fogging up. "What the hell? I should be building an ark. So Delacourte didn't come here. He would have been here by now. Even allowing for the weather. So he left the Everglades in a hurry, taking a guy's car. That's not someone just returning to home for a warm bath and a turkey sandwich. If he's not gunning for Petrovski, who?"

James wiped water from his face, drying it with a handkerchief. "The big guy. Stan. He's got a regular beef with him. If he's done Grigory it would make sense to find and finish Stanislav."

"That would put him directly in Petrovski's path. Ballsy."

"That's loyalty for you. All because Coates wants to get out from under the Russian's thumb."

Mac shook his head. "Loyalty is all well and good, but he's breaking the law. We need to stop him."

James took out his phone. "So we find out where this Stan guy is and get to him before this Delacourte guy does."

~~~

Stan smiled. "They don't make doors like they used to. Both of you, over here. We're going for a ride."

Stephanie stood. "I don't think so."

"I can kill you here. It's the other one Petrovski wants."

"Petrovski?"

Stan looked at the girl, annoyed at the intrusion. He just wanted to grab the old guy and get back to the club. His leg ached and his wrist, with the limited protection of the now soft cast, throbbed waves of pain up to his shoulder. "What difference does it make to you, bitch?" He pulled out his gun. "You're gone."

"He's my uncle. Check with him before you kill me, or you'll be in big trouble."

Stan lifted the gun and looked closer at her. "Bullshit."

Stephanie took a step closer. "Call him. He'll tell you."

Stan lowered the gun and awkwardly pulled the slide-action back with his right hand. "You're lucky Petrovski wants the man alive. I'll take you alive too. You might be right. I don't want to piss him off any more than he already is."

Stephanie walked closer. Stan put his right hand out, the gun in his left hand pointed to the ceiling. "Stay back. I don't mind hitting women. Most of you are more vicious than men."

She took another step forward and Stan sighed and placed his hand on her shoulder. "I said to stay back. Are you deaf?" He cocked his head, confused. She smiled. She should be terrified.

She grabbed the back of his right hand with hers. She twisted and pulled back, tearing a gaping big hole of pain in his arm. He squeezed instinctively with his left and shot into the wall as he followed his head to the ground. The twist on his arm wouldn't bother him normally, but any resistance now felt like daggers into his wrist. He fell face down on the ground, right arm twisted at the shoulder and torsion applied to his wrist by a little girl less than a third of his weight. His left arm, hand and gun were pinned under him. He craned his neck and saw Coates get out of his chair.

With gritted teeth he used his bulk to roll off his hand and gun and shot Coates in the arm. He leveled the gun at the girls head. "Let go before I splash brains all over this guy's apartment."

His arm dropped to the floor as she stood back, hands in the air. The drummer yelled an oath, and held his wounded arm. Stan pushed

310

himself to his feet, a bit wobbly. He waggled the gun at Stephanie. "Come here."

"Why?"

"Fuck you and come here. You're expendable. Remember that."

She walked closer. Stan kept the muzzle trained on her head. "I've got a bottle of pills in my right pants pocket. I can't use my right hand any more, bitch, and I'm not going to put the gun down. Take the bottle out and give two of them to me."

"Seriously?"

He pushed the gun against the side of her head.

"Fine, okay." She dug in his wet jeans pocket and fished out the small bottle of pills. No prescription label, no child-proof cap. "These?"

"Open the bottle and take two out."

She looked at him while opening the bottle and pouring them on the floor. "Oops. Bet the cops get here before we get all these picked up."

"You bitch. What cops?"

"You just shot a hole in the wall. You think maybe somebody noticed that?"

He pushed the gun hard against the side of her head. "You're dead."

She closed her eyes. "My uncle is going to be very pissed if you kill me. You *really* should call him first."

Stan debated the consequences. He wasn't brain surgeon smart, but he knew that there were two kinds of mistakes, and it was better to make the mistake with the least adverse consequences. If he killed her and she was Petrovski's niece, he'd be joining Sergei in the Everglades. If he brought her back and she wasn't Petrovski's niece, the worst that would happen would be a yelling at. He pulled the gun from her head. "Move it. I can shoot you without killing you. You too, drummer boy." He stepped to one side and corralled them out of the apartment. "In the elevator. Move your feet faster."

"Hang on, he's bleeding." Stephanie grabbed a tea towel and wrapped it around Paul's arm. "Hold that tight."

Stan followed them into the elevator. "I'm going to have the gun out of sight when we get out of this thing. Just outside the front door is a yellow Camaro. Drummer boy, you get in the back seat. Chippie, you sit up front with me. Buddy, if you try anything from the back remember that my gun will be pointed at her the entire trip."

~~~

John ran around the corner of the apartment building to the entrance. Stan's had parked his Camaro out front by the door. "Shit." He hit the buzzers at the front door and heard a gunshot from inside. He punched the buttons again and someone buzzed the door. He ran to the elevators and pushed the button. He poked it a couple of more times then turned to the stairs and ran up them two steps at a time, his calf and chest screaming. He exited the stairwell onto Coates' floor. The door had been kicked off its hinges.

He stood by the door frame. "Paul? Steph? You guys in there?"

The door opened behind them. "Hello?"

"Amber? What the hell is going on? What happened here?"

"This really big dude? The one you shot before? He kicked in the door and shot Paul and took them both."

"Stan. Dammit. Did he say where he was going?" He heard sirens in the distance. "Quick, where did he say they were going?"

"Stephanie said something about her uncle. Who's her uncle? I peeped through the, you know, peephole so I couldn't really hear them very well."

"Shit, shit, shit." John stepped into his friend's apartment, quickly, for a look around. Green pills were scattered on the floor. Percs, by the look of it. A bullet hole in the wall near the TV, and a pool of blood in the dining area, and drips out the door and to the right told the story. Fresh blood, still damp. The sirens got louder. "Were both of them walking okay? Paul and Stephanie?" He grabbed Paul's phone off the table and slid it in his back pocket.

Amber nodded. "Paul's arm was bleeding? He made them both walk to the elevator. He was going to kill Stephanie, the girl, but she said something to him, and he didn't shoot her."

He pushed her, gently, back into her apartment. "Amber, these people are very dangerous. Pack whatever you need and get out of here. Go to a friend's place, then find somewhere else to live."

~~~

Mac and James pulled up to Stan's apartment.

"It's a death trap, if you ask me." James got out of the car and sheltered himself against the rain as he sprinted to the front door.

313

Mac followed. "If only." He looked for the Superintendent's buzzer when his phone rang. "MacCready."

"Hey, Collins here. I'm on the desk today. Call came in about a shooting and home invasion at that Coates guy's place. Thought you'd want to know."

"Absolutely. Thanks. Who's the victim?"

"No bodies at the scene. Some blood, smashed in door and an uncooperative witness."

"Any word on who did it?"

"No, but a yellow Camaro left the scene. Same make and model as one of the APBs you've got out."

"Shit. Thanks." Mac closed his phone. "Back to the car."

"What's going on?"

"Shooting at Coates place and it looks like Stan has taken him."

"Where?"

"Not back here. Short odds on back to the Everglades. The stubborn old man should have listened to me. Shit."

Chapter Thirty-One

John sat in Hector's car, rain drumming a tattoo on the roof. They were still alive. For now. And it sure sounded like Stan took them to Petrovski.

But he didn't know where Petrovski was. He knew someone who did, though.

He dialed the restaurant number from memory. "Izzy? Got to talk to Rico. It's important."

"Who's this?"

"John Delacourte. Sax player."

"It's important?"

"Extremely."

"Hang on a sec."

John turned on the wipers while he waited for Rico. Wasted effort. Sheets of water streamed down the windshield and the blades made no headway.

"JD, what's going on? I'm hearing a lot of noise on the streets, and it ain't all thunder."

He rubbed the back of his neck. "One of Petrovski's thugs, the giant, has picked up Coates and Stephanie. I think he's taking them back to wherever Petrovski is. I need to know where that might be. Actually, I need you to tell me everything you can about that asshole."

"If it's Stan, he could be taking him to the Everglades. He likes it down there."

"Nah. Someone overheard him talking about taking them to Petrovski. But I don't know where Petrovski is."

"You're going to just march into the lion's den, right? You're nuts."

"He's got Coates, and his daughter."

"Petrovski's daughter? Petrovski's got a daughter?"

"No, Stephanie is Coates's daughter. And she happens to be Petrovski's niece."

"You're shitting me."

"I shit you not. Where does this guy hang out?"

"When all of this is finished, you and I need to sit down for a long chat, and you can catch me up on what the hell is going on. Petrovski's main hangout is at a club called *The Natalia*. High-end strip joint near the airport. This weather, though, he might be at home. He's got digs on the Inter-coastal." He gave John the addresses. "Check out the club first. And if you get out of that alive, give me a call."

~~~

Petrovski checked the time and continued pacing. He reached over to his desk phone, hit speaker and pressed a speed dial button.

"Who is it?"

Petrovski could barely hear the voice over the rain. "It's me. Your boss. Where are you?"

"A few minutes away. Look, I can't really talk right now. My good hand is holding a gun on these two and my bad hand is holding this phone. I'm steering with my knees, and it's raining so hard my wipers are useless. I'll see you in a couple of minutes."

The desk phone reverted to dial tone.

He reached across the desk and hung up. He pulled his hand back, and it rang. He poked the speaker button again.

"Yes?"

"Petrovski?"

"Who is this, and how did you get this number?"

"Your ape has just picked up my friend, and your niece, and is taking them to you. He's ahead of me in a car faster than mine or I'd try and get there first. Know this, Vladimir, I will drop you like a third-string quarterback if anything happens to either one of them."

"How did you get my private number? Did Rico put you up to this? You're that guy Stanislav said he killed in the Everglades, aren't you?"

"He's a pretty crap employee. You should probably fire him. Be smart, Petrovski. Let Stephanie and Paul Coates go. They don't care about Sergei or how you killed him."

Petrovski stopped pacing. "You know way too much information, Mr. Delacourte. When I finish with Coates, and my niece, you'll be next on my list. I look forward to meeting you face to face." He punched the button and hung up.

~~~

John looked at his phone, clenched the wheel and floored it. Petrovski was dead. It didn't matter what he did to Coates and Stephanie, he was dead. Although the death would be a lot slower if he did something to Stephanie.

The Natalia was close to the airport. He headed south and west and slipped around the traffic as fast as he dared. The wipers flailed. Lightning lit up the sky to the southeast; deep, resonant thunder thrummed through the car seat and steering wheel. The storm created the perfect backdrop for his all-or-nothing situation. Petrovski was dead.

~~~

"Okay, you two. This is the back door of where we're going. We're getting out slowly. Chickie, you get out and pull the seat forward so pops can get out. Slowly. I will sit here and point my gun at you. If there's any kind of fast movement, I will indiscriminately start shooting either or both of you. I really don't give a fuck now. So get out, slowly, and then stand in the rain while I get out."

He held the gun on them and they slowly extricated themselves from his car. Coates looked pale and favored his arm, the tea towel soaked with blood.

"Hurry up. I've got to piss." Stan waited until they both stood beside the car. Rain hammered the car roof and soaked Stephanie and Coates in seconds. "Place your hands on the roof of the car. Both of, you, both of your hands. Even you pops. I don't give a shit if it hurts."

Their hands disappeared above the window line and he got out, favoring his right leg and his right wrist. He leaned on the roof. "Lovely weather. I'll take snow over this." He pointed with his gun. "That door there. Knock on it, three short knocks and two long."

"What the hell is a long knock?" Stephanie took her hands off the car and crossed her arms.

"Do it or I'll shoot you. Stop being such a difficult bitch. I'm tired." He waved the barrel of the gun at her. "Knock."

Stephanie shook her head and pounded on the door, the pattern not even remotely similar to the one Stan told her.

A small door slid open at eye-level. "What?"

Stan crabbed over, gun pointed at Coates's head. "It's us. Open the fucking door. We're getting pelted on out here."

It swung inward, and Stan prodded them forward. "Get in. Quickly."

The guy at the door shut it behind them. "Wait here. I'm not taking you into the boss's office drenched like that."

"I've got to piss. Wait until I'm back, then get him. Watch these two, and be careful of the girl. She's a nasty bitch." Stan limped to the back, water dripping off his clothes.

~~~

Petrovski picked up his phone to call Stan again when his office door cracked open. "Stanislav is here with guests."

"Bring them in here."

"They're soaking wet from this rain. It will ruin the rugs in here. Best you see them in the back."

Petrovski nodded agreement and followed the man to the loading area. "Where is Stanislav?"

"Taking a piss. He'll be here in a second."

Stan came out of the bathroom pulling up his zipper awkwardly and with a hitch in his step. "I'm here now. I told you to wait until I got back before you brought the boss back, you idiot."

"And *I* am here now, Stanislav. You're not looking well. Are you okay?" Petrovski cocked an eyebrow at Stephanie. "Why are you smiling?"

"Because JD, half this ape's size, took this guy down twice, and I just had him face down on the ground all by myself. The big guy is a big poof."

Petrovski held out a hand to stop Stan from lunging forward. "Enjoy the time you have left on this earth, young lady. It will be very brief."

"You're actually going to kill family?" She shook her head. "My mother warned me that you weren't to be trusted."

"I'll do whatever I have to do to survive. That's not negotiable. If that means killing you, then I will do it with regret. I do like your voice." He looked at her father. "And you, well, absolutely no regrets with your death. Make them kneel and make sure they go nowhere. Stanislav, we need to talk."

He led his enforcer to a corner of the loading dock area. "The sax player is still alive."

"Impossible."

"No, quite possible."

"The cop just fucked with your head."

Petrovski smiled and lightly slapped Stan on the face. "I talked to him myself not fifteen minutes ago. He's alive. He threatened to kill me. Stanislav, my friend, you are useless to me if a bantam rooster runt like that sax player can beat you so easily. He should have been dead three times now. He lives. And you're looking much worse for wear as a result." He pointed across the small warehouse to Stephanie. "Even she managed to beat you."

"She's here, isn't she? Let me kill her. You can kill the drummer, but I really want to kill her." He cradled his wrist.

"No, Stan, you are going to find the sax player, and you are going to empty your gun into his head. No fucking around, no long chats, just find him and kill him. I am clear?"

"But -"

"No buts. Am I clear?"

Stanislav nodded. "I just need to find him."

"I will call our cop and get him to track the rental again."

Stan rubbed the back of his neck. "That won't do any good."

"Why?"

"I disabled the rental at Hector's place."

"Why? You thought you had killed him, did you not? Left him in the Everglades? You told me he would be 'gator burps or some such bullshit. So why take the time to trash his car?"

Stan scratched his jaw. "He really pissed me off. I vented. What difference does it make? I thought I killed him."

"What difference does it make? If you hadn't wrecked his car, he'd be driving it now, and we'd be able to track him." Petrovski rubbed his forehead. "He must be in Hector's car. Call him and find out the make, model and tag number."

Stan stood there.

"Go on, call him."

"And then I'll give it to you, and you call your cop friend, and we get its location?"

"No. Then you find out where the sax player likes to hang out and find him and kill him. You know where he lives, right?"

"Yeah."

"So go back there and rip the joint apart. Ask neighbors where he goes. Do some fucking leg work. Now go, and don't come back unless he is dead. Or you are."

Stan grumbled and left, his phone to his head. A gust of wind blew in a flood of rain before he closed the door.

Petrovski walked back across the warehouse. "So, my guests. It has come to this." He pointed at Stephanie. "For you it will be fast. For your father, not so much. But first, we talk."

He sat in an old office chair. Stephanie and Paul kneeled in front of him, armed thugs on either side of them. "Paul, how fast you die will depend entirely on how much information you have already given Detective MacCready or his partner, Agent James. And don't say you have told them nothing. They would not have hidden you away in anticipation of a WitSec application, and subsequent mandatory testimony against me, if you did not give them at least a sniff. So what did you tell them?"

Paul said nothing and slowly raised his right hand and gave him the finger.

"That was not nice, Mr. Coates. Sven." He nodded at the man beside Stephanie who put his pistol under Stephanie's chin and pushed upward. "I will not hesitate to tell Sven to blow the top off her skull. That is a big gun." He picked at the hair in his goatee. "Tell me what you told MacCready and James."

Paul put up his hands. "Okay. Take it easy." He looked at Stephanie, then back at Petrovski. "What do you want to know?"

"You met them or did you talk to them on the phone?"

"We met. Last Thursday morning. I went into the station and met them and talked. Okay? Let's get this over with."

"We're not finished talking. What did you tell him? Actually, first, tell me what you saw last Monday morning."

Paul took a deep breath. "What the hell, I'm dead regardless of what I tell you, so go fuck yourself."

Sven cocked his pistol.

"Okay, okay. I go out every week or so shooting 'gators. Went out Monday. Didn't actually see any, by the way, so overall, not a real fantastic day. Came around the point of Gator Hammock and saw you with your gun against the young kid's forehead, then the kid fell in the water. A second or so later I heard the shot. I bugged the fuck out after that."

"And you told all this to MacCready?"

"Pretty much, yes. So let's get this over with." He held out his arms. "Shoot me. Don't shoot her, she doesn't have anything to do with any of this."

"I think she does." He took out his handgun and pointed it at Stephanie. "Sven, bring my car around to the back. You will be driving. We're heading back down to the scene of the crime. Fitting, don't you think? You two will meet the same end as Sergei."

A crack of thunder rattled the windows.

"Getting pretty nasty, boss."

"Fuck off, Sven. Get the goddamned car."

Chapter Thirty-Two

John's pants and shirt were soaked. And torn. And covered in the sludge from the bottom of the Everglades. His sneakers were soaked and stinking. He'd ruined Hector's upholstery. Fortunately, his route to *The Natalia* passed by his apartment.

He had to pick up a weapon. Facing off against Petrovski unarmed was stupid. And he wasn't stupid.

He parked at the front door to the building and ran in. His apartment was as he left it. He dropped his clothes in the tub and went to the kitchen wearing boxers and dry socks. He grabbed an almost empty box of cereal and a filleting knife. He cut the cereal box to use as a sheath and wrapped a couple of layers of duct tape around it. He placed it on the counter and crossed in front of the apartment door when it smashed open.

He slid off his feet and landed on his ass as Stan pushed in, pulling out his gun and cocking it. "Stand up."

John pushed himself to his feet, hands extended. "Hey, Stan. Long time, no see. What's up?"

"I'm going to kill you now."

"Again?" John took a step forward.

"No, no, no. No closer. I know you know all those fancy disarming tricks. Turn around."

"You going to shoot me in the back of the head? Like a coward?"

"Call me a coward if you want, but I'll be eating dinner tonight and you'll be gator bait."

"Again? The Everglades, again? You've got no imagination. If I were you and you were me I would have shot me by now. Roger Ebert has these movie definitions and man, you are exactly the 'talkative killer' to a 'T'. Just shut up and shoot me." He took another step forward. "Or do you have to explain to me everything I've done wrong so far?"

"Turn around. Into your room and get dressed. I can't take you out to the car with your dick hanging out."

JD looked down. "Has it slipped out again? I hate boxers. Don't know why I buy them." He slowly turned and faced down the short hall to his bedroom. "This way?"

Stan jabbed the gun in the base of his neck. "March."

~~~

Petrovski marshaled his captives out to his car. "Get in the back." He flicked the child safety locks on both doors. He got in the front passenger seat, locked the back windows and sat sideways, gun between the seats pointed to the back passenger cabin. "Sven, to Hector's place."

"Down south?"

"There is no other Hector's place."

"Pretty nasty weather, and it's going to be dark in a couple of hours."

"Sven, Hector's place now or I shoot you in the knee."

Sven started the car and pulled away from the club. "Got it boss."

"Good." He looked back into the rear of the car and waved the gun at Stephanie. "There is a switch on your center console. Hit it and turn the lights on back there. I can't see you."

She complied and soft yellow light, like warm butter, lit the cabin. "How do you sleep at night?"

"I usually have a shot of whiskey and sleep like a baby." Petrovski smiled. "I was about to suggest that you try it, but you will not have the chance. Shame.

"There's so much blood on your hands. I can't believe you and my mother are from the same family."

"How is she? It's been years and years. She still in Nebraska?"

"She's dead, but I'm not surprised you don't know. Cancer, five years ago. You've never asked about her before."

Petrovski shrugged. "I didn't really give a shit. Still don't. Making conversation. It's a half-hour drive there. Maybe longer." He looked at the driver. "Sven, can you step on it?"

"Hey, boss, it's pissing out. Hydroplaning all over the place. I can't push it any harder."

"A little bit harder."

"We'll go off the road."

Petrovski pointed the gun at Sven. "I said a little bit harder."

Sven shrugged and pressed harder. "Your funeral."

"No, Sven, I didn't tell you to crash. Go faster and get us there safely." He stared at him for a second then redirected his attention to the back seat.

Stephanie wiggled the door handle on her side.

"No, that's not going to work. We're doing over thirty. You'd be killed on impact if you went out the door."

"I'm willing to take the risk." She stopped working the door and sat back. "JD's dead, isn't he?"

Petrovski narrowed his eyes. "Stan is taking care of him now. He's a very resourceful man, your Mr. Delacourte. He should have been dead a few times now. Stan will make sure this one is final."

"You sure about that? I had that big guy down pretty quick. Stan isn't in very good shape. I hope he brought a gun. A big one."

~~~

John took a deep breath. Behind him with a gun was just as good as in front of him with a gun. Better, actually, since the guy holding the gun didn't expect resistance.

Stan pushed the barrel hard against the back of his neck. Rookie move.

He took a slow step forward, paused and then took a second one. He wanted Stan to be a bit more relaxed, assuming control, and he wanted the restricted space of the hallway. He had another three or four steps to get Stan into that comfortable mindset. "So, what should I wear? Is this place we're going to formal or informal?"

That got him another poke to the back of the neck. He took another step forward. "I'm just asking, Stan. I don't want to embarrass you."

"Tell you what, smart ass. Wear whatever you will be comfortable in on the table at the morgue, okay?"

John took another step forward and shrugged. "I guess it doesn't really matter then does it, because if I'm on a table at the morgue, I'll be dead, right?"

Stan chuckled. "You're a genius."

John had stepped two steps into the confined hall when Stan chuckled. Now or never.

John spun hard to his right, rolling his head out of the way and following through with his raised right arm. He caught Stan by surprise and smashed the gun hand into the wall. The revolver went off and clattered to the floor as he drove his left fist up under Stan's hanging ribs.

He clenched his right fist and smashed Stan in the throat, then kicked out his right knee. "This is the last time, you shit."

Stan brought his left hand to his throat and swung at John's head with his right elbow as his right leg collapsed, catching John just above the ear. John's follow-through drove Stan to the floor. He instinctively put his right hand out to break his fall and John heard the bones in his wrist grinding together. Stan continued rolling to his left to get on his back but the wall stopped him.

John shook his head. The skin above his ear had split and was bleeding like an open faucet, but it wasn't deep. He pushed himself up the wall opposite Stan and stepped on the gun. Stan saw it at the same time and lunged for it. John kicked him on the bridge of his nose with his heel.

They say everyone has a plan until they're hit in the nose, and that seemed to be the case here.

Stan covered his nose with both hands, and John scooped the gun. "Next time remember Tuco's advice. 'If you have to shoot, shoot, don't talk.'." He leaned down and smashed the gun against the side of Stan's head and watched his eyes roll back.

He rolled Stan onto his front, took the duct tape he'd used to make the sheath and taped his hands, elbows and ankles.

He stood and looked down at himself, still in boxers and socks. He needed to get dressed before he hit *The Natalia*. He grabbed Paul's phone and called MacCready.

"Who's this?"

"Delacourte."

"You're still alive?"

"Just. Look, there's a guy restrained in my apartment. I'd hang around and make a statement and all that, but Petrovski has Paul and Steph. I've got to find them." He padded into his bedroom and pulled open the dresser drawers. "Purely self-defense, you understand. More than happy to make a full statement tomorrow. If I'm still alive."

"Who'd you kill this time?"

JD stopped pulling on his pants. "He's not dead. And what do you mean by "this time"?"

"You broke Grigory's neck, right? And then cut the tips off his fingers and torched him in his car."

"I broke his neck, also self-defense, but his car and his fingers were whole when we left."

"We?"

"Me. I'm not going to implicate anyone else. How'd you figure out I did it?"

"Very professional neck break. You've got a beef with his boss. If you didn't cut off the fingers, who did?"

"Don't care." He pulled a t-shirt on and winced as it slid across the cut above his ear. "Big Stan is trussed up like a turkey in my hallway. Didn't break his neck. Smashed him in the head with his gun. He's got a bit too much muscle on him for a fair fight. He might have a concussion. He's waiting for you."

He grabbed a facecloth in the bathroom and wet down the hair above his ear, wiping as much of the blood away as possible. Too much hair there for a bandage and not enough time to shave it. "I'm fine, though. Thanks for asking. Mac, if I see you again I'll tell you the whole story, right now I've got to stop Petrovski."

"That's our job."

"And a bang up job you're doing of it. Behind the curve all week." He terminated the call and slid the phone into his pocket. He stopped on the way out to look down at Stan. "I'm going to need to find a different place to live." He dug the Camaro's keys out of Stan's pocket, slid the pistol in the small of his back and left.

~~~

MacCready tossed his phone to James. "We have to go to JD's place. Call Gloria and tell her we need a crime scene crew there."

"We're looking for Petrovski, right? Isn't this a diversion?"

"Stan is there, disabled, disarmed and out of circulation. We have to attend. Even if it's only briefly." He pulled a U-turn on Biscayne Blvd. "We'll be there in ten."

"JD took out Stanislav? My estimation of him grows. That's truly impressive."

Mac shook his head and turned left. "Taking the law into his own hands."

"I'll chastise him when we get there, then buy him a bottle of scotch."

"He's not there. Or he won't be by the time we get there."

"Where's he going?"

"After Petrovski. Says we've been behind the curve all week, and I can't say he's that far wrong."

James held onto the 'holy shit' handle above the door as Mac drifted into a corner. "He's got the benefit of doing and going where he wants. We've got to follow certain steps. I envy him."

~~~

Sirens again. It seemed to John that he spent the majority of his time lately staying just ahead of the police. Reminded him a lot of high school. A bit more serious than a dime bag of weed this time, though.

He ran out the front door of his apartment building into the rain. Stan's bumblebee Camaro blocked in Hector's car, his only other mode of transport. "Right-o. Better to be lucky than good some days." He climbed behind the wheel and smiled at the sound and feel of the V-8 rumbling under the hood. "That's more like it." He revved the engine a couple of times and rolled out of the parking lot and pointed himself toward the airport and a meeting, once and for all, with the man behind the last week of crap.

Chapter Thirty-Three

Mac and James arrived at John's apartment building third or fourth in line. Black and whites clustered around the door and a SWAT team readied for their assault. Mac walked up to the Sergeant in charge. "What's with the assault team?"

"Reports of gunfire inside and we're not sure if the shooter is still there."

Mac pushed past him. "The place is clear."

"Hang on, pal, there's no way you could know that."

"I talked to the apartment owner about five minutes ago. He's gone. There's a bad guy in the apartment, disabled and restrained. You writing this down? I'm saving you guys hours of time in the rain. The mug in there works for Vladimir Petrovski, who we are currently investigating." He pushed through the front door of the apartment building and took the stairs two at a time, James and the sergeant on his heels.

"If you've just talked to him, why aren't you going after him?"

"In good time." They stepped into the apartment. Mac pointed at the shoes sticking out of the hall. "Stanislav what's-his-name."

"Gorski," offered James.

"Exactly. Roided out thug, sits at Petrovski's right hand. Well, he did. No longer." He leaned down and looked at Stan's face. "He's out like a light, just like he said. Get the paramedics in here."

"Okay, partner, where's he going next?"

"His piece of crap Honda is still in the parking lot, as is Hector's car. He's driving something else. And he'll be looking for this guy's boss. Back to *The Natalia*?"

James tapped his lips. "Probably. And Stan drove that Camaro. Yellow one. I didn't see it outside."

Mac waved a crime scene tech over. "Check this guy for car keys."

The gloved tech patted Stan's pockets and shook his head. "Nothing."

"Okay, to *The Natalia* and on the lookout for a yellow Camaro."

James shook his head as they walked out. "He's right, you know."

"What?"

"Delacourte's right. We've been a step, at least, behind the curve all week."

"Lights and siren, maybe we catch a break."

~~~

John hydroplaned to a stop in front of *The Natalia*. He slammed the car door and jogged through the rain to the entrance. The security under the awning at the front door held out his hand for him to stop and John drove the inside edge of his right hand into the beefy Slav's throat and followed through with an elbow to the side of his head.

He barely broke his stride, pushing open the door as he slipped the gun from his belt. He pushed the barrel under the jaw of the first guy he saw. "Petrovski. Take me to him."

"He's not here."

John cocked the gun. "No bullshit. I need to see him now."

The bartender moved from behind his counter with a shotgun. "You don't want to be doing this, son."

John pulled the man in front of him, grip tight just above his elbow and pushed the pistol even harder under his jaw. "Shoot us both, if you want, but you might want to tell Petrovski that I'm here, first. Let him know that Stan is out of the picture, and he's next."

"You suicidal?"

"Not generally, but I've had better days." He pushed the man toward the shotgun-wielding bartender. "Is he in the back? These guys usually have an office in the back. I need to see him."

"It's not going to happen, buddy. First of all, there's no way I'm going to let you back there without his permission and second, he's not here to give you that permission." He shouldered the shotgun. "I'm in no mood for cops today and I'm a little shorthanded with muscle, so why don't you fuck off out of here."

John looked at the bartender and then around the club. No dancers on the stages and only one customer at a table, a fat guy with no aura of threat around him. "So if he's not here, where is he?"

The bartender took another step forward, nestling the stock into his shoulder. "Get the fuck out, son, before I change my mind."

John nodded. "You're just delaying the inevitable, but okay." He backed out, pistol still firmly wedged under the shield's jaw and a strong grip on the pressure point just above his elbow. "I'll be seeing you all later."

He stepped out into the weather. The security still laid flat on his back, unconscious. He pushed his human shield into the bushes around the door and got back in the car. He wiped the water from his face and slammed the steering wheel. "Where in the hell are you?"

He started the car and pulled away from the club as the bartender came out, shotgun over his shoulder. He stood under the awning, watching him, as John left the lot.

Intelligence. He needed intelligence. He called Rico back. "Buddy, I need your help."

"Sax man. What's happening? You find Petrovski?"

"No such luck. He's got Paul and Stephanie and he's taking them somewhere to kill."

"I don't think so. The Russian is almost anal about not getting his hands dirty."

"He got his hands dirty a week ago, and that's what started all this shit. He's got Paul and Stephanie with him. And he's not at his club. Call me crazy, but I don't think he's going to take that kind of mess to his house, wherever that is."

"You're not crazy. You've been at *The Natalia*?"

"Just left. I don't think I'm welcome back."

"Right. So if he isn't there and he has a couple of bodies to dispose of he'd be going to the Everglades. But doing that in this weather is insane."

"Is he sane?" JD turned south on Brickell. "I don't think he's sane."

"Good point. He's got this thing. He loves dumping his trash at the same place every time. Has his guys go back to the same location. It's just west of Gator Hammock. You're going to need a good set of charts -"

"I know where it is," interrupted JD. "Been there a couple of times already. Hector's going to be pissed when I don't show up with his car."

"I wouldn't worry about Hector. Wherever Petrovski is, Stan is. I'd be worried about him."

"No need. He won't be bothering anybody again. If MacCready's on the ball, Stan is in custody now."

"Okay, you really need to be careful. When Petrovski finds out you took out Stan he's going to let you bleed out in the Everglades. There are 17-foot pythons in that water. Watch your back, sax man."

~~~

Rico hung up the phone. "Holy fuck."

Simon stopped his beer halfway to his mouth. "What?"

"That sax player has giant, pendulous elephant balls." He pushed his chair back. John's call had interrupted an early dinner with Simon, his daughter and her boyfriend, Barry. "Sorry, Izzy."

Simon finished his drink. "He really got rid of Stan?"

"That's what he said. Heading to the Everglades for a face-off with Petrovski."

"I can go and help him."

"No, Simon, you stay right here." Rico tapped the table with his finger, thinking. "I don't want anyone associated with me or my organization involved in this." He chewed on a mouthful of pasta. "But there may be a way. Call your brother. Petrovski is on his way to a place just west of Gator Hammock. If your brother gets good charts he can find it. Hopefully there's enough time."

Simon pushed back for the table. "I need to do this with some privacy. He needs to think I'm sneaking him some info. Wouldn't do to have you drunks laughing in the background."

Simon walked to the far corner of the nearly empty restaurant. He flinched as a clap of thunder rattled the windows. "What a day." He dialed his brother's mobile.

"MacCready."

"Me too, brother. You out in this shit?"

"Kinda busy Simon. What's up?"

"Passing on some info that may be germane to whatever you may be working on." A bright flash preceded almost immediately a sharp clap of thunder and the lights in the restaurant went out. "Great. Just lost power."

"Speak up, Simon. Can't hear you over the rain."

"Petrovski is heading to the Everglades. There's a favorite place of his just west of Gator Hammock. He's got Coates and Stephanie Peters with him. And there's a guy chasing him. That Delacourte guy."

"Gator Hammock? Do you know where exactly that is?"

"Sorry, bro, that's all I've got. Stay safe." Simon hung up and turned back to the table on the far side of the restaurant. Candles lit the occupants, even though it was still just late afternoon. "Great. All romantic and shit and my date is Rico."

~~~

Petrovski held the gun tighter, the grip slick from sweat. Sven pulled into the parking lot beside a beat up Toyota. "It looks like he's closing up."

Petrovski shook his head. "Go tell Hector I need a boat, and I need it now and I won't be taking no for an answer. Then hurry back here and help me prepare these two."

He smiled at the two in the back seat. "End of the line for you. Touching family scene."

"Why don't you just shoot us? Why are you going through all of this? You could have killed us hours ago." The rain and thunder almost drowned out Stephanie's.

"The personal touch. And to symbolically put you," he pointed at Coates, "where you belong." He shrugged. "You, missy, are just in wrong place at wrong time. But I can't risk leaving you alive. There's too much at stake. With the sax player gone, and you two alligator food, or maybe python food, I can get back to business. I've had enough distractions this past week to drive a normal man insane. But I'm not normal."

"You sure as hell aren't." Coates spit at him. "You're a psychopathic bastard."

Petrovski wiped the spit off his face with his sleeve. "Extra-slow death for you." He waved his gun at them. "Both of you out. On his side."

Paul Coates climbed out and turned to help Stephanie. They stood in the pounding rain, the temperature now cooling in the late afternoon. Wind drove the rain almost horizontally, forcing them to lean against the car for support.

Sven ran back from the shop, leaning into the wind. "Hector says, and I quote, if you take a boat out and die, it's on your head. He also said not to bother with the paperwork since it doesn't really matter anymore anyway."

"What's that supposed to mean?"

"He's in a pissy mood. He's collecting the chains to lock the rest of them up for the night. I'll wait in the car, okay?"

"Help me with these two first. Get some duct tape and do their hands behind them."

Sven produced a roll of tape and stood them facing the car while Petrovski held his gun on them. "Hands behind your back, you two." He taped the girl's first with a smile on his face.

"You enjoying yourself, Sven?"

"More fun than I've had in weeks."

"Hurry up."

"All done."

"Good. To the boat then tie them to the frame."

The wind pushed them down the wharf, forcing them to lean back to support themselves. Petrovski poked Coates in the back with his gun. "Faster."

Sven braced himself against the wind. "Fucking hell, man. You really think this is a good idea? You know how to fly one of these things, right? Because I'm not going out in this weather. I'm not *that* crazy."

"I want you to stay with the car. If anyone other than me comes out of the marsh, shoot them between the eyes. Don't ask them what happened. Just shoot them."

"I can do that."

They came alongside the airboat at the end of the wharf. Whitecaps ripped across the top of the shallow water, rocking the boats like a hydraulically enhanced low-rider.

Sven tied a rope at the wrists and then to the frame of the boat for both of them, giving them about six feet slack. "That good boss?"

"Yeah. Give me a knife. I'll have to cut them loose after I kill them."

Sven pulled a folding knife out of a sheath on his belt. "This is a Swede 10. Cost me a hundred bucks. Don't drop it, okay? It's my favorite."

"I'll buy you a new one if I do. Start the boat. Push that button on the back."

Sven poked the ignition switch as Petrovski climbed onto the pilot's seat. Stephanie and Paul sat huddled from the rain on the deck. Petrovski smiled. Making them wait until their death, them knowing they were going to die, was more than suitable punishment for the shit they'd put him through.

Sven yelled over the combined noise of the storm and the boat. "You know where you're going, boss?"

Petrovski nodded and smiled and accelerated into the dark and stormy night.

Chapter Thirty-Four

The Camaro's throaty roar carried across the flat landscape in the brief lulls in the storm. Sven smiled. He recognized the car's sound. He helped Stan work on the engine after he "inherited" it from Carl.

Good. He'd have some company. Maybe Stan would share a drink or two with him. At least he'd have someone to talk with.

The roar drew closer and Sven saw the yellow Camaro turn into the parking lot.

The streams of rain running down the car's window distorted his view as the Camaro approached and slowed beside him. The tracks of water made the car look like a reflection in a funhouse mirror. The distortion masked the driver also. He cocked his head and squinted and was struck with a major case of cognitive dissonance. Stan's car idled into the parking lot. Stan never allowed anyone else to drive his car, a fact he made plainly and painfully clear to any young up and comer who made the mistake of even sitting in the driver's seat

Yet the face behind the wheel wasn't Stans's. He rolled down the window to see better. "Hey, you. What the he -"

His breath caught as a muzzle lifted up above the window line.

345

~~~

John looked at the guy behind the wheel of Petrovski's C300. "Sorry, buddy. No time to talk. Don't have the energy for an argument. Get both of your hands out of the window, now."

He waited until he could see both hands, then got out of the Camaro. "Open the car door from the outside and get out slowly." He stood back. "What's your name?"

"Sven. You going to kill me?"

"Tired of killing people, Sven. It's your lucky day. Start walking home."

"What?"

John fired a shot into the ground at Sven's feet, spitting gravel into the side of the car and Sven's shins. "Walk. Now, or you'll have to walk with a hole in your foot."

Sven sidestepped toward the road. "The rain. It's bucketing down."

"So you shouldn't overheat. Start running now."

Sven started up the road, slowly jogging and looking over his shoulder. John fired another shot into the ground near his feet. "Faster." He watched him pick up the pace into the rain.

Flashes of light and cracks of thunder were so frequent now JD found it impossible to tell which lightning triggered which thunder. The storm surrounded him.

He ran down the wharf. Chains and padlocks through the fan housing of every boat stopped him. If he started the boat, any boat,

346

the fan blades would disintegrate in seconds. "Hector, you son of a bitch."

He ran back up the wharf and up the stairs to the store. He hammered on the locked door, then ran around to the back. The door was slightly open. He stepped in and met a shotgun muzzle to the neck. "Hey, be careful with that thing. You could kill someone."

Hector lifted the shotgun. "You."

"Me. I need a boat."

"You wreck my boats. Where's my car? I need to get home."

"Your car? It's at my apartment. I'll give you the address." He reached into his pocket. "Here's the keys."

"How'd you get here?"

"Took Stan's car. He didn't need it anymore."

"Really?" Hector placed the shotgun in the rack on the wall.

"Absolutely. I need a boat, Hector."

"I've already locked everything up. And this storm is the absolutely wrong time to go out. The only time worse would be during a hurricane."

"Petrovski's out there with two of my friends. He's planning on being the only one coming back. If I can't get to him in time to stop him from killing my friends, at least I can make sure he stays out there with them."

"I didn't think Petrovski had anyone with him."

"What do you think he came out here for? Seriously? In this weather? I don't pretend to understand the total fucked up brain that would make a guy take bodies out to the same place to kill them, but that's what he's doing."

Hector's shoulder's slumped. "You really took care of Stan?"

"Really did. Is he a good friend?"

"God, no. Despised that asshole. I hope it was painful. I held out hope when you were beating on him out back that you'd finish him then."

"This catch-up is great and all, but I need a boat."

"He left a guy waiting down by the wharf, like a sentinel."

John shook his head.

"Him too?"

"Didn't kill him. Sent him on a long walk home." He looked at the tools in the shop. "The key Hector, or I'll take these bolt cutters and get rid of the lock myself.

"It's hardened steel."

"The chain isn't. I'm going one way or the other. Help me."

Hector tossed him a ring of keys. "Give me the keys to Stan's car so I can get home."

"No can do, buddy. But Petrovski's not going to need his after tonight. The keys are still in it."

Hector grimaced. "You don't kill Petrovski, he's going to kill me if I do that."

"You don't worry about the Russian. He's mine."

John jogged back out to the wharf and spooled through the keys until he found the right one for the padlock. He tossed the chain on the wharf with the keys and started the airboat.

As soon as he untied it the wind started blowing him and the boat west. He adjusted the direction slightly south and opened the throttle. He over-steered, fighting against the strong tail wind. And as the prow bounced of the white caps he thought he was going to lose his teeth. The storm and heavy clouds made visibility like twilight. The strobe of lightning and occasional breaks in the rain kept him from colliding with submerged logs twice and then with a smaller hammock only a few minutes into the ride. He swerved north around it and tried to compensate by pointing the boat slightly south of where he should aim. He piloted into the heart of the storm, lightning striking repeatedly around him.

Like a sitting duck.

~~~

"Where are we going to get charts?" MacCready had already realigned the car south.

"No need. I'll make a call. Cruz will help *us* this time."

"He's going to tell Petrovski."

"Maybe. It'll be instructive if he does." He stuffed the bud in his ear to overcome the rain noise. "Cruz? Where are you?"

"Who is this?"

"James. Special Agent Stephen James. Are you near a computer?"

"I'm home. The power is out."

"Shit. I need mapping info. Can you head to the station and give me a call when you get there. Critical. Life and death."

Mac leaned close. "Put it on speaker."

James pulled the headphone out and popped it on speaker.

"Cruz," yelled Mac, "this is number one priority. Get to the station and find out where in the Everglades Gator Hammock is. It'll be almost due west of Kendall."

"Hey Cruz, James here again. Find the location then email it to us, okay? We can find it on our smartphones, but it'll be a lot faster if you do it. Need it in the next fifteen to twenty minutes. Very urgent."

They heard him grumble something about overtime before James hung up. "What do you think, Mac?"

"I think you better start looking for that damned place on your phone, just in case."

"No, I mean do you think he's going to let Petrovski know we asked for this."

"Maybe. But Petrovski is allegedly out in this storm. Not sure how successful he's going to be reaching him. It's a risk we have to take. No other options at this point."

"Yeah, nothing we can do about it now."

James opened the mapping app on his phone and scrolled to Kendall, southwest of them. He zoomed and panned until he found Hector's launch. "Found the wharf. It's about twenty minutes from here."

"Almost due west of there, I don't know, a couple of miles should be Gator Hammock."

"Shit."

"What?"

"Only three of them are labeled. None of them Gator."

"Okay, we got the general area, we rely on Cruz for the rest."

~~~

Mario ran from his car to the station and waved at the desk Sergeant as he climbed the stairs to the squad room, shaking rain off his jacket. His phone rang. He looked at the display and directed it to voicemail. His wife had called him three times in the last five minutes and he knew what she wanted, so there was no point in answering. He'd stay out late. She'd be asleep before he got back.

He logged onto the internet, selected the departmentally approved mapping program and searched for Kendall. He panned west of that and looked around the squad room. Skeleton staff. He opened his burner phone, calling the only number he ever called on it and held it to his head while he searched for Gator Hammock.

It rang out to voicemail.

He sent Petrovski a text message. "Cops on their way to where you are, if you're out by Gator Hammock. I'll give them bad directions to buy you time."

He closed his phone and hovered the mouse over Gator Hammock, clearly marked on the map.

He moved the mouse to a mile and a half west of their desired destination, right-clicked and selected "share".

~~~

James phone blurped with an incoming message. "Huh. Cruz has come through." He clicked the link and waited for it to resolve on his mapping program. "Or maybe not."

"What's up?"

"He says in the email that this link is to Gator Hammock, but it ends up pointing at Poinciana Hammock."

"When we get back from this I'm going to punch that asshole in the neck."

"I'll hold him."

"So we're flying blind." Mac turned west on Tamiami Trail.

"It is what it is."

"Getting tired of hearing that, James."

"Sorry, partner, but, you know, that's what it is."

~~~

The wind shifted. The steady push now came from his right, sliding him south. John adjusted the steering lever slightly to compensate for the crosswind and pressed harder on the throttle, a wasted effort as the airboat was moving as fast as it could.

In the very brief respites from the rain, the landscape changed just enough to make him question his confidence.

The wind shifted again, coming around to his front, messing with his sense of direction. Especially with the airboat's bullshit steering system. But the hammock ahead of him got closer, and the one behind him receded. His wake was still in a straight line, relatively, although it disappeared quickly in the high wind.

He snuck a look at Paul's phone. It was after 5:00. There were still two hours of daylight, but the low, heavy clouds darkened the sky. He wiped the rain off the phone and slid it back into his pocket realizing as he did the futility of his actions. Rain and swamp water soaked his shirt and pants and he doubted that he'd ever be dry again.

He passed another hammock; a smallish tear-shaped raised island in the Everglades, populated with hardwood, mostly mahogany and oak. As he passed the northern tip, he squinted through the swirling rain. An airboat had stopped about a mile ahead, right on the southern tip of another hammock. He must have drifted farther south than he intended. He planned on coming in on Petrovski's blind side. He pulled the lever back hard and veered right, north, getting the stand of trees between him and the airboat. It looked like three on the airboat. Three tiny specs. He couldn't tell if all of them were alive, but there were three.

It might not yet be too late.

~~~

Mac turned left onto SW 187. "Call Patrol and let him know we're going to need some black and whites at the boat launch."

"Expecting trouble?"

"Petrovski wouldn't have gone there on his own. He's going to have muscle and we need to get them out of the way."

"How far away are we?"

"Twenty minutes, max. Get them moving."

Chapter Thirty-Five

Petrovski looked around at his surroundings, getting his bearings. This was it. About 20 yards to the west of Gator Hammock. "We're here." He braced himself against the wind from the west.

Stephanie continued to struggle against the tape. "You're a sick fuck."

"Shut up." He eased off on the throttle and flinched as a flash of lightning barked a clap of thunder less than a second later. He looked up at the sky. "That was close."

"And you're the tallest guy around."

Petrovski pointed at the stand of trees to their east. "I'm not a complete idiot. Lightning will hit those trees first." He pulled the .22 from the back of his pants. "I used this to kill Sergei, and now I'm going to use it to kill you, too."

Coates chewed the inside of his mouth. "The cops assumed you tossed that in the water."

Petrovski examined the handgun. "No, I like this. Small. Compact, even. Does a fantastic job up close. Not too loud. Although the noise won't be an issue today. I only wish I could have killed your sax player with this too."

355

"So he isn't dead?"

"Stan had that pleasure."

Stephanie visibly slumped, her shoulders dropping. She fell to one side, onto her shoulder, then rolled to her front, her hands still bound behind her.

He grabbed her by the hair and lifted her head. "You should watch this. I'm going to make him suffer. Teach him to stick his nose in where he shouldn't. Did you hear they picked up a seventeen-foot Burmese python in here about a month or so ago? Seventeen foot. What I wouldn't do to watch that thing take him. While he breathes."

"You can't be my mother's brother. You must have been adopted."

"No, sweetie, I'm just the only one true to myself. Your mother could be a vicious bitch when she wanted to. But out of respect for family, I'll make sure you go fast. Shot to the head. Almost immediate death." He held up the pistol. "With this thing the bullet won't even leave your skull so the funeral can be open casket." He grimaced. "Oh, I almost forgot. The alligators. Or pythons. Maybe no open casket after all." He squatted beside her. "You know your mother and I never got along."

"She only spoke the worst of you."

He pressed the muzzled lightly between her eyes and slowly dragged it down to the end of her nose, giving it a tap before he stood. A wave caught the boat and he had to steady himself by holding on to the raised seat. "I do apologize for the inclement weather, but this really could not wait until tomorrow. I'm firmly in the anti-procrastination camp."

Coates grunted. "Lucky for us."

"Yes it is. No spending the night terrified about the fate that awaits you." He wiped the rain from his face. "And I can go home tonight, comforted by the fact the only person who held any threat over me is dead."

~~~

Paul Coates reviewed his life to date and while he didn't regret any of his actions, he realized there were plenty of times he looked the other way for convenience. His decision to go against that ingrained belief put him in his current predicament, but he sincerely doubted he'd have done anything differently, given the chance again.

Stan cracked one of the bones in his forearm when he shot him, but the rain had washed away the blood and the flow had been staunched, Mother Nature doing its best to keep as much of the precious fluid contained to his body as possible.

Not that he would be needing it much longer, it would appear.

He used his elbow for support and pushed himself to his feet, spreading his legs against the wind and the rocking deck. "Petrovski, I'm not going to beg with you for my life. Do what you have to do, but let her go. She's innocent of anything, except being in the wrong place at the wrong time. And she's family, for Christ's sake."

"Sit back down on the deck of the boat."

"Or what, you'll shoot me? You're going to do that anyway."

He saw the swing coming a mile away, but the rocking boat threw his timing off and he ducked into the hit. Petrovski caught him with a glancing blow under the left eye with the butt of the gun. The momentum of the swing, combined with another wave and a slippery deck tipped Petrovski over the side and into the marsh.

Coates fell to his knees and tucked his bashed cheek into his left shoulder, squinting through the rain with his right eye. "Fuck, yeah. See that Steph? In the drink."

He stopped chuckling as the Russian pulled himself out of the shallow water, covered in mud and marsh grass. "Son of a bitch." He took a long stride forward and kicked Coates in the ribs. "Stay there until I tell you it's okay to die."

~~~

John drifted along the east side of Gator Hammock. The teardrop-shaped island ran northeast to southwest, no more than 300 yards long and barely 100 yards wide at its widest, twenty at its narrowest, the southernmost tip. He could see Petrovski through the trees on the other side. The wind pushed the Russian's airboat toward the hammock.

John saw the smash to Paul's face and Petrovski's resultant fall into the water. "Beautiful." He applied throttle and swung around the southern tip of the hammock, taking a bead on Petrovski's boat.

The wind whipped his face, and the rain seemed to crank up a level. He saw Petrovski, standing on his airboat, stance wide against the wind and the waves, Paul and Stephanie on their knees in front of him. The Russian wiped the muddy water from his face, pistol at arm's length pointed at the top of Paul's head.

"No," he yelled, but the wind and rain and thunder took his voice and threw it back at him. He sideswiped Petrovski's boat as the mobster shot, hitting Paul off-center. He watched the body fall into the shallow swampy water and Petrovski fall to his knees. The Russian scrambled to his feet, looked at John turning his boat and faced Stephanie. John saw him smile and say something and she closed her eyes.

He approached from less than fifteen feet away and closed fast. Petrovski lifted his head and looked at him just before the collision.

John jumped before impact and landed in waist-deep water a few feet from his boat. Petrovski fell off the edge of his, backward.

John grabbed Stephanie. "Get over on my boat and get the hell out of here now."

"I'm tied. I can't." She showed him her hands behind her back.

"Okay, stay here and stay down."

Paul floated face down in the water. He rolled him over and ducked as a shot hit the water beside them. "Shit." He lifted Paul onto the airboat. He bled from his right forearm and left shoulder. "Steph, stay down and keep him from rolling off."

Petrovski had pulled himself onto the airboat John had piloted and stood on the deck, bracing against the wind and the rain. The storm was neutral; it attacked everyone equally. Clusters of lightning crackled to the west and the thunder sounded a steady bowel shaking roll. John glanced at Stephanie and Paul - she held on to him and he appeared to be barely conscious.

He pushed through the water, at times almost up to his waist, keeping his gun trained on Petrovski. The Russian looked between the threat approaching him and the two targets on the boat, about ten feet away and slowly drifting toward him.

John had to yell above the thunder and the wind. "Don't try it Petrovski. Drop the gun before I shoot you." Petrovski turned his gun on John and staggered to a knee as another gust rocked the airboat. He took a shot but missed. John didn't know if it was the wind, the rain in his eyes or the sting in his ear that threw off his shot, but he didn't care. He leveled the gun he liberated from Stan and squeezed off a shot at Petrovski.

The slide stayed back. Last shot.

"Fuck." He scrambled toward the boat as Petrovski grabbed at his right arm and staggered against the raised pilot's seat. As John climbed onto the boat, the Russian switched his handgun to his left hand. He raised it at the charging John. Another close lightning strike caused them both to flinch. John thought he saw a flash from the barrel of the .22, but he couldn't hear it above the thunder.

He felt the sting, though, as the lead grazed his shoulder. "We're both not doing well in the shooting department." He pushed Petrovski's gun hand to one side and grabbed him by the throat. "Not so tough now, comrade."

Petrovski smiled.

"What's so funny?"

The Russian dropped his gun and slid a knife out of his back pocket, flicked it open and slashed at John.

He jumped back and fought to keep his balance on the shifting, slippery aluminum deck. "Son of a bitch. You assholes and your knives. That's dangerous, pal."

Petrovski advanced on him, swiping the knife left and right. "I cut you couple of times and leave you out here. Just like I am going to do to your to friends. I take it by your presence that Stan is no longer?"

John jumped back again, at the edge of the boat. "Stan's kinda tied up right now, and the schmuck you left at the wharf has gone for a jog."

A triple strike of lightning, less than a mile to their west, ignited the damp grass. Flames and smoke, fanned by the wind spread north and south and started coming toward them.

Petrovski smiled again. "Running out of time." He swung the knife at John again. As he reached across his body, John stormed him, pinning the knife arm against the Russian.

"You're right, comrade. No time left at all for you." He hit him under the chin with the heel of his hand, snapping the Russian's head back into the boat's fan housing. He heard the crack and watched Petrovski's eyes roll back.

John picked up the small .22 caliber handgun and looked back to Stephanie and Paul. They were both lying flat on the boat. A wall of flame and smoke approached with alarming speed, whipped by the wind and fueled by the marsh grass.

~~~

MacCready and James stopped at the wharf. The wind blew stronger, but the rain had eased off. Mac pointed at the yellow Camaro, the only car in the lot. "That's Stan's, right?"

James nodded. "Looks like it. But Stan is out of commission, so that means the sax player is here."

"And where's the Russian's car?"

"Been and gone? This doesn't look good. The shop's shut down too, so no Hector." James got out of the car and braced himself against the wind.

Fire lit the horizon, cutting through the rain. "How's it do that?" James pointed at the fire line.

"What?"

"Burn when it's pissing rain. You'd think the rain would put out the fire."

"It's a really hot fire. Multiple lightning strikes in the same vicinity." Mac looked at his watch. "What time are the black and whites supposed to show up?"

"Any minute now. We need to get out there and see if MacCready or Petrovski or the others are out there."

Mac nodded. They ran out on the wharf. "They're all locked. Track down Hector and call him back here."

"No time for that, Mac."

"Yeah, you're right. Keys might be inside."

They ran back up the wharf to the boat shop. Mac elbowed the glass and reached in and opened the door. An alarm went off inside. "Great, maybe those black and whites will step on it."

James followed him in. "Check the counter for keys. I'll look for a tool."

"Fuck the keys." Mac grabbed the bolt cutters off the wall. "I've found the master key."

~~~

John crawled on the airboat. Smoke billowed around them. "We've got to get out of here, kids."

Stephanie looked up. "Is he gone?"

John nodded. "Don't worry about him. He's out. If he survives this, I've got the gun he used to kill Sergei. He's no longer a threat. Hurry. We've got to get out of here. How's Paul?"

"I hurt like a son of a bitch, but I'll live unless this fire gets us."

"Yeah." John reached around the back of the airboat and pressed the ignition button. The boat sputtered twice and then caught.

Stephanie cried with relief. "Let's get home."

"We're not clear yet. That fire is coming at us pretty quickly. Hang on. This isn't going to be a comfy ride."

~~~

"You ever ride one of these?"

"I'm from Jersey. When would I have had the chance to ride one of these?"

Mac pulled the chain through the housing and tossed it on the wharf, beside the other one. "Just asking. I'm a little rusty. Starts with a switch on the back. Find it and give it a poke."

"Hang on. I'll be right back."

"What are you doing?"

James yelled over his should as he ran to the shop. "Thirty seconds."

Mac grunted and climbed off the pilot's seat and reached around the back and started the boat. "What the hell is he doing?"

James ran back down the wharf, two heavy-duty flashlights in his hands. "It's getting dark. The boats don't have lights. We're going to need these. You can thank me later." He jumped on the boat. "How fast do these things go?"

"We'll find out. Hold on." He opened the throttle and headed west into the Everglades.

James turned on both lights and started sweeping the beams across the marshland in front of them. "Hang on, Mac. Look at that." He held the beam on an approaching airboat. "Head back to the wharf now."

Mac slowed and turned, and slid up against the dock. They both jumped off and James tied down the boat.

They steadied John's boat as he stepped off and stood face to face with MacCready. "Still behind the curve, Detective."

"Where's Petrovski?"

John jerked his thumb over his shoulder. "Out there, somewhere." He handed MacCready the handgun. "This is his. Said he shot Sergei with it. Might be useful. Help me with Steph and Paul. Paul iss injured. He's going to need medical help."

"Hang on a second. You killed Grigory, you took out Stanislav - we saw that first hand - and now you say you've killed Petrovski? You've completely dismantled a criminal organization we've been trying to bring down for the last year."

John smiled. "I didn't kill Petrovski. Just subdued him." He looked out at the fire. "But I doubt that he'll survive this." He looked at MacCready and James. "You're welcome." He held out his hand. "Knife?"

Mac handed him a folding knife and followed him to the boat. "Self-defense for all of them, right?"

"That's my story and I'm sticking to it."

"We're going to have to investigate this, Mr. Delacourte. If you've broken any laws I'm afraid we're going to have to charge you."

"Are you going to arrest me tonight?"

Mac shook his head. "We know where you live."

"Good. Paul has at least a shattered ulna and a nasty shot to his shoulder. Maybe a cracked cheekbone. Hard to tell. Stephanie's in a bit of shock and I'm starving. I'll talk to you guys later."

Chapter Thirty-Six

Paul Coates, arm in a cast, stood at the mic. "Welcome, folks, to one of the hottest jazz bands in South Florida, Stephanie Peters and the Paul Coates Quartet. On drums, sitting in until my arm heals, is Larry. He's praying I never get better. This is the best gig he's ever had. Our resident Canadian, Ned, is tinkling the ivories, and craps his pants every time the cops show up. He won't say why, but I think he's an illegal alien.

"Big man Henry thought that was a fiddle when he bought it, and he could probably play it like one, but today he's playing it like it was meant to be played, upright.

"Johnny D, the Sax Machine is on sax. Mr. Delacourte is the newest member of this motley crew if you exclude the stand-in on drums, but he's a rock solid member, without whom we wouldn't be here tonight. Long story I might tell someone someday.

"Finally, with a voice I've heard described as Bailey's poured on velvet and wrapped in moss is my lovely daughter, Stephanie Peters.

"Ladies and gents, it's been over a month since we last played. We're a bit rusty, so bear with us."

Coates slid the microphone back in the stand and sat at a front table. He lifted his glass of with lemon infused sparkling water, saluted his band and took a deep breath. Back in the saddle. The band played well.

Someone sat beside him at the table. "Good to be back?"

Coates looked over and smiled. "Rico. You fat fuck. What brings you out of your hole?"

"Your daughter's exquisite voice." He waved for a beer. "Your drumming too, but I guess that'll have to wait for a while. When will it be good?"

"Another couple of weeks they say."

"I have to thank you."

Coates sipped his drink and looked warily at Rico. "Why?"

"For the past month I've been successfully and rapidly expanding my territory, taking Petrovski's business almost at will. His organization was decimated."

"That wasn't the plan."

Rico shrugged. "Maybe not, but that's the end result." He pointed at John. "Word has it, the little guy did all the damage."

"Word has it?"

"Through the grapevine. You know." He pulled on his beer.

"I had no idea before all of this you were mobbed up."

"Seriously? Are you blind?"

"Naive, I think."

"Does that mean you'll stop coming to my joint for lunch? I haven't seen you guys for almost a month."

"Nah, your food's too good to pass up. We've been on a bit of a hiatus. Taking a break. Getting our heads back together." He held up his cast. "Had a bit of a rough time, if you recall."

"The grapevine also tells me you and your singer were knees down on an air boat with Petrovski ready to finish you both."

"The grapevine again?"

"Such as it is. Is it true?"

Paul sipped his drink and laughed. He leaned back as a server left a plate of stuffed potato skins on the table. "That falls into the 'alleged' category, Rico. Surely your grapevine made that clear."

Rico chewed the inside of his mouth and stared at Paul for a good minute. "You guys accomplished in a week what I've been trying to do for a year. I'll forever be in your debt."

"No, no, no. We didn't do anything for you. We were just trying to stay alive."

"No matter." He tapped on the table. "You got contingency plans?"

"For what?"

"If the little guy takes the fall for this, you're going to need another sax player. And since my grapevine says he was instrumental, if you'll excuse the pun, I can't see him not taking the fall." He looked toward the door. "And that's my cue. Catch you guys later. Your daughter has an incredible voice. I'm glad she didn't quit."

He stood and finished his beer. "Thanks for the drink. Come by my place when you're finished. Everything's on the house."

Paul grunted and turned back to the band. Stephanie sang *Ochi Chernye*, a Russian jazz standard. "Dark Eyes". He smiled at the irony of, not a month ago, almost being killed by a Russian mobster and now the song that brought the house down was a Russian tune.

He had a potato skin in his hand, stuffed with cheese, chives, chunks of bacon and a slather of sour cream, and his mouth open, when someone else sat beside him. Two someone else's. "Ah, if it isn't Special Agent Stephen James. And his sidekick, Detective MacCready."

Mac tapped on the tabled with his forefinger. "Hey, he's the sidekick. How are you doing, Paul? Arm healing up okay?"

"Just fine, thanks. What are you here for?"

"Want to have a chat with you, and Stephanie and Mr. Delacourte."

"We're in the middle of a set, boys. You want us to break it down now, or can you wait?"

"How long?" James looked at his watch.

"Steph finishes this song then there's an instrumental, non-vocal tune to close it out."

"Okay, just a couple of songs then."

"Not much more than one. Steph's almost finished."

She wrapped it up to rapturous applause, thanked the crowd and came and sat with Paul. "What are the coppers here for, Paul?" She sounded just like a moll from the 1920s.

MacCready laughed. "You've got a great voice. How are you doing Miss Peters?"

"Fantastic. What about you two?"

"I'm good. What about you, James? You good, too?"

"Bloody fantastic."

Mac leaned forward, as if sharing a secret. "He's seeing a British girl. He's added some really strange slang to his vocabulary."

James leaned back and fixed Paul with a stare. "We've come to a point where we need to close off a few things about the Petrovski incident."

"Incident?" Paul held up his cast. "A bit more than an incident."

"Vladimir Petrovski, Stanislav Gorski, and Grigory Belov, collectively, are being referred to as the Petrovski incident. Perhaps it would be better if we waited until Mr. Delacourte finishes this song and joins us ."

Stephanie pointed over her shoulder at the band. "This song? It never ends, gentlemen. They'll feed off each other for hours, if we let them. Just becomes a killer jam session."

"We don't have that long. Any way you can signal him to keep it down to regulation length?"

"Minimum five minutes."

"It'll have to do."

She turned and caught John's eye and held up five fingers and gave him the wrap up signal, her index finger describing circles. He nodded and continued playing.

"Okay, coppers. What do you want from us?" She held out her hands, wrists up and touching. "You gonna cuff me?"

"Not as yet. But who knows what the future may bring." Mac smiled at her. "Any nightmares?"

"Only about you guys, not the bad guys." Paul saw a twinkle in her eyes. She was winding them up. "Actually, in one of the nightmares the bad guys rescue me from you guys."

Mac pulled his cuffs from his belt. "Maybe we do need to detain you, Miss Peters. It appears you may be under a bad influence." Mac stopped when he saw the look in her eyes. "I'm just messing with you, now. Relax. And I apologize."

"Not funny. What's the deal? We talked to you guys for almost three days straight, together and separately, then we hear nothing from you for over three weeks."

"Weren't you guys out of town? R&R? Coates told us you guys were all taking a much needed break." Mac looked at his partner. "Isn't that true?"

James nodded. "And that worked great for us. Gave us some space to investigate the hell out of this." He nodded at the band. "Here comes number three."

John parked his sax and came over to the table. Coates saw the concern in his eyes. He pulled out a chair. "Sit here, Johnny. The nice men want to talk to us."

John shook both Mac's and James's hand. "Gentlemen. What's new?"

"We're wrapping up some loose ends. By my count, there's assault against both Grigory and Stan, and murder of Grigory, assault again on Stan and, well, we're not sure what happened to Petrovski in the 'glades. He hasn't been seen since then." MacCready looked up. "You're a very resourceful man, Mr. Delacourte. Extremely resourceful."

"I don't understand what you're saying."

"Are you denying what I just said?"

"We talked about this for days, Detective. I don't deny it. How could I deny it? I admitted it to you up front. It was self-defense, every bit of it."

"For the fight, we've got Hector, the airboat guy as a witness. I've got his statement that you were attacked, and given that Stan and Grigory combined are triple your weight in muscle, we kinda believe that you wouldn't have started that one.

"Stan's subsequent beating, Grigor's death, I've got no witnesses. I'm more than willing to concede on the second Stan beating, though, since he showed up at your place and with the recent history you had with him. Petrovski, well, these other two were there, but they both claim they can't remember a thing. Pops was knocked out and girlie was hiding her head."

"I object to that sexist characterization."

"Fair enough. *Miss Peters* was hiding her head."

"I was. It was scary out there."

MacCready threw his hands up in despair. "There you have it."

Coates shook his head. "Have what?"

"No case. At least not one we would have a hope of proving. It was evident from the beginning actually, which is why we never formally pressed charges. No case. Stanislav is in the hospital still, under guard, charged with a multitude of crimes. He's not saying anything about the fight he had with you. And Petrovski has never been found. The airboat showed up, charred, but not him. The gun you gave us conclusively ties him to Sergei's death. His prints were on the outside of the gun and the magazine and ballistics matched it to the bullet in the kid's head."

"So this is all over?"

"Completely." MacCready smiled. "Now if you'll excuse us, we've got to go. You sounded great tonight. We'll probably bump into each other again."

Paul, John and Steph watched Mac and his sidekick leave. Stephanie threaded her fingers through John's. "Next time my dad wants to go hunting alligators, sit on him will you?"

Playlist

The Coates Quintet - sorry, Stephanie Peters and the Coates Quartet - played some very good tunes during the course of this book. Links are below:

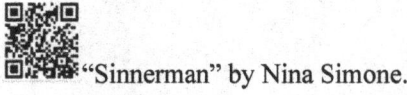 "Sinnerman" by Nina Simone.

 "My Heart Belongs to Daddy"

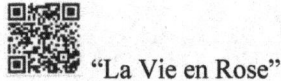 "La Vie en Rose"

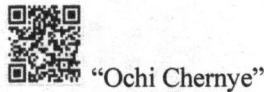 "Ochi Chernye"

 "Lazy Bird"

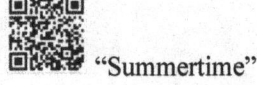 "Summertime"

 "It's a Man's Man's World"

<<<◇>>>

What follows is the short story **Ten Million**. It follows Petrovski from the end of this tale to ten years into the future, the beginning of **Dead Tomorrow**, my next book.

Ten Million

A Miami Mob
Short Story

Florida.
November 2012

Chapter One

Rain hammered on Vladimir Petrovski's back as he crawled out of the muddy Everglades water onto the equally muddy Gator Hammock. He choked on the acrid smoke from the burning sawgrass and rolled onto his back. The driving rain stung his eyes and the left side of his face. He felt nothing on the right. His right eye felt like it was encrusted with blood.

He lifted his right hand to his face and passed out.

The rain had stopped. He had no idea how long he'd been out, but it was still night. Or maybe night again. His left eye looked up at the stars while he tried to recall what had happened. He couldn't open his right eye, and everything hurt.

He shot somebody. Or at somebody. He couldn't remember if he connected. Some fucking saxophone player who stuck his nose in where he shouldn't have.

He shook his head. That didn't make sense. It was the drummer he had to kill. A wave of nausea rose in his throat, and he rolled over and pushed himself up and screamed in pain as he put weight on his right hand. Vomit bubbled through the scream as he collapsed face-first in a pool of his bile.

Petrovski tried calming his shuddering breath. The pain bloomed, flooding his right hand and arm, the right side of his torso, and the right side of his face. He held his right hand close to his left eye. It was too dark to see.

But he could smell it. Like if a burnt leather wallet and a rain-drenched dog had a baby. He gingerly touched his right hand with his left and screamed.

And passed out again.

The sun had risen before Petrovski regained consciousness. His mouth tasted like the ass end of a sheepdog. His right eye was still stuck shut. Pain consumed his body, but at least that proved he was still alive. And now he could see what was causing it.

He slowly pushed himself up to a sitting position with his left hand, cradling his right arm across his chest. It was horribly burned, his hand a claw. He tried straightening his fingers and immediately stopped as pain threatened to overwhelm him again.

He inhaled through his nose and slowly let out his breath. He took stock.

His shirt was burned. Mosquitos were making a meal of him, but he didn't notice. The skin on his arm was a mottled red and black, with blisters starting to form. It stunk. He slowly moved his arm and looked at the side of his body. The burns stopped almost at the centerline of his body. His left side, with what was left of his shirt, was untouched. The right side of his torso looked like a poorly cooked side of pork.

He grimaced and stood. His clothes were drying out, what he had left. He reached across his body with his left hand and dug his mobile phone out of his front pocket. He flipped it open with his thumb. The screen was blank. He tried powering it on, smacking it against his leg when it failed to come alive. *"Kusok der'ma!"* He awkwardly threw the phone into the water.

Just beyond the ripples left by the dead phone floated an airboat, about twenty yards off Gator Hammock. It was a ten-minute airboat ride back to the dock, and whatever waited for him there. But there was an alligator — actually the eyes of an alligator — floating a few yards away. He eyed it. It eyed him. He walked to the far side of the hammock, making as much noise as possible, then slowly and quietly walked back to the side facing the boat.

The alligator was gone. Or submerged. "Well, fuck it."

Petrovski jumped into the waist-deep water and pushed his way through the turgid water, unscathed, to the boat. Getting on board was awkward, with only one working arm. But he managed. He pulled himself onto the seat behind the controls and took a deep breath. He leaned his head back and closed his eyes. Sven had started the boat for him when they came out here. Someone else had always started it for him.

It was something in the back of the boat. A switch. He leaned to his left and looked over his shoulder. His peripheral vision caught a bullet hole in the engine housing. He stood and inspected it. He closed his one good eye and shook his head. "FUCK."

The bullet hole went into the engine casing. He checked the other side and couldn't find an exit hole. Somewhere inside, a piece of lead was ruining his life. Wouldn't matter what steps he needed to follow to start it, it wouldn't. The ten-minute trip was going to take a lot longer. A whole lot longer if he didn't find some method of propulsion.

He looked back at Gator Hammock. Lots of sticks there to use as a pole. Lots of possible alligators between him and them.

He eased back into the waist-deep water and trudged slowly, easing through the water as quietly as he could, pulling the airboat along with him. He scrambled onto the hammock of land and picked through the deadwood until he found a stick about 8 feet long and as big around as his forearm. Getting onto the airboat was a challenge with only one working arm, but he got on carefully, the pole under his left arm.

He sighed, leaned against the engine housing and used the pole to push off from the small island. He slowly, painfully, made his way around Gator Hammock. Ahead of him was about two miles of heavy slogging to get back to Hector's airboat dock.

He let the pole drag through the water, and he weighed the odds of a police presence at Hector's. After some thought, he angled south. There was a decent chance there would be someone at Hector's, possibly fire or police, but the dock half a mile south of Hector's, abandoned for the past few years, would be clear.

He had a little more than two miles, at least an hour of pushing, ahead of him.

Petrovski dropped the pole and stepped off the airboat onto the battered dock. The shop at the end of the dock had lost out to Hector's business years ago. It was weather-beaten, dilapidated and of dubious structural soundness. It was once a rental point for airboats. They used to sell bait and beer, issued fishing licenses and was the gathering place for the local rednecks.

Petrovski cradled his right arm as he pushed through the open front door of the shop. It smelled of mildew and dead animals. The floor was damp. He looked up, through the roof to the sky.

His head swam. The pain from his burns was reaching levels he had never experienced before. He braced himself against the wall with his good hand and slowly eased himself to a sitting position on the floor. He felt the dampness on the floor seep through his trousers He leaned to one side and dry-retched. He needed food, he needed water, and he needed someone to look at his injuries before he died.

Nothing here could help him. He wiped his mouth on his cuff and struggled to stand. Hector's place had a phone. It might have cops, but it would have a phone. And water. He'd walk there and wait until they left if he had to.

He trudged north up the poorly maintained single-lane road. The Everglades were on his left, and empty fields on his right. An increasing number of flies were landing on his face and right arm. He didn't have the energy to wave them away. He stumbled as he walked. Nothing in his brain worked except attempting to block the pain while placing one step in front of the other until he reached Hector's place.

The sun was high in the sky when he finally saw the small shop. He slowed, checking for police cars. He squinted his left eye. The only car there was the piece of junk that the sax player drove, disabled by Stanislav the night before.

He could see the fluttering of police tape on the door of Hector's place. But no police. He peered through the door's window. The shop was empty. He pulled the tape out of the way and pushed at the door. Hector had locked up. He pulled one of his shoes off and broke the window nearest the doorknob with its heel. He pulled his shoe back on and reached through the glass, and unlocked the door.

An electronic chime announced his arrival.

He grabbed a bottle of water out of the cooler and struggled to open it, gripping the plastic cap with his mouth and twisting the bottle with his left hand.

When it broke free, he spat the cap on the ground and poured the bottle into his mouth. Half of the contents spilled down his chin and over his torso, stinging when it hit the burns on the right side of his body.

He tried twisting away from the pain, spilling more water across his body. "Shit!" He threw the bottle to the back of the shop. He leaned over and groaned, then took deep, slow breaths trying to quell the agony.

He staggered to the counter and lifted the receiver. Dial-tone. He put the receiver between his chin and his neck and called his restaurant.

"*The Natalia*. May I help you?"

Petrovski closed his eyes. "I need to speak to Sven."

"Mr. Petrovski? Is that you?"

"SVEN. NOW." Yelling drained him. He waited and listened to the footsteps and kitchen noise in the background.

"Boss?"

"Where's my car, Sven?"

"I-I-I was told you were dead."

Petrovski closed his eyes. He took a long, slow breath. "Do I sound dead? Get my car and return to Hector's NOW."

"There are police there."

"You idiot. I'm at Hector's now, and there are no police. You need to come back here and get me and take me to our doctor."

Miami

Three Years Ago

Chapter Two

A single desk lamp provided illumination in Petrovski's office. It cast a warm yellow circle on his desk, highlighting a leather-bound folder with a fountain pen lying across it and a series of gouges and scars along the right side of the mahogany desk top.

He sat behind this desk, facing his right, leaning back in his chair in thought. Maintaining an illusion of legitimacy got harder every year. The hardest part was cleaning the dirty money. The financial arms of federal law enforcement, globally, were getting very good. And he could only hide so much in his restaurant. The IRS had excellent accountants.

A light blinked on his desk phone. He stared at it for a minute. One-eyed. He held his finger over the speaker button for a second, then depressed it. "What?"

"You have visitors." The accent was strong, a recent arrival from Russia. From a small town just south of Moscow.

"You were told not to disturb me."

"They have badges."

"I don't care, Mikhail."

There was a pause, and muffled sounds as Mikhail covered the phone handset with his hand or chest.

"They say they are old friends. MacCready and James."

Petrovski sighed. "Not friends. But they can come in. They won't leave until they see me, and if past visits are any indication, they'll make a scene until they do. Send them through." He tapped the same button, cutting off Mikhail's response.

He turned to face his desk. He wore an open-collared shirt. His days of crisply starched collars and ties were long gone. The scarring from his burns almost perfectly bisected his face.

His right eye socket was completely scarred over. There was no eyebrow. Scarring reached up to and beyond his hairline. The corner of his mouth drooped, and a landscape of rugged scar tissue reached back to where his right ear used to be. It had smoothed somewhat over the intervening seven years, looking like melted wax ridges. The scarring followed his neck under the collar of his polo shirt, visible again on his right arm just before the leather cup covering the stub of his forearm. The hook at the end of the leather cup was as polished as the leather, reflecting the light from the desk lamp.

The door opened and light spilled in from the hallway.

FBI Special Agent James reached over and flipped the light switch on as Detective MacCready of the Miami Police Department sat in one of the chairs across from Petrovski's desk. James took the other and leaned forward, elbows on the desk.

"You're looking as good as ever, Vlad," said James. "Isn't he?" He turned to MacCready, who was flipping through his notepad.

"What's that?" MacCready looked up. "Yeah. Right. Charming as ever."

"It's been a whole year already?" Petrovski leaned back in his chair. "Time flies, doesn't it? What do you want?"

"The same thing we always want. Some insight. Seven years ago, you were decimated."

"No, Mac. Not decimated," said James. "That implies he lost only a tenth of his business. He was eradicated."

MacCready looked at his younger partner for a moment, then nodded. "Pedantic as usual." He turned back to Petrovski. "You were *obliterated* seven years ago. Your criminal enterprise was subsumed by the Italians, and you were left for dead in The Everglades."

Petrovski tapped his hook on his desk. "I am a legitimate businessman, gentlemen. I own the club and pay taxes on my legitimate revenues."

"Do you pay taxes on your illegitimate revenues?"

"James…"

"Special Agent James, Petrovski."

"Special Agent James, why would you say that? We do this dance every year. Don't you have better things to do? Are there no criminals in South Florida for you to harass? What did I do to get this honor every year for the past six?" He shook his head. "I could see it when you thought you had a witness to one of my alleged crimes, but that didn't even make it to trial, did it?"

James dismissed that with a wave of his hand. "DA didn't think he could make the case with just the witness."

"Why don't you do anything about that scarring?" asked MacCready. "You're a wealthy man. You say you run a respectable business. You'd think a respectable businessman would want to present a respectable front to his respectable clientele."

Petrovski shrugged. "Same thing I tell you every year. Maybe someday I will. But this is working for me now. Gives my clientele a sense of attainable, safe danger." He smiled with the left half of his mouth. "Are you staying for dinner?"

"We're tracking your money very closely, Vlad. Very closely."

Petrovski leaned forward, dragging his hook across the top of the desk. "And what have you found? Nothing out of the ordinary, right? I am clean. I have a high-end Russian restaurant that does quite well and a related catering business that does even better."

MacCready flipped through his notepad. "You know, you're one of the luckiest men I know."

Petrovski gently rubbed the scar tissue on his cheek with the back of his hook. "Lucky?" He leaned back in his chair. "How's that?"

"Lucky. We had, actually, still have, the weapon you used to kill Sergei and used to attempt to kill Paul Coates. Ballistics match. The serial number was removed with acid, but it has your prints."

Petrovski held out both arms. "So, cuff me."

"And here's the luck. Your prints aren't on file. And we would have arrested you with probable cause — really strong probable cause — and take your fingerprints to close this out, and your career, once and for all, but," MacCready grimaced, "the weapon only has prints from your right hand."

Petrovski lifted his hook and looked at it. "So fucking lucky." He stood and leaned on his desk, his weight on the hook and his left hand. "I'm getting very bored with this harassment. You two used to have witty repartee in your arsenal, but now you're just boring old men nearing the end of your careers." He smiled again, a grotesque imitation of a smile. "Maybe you can come work for me as security when you retire. I'm pretty sure I pay better than your respective bosses."

"He's trying to bribe us, Mac."

MacCready shook his head. "That's not a bribe. It's a threat." He flipped his notepad shut and stood. "Always a distinct pleasure, Vlad. Keep your nose clean."

MacCready got behind the wheel of his unmarked car. James slid into the passenger side. "He's still dirty."

James nodded. "And we still can't prove it. Look at a map of the crime in South Florida, and there are conspicuous clean spaces I know he has his hook into." He smiled at MacCready. "See what I did there?"

"Punk." MacCready's stomach rumbled. "We should have eaten there."

James sat in silence.

"What are you thinking?"

James looked up. "What if it's not in South Florida? What if it's not even in the US? What if he's running something overseas, out of our reach?"

"You're FBI. What possibly could be out of your reach?"

Chapter Three

Petrovski waited until the door closed behind his uninvited guests. "Son of a bitch." He stabbed another hole in the side of his desk. They'd been on his ass for almost a decade. Nowhere near close to causing problems, but an annoyance nonetheless.

He shook his head. Seven years ago he had two people on their knees on an airboat, prepared to put bullets in each of their brains. And he was interrupted. They lived. But they never went to the police. The drummer could put him away for life.

It worried him that their potential threat hung over his head.

He used his good hand to rub the stubble on the back of his head. He had a good international scam going. All offshore. No local players. Millions of bitcoin dollars monthly.

But illicit gains were useless until they were cleaned, and the old Irish man and his daughter were the best in the world.

He had a number of what the media distastefully called Pig Butchering operations, mostly out of SE Asia - Cambodia, Laos, Thailand. No pigs were actually butchered. His organization trafficked mostly young Chinese men and women to SE Asia, promising them new careers with great pay and benefits. Once his syndicate got them out of China, he confiscated their passports and got them scamming unsuspecting westerners in a type of Ponzi scheme, fattening them up with fake investment successes until they started putting real money in. Once the marks were pumped hard, their account would be drained due to 'market fluctuations'. More often than not, they'd chase the bad money with good until they were so far underwater that they had no way out. Then they'd be ghosted.

He's recently branched out, trafficking young Cambodian and Thai girls to the west. His organization in those countries had access to prime products. He anticipated making more money facilitating the sales than when he was on the receiving end of the trafficking that used to put girls in his strip clubs.

But for now, the pig butchering money needed to be cleaned.

He knew his phones were tapped and was positive the feds could monitor all mobile communication traffic without actually having a tap on the actual phone. Fortunately, there were other ways to communicate. Cheaper, cleaner and worry-free.

He opened his laptop and unlocked it with his fingerprint. He launched one of the multiple encrypted messaging apps and tapped the top contact on the list.

A warbling tone echoed the ringing on the far side. Ireland, he suspected, given the nationality of the man he was calling, but he didn't care where. The Irishman always answered, regardless of the time where he was.

On the third ring. Every time.

"Vladimir, you're as ugly as ever." O'Shea was a large, florid man with graying red hair and a web of veins spreading across his nose like the Mississippi delta. "What's new?" O'Shea looked off-screen for a second. "Terri says hi. You've got some funds to clean, I take it. Same deal? Cayman bank?"

Petrovski shook his head. "You should eat a salad once in a while, O'Shea. The source account is the same, but the destination is a new account in Belize."

"Where the fuck is that?"

"Little country on the Yucatan Peninsula, on the Gulf Of Mex -- it doesn't matter." He tapped a couple of keys. "I've just sent you the bank details. There's a surf shop in Belize City, right on the beach. Make it a charter operation. Run the money through that."

"Sounds like a plan, mate." O'Shea was tapping on his keyboard as he looked slightly off-screen. "Just pulled that place up on that mapping program. Looks like a nice place to retire." He leaned in close to his camera. "You looking to retire?"

Petrovski smiled his half-smile. "Not for many years. I'm enjoying my life. Many years left in me." He paused. "Same percentage, I trust?"

O'Shea chewed the inside of his cheek. "New bank, new business set up. Let's make the first one a point higher. All remaining transactions after this first one are back to usual. Reasonable?"

Petrovski nodded. "Reasonable. You and your daughter do good work. It's worth it. Message me when it's arranged. I've got new revenues coming through in a couple of days I'll want to talk to you about. Will this still be a good time?"

"Yeah, mate. For you, any time."

"Always a gentleman. Talk to you later." He tapped the 'Leave' button on his screen, and O'Shea's image disappeared.

He scratched at his chin with his hook. The cold steel felt good against his skin. The point of the hook caught a wrinkle, and he winced. He opened his phone and turned on the front-facing camera. A bead of blood seeped from the small cut. He dabbed it with a tissue and tapped the screen to make another call.

His laptop warbled four times before an Asian man appeared on his screen. "Comrade Petrovski."

"Don't call me that, Peng Ho. You know I don't like it." He held the tissue against his chin. "And how are things progressing?"

"By things, I assume you mean the forty-seven girls we're placing through the Middle East and Europe?"

Petrovski nodded.

"Payment has been received from all the pre-sales, and the auction for the remaining ten is in," he looked at his watch, "three hours. We're expecting your share to top out at a bee's dick more than ten million US."

Petrovski raised his eyebrows. "Nice."

"Well, Comrade," Peng Ho smiled, "More than double than I could have done. It was your contacts. We're going to keep this going, right?"

Petrovski ignored the Comrade jibe. "If you keep finding quality merchandise like the last batch, you can be sure we'll keep this going."

"There are plenty more. Years' worth. We're going to keep it going?"

The Russian nodded. "I'll line up more buyers. Get back to me with dates for the new product, and send me the financial details for the most recent transaction."

Peng Ho winked. "You got it, boss. Details are in the chat." His hand reached up, and his image disappeared.

"So that's a goodbye, then." Petrovski looked at the bank details in the chat, committed them to memory, and deleted all records of that call and the one with O'Shea. He executed an application that scrubbed all internet history, all call logs and sat back in his chair.

Pig butchering brought him somewhere around a million a month. The girls would eclipse that by at least a factor of ten.

And all of it offshore.

Chapter Four

"Mr. Petrovski. It's been a couple of days. Still working on the Belize thing. You should have money moving through that dive shop later this week and a growing balance in the bank account by the end of the month. You're going to be chartering some very high rollers. You've got something new?"

Petrovski tapped on his desk in approval. "Good work for two days, O'Shea. The full amount will take how long?"

"It converts from bitcoin to just a bit shy of $979,000 American. A couple of weeks to push it all through in an unobtrusive manner. I'll start in a couple of days"

"Does Belize care about obtrusive?"

O'Shea laughed. "Always to the point." He waggled his hand. "Not so much. But it pays to be careful, I find."

"I only ask because I've got a larger pool of money I need managed. Can I use Belize, or will it be smarter to hit Singapore or Switzerland?"

"Parameters?"

Petrovski rubbed his hand over the stubble on his scalp. He'd need to shave it in the morning. "In the neighborhood of ten million every couple of months."

Petrovski saw O'Shea lean forward and glance quickly to his right.

"Are you alone, O'Shea?"

The Irishman adjusted his camera, and his daughter Terri slid into view. She was in her thirties and had close-cropped blonde hair. "Not quite. Terri's here. Tell us about the ten mill."

Petrovski gave her a quick nod. "Terri. Good to see you again. So, Belize. Your suggestion?"

"That's a big jump, Vlad," said Terri. "You're not running guns, are you? We stay away from that. Too many opportunities to get 'disappeared'." She looked at her father. "Though our cut on ten is pretty good. Almost good enough to handle weapons. Almost."

Petrovski shook his head. "No, not weapons. Margins are too thin. I'm moving some women out of SE Asia into the Middle East and Europe. The margins are huge, and the pipeline is full, at least, for the foreseeable future. Your cut works out to seven hundred thousand American for every shipment. Minimum." He took a deep breath. "So, Belize?"

Terri moved off-screen, and O'Shea centered himself on the camera. "Yeah. We'll come up with a way." He glanced in the direction Terri had gone. "Give me twenty-four hours and call me back." He reached for the screen and hesitated. "Same account?"

Petrovski nodded. "Tomorrow." He tapped the screen and dropped the call.

"Sex trafficking? We're not going to launder for a sex trafficker."

"Terri, Seven hundred grand a month. On top of everything else he's bringing us." O'Shea pushed his massive girth away from his desk and ran his hand through his thinning hair. "We've got a good life. We've got steady clients, and sweetie, you're excellent at what you do."

"There are ethics involved. Drugs are okay. There's a buyer and a seller. And god knows there are plenty of dealers looking for a way to clean their money. The scam deal the Russian is running is, I admit, unique, but dummies gotta pay, right? You click a link on your phone from an unknown sender, you deserve what you get. But we agreed we wouldn't facilitate anything that hurt innocent people. Definitely no arms dealers." She slammed both hands on the desk and stood. "And sex traffickers? Are you fucking kidding me?"

Her father frowned in thought. "He said nothing about sex. I got the impression it was a nanny-for-hire situation."

"You don't believe that for a second."

"I choose to believe it. Until I get something that tells me differently, we're going to clean his money." He watched his daughter's face. A wall had slid over it. "You can handle this?"

She clenched her jaw, stared into his eyes for a moment and then gave him a sharp nod. "Leave it with me."

"You sure, lass?"

"Leave it. With. Me."

O'Shea nodded. "Okay. Hey, smile. This is big money. You like money. I like money."

"Noted. I'll take care of it."

Petrovski checked his watch. Twenty-four hours had elapsed. The bitcoin had left his wallet, and there had been no signs of any activity related to it since. He called O'Shea.

"Petrovski. Punctual as usual."

"Where's my money?"

"It's a process, Vlad. Terri is working on it." O'Shea adjusted himself in his chair. "You know how good she is. It's a lot of money, Vlad, and we need to be careful how it's set up. For your protection as well as ours."

Petrovski rested his chin on his hook. "Okay. I understand. Don't take too long. This time tomorrow I need to see the plan and a clear indication of progress. Am I understood?"

"You am." O'Shea smiled. "It's all good, mate. Wheels are in motion. Belize is still looking good. Twenty-four hours, right?"

O'Shea pushed away from his desk and scrubbed his face with his hands. "Fuck." He double-checked to make sure his connection with Petrovski was closed and slammed his laptop shut. "FUCK."

He called the phone number he'd been calling every five minutes for the past three hours and grunted with frustration when he hit Terri's voicemail. It was full, or he would have left the same message he left the first thirty times he called. *Where the hell are you, and where in the FOOK is the money?*

He threw it. The phone bounced off a brick wall and scattered in pieces across the hardwood floor. He was in rural Italy. Just outside a small town called Bottai. He owned an old brick house on twelve acres with a vineyard he paid more to maintain than he generated in wine revenue. She hadn't shown up for breakfast, and after a quick search, he'd realized she was gone.

There was no way he could unload it fast enough. He had to leave now and take the loss.

He swung a fake Rembrandt out of the way and opened his wall safe. He had to go deep. Five passports went in the fireplace before he reached the black one from New Zealand.

He tapped it on the edge of his safe and then thumbed it open to the main page. He'd be Gerry O'Riordan until things cooled off.

And as an added bonus, it was spring in Auckland.

He gathered any personal papers he had and added them to the fireplace, turned on the gas, sparked the flame and removed any evidence of his existence in Italy.

Current time

Chapter Five

Petrovski leaned back in his chair in thought. Maintaining an illusion of legitimacy was still very difficult. The hardest part, still, was cleaning the dirty money. The financial arms of federal law enforcement, globally, were getting extremely good. And with the O'Sheas out of the picture – he clenched his jaw thinking about them – he had to work with the second-best launderer in the business.

A light blinked on his desk phone. He held his finger over the speaker button for a second, then depressed it. "What is it, Mikhail?"

"You have visitors. The badges." The accent was still strong, unchanged after three years in America.

"You were told not to disturb me."

"They have badges," he insisted.

Petrovski sighed. "Fine. Send them through." He tapped the same button, cutting off Mikhail's response.

The door opened, and light spilled in from the hallway.

Special Agent James reached over and flipped on the light switch as Detective MacCready of the Miami Police Department sat in one of the chairs across from Petrovski's desk. James took the other and leaned forward, elbows on the desk.

"Deja vu, all over again, Vlad." James flicked a crumb off the desk.

"Like clockwork, the two of you." He smiled, the scarred right side of his mouth refusing to keep up with the left. "Is this like an anniversary thing? Should I have some cakes brought in?" He spread his arms, the light glinting off the hook where his right hand used to be. "I'm flattered by your attention, gentlemen, but as I keep telling you, I have no involvement in any criminal activities in Miami anymore."

"This will probably be our last year, Petrovski. Unless James wants to keep it going. I'm retiring in March." MacCready leaned forward. "But only Miami? Do you have involvement in criminal activities in other cities? Or countries?"

"Me? I own this club, and its very popular restaurant. Nothing more." He rubbed the bottom of his chin with the curve of his hook. "Not anymore, anyway."

"Those were the days," said James. "Weren't they, Mac?"

"I don't miss the gunplay. And you never did replace the Turk, what's his name."

James snapped his finger. "George something or other. Sajok."

"Yeah. Nasty son of a bitch."

"Guys, I've got a busy evening ahead of me. This chit-chat is delightful. Call ahead next time. I'll buy you dinner. My chef is fantastic."

MacCready stood. "I prefer Indian." He leaned on the desk, standing over Petrovski. "We know you're dirty. There's no way the money coming in from this joint can support your lifestyle." He held out an index finger. "We're almost there. And when we are there, we'll be shutting all of this down."

Petrovski stood and leaned close. "Ten years and your 'almost there' is not as impressive as you think it is. I've been friendly, gentlemen. If you persist in being jackasses, you can stop coming by unless you have a warrant. I'll instruct Mikhail to block your entrance."

"Maybe we'll have a warrant next time." He tapped James on the shoulder. "Let's go."

"Hang on. Before you leave. It's always bugged me. You were going to charge me with the attempted murder of a couple of people. Out on The Everglades," he held up his hook, "where this happened. You never followed through with that. You still waiting for evidence of that, too?"

Mac looked like he wanted to jam Petrovski's hook in one eye and out the other. "Let's go, James."

Petrovski watched them leave. Mikhail came in a minute after they left.

"Boss, they have left the shop."

"You've been with me a little over three years now, isn't that right, Mikhail?"

The small, wiry Russian sat in the chair MacCready had just vacated. He nodded. "Three years and two months. You have been very kind. I would like to do more."

"And I'd like you to do more." He tapped his desk with the back of the hook. "You've never asked me what happened to my face."

"Is not my place."

"I want to tell you." Petrovski looked at the hook and sighed.

"Ten years ago, almost to the day, I was in The Everglades on an airboat preparing to kill a witness and my niece."

"Your niece?"

"Yes. My *plemyannitsa.*" He waved his hand. "Long story which one day I'll tell you. It doesn't matter. They both had to disappear." He smiled at Mikhail. "Your expression hasn't changed. You're not surprised?"

"Is not for me to be surprised." He shrugged. "But I am not idiot. I know you have history. The scarring?"

Petrovski nodded. "I was about to shoot the witness when I was interrupted. This was in the middle of a thunderstorm, by the way. Lightning strikes all over the place. It was a wild night."

Mikhail raised his eyebrows. "They are still alive? This witness and your niece?"

Petrovski nodded. "Let me finish. There was a fight. I was left in The Everglades, in the middle of a fire, thought to be dead."

"But you are not."

Petrovski smiled with the left half of his face. "You miss nothing."

"And?"

"The witness and my niece are both in a fairly good jazz combo. They eventually went into Witness Protection. Last I heard, they were touring Asia. It's not a concern for me right now."

Mikhail chuckled. "Why do these police come every year?"

"They were investigating me a decade ago when this happened. Almost had me." He held up his hook. "But the prints don't match anymore. That really pisses them off. There was a preliminary hearing about a year after the fact, and the judge determined there wasn't enough to make a case." He smiled. "That cost me $50,000."

He leaned back in his chair and looked at his nails. "Those two are fighting organized crime in south Florida, and I'm the one that got away. I could have left Miami and set up shop somewhere else." He pointed to his face with his hook. "I could have cleaned this up also. But I take great delight in being a permanent reminder of their failure while I continue to succeed."

Mikhail chuckled. "I like."

Petrovski adjusted himself in his chair. "You're good with a knife, I understand."

"I have skills."

"I've been told."

"Why?"

"Those two idiot cops reminded me of a man who used to work for me who did," he paused, "extermination jobs for me. You understand extermination?"

Mikhail nodded. "*Da*."

"His skill went beyond what he could do with a knife. He could make it messy or very clean, but he never left a single piece of evidence implicating him or me behind." He smiled. "He was very useful." Petrovski cocked his head. "Would you be interested in helping out in a similar way?"

"How would this work?"

"We'll sort out those details later. First, we need to talk about how to be clean, forensically."

Auckland was having an unseasonably wet and cold spring. O'Shea read something about it being El Nina, but the reason, as far as he was concerned, was irrelevant. It was wet and cold. He was cold. His bones, getting older every advancing year, really hated the damp chill.

He paced the living room. "Reggie, lad. Where the fook are ya?"

An extremely tall, muscled man came out of the kitchen, wiping his hands on a tea towel. "Cleaning up your mess, like I've bene doing for the past three years. What are you yelling about?"

"We're going to your home country for a spell. Warm up my aching bones."

"Brissie?"

O'Shea scowled and shook his head. "Sydney. The food is better. None of that BrisVegas bullshit."

Chapter Six

\

Mikhail stopped at the office door. "You like me leave it open or close?"

"Close it, please, Mikhail. And I need an hour undisturbed." Petrovski smiled. "Even if MacCready and James return."

"Understood."

When he heard the door latch, he opened his laptop and launched the anonymous browser. He checked his now shielded IP address, and it informed him that he was in Calgary, Alberta.

He started a video call.

"Vlad, you're early." The man on the other side of the call was wiping his mouth with a napkin.

"I could call back later, Martin."

"No, it's fine," said Martin. "I was just finishing." He tossed the napkin off-screen. "You've been doing well."

"When I do well, you do well. The scam work is picking up."

Martin nodded. "About 30% of your revenue now. Up from twenty last quarter."

"It's bigger growth than that," said Petrovski. "The trafficking has increased by over 50%."

"That's what we need to talk about. The opportunities to launder are getting more difficult. Your incoming is more than can be reasonably explained by your current legitimate and quasi-legitimate businesses. Even on a good day." He scratched his head.

The room behind him was a wood-paneled office with nature paintings arranged haphazardly on the wall. He wore a checked shirt with pearl buttons, like an urban cowboy.

"So what are you thinking? Any opportunities in Chicago?"

"Too close to home." Martin paused. "You have a dormant charter operation in Belize."

Petrovski shook his head. "Bad luck."

"What?"

"That place is bad luck. That place is the reason you and I have had a relationship for the past three years. Something else. Maybe the same set-up, but in Costa Rica."

"Belize has better privacy laws. I could do it, but it'll take a month or so to set up a believable presence in Costa Rica. Belize is ready."

Petrovski rubbed his forehead with his good hand. "That was set up for the first trafficking funds. Ten million."

Martin looked confused. "It's dormant. As near as I can tell, and I'm pretty good at this shit, it's never been used."

"The fat Irish git who was supposed to use it to clean that ten million fucked off with the money."

Martin's eyes narrowed. "Fat Irish — O'Shea?"

"You know him?"

"It's a small industry. I haven't heard from him in a while." He nodded. "About three years, now that you mention it. Fell off the face of the earth."

"He might be dead. He was in poor health. But his daughter should still be around. She was the brains, anyway."

"She's gone, too."

"I know." Petrovski shook his head. "If you ever hear about where they are, let me know, okay?"

"I want him, too." Martin tapped his chin. "I think you should reconsider Belize."

"Why in the hell should I reconsider Belize?"

"Well," said Martin, "O'Shea set that up for you, right?"

"He did. Then didn't use it."

"So maybe if you do use it, and I suggest you do — it's a great set-up, we might flush O'Shea out of the weeds."

"He's not that dumb." Petrovski sighed. "But what the hell. Use it. It's a good arrangement."

"Okay. That'll cover part of it." Martin smiled. "The cost of success. We could do something similar in the Caymans. There's a bit more competition for that kind of business in the Caymans, so it might not absorb as much."

"Maldives?"

Martin nodded while he considered. "I'll look into it and get back to you."

"Thanks. Apologies again for interrupting your meal."

Martin waved it off. "Not a problem. Talk to you in a week?"

"In a week." Petrovski tapped his screen and disconnected.

O'Shea was as tired of being O'Riordan almost as tired as he was of living in Auckland. It was a lovely town, but the wonder ran out after six months. The last two and a half years were interminably boring. And the winters were cold. Colder since the houses weren't built for cold. Sydney would be a nice change. He might make it permanent.

"Reg, make sure my insulin is packed in the mini-cooler."

"You better pack it. I don't want to be responsible for you going into a diabetic coma."

He shook his head and muttered under his breath. "What do I pay you for?"

He had a laundering business. Without his daughter. He didn't know where Terri was. He knew she was working. He bumped into her customers every six months or so. She was good. He was proud of her but needed to find out where the Russian's ten million ended up. If he poked his head up before he was able to return the money to Petrovski, he'd end up in a weighted bag on the bottom of the ocean.

Terri O'Shea sat on her balcony in Floriana, Malta, sipping an espresso and reading the International Herald Tribune. Her laptop was open beside her. The screensaver was slowly sliding photos from her travels across the screen.

Brussels. Halifax. Quito. Buenos Aires. Beirut.

An early morning cruise ship docked in the distance, what the locals called "boatloads of money". It was a good place to hide. The population fluctuated wildly and frequently. She was just another face.

It had taken her some time to get her business going. When she and her father worked together, the old man got the clients, and she set up the laundering activities. Three years ago, the Russian's ten million seemed like good seed money. Until she remembered how he made it. She converted it to cash and stowed nine million of it in a large safe deposit box in a boutique private bank in Sydney, Australia, with very restrictive services and tight international security, and deposited the remaining million in an account there.

Waiting.

She used her own money and connections to launch her money laundering house. A couple of reliable drug organizations kept her in a comfortable lifestyle.

She folded the paper and unlocked her laptop. She had an alert set up on the Belize bank she and her father ended up not using for Petrovski. She wanted to use it at some point. She thought it would be fitting to take Petrovski's ten million and launder it through Belize and donate the money to fight human trafficking. She checked it every couple of months. The charter business was still dormant, and the account still only had a minimum balance.

Three years was long enough. It was more than likely he'd forgotten about it. She had set it up, after all. Very unlikely he even remembered it existed. Time to make use of it.

Terri flipped through her literal little black book until she found the details of her Sydney bank account. She put her headphones in and made a VOIP call from her laptop.

"Personal banking. Nigel McInnes speaking."

Terri glanced at the notes against the bank details. "Good morning, Nigel. This is Grace Rawlston."

"Miss Rawlston, how delightful to hear from you. It's been a long time. How may I help you?"

"It's Grace. Please. Nigel, I bank with you precisely because there is no access to any accounts electronically. I am not a big fan of electronic bank access. So many people hacking and breaking into people's accounts and taking their money." She paused. "I'm sure that must limit your client base, with such restriction in this day and age."

"You'd be very surprised, I'm sure, by the number of high-end clients, such as yourself, who prefer such arrangements. How may I help you today?"

Terri glanced at her notes. She had $1.1M written beside the bank name. "Is my balance still a bit over a million US dollars?"

"It has earned a little bit of interest over the past few years. I hope you have a use for this money, Miss — Grace. It's a shame to let it sit around and not work for you."

"I appreciate your concern, Nigel. That's my rainy day money. And I'm planning on spending some time diving in Central America. Snorkelling, actually. I'm calling to have a hundred thousand, no, a hundred and fifty thousand transferred to an account I have set up in Belize. Can you help me with that?"

"I certainly can. We will need to go through the usual security questions."

"Of course." Terri read the responses to Nigel's questions from her notebook and gave him the bank details in Belize. The transaction was completed, and Terri thanked him and hung up.

She logged back into the bank in Belize. The balance was $155,000. She smiled and closed her laptop. She'd head to Sydney and transfer the rest, save for half a million in the bank to keep Nigel happy.

She left the patio and opened the small wall safe. She flipped through the passports until she found Grace Rawlston's.

Chapter Seven

The laptop on Petrovski's desk warbled. He looked up from his book and shook his head. Martin. He sniffed and tapped the screen to answer the call.

"Martin. We just talked. Problems already? Why are you frowning?"

"You're already using the Belize account? You need to give me a heads up when you do that or," he scratched his chin, "or I'll end up getting us both in trouble."

"What in the hell are you talking about?" Petrovski cleared his throat. "It's been dormant for three years. $5000 initial balance just sitting there. That's why we agreed to use it. Now you look confused."

"That's because I'm fucking confused. $150k just landed in that account. If you didn't put it there, who did?"

Petrovski leaned back in his chair. "Well."

"Now you're smiling?"

"Can you do some digging and find out who deposited it?" He rubbed his chin with the curve of his hook. "Discretely?"

"Everything I do is discrete. You know who it is, don't you?"

"I have a suspicion. How long will it take?" He tapped his hook on his desk. "Discretely."

"An hour or so. Who do you think it is?"

Petrovski shook his head. "You tell me. Talk to you in an hour."

O'Shea stood on the pool deck of the three-level flat he was leasing in downtown Sydney. He wore a pair of swimming trunks and a robe. "Reg, lad, the view is spectacular. I may move here permanently."

"It gets shitty in the winter. Brisbane is better."

"Too many cyclones and too much flooding up there. And those fucking toads, whatever you call them." O'Shea padded down the stairs from the roof into the living area. He reached into his robe pocket and handed a prescription to Reg. "Get my insulin for me, would you? Some syringes, too. Thanks." He looked at the scowl on Reg's face. "Hey, this is the kind of shit I pay you to do."

"You've got insulin. Brought it with you."

"I'm on my last vial. Two weeks' worth. Just go get it."

"Fine, old man. I'll be back in a couple of hours."

"There's a fucking chemist right across the street."

Reg held up the script. "You need this right now? No? I know you don't because you just told me you don't. I'm catching up with some friends for lunch and a beer. I'll see you in a couple of hours."

O'Shea waved him off. "Enjoy." He picked up the remote and turned on the television. He flipped through channels until he landed on a gorgeous talking head on one of the local channels. Perfect blonde hair, plump lips and a healthy tan. O'Shea smiled. Not much he could do more than smile.

The reporter was talking about something, but O'Shea didn't

notice her anymore. "Reg. Get the hell back in here." He grabbed the remote and held it at arm's length, trying to read the buttons. "Reg!"

"I'm going out the door."

"Two minutes. I need to figure out how this remote works."

"Fucking hell, old man. Figure it out yourself."

O'Shea looked over his shoulder at his bodyguard. "I think I just saw Terri." He rewound the vision on the television. "I need you to go find her." He jabbed a finger at the television. "See? Right there."

Reg shook his head. "Might be her. Might not be her." He sat on the sofa beside O'Shea. "I'm going to need some help."

"Yeah, I might know somebody."

Petrovski tapped the screen to answer a call. "Well?"

Martin was offscreen, just his left shoulder visible. "Hang on a sec." He typed something offscreen, then moved into frame. "Do you know a Grace Rawlston?"

Petrovski shook his head. "Don't know that name. Why?"

"She transferred the money."

"Where did it come from?"

"Sydney. Australia, not the Canadian one. And she bought a ticket on Emirates from Malta to Sydney." He held up a finger. "Hang on. She was pretty good, but the credit card used to buy the ticket was in the name of Terri O'Shea." He smiled. "I thought she was supposed to be smart."

"She is." He tapped his forehead with the curve of his hook. "She is. Unlike her to slip up. When does she land in Sydney?"

"It's an ugly flight from Malta to Sydney. Two stops. Thirty hours travel time." He looked at his watch. "She would have landed a couple of hours ago."

"Dammit." He scribbled a note on a pad on his desk. "Thanks, Martin. Hold off on the Belize thing for now. I'll get back to you when it's safe." He tapped the screen and dropped the call. He looked at his watch and picked up his mobile phone. "Mikhail, where are you?"

"At the front, boss."

"Come to my office. I have a job for you."

"The bar is almost closing. I will need to help remove the, um, stubborn customers from the bar."

"They can survive without you. Now." He dropped the phone on his desk.

Mikhail cracked open the office door and peered in. "Boss?"

"Come in. Sit." He waited until the young Russian was seated across from him. "Have you ever been to Sydney?"

Mikhail looked confused. "Sydney?"

"Australia."

Mikhail shook his head. "No. Not Australia. I have not been there. There are kangaroos, right?"

Petrovski looked at him over his glasses. "Yes. Probably. Not relevant. You have a US passport?"

"No, I do not. *Russkiy*. Two years remaining. Why do you ask?"

"It will have to do." Petrovski leaned forward. "I need to send you to Australia to find somebody."

"Find them?"

"And kill her."

Mikhail shifted closer in his chair. "Her?"

"Problem?"

"None."

Petrovski nodded. "Good. I thought as much. Her name is Terri O'Shea. She may be travelling under the name of," looked at his notepad, "Grace Rawlston."

"Do you have picture?"

Petrovski shook his head. "Unfortunately, no. I might be able to dig something up on the internet, but she's very private. Would that be a problem?"

Mikhail thought a moment, then shook his head. "Not a problem. I can find people." He scratched the back of his head. "But I have no contacts in Sydney. I will be, what is the word, disadvantaged."

"There will be someone meeting you at the airport. They will find a place for you to stay and help you in your search."

"They can get me weapons? I cannot fly with weapons."

Petrovski smiled. "I understand they have very large knives in Australia."

Chapter Eight

MacCready tapped on his monitor. "James, did you see this?"

They were in a small office in the bowels of the FBI field office in South Miami. MacCready was the Miami PD liaison with the FBI's organized crime task force. He had been for almost the last decade. They had done a good job of keeping the crime levels to a dull roar, and the inter-family squabbles had almost disappeared.

Petrovski was an ongoing frustration, though. They knew he was dirty. How dirty and in which manner continued to elude them. Ironically, he had the lowest profile, and lately, they were giving him the most attention.

James rolled his chair over and looked at Mac's monitor. "What am I looking at?"

"That digital tap we put on his computer may be finally bearing fruit. He makes regular video calls, usually at the same time of day, and usually a week apart." He pointed at three consecutive entries. "Then these three, all within hours of each other."

He changed tabs on the browser. "Then credit card activity under an alias we know to be his and some transaction on an online airline ticket portal."

"Online airline?"

421

"Shut up."

"Where'd he buy tickets to?"

"Single business class ticket, Miami to LA to Sydney for Mikhail Sidorov."

"Business class. The runt is moving up in the world." James rolled his chair back to his workstation and stood. "Let's go pay the ugly fucker a visit."

The large suited man at the front of *The Natalia* blocked their entrance. "Mr. Petrovski is not having visitors today."

MacCready and James pulled their badges out simultaneously.

"Yes, he is." James moved his badge within an inch of the Russian's eyes. "Please move. I don't want to arrest you. It would take two sets of handcuffs to restrain you. And you might get hurt."

The Russian smiled.

MacCready unclipped his holster and rested his hand on the butt of his service revolver. "He's the good cop. We're going in."

"Do you have a warrant?"

"This is a public establishment. We don't need a warrant." James pushed past the large man, giving him a bit of an extra shove.

MacCready winked at him and followed James. "Catch you later, champ."

Petrovski was on the phone when they pushed into his office. "Hang on," he said. He pressed the receiver to his chest. "What are you doing here? I wasn't meant to be disturbed." He held up the receiver. "I'm on the phone. Get the hell out of my office."

MacCready sat on the corner of Petrovski's desk and depressed the receiver hook. "You're not on the phone anymore. Why are you sending the runt to Sydney?"

"Where's your warrant?"

James looked around. "We probably should have one." He glanced at the closed door and shrugged. "But we're here. Let's talk."

"You were here a couple of days ago. We talked enough then." He pointed at the door with his hook. "Piss off, come back in a year."

Dan glanced at the notepad on Petrovski's desk. Then he cocked his head to read the note on the desk. "Australia? What's in Australia, Vlad? And why is young Mikhail going there?"

"I've never been, Mac," said James. "You should take some vacation, Vlad. You deserve it. You're all work and no play, bringing all that money into your coffers." James walked while he talked and clapped Petrovski on the shoulder. "You deserve a break, mate. Go put a shrimp on the barbie."

"Hey, James, they call them prawns. Not shrimp."

James glanced at the door again, then walked back and sat in a chair across from the Russian.

"We've noticed a big bump in activity the past couple of days." MacCready took a seat beside James.

"I'm going to have to escort you out."

James stared at the door and said, "Why is Mikhail in Australia?"

"It's his day off. He wanted to explore the world." He stood and moved from behind his desk. "Detective MacCready. Special Agent James. One day, far, far into the future, we will look back at this day and laugh. Remember that." He opened his office door and held up his hook. It was polished, as usual, reflecting the ceiling lights. He looked at the sharp point, then back to James and MacCready. "I have dozens of these. I'm asked, frequently, why I don't have a prosthetic that is a little less…intimidating."

"Are you intimidated, James?"

The FBI agent shook his head. "Not by this punk."

Petrovski stuck the hook in the doorframe and dragged a gouge in the wood, leaving splinters on the carpet. "Maybe you should be. Get out of here."

"How do you handcuff a guy with a fake hand, Mac?"

"Why would we have to handcuff him?"

Petrovski took two steps back, fully opening the door. "You misunderstood me. Maybe it's a language thing. I've only been in this wonderful country for twenty years. I said get out."

"It was a threat, Mac. A clear threat. And look, if we're not going to actually cuff him today, we will definitely be cuffing him in the near future. We should figure out the logistics."

"You have a point. We'd have to take that hook off him. The bracelet would slip right off his arm."

"We might have to knock him out or something."

"Gentlemen, I'm getting tired of this horseshit. That's the right word, no? Horseshit?" He clenched his jaw. His scars amplified the menace from his scowl. "Get out."

"You're repeating yourself." James held his hands out in surrender. "We're leaving. But leave a note with the meathead at the front, okay? Use pictures of us if you have to. Don't stop us from coming in here again."

MacCready slammed his car into gear and accelerated out of the parking lot. "I really hate that sonofabitch. We're digging deeper and getting enough to get a warrant. We know something is up now, and we know that little scary fucker is involved somehow."

James nodded. "What do we know about him?"

"Mikhail Sidorov. Three years in the country. Valid paperwork. Legit visa. Nothing to hold him on. Not even charged with littering."

"And he's on a flight to Australia right now."

"And in a hurry," said Mac. "We should probably figure out why."

<<< >>>

The story doesn't end here. Read 'Dead Tomorrow', available online and in bookstores on May 1st, 2023

About the Author

Tony McFadden is a displaced Canadian now calling Australia his home. He and his wife and two children live near the beaches, where he spends as much time as possible writing.

More about Tony and his writing can be found on the interwebs at

TonyMcFadden.net/mybooks, Facebook

and Twitter.

Also by Tony McFadden

G'Day LA • G'Day USA

Matt's War • Daly Battles: The Fall of Pyongyang • Target: Australia

Book 'Em - An Eamonn Shute Mystery • Unprotected Sax • Family Matters

Have Wormhole, Will Travel • Killing Time

Mac D: Private Investigator • A Step Too Far (A Mac D Case) • Hunter/Prey (A Mac D Case)

The Murder of Jeremy Brookes (A McGinnis Investigations Case) • Number Fifteen (A McGinnis Investigations Case)

Batteries Not Included (A Nick Harding Case) • Broken (A Nick Harding Case)

Coming in 2023: Dead Tomorrow (A Nick Harding Case)

Chapter One

The full moon reflected off the ripples in the harbour. The air was sweet with the smell of Orange Jessamine flowers.

And grilled steak.

Lucy watched Nick dig into a rib-eye and smiled as she used her fork to pop the poached egg on top of her Portuguese grilled chicken, which sat on a bed of rice. "Hungry?"

He nodded. "Famished." He dipped a piece of steak into the small cup of mushroom gravy and nodded at her plate. "That looks good. I'll have to try it next time."

Lucy raised her eyebrows. "You're assuming there'll be a next time? I might not go along with that."

Nick looked at her. Despite the never-ending Australian sun, her skin was alabaster white, speckled with freckles. Her long, curly red hair was up in a bun, showing off her long neck. Nick was smitten. He smiled. "I'll win you over before the night is through."

"Do you normally go out with your clients?"

"Ex-client. Your company has paid my invoice. This is extra-curricular." Nick sat back and took a sip of his wine.

"Oh, really? A hobby?"

"Oh, I'm hoping more than that. But time will tell. Are you enjoying yourself?"

"You're acquitting yourself well, Mr Harding." Lucy smiled. "Paddle-boarding this afternoon in the Narrabeen lagoon and dinner on the beach? One would almost think you're trying too hard. And what's a Bondi boy doing on the Northern Beaches?"

Nick speared a tomato wedge. "Grew up in Warriewood, just up the road. As dad's law firm grew, we moved to Rose Bay. But I still love it up here. Don't get enough chances." He smiled at Lucy. "Thanks for giving me an excuse."

The server collected their plates, and they ordered coffee.

"So," said Lucy. "Are you an only child?"

"That's me. The parents quit at one."

"Are your parents still working?"

"Mum was an ER Nurse. She left that a few decades ago. My father has just started backing away from his law firm. They're both somewhere in Italy looking for a villa in Tuscany to use as an intermittent retirement home."

Lucy raised her eyebrows. "Wow. Serious family money."

"He's promised he'll spend the last dollar on his deathbed. What about you? Only child?"

"A younger brother. Bobby. By three years. He's a telecommunications engineer at one of the carriers. He's bounced around a couple of times. Not sure which one he's at this month." Lucy leaned forward. "You've got to tell me how you managed to convince what's his name - Tom Goulding - to make full restitution to my company."

"He offered. He needed to wait until the executor sorted his father's estate, but he told me he'd make sure all of it was accounted

428

for and returned. Drop in his financial bucket." Nick leaned back while his coffee was delivered. "I'm glad he came through."

"Got me a promotion."

"Oh, so you're paying for dinner? I'm currently between clients."

"I know how much we paid you, Nick. This is your treat.?

"Yes, it is."

Half an hour later they were walking down Narrabeen beach, warm water lapping at their feet, the full moon now higher in the sky and casting night shadows against the wet, packed sand. Nick's trousers were rolled up to mid-calf. He carried his shoes, socks stuffed in them, in one hand and held Lucy's hand in the other.

"Trade sides," she said. "You're getting all the surf. She swapped her shoes to her other hand and moved to the down side of the beach. The waves lapped around their feet.

"You ever surf?"

Lucy looked up at him. "Are you kidding? My sports are indoor sports. I was cursed with Irish genes. I sit too close to a glass of orange juice and I burn. I wear SPF1000."

He chuckled. "What indoor sports? Badminton?"

"Various martial arts. Tae Kwan do, Karate, Wu Shu, Hapkido."

Nick stopped and turned, and looked at her closely. "Really?"

"Why are you surprised?"

"I'm not falling for that. Listen, Miss Simpson, to what level of expertise have you reached in these acts of war?" He rubbed his no-longer straight nose with his thumb and smiled. "And where were you when I was getting pummelled while tracking down your missing money?"

She laughed. "Black belts in all. Different levels of black for each of them." She reached up and tapped hm on the end of the nose. "Not that I would be any good to you in a street fight. Ours is a very controlled and disciplined sport."

He took her hand and they walked back up the beach to the parking lot. "I don't know. I think you'd be an asset in the field."

She shook her head while she smiled. "Too rough for me. I want an official keeping an eye on the match up, ready to step in if things got out of hand."

"Definitely could have used one of those officials."

"Hey. It all worked out in the end."

They reached Nick's car.

"The moment of truth, Lucy. And it's entirely your call. Do I drive you home and we make plans for our next date? Or do I drive you to my flat and we continue this discussion over a final drink?" He unlocked the car and held the door open for her. "I'm perfectly fine either way, but I'd be lying if I didn't say drinks at my place was my preference."

Lucy leaned in and took his hands. She kissed him and was enveloped by his arms. "Want to know my preference?"

The car door slammed shut and Lucy was roughly pulled from Nick and tossed onto the pavement. She rolled and sprung to her feet as a large black sedan pulled up behind Nick's car. The back doors opened and two men stepped out, grabbing Nick by his arms before he reached the man who threw Lucy.

He struggled against the grip. "Are you okay?"

Lucy fought to get past the man who pulled her from Nick. The man was a head taller and had muscles on his muscles. He had her wrapped up from behind, her feet dangling half a metre off the ground.

"I'm okay." She kicked back at her captor's knees, trying to connect. "If this arsehole would let me go."

Nick was pinned on either side. He couldn't move his arms. "Don't waste your energy, Lucy." He looked at the man on his left. "You want money, just ask. We'll give you our money. No big deal. It's only money."

The man holding on to Lucy cleared his throat. "I really apologise for the way this has turned out. We just want to talk."

Nick tried to wrench his arm free. "So let us go and talk."

"Rules of engagement, first. No screaming, no trying to run, you listen and comply."

"Comply? Like hell." Nick tried again to pull his arm free.

"Look, mate. Settle down. I'm here on behalf of a client. You're going to take a little ride with us — just you. Miss Simpson can take your car to her place — and I am going to deliver you to my boss. He'll decide what happens at that point."

"That's not how it works, mate. Luce, call the cops."

"Hey Siri, call-"

The man holding Lucy dropped her and grabbed her bag. He managed to get her phone out quick enough to stop the call. "Nope. No police." He turned off the phone and slid it into his back pocket. "Anybody calls the police, and Nicky's going to get hurt. Just let it go. You can do that, right Lucy? Nick is fine if everybody plays along."

Nick shook his head at Lucy. "Let it go, Luce. I'll be fine." He underhanded his car keys to her. "I'll call you as soon as I'm free." He looked at the big guy behind her. "Do you guys have names?"

"Of course we have names." The guy from behind Lucy walked forward and stood in front of Nick. "Why wouldn't we have names?"

"Are you going to tell us your names?"

"Hell no. You don't need to know them."

He turned and looked at Lucy. "After we leave, you're going to be busting to call the cops. Don't. We have friends there. We'll know if you call them. This really needs to stay off their radar." He leaned against the black sedan. "We could have just dropped a sack over Nick's head and stuffed him in the boot. Popped you on the head and left you in the sand, prey for whoever - whomever? Never get that right - whomever might happen along. But we're not doing that. Asking for a bit of patience and consideration. Nick won't be harmed if you sit tight."

He pulled her phone from his back pocket and held it between his thumb and forefinger. "You'll sit tight?"

Lucy glanced at Nick who gave her a quick nod. "I'll sit tight." She grabbed the phone. "For twenty-four hours. If I don't hear from him by then, I'm calling the police."

The big guy grabbed the phone back. "That's not how it works. Do not call the police. You'll hear from Nick soon enough. If you call the police, you won't see him again. Do you understand?"

"Jesus. Okay." She held out her hand. "Give it."

432

"So you won't-"

"For Christ's sake, I said I wouldn't." Lucy grabbed the phone back and turned it on. "So help me god, if anything happens to him…"

Nick smiled. "These guys want to hire me for something. I'll be okay. Stay at my parent's house, if you want. The address is in my car's GPS, and the key is on the ring."

"See?" The big guy smiled at Lucy, then turned and smiled at Nick. "We're all getting along." He held out his hand to Nick. "Hand it over."

"What?"

"Your phone, mate. Don't make me ask again."

Nick frowned and handed over his mobile. "I'm definitely not going to call the cops while you've got me jammed in the back of your car."

The big guy took a pin from his pocket and used it to extract the SIM from Nick's phone. He took a small glassine envelope from his shirt pocket, slid the SIM in and put it in his wallet. He handed the phone back to Nick. "I know you won't call the cops. But we can't have your little girlfriend tracking your location. You get the SIM back when you're finished."

"Finished?"

Big guy shrugged. "Finished. Whatever it is the boss wants you to do."

Nick took the phone back. The display, where it normally showed the name of his carrier, said 'SOS calls only'. "Excellent." Nick opened the sedan's back door. "Let's get this over with. Lucy, don't worry. I'll call you as soon as I can. Tell Davie."

Lucy watched the other men get in the car: Two in the back, either side of Nick, and the third, the one doing most of the talking, in the front passenger seat.

Lucy took pictures of the receding licence plate as the car drove away.

Then she unlocked the phone and made a call. "Bobby. Wake up and put on a pot of coffee. I'll be there in fifteen minutes."

~~~

Vladimir Petrovski sat at his table in the kitchen of *The Natalia*, just north of Miami's city centre. He picked at his food. He had lost his appetite shortly after he heard Terri O'Shea was in Australia. It took him almost a year to recover from her theft. That year was a rough year. He almost lost his restaurant. This restaurant. His legitimate base of operations.

Getting the money back didn't matter to him as much as making her pay with her life.

He hated being in Miami when the action was happening on the other side of the world. He dabbed a slice of roast potato in the gravy smothering his prime rib. His phone was face down on the table. He tipped it up to check the time. Mikhail would be in LA by now, with a four-hour layover before the next leg of his flight.

His phone buzzed with an incoming video call. He sighed and answered. "Martin, This isn't a secure device. I'll call you back from my laptop."

"No need. Quick message with no financial implications." Martin, Petrovski's money laundering contact, gave him an exaggerated wink. "Absolutely confirmed it's Terri in Sydney, and she's definitely travelling under the name Grace Rawlston. And she is leaving Sydney in three and a half days." The call terminated.

Six miles from *The Natalia* Special Agent James and Miami PD Detective MacCready sat back from a surveillance station in the bowels of the FBI office.

"Ten bucks says this Martin guy is his money launderer," said James.

"No bet. And Terri O'Shea is in Sydney for another three days. How fast can you get approval for international travel?"

James laughed. "I'll reach out to the Australian Federal Police." He looked at his watch. "It'll have to be tomorrow."

"You know anybody there?"

"A kid by the name of Nick Harding. I worked with him about five years ago. He's a whiz kid. He's in the Financial Crimes unit. Really knows his way around secret bank accounts."

"Sometimes you don't have to be good, just lucky. Most days Petrovski would never take a business call on that phone."

Coming in 2023: Dead Tomorrow (A Nick Harding Case)